SHADOWS OVER TIME

SHADOWS OVER TIME

C. J. Christensen

QUARTET BOOKS

First published in 2011 by
Quartet Books Limited
A member of the Namara Group
27 Goodge Street, London WIT 2LD

A catalogue record for this book
is available from the British Library

ISBN 978 0 7043 7213 9

Typeset by Antony Gray
Printed and bound in Great Britain by
T J International Ltd, Padstow, Cornwall

FOR CHARLIE AND FELIX

Where the light is brightest,
the shadows are darkest.

JOHANN WOLFGANG VON GOETHE
1749–1832

RENATA

Dresden, Germany. Shrove Tuesday, February 13th, 1945.

Dense clouds, thick like a winter's quilt, hung low and unbroken across Germany, except over Dresden, a city in the east, where the clouds were sparse. Here, an unfamiliar burst of sunshine warmed the city's spirits, little realising the countless amongst them who were condemned to death by a sunny day.

Renata woke early. She lay still, anxious not to wake the children who slept beside her, but she was joined at once by hunger and worry, her frequent companions in the early morning hours. Dark indigo sky was slowly stripped away, and replaced with pale strips of candyfloss clouds that promised respite from the relentless grey of the previous weeks. The delicate morning light took her thoughts back to gentler times and for a moment she smiled, remembering the days of her marriage when she and her husband Sebastian would wake early, and in that still soft time before the dawn, unite.

Small eyelashes, fragile as butterfly wings, eased open on the pale face of the child beside her. Renata gently kissed Sabina's forehead then stroked the soft cheek of little Joachim to wake him, never imagining that this would be her last ever morning to enjoy such a simple pleasure with her son. She would regret forever more that she rushed through the morning's activities: a quick damp cloth across their faces, a hurried *Frühstück*, if you could lend the name breakfast to a shared slice of stale *Lebensbrot* and some indeterminable cheese. Hardly enough for two growing children Renata knew, although it was the best that she could manage under the difficult circumstances.

9

SABINA

London, England. March 1967.

The thud of the door closing as her husband left for work sent a jolt through Sabina's pounding head. She hated waking. Another day to haul through the terrible, guilty images in her memory.

She immediately reached beneath her bed, fingers splayed, anticipating the cool texture of glass and the promise of comfort from a bottle of gin. She'd have a small swig: just the one. It wasn't a habit and she could stop at any time of course, just not today. Maybe tomorrow, or next week, definitely.

It was gone. The bottle wasn't there. Sabina was on the floor in an instant, still naked, scrambling frantically amongst scuffed shoes and old magazines. Perhaps she'd hidden it elsewhere. She didn't remember if there was food in the fridge or clean clothes for the children, but she was certain where she kept her drink. She opened her wardrobe and searched it anyway, delaying the inevitable a moment longer. Anxiety and cold sweat pricked her thin, sagging skin. Sabina put on her dressing gown and found in the pocket, thank God, a packet of slightly crushed cigarettes. The lure of caffeine took her mechanically to the kitchen, and there, accusingly, was the missing bottle, placed upside down and obviously empty, in the sink. Her husband's triumphant exclamation mark.

Guilt, anger, nausea: they came all at once. Her emotions erupted in a blur of breaking crockery and shattering glass while two small frightened faces stood tear stained by the kitchen door.

*   *   *

The rage finally abated, Sabina, a spent force, slumped against a wall. Ellie, a sobbing bundle, cowered at the bottom of a cupboard whilst Justin was half-hidden beneath a chair. His normally gentle eyes were filled with terror, confusion, and pain. As blood trickled down his forehead, stark, undeniable evidence of Sabina's maternal betrayal, the image that filled her mind was of Joachim her brother, who, in the moments before his death all those years ago, had looked at her that very same way.

ELLIE

London, England. August 1981.

Five days of searing sun and nights without breeze had left the city streets deserted. Most Londoners were spending the weekend, or at least the day, at the coast or in the country.

Having woken late in the morning it was still a while before Ellie was due for work at the Theatre. She took the tube to Covent Garden for a few hours of window-shopping and people watching. She wandered in and out of the many boutiques, flicked through rails of jewel coloured dresses and glanced at quilted handbags costing more than she earned in a month.

Along the main roads a few cars cruised slowly by with their roofs pulled down and music turned up, the drivers and passengers catching the sun and a breeze all at once. In the Piazza she stopped for an ice cream and watched a street performer struggle under the sun. Then, wilting herself, Ellie decided to head to the British Museum a few streets away, where she could pass the time in respite from the heat.

Passing the shop front of 'L. Cornelissen & Son', her eye was drawn to the rows of old pigments and a display of artists' brushes fanned out on a palette in the window: rounded fitches, camel hair mops and blunt cut hog hair stencilling brushes; gliders with thin silky bristles and fat badger blenders, stippling and dusting and lining brushes. Ellie was pleased that at last she could name them all.

On days when the box office phones were quiet she would leave the foyer opulence for the stark backstage, the myriad rooms and countless corridors that filled as much space as front of house. Time and again she would arrive at 'The Run' – the corridor behind the back wall of the stage – and go through the steel dock doors that stretched some fifty feet to the roof above into the cavernous room that housed the paint frames. The colourful worlds that the artists conjured from chalk white canvas always amazed her. The Master and Scenic Artists would indulge her, and she had watched them work on the scenic cloths at every opportunity. From time to time Ellie had been allowed to help mix the paints or clean their brushes if the studio assistants were away for some reason, but more recently it was accepted that she would pitch in regardless, and, slowly, she learned about their craft.

Usually they went to 'Brodie and Middleton' on Long Acre to get their art supplies. Ellie had been there on errands a couple of times, but, if they needed something rarer, a particular gum arabic crystal or gesso or gilding materials, than they came to the shop. She'd passed 'L. Cornelissen & Son' on endless occasions but had never before gone in, never really had the time or reason to, but, with an hour to go until she was due at work, Ellie went inside to browse amongst the oils and inks and acrylics.

GERMANY – THE TWENTIETH CENTURY

Eleanor Von Steindorf, Moderne Kunsthalle, Berlin
November 15th, 1995

PENUMBRA

283cm x 338cm. Oil on canvas.

SCHRECKLICHKEIT

252cm x 206cm. Oil and acrylic on canvas.

SEPARATION

222cm x 285cm. Oil and acrylic on canvas.

STURM

244cm x 215cm. Oil on canvas.

ISOLATION

200cm x 350cm. Oil on canvas.

PERDITION

363cm x 254cm. Oil and acrylic on canvas.

AMELIORATION

150cm x 300cm. Oil on canvas.

MAELSTROM

330cm x 300cm. Oil and acrylic on canvas.

LUSTRATION

330cm x 330cm. Oil and pastel on canvas.

1

PENUMBRA
Oil on canvas
283cm x 338cm

Berlin, Germany. November 15th, 1995.

A bitter wind that swept in from Siberia had sliced across the city throughout the day. Collars were raised; hats lowered. Careless gusts scattered pedestrians, ripped autumn's last remaining leaves from trees and gnawed at workers atop the cranes around the re-emerging Reichstag. In the seasonal rush towards the winter solstice, day faded quickly into night. Neon and halogen cast their glitter, hinting at warmth and the comfort of coffee and cakes in *Konditorei*, or sausage and beer in the many *Stübe* that were strung across the city.

Ellie Tyler had arrived in Berlin for the first time that morning and since lunch had walked for hours, ignoring the cold and enjoying the solitude. A stranger searching anonymous streets, she was hoping to elicit the secrets of both the city's difficult history, and of her own.

Anxious to exorcise the remnants of war and destruction, occupation and division, the city was re-inventing itself yet again, erasing the scars that conflicts across the past century had inflicted. Sand-grey Wilhelmian houses of faded grandeur stood awkwardly beside the drab, functionalist relics of Soviet occupation whilst gleaming skyscrapers rose optimistically through a forest of cranes near streets still pockmarked with bullet holes and wastelands where weeds had conquered long forsaken bombsites. Each building reflected a different era along

Berlin's tumultuous journey from Prussian and Imperial capital, through revolution, Weimar decadence, Nazi bastion, to a divided epicentre along the fault line of the Cold War, and, since the fall of the Wall, a global symbol of hope and reconciliation.

Berlin, once more the country's capital since the reunification of Germany in 1990, was actively building on the benign image of its arts heritage. In this chameleon city where a brighter future lay on the canvas, Ellie knew that she'd found her spiritual home.

Leaving behind the cranes and the cold, she returned through the stark streets of former East Berlin at last to her hotel. Her room was heavy with scents from an abundance of flowers that had been delivered a short time before: moss roses, mallow and Japanese maple in a cascade of crimson and russet and gold. There were endless messages as well: good luck greetings from friends, requests for interviews from journalists, and on top a note in the hurried scrawl of Justin, her younger brother and art agent, that said 'DON'T be late'.

In a few hours her exhibition, 'Germany: The Twentieth Century', would open at the *Moderne Kunsthalle*. The good and the great would be on hand to admire and criticise her work. This, she felt, was the arduous part of being an artist, and why she had intentionally avoided the chaos of all the last minute preparations. In any case she had wanted to spend a rare day on her own, without responsibilities – to avoid the world for a few hours at least, as she knew that later on there'd be so much to confront. Her mother Sabina, and her grandmother Renata, both for so long estranged from the other, were due to be there too, reunited once more after the divisions that war, loss and recriminations had inflicted upon her family.

It had seemed such a good idea for her to invite them to assemble at her exhibition in the city of her grandmother's birth, just days away from her eightieth birthday, and make peace with their past. But now that the evening had finally come, Ellie wondered if it would be the cathartic event she had wanted. She'd not heard from either of them since the weekend before, which she didn't take to be an encouraging sign, and she was worried that she'd set herself up for disappointment or even debacle. Worse, she worried that she had set Justin up for a fall as well. Having spent so much of her life applying balm to his emotional wounds she knew that he didn't need any more falls.

'What the fuck for?' had been his typically blunt response when she mentioned the idea. 'Why would you even *think* about inviting mother?'

Renata, their grandmother, was always welcome, but she and Sabina had previously always been a ferocious mix.

'I hate this rift between us,' Ellie had replied carefully, feeling her way slowly forward into a subject that they usually kept off limits. 'We should at least *try* to change things for the better, and I think that this is the perfect opportunity.'

'I think you're being naïve.'

'They can't carry around their bitterness forever. Mother . . . well mother is what she is. But don't you think that Grandma is too old for all this animosity?'

'We didn't create this rift, and we aren't going to mend it.' His arm reached automatically to the back of his head and he scratched at his scalp, the way he always did when he was anxious.

'Maybe mother wants to,' Ellie had suggested after a short pause, 'But now it's gone on so long that she just doesn't know where to begin.'

'It's really not difficult: you apologise. You pick up the phone or you write a letter and you say sorry, it's that simple. Even mother could figure it out.'

'I think we're all old enough now to live without apologies. Why couldn't we just leave it all behind us?'

'I have. But you clearly haven't. As far as I'm concerned we haven't done anything wrong . . . if mother wants to patch things up then it's up to her.'

'Yes, but I'm tired of papering the cracks. I'm sick of it. Aren't you? Don't you at the very least want some sort of closure?'

'I closed the door on that part of my life long ago, and I've no desire to re-open it.'

'*Closed* it? You slammed it. You walked away from mother, but you've never resolved your feelings, you just hide from them. You bury yourself in work and women and booze and cigarettes, and spend ridiculous money on . . . God only knows how many varieties of substances – and that would all be fine if any of it made you happy, but it doesn't. How someone could have so much going for them – the big career and glitzy lifestyle, the good looks and endless girlfriends – and still be so miserable. It's unbelievable.'

Ellie regretted the words immediately. A confrontation with Justin had been exactly what she hoped to avoid, and it seemed that once again they were fighting for peace.

Justin grimaced, looked directly at his sister and opened his mouth as if to say something, but after a second or so he exhaled sharply instead and bit down on his lower lip. He then reached for his packet of cigarettes, lit up yet another and shrunk back into his chair.

'Stick to painting Ellie,' he said wearily, his eyes glazing over as he retreated back into his inner sanctuary. 'If I wanted a bloody therapist, I'd pay for one.'

They didn't discuss it any further and a few days later he watched silently as she addressed and stamped the envelopes containing their invitations.

Later on, having watched him wrestle with increasing anxiety as the exhibition drew nearer, doubling his nicotine intake and dabbling more than ever with cocaine and cannabis, Ellie realised that she'd not been fair on Justin: whatever resolution she was hoping for, she didn't want it at her brother's expense.

Cosseted in her Berlin hotel room, she flirted with various means of procrastination whilst making the metamorphosis from

Ellie Tyler to the public persona of Eleanor von Steindorf. She languished in a hot bath; phoned home and spoke with her young daughters, Joanna and Millie, in London; caught the headlines on the CNN news; brushed soft coral blush across her cheeks and a rich sable over her lashes; changed from dress to dress several times and then back again to the sage green shift that matched her eyes; untied her carefully piled up copper blonde hair and then artfully re-arranged it beneath the pale coral wool of a winter beret. She felt more comfortable in jeans and jumpers and rarely wore make-up, but had come to realise that a certain flamboyance was expected of an artist at events such as these.

Eventually, when it was no longer possible to ignore the car and driver that Justin had waiting for her outside, she applied a last gloss to her lips and finally left her hotel room. She was unsure of which she was avoiding more – the demands of the art world circus, or of her family.

Only her loyalty to Justin, and the thought that their grand-mother Renata might actually have come to Berlin, restrained the urge in her to ask the driver to head for the airport and the last flight back to London. Instead they crawled, stopped, and crawled their way towards the *Moderne Kunsthalle* in the familiar rhythm of rush hour traffic the world over.

From the back seat of the car the frantic swarm of the early evening cityscape provided an endless distraction: the sudden shift from austerity to affluence as they passed near the Branden-burg gate; buses, bikes, cars, pedestrians; tired workers bracing for the cold as they spilled out from buildings; shoppers and browsers and tourists braving the sharp night air and the first heavy drops of encroaching rain for an evening's entertainment. An endless flow through the city's winter streets: vivid, vibrant, and timeless.

Berlin, Germany. November 18th, 1915.

The evening crowds had slowed Herr von Steindorf's progress and he was anxious to return home at once. Six-foot, with dark brown hair that swept across his forehead, he had a pleasant, sensitive face that was spared from being handsome by a broken nose, the result of a childhood beating from his father who had insisted during an argument that his son's slight stammer was a deliberate taunt to him. He strode with the bearing that you would expect of someone for whom the terms lawyer, politician and member of a patrician military family would rightly apply, though they equally misled, suggesting as they did an unswerving path through conservative thinking. As ever, he was elegantly dressed, although that owed more to his wife's devotion to shopping and eye for the aesthetic, than any innate vanity.

Although a war was on and winter had come early, still the streets were teaming with life. Herr von Steindorf increased his step as he passed by the *Brandenburger Tor* – the news he had just received would change his life forever. Along the boulevard Unter den Linden, glamorous women, fur wrapped and jewelled, peered from carriages on course for Charlottenburg and the Deutsches Opernhaus. Starched governesses, threatening bed-time and promising stories, peeled excited faces from the enticing windows of Schneidermann's toyshop in Friedrichstraße. Office workers who had left their ledgers now headed for home, whilst street vendors seduced them all with apple fritters and cinnamon biscuits; prices were high, but business was brisk.

The headline from the *Berliner Tageblatt* caught von Steindorf's attention. Hurriedly, he crossed the road, passed the pale and hungry looking newspaper boy a fifty-pfennig coin, but declined the change, and then scanned the front page before resuming his pace.

Once more the Supreme Army Command was peddling their lies. The hypocrisy and subterfuge of those who clung to power never ceased to incense him: 'The End of War in Sight!' 'Victory Assured!' He thought it preposterous to dangle false hope before the public in this way. Little wonder so many Berliners continued their lives with apparent nonchalance, for the press pronounced with such certainty that annexations and reparations would soon be Germany's reward, and that peace lay just around the corner. The reality of the situation, so removed from the propaganda, would have astounded and terrified them all; after barely three months of fighting, the War Minister had pleaded to the Chancellor to broker for peace. 'Victory is beyond reach,' he had advised him categorically. And while von Steindorf had come to see the truth in these words, those in power chose to fight on regardless, with too much to lose in defeat. Memories from the previous year lay like concrete slabs across his troubled conscience.

*   *   *

The fatal shot fired at Archduke Franz Ferdinand on June 28th 1914 by Serbian dissident Gavrilo Princip, had ricocheted through the cities of Europe. For weeks politics and palaces had been awash with poisonous gossip and unbridled aspirations that had stripped good men of integrity, and empowered lesser ones with megalomania. Austria, assured of the 'faithful support' of her neighbour Germany, had demanded retribution from the Serbians, who in turn sought and found a pledge of protection from Russia.

Resentments and ambitions, long suppressed or restrained, now found the oxygen to ignite. Ultimatums were demanded and rejected, deadlines issued and ignored. On July 29th the brinkmanship ended when Austria bombarded the streets of Belgrade.

Within hours Russia ordered a general mobilisation, deploying troops along her border with Austria. Germany demanded disbursement of the Russian army by August 1st, and when no reply was forthcoming from St Petersburg the Kaiser was then able to lament, 'The sword has been forced into our hand.' Towards evening that day he signed a declaration of war against Russia, and then issued a call to colours for Germany's army, announced at once to the jubilant crowd gathered in the summer dusk outside the Neues Palais in Potsdam.

The order for mobilisation unleashed the formidable plans of General Schlieffen. Fifteen years and a pedant's dream in the making, the Schlieffen Plan, on paper at least, held a military logic that few had questioned: sweep in behind the French enemy and destroy them from the rear. A route through Belgium offered fewest obstacles and therefore the advantage of speed, although the fact that this violated the small country's neutrality was deemed a 'military necessity'. Belgian resistance was expected to be minimal and her invasion thought unlikely to provoke a response from the English, the originators and a guarantor of her Neutrality Treaty.

August 2nd, a Sunday, was anything but a day of rest through-out Europe. At six that morning, as Germany's declaration of war was presented to the Russian Foreign Minister in St Petersburg, the field grey uniform of her army crossed the border into Luxembourg. That evening, the Brussels government received Chancellor Bethman Hollweg's demand for an unopposed passage through Belgium, and within two hours the Belgian Council of State had convened at the Palace with the monarch, King Albert, presiding. There was no hesitancy, no ambivalence: Belgium would not concede. The King's firm declaration, 'Our answer must be "No", whatever the consequences,' was delivered to the German Ambassador in the early hours of the following morning.

The Belgian reply echoed in London where overnight Prime Minister Asquith had issued a call to arms, and then confirmed to Parliament that Britain would honour her commitment to Belgian neutrality. That evening, the German Ambassador to France had taken his carriage the short distance through the

Parisian streets to the Premier's residence to officially deliver Germany's declaration of war. Through the capitals of the continent, peace, with every hour, was flailing.

August 4th brought searing sun and heavy air to Berlin. Sharp light filtered through the windows, bleaching the parquet flooring and antique furniture in the dining room where Herr von Steindorf picked through the morning papers and his breakfast, his appetite that morning as subdued as his mood.

Events were escalating at an alarming rate, and he shared none of the optimism that gripped the capital. It seemed that the entire nation was eager to leap forward into the war, and he alone suffered from vertigo. Beneath his silk ascot tie, starched wing-collared shirt, and the charcoal morning coat with matching woollen waistcoat, he already felt too hot.

His wife Katarina eventually joined him. She mumbled, '*Guten Morgen*', although the words appeared as much directed to the food spread out along the mahogany sideboard, as at her husband.

Herr von Steindorf glanced up over his newspaper and offered the back of his wife's tailored sailor tunic an equally half-hearted, '*Guten Morgen*'. Her ironic gesture of wearing seaside attire in the city, intended to emphasise her irritation at their early return home from the coast, went entirely unnoticed by her husband.

Anxious to maintain her enviable waistline, she ignored the fresh rolls and soft boiled eggs that had been prepared, settling instead for black coffee and a Muratti Gold cigarette, a gesture calculated to annoy her husband who, unusually for a Berlin man, loathed tobacco in all its forms. Behind the pages of the *Berliner Tageblatt* he barely paid attention. The silence between them hung heavy and troubled, like the summer air. Storm clouds gathered inside and out, and across Europe.

Katarina loathed the city in August and had long looked forward to escaping the capital's stagnant summer air for the Baltic sea breeze. When their holiday at the elegant coastal resort of Heiligendamm had been abruptly cut short by the arrival of the

Chancellor's telegram demanding her husband's return to Berlin, she had been furious. Most of her friends were installed for the season in grand villas amongst the cluster of seaside towns along the pristine white sands of the Baltic Sea. They had already made the most interesting introductions, including the renowned artist Herr Max Liebermann who was there for the summer to paint, and their hosts had organised a summer of fun. There were tea dances and tennis parties planned, even a ball. She struggled with the thought of missing out on it all.

'Don't be so ridiculous Gustav,' she had protested when he insisted that they did in fact have to return to Berlin. 'I'm certain that this is just another "crisis" that will be forgotten by next week, and if not, I'm sure they'll manage to sort out whatever it is just fine without you,' a comment which he felt was not entirely flattering.

Ahead of her stretched the dullest of days, with her husband busy – as ever, she thought wryly – and her friends all out of town. Her options were indeed very limited; after all, she could hardly ride in the *Tiergarten* unaccompanied, or take luncheon in a restaurant alone. Instead, she spent most of the morning up in her room writing letters, and trifling with her wardrobe as a child might play with its toys. Out of boredom she changed her outfit a couple of times, then sorted through her many powders and lipsticks and perfumes.

'Annette,' she called to her personal maid. 'Would you please help me with my hair? I want to try out some styles that I've seen in a magazine, and work out the best way to wear some new clips which I bought at the coast.'

This successfully passed the time for a while. Annette patiently rotated an assortment of ivory, tortoise and seashell clips in Katarina's thick auburn curls, holding up, when required, a silver hand mirror so that her employer could closely scrutinise each one, and then Annette curled and pinned the hair in as close an approximation of the styles she had been shown, as possible.

Eventually, when even preening had lost its appeal, Katarina settled on a sap green velvet ribbon that almost matched her eyes, and which Annette carefully pleated through Katarina's thick, glossy hair.

She then sent Annette downstairs with most of her shoes. 'These ones just seem to need a good polish,' she told her, pointing at several pairs that had acquired a faint bloom of dust. 'But you can throw those away,' she said, gesturing towards a pyramid of shoes that she had assembled beside her closet and which she deemed to be no longer in vogue.

'Of course,' replied Annette, who was excitedly eyeing the shoes for herself.

For a while Katarina lay supine on her bed, weighed down by the heat and her boredom. She thought about shopping, but even that held little appeal as it was far too hot to visit the stores and their housekeeper, Frau Braun, had reported that the streets were jammed with crowds intent on either celebrating the call to arms, or stockpiling goods because of it.

Katarina hated days spent alone; she took no pleasure in her own company. Brought up on an exacting diet of Kant and Goethe and Schiller she had never warmed to the company of books, whilst hours of arduous piano tuition had failed to reveal any talent. Children would have given her life some purpose and relieved such moments of loneliness, but throughout their nine years of marriage her blood had come quite regularly each month, like a stab of disappointment, and she thought it was now probably too late as she had recently turned thirty.

On a whim, she wrote out a list of items for Frau Braun to purchase: pencils and papers, erasers and inks, red sable brushes and watercolours. She would, as she had planned had they stayed at the coast, spend the day painting. For the first time in many long months she felt truly excited. Maybe, finally, she would ease the boredom that she so often fought.

Herr von Steindorf had been truly appalled by his wife's

behaviour during the preceding few days, and, although he never said it, her naivety. The country was at war, the army mobilising, pro-war revellers and anti-war demonstrators were flooding the streets of Berlin, yet Katarina seemed more concerned about her holiday and friends than his responsibilities to the Reichstag. He adored her completely, she could be witty and charming, and with her still slender curves and fine featured face she was as alluring as ever. However, he had overindulged her – as had her parents beforehand – and if he was honest, at moments such as these, he thought her shallow and spoilt.

They had argued rather publicly over an elaborate dinner at their friend's villa in Heiligendamm, caused quite a scene in fact, and no doubt provided ample amusement for the gossipmongers who were seated all around them. They were savouring a schnitzel of artichoke with roast loin of rabbit and a fine Pouilly-Fume, the third of eight courses and accompanying wines that they would enjoy as the long, hot dusk had slowly blended from ultramarine to a deep sapphire blue.

Katarina had been in an exuberant mood all evening. The unspoken contest amongst all the women at any event during the summer season was that of fashion, and that night Katarina had triumphed.

'Frau von Steindorf, wherever did you get that heavenly outfit from?' the aged Countess seated across from her at the table, had asked.

'I had the dress made by a *couturier* in Paris; it arrived just last week. And this,' gesturing at her neck, 'Is the latest indulgence from my husband.'

'Herr von Steindorf, I must ask you to talk to my husband and give him a few lessons about indulging me!' the Countess quipped rather loudly.

'I'm not sure whether I really indulge my wife, or just eventually succumb to her hints. So the skill is all hers I'm afraid, as beyond writing a cheque I can take little credit,' he replied to general laughter and approval from the ladies.

Amongst the endless ruffles and feathers and frills, and the deluge of broaches and necklaces and earrings, Katarina had basked all evening in the attention that the simplicity of her organza sheath dress and elegant pearl choker provided. She looked truly beautiful, like one of the Three Graces from Botticelli's *Primavera*, Herr von Steindorf thought, although a number of the female guests whispered amongst themselves that the effect was somewhat diminished by her obvious air of self-satisfaction. Emboldened by it all, she certainly enjoyed each of the different wines that accompanied the meal's eight courses, and was perhaps feeling more than usually fortified by the end of meal champagne and cognac, when she'd addressed her husband across the table.

'*Liebchen*,' she began quite flirtatiously, offering a dazzling wide smile for the benefit of the whole table. 'If you really do have to return to Berlin tomorrow, than maybe you could go ahead without me and I could join you later?'

Herr von Steindorf, who had drunk rather less than his wife, noted the quietening of the conversation and the gleeful sneers as the other guests lent an ear to this conversation, and, as someone who had guarded his privacy all of his life, he felt instantly embarrassed. He thought that if they were to have such a ridiculous discussion, than at least they should do so alone.

'No Katarina, we must both leave for Berlin in the morning,' he replied sharply, his shoulders suddenly set square in his white tie and tails. Had she been more alert at that moment, Katarina would have realised from the clipped monotone of his voice, which he usually preserved for cross-examinations in Court or to make harsh pronouncements in the Reichstag, that she should leave the matter alone.

Unfortunately, she had not been so easily swayed.

'But I'm having fun here with my friends,' she giggled. 'And in any case, what use would I be to you in Berlin when you'll be at the Reichstag all day? The city's so stifling in summer, and here I can ride on the beach each day, or take the waters at the Kurhaus, and Herr Liebermann has promised that I may set up an easel beside him and paint.' Her voice had become slightly shriller, edged with indignation; her cheeks blushed with wine and the excitement of capturing the attention of the entire table. 'Why can't I return at the end of August, as planned?' She added petulantly, curling a perfect auburn ringlet around her delicate forefinger.

Herr von Steindorf felt both anger and humiliation at this ludicrous suggestion, for Katarina knew well enough what a scandal would have ensued had he left her, a renowned Berlin beauty and the wife of a politician, alone at a seaside resort. But, uncomfortable under the unwelcome gaze of the eighteen other diners around the table, he masked his feelings with feigned tiredness and a faux jovial suggestion that they both retire to bed. They had barely spoken since.

The following morning they took the train south to Berlin in silence, Herr von Steindorf hiding behind a defensive mound of correspondence. Katarina meanwhile, fragile from the previous evening's excesses, languished wearily against the deep velvet seat of their first class compartment, suffering with the suffocating heat and each blast from the stationmaster's whistle and every jolt of the carriage as the train stopped, then started, struggling to find fresh steam at all the towns and villages on the long, dusty, journey back home. On their return Katarina retired early to bed, claiming fatigue. By breakfast the following day they had still not discussed the matter, although the tension between them had far from eased.

Herr Von Steindorf was pleased when an urgent telephone call required his presence in the study. Katarina poured more coffee and lit another cigarette, and was not surprised when Frau Braun relayed a message from her husband that he was gone on urgent business and should not be expected back till late.

Every Member of the Reichstag had received a summons to hear Chancellor Bethman Hollweg deliver Kaiser Wilhelm's address at three that afternoon, and in the preceding hours they had begun to assemble noisily at the building.

The morning sun gave way to a grey, oppressive afternoon, and even the constant rain from lunchtime onwards had failed to clear the heavy summer air. Herr von Steindorf sat in the packed Chamber, the unopened windows adding to his discomfort.

'What do you believe of the rumours that the invasion of Belgium begun this morning?' asked his colleague seated beside him.

'Absolute nonsense,' he replied gravely. 'I struggle to believe that Germany would risk increasing her enemies for so small an advantage; an easier route to France is surely not worth the addition of Belgium and England as adversaries.' However, tension kneaded the pit of his stomach.

His peer looked to retort, but instead sat back as the chamber quietened. The Chancellor, whose naturally distinguished features and sombre demeanour lent themselves well to the occasion, stood up and began his address, 'We now draw the sword with a clear conscience and with clean hands.'

Herr von Steindorf strained to hear the words. Bethman Hollweg's lone voice was no match for the clatter of hooves on the cobblestone roads as the passing cavalry headed out of the city, or the excited crowds that lined the streets and cheered them on.

Eventually, Chancellor Hollweg took his speech towards Belgium and the nation's destiny.

'The invasion of Belgium may have already begun,' he told the house, fully aware that it had, just after eight that morning. 'And yes, the invasion violates International Law.' However, it was, he continued, 'A military necessity, and the wrong that we are committing we will make good as soon as our military goal has been reached.' Excitement surged through the Reichstag as the Chancellor concluded, 'From this day on I recognise no parties, but only Germans!'

The speech was a masterful piece of political manipulation, designed to unite a political divide that ran as virulently through German home affairs as through her foreign policy. 'Germany the defenceless!' 'Bravely confronting her encircling aggressors!' Chancellor Hollweg held up handfuls of 'documentary evidence' that he extravagantly displayed to them all to support these claims, although later many were proved to be blatant forgeries.

For too long Herr von Steindorf had listened to aspirant dreams of German pan-European domination and colonial expansion, and his calls for moderation and attempts to rein in the ambitions of his colleagues had only left him increasingly isolated. He had watched a cancer of greed spread through the Reichstag, and knew too well the true aims that lay concealed behind the Chancellor's clever rhetoric.

No debate followed, only the ballot, duplicitously phrased to ensure a majority vote and to allow the passage of the all important war credits, and, lastly, the Members' adjournment. The wording offered no room for any vote other than, '*Hoch*! For Kaiser, the People and the Fatherland.' The Chamber erupted. Applause and the jubilant stamping of feet from Reichstag deputies created an ominous overture to the war, but Herr von Steindorf sat silently, and, watching their excited faces, realised that he had never felt more alone, or more despondent.

'These proceedings are a sham,' he declared vocally to those around him. 'This war will only bring shame to us all.'

'You're behind the times, von Steindorf. This is Germany's hour and nothing's going to stand in the way of the *Furor Teutonicus*!' A voice declaimed pompously from behind.

'Do not doubt that these lies will come back to haunt us all yet,' replied von Steindorf tersely, though in the squall of conversation that had erupted around the Reichstag, the other politicians paid little attention to this last remark.

There was chaos as the Members cleared the Chamber. Generally a spirit of elation pervaded, although Herr von Steindorf felt much closer to shock. He was in no mood to join his colleagues from the right, who, eager to celebrate the occasion, poured into Fraction Schulze, the house restaurant, and of course he was shunned by the Social Democrats who sought solace in the bars and cafés along Wilhelmstraße. Instead he slipped from the Reichstag unnoticed, and went in search of solitude.

War fever gripped the capital. With the certain victory that was predicted, Germany, a young country only unified since 1871, would finally be conferred her status as a world class nation, with Berlin, Europe's newest capital, at the epicentre of power. Berliners, confident that their hour of glory had finally come, took to the streets to celebrate. The storm clouds had dispersed to reveal a lustrous sunset, as burnt sienna brushed across the city's still wet rooftops.

For livelier women, the revelries were the perfect excuse to show off their prettiest frocks and most fashionable hats and approach the better looking young men to pin a flower for good luck to their lapel. For the men it was a perfect excuse to spend a summer's evening in a *Biergarten*. A press car from the *Berliner Tageblatt*, its horn pounding, weaved through the crowds along Unter den Linden trailing a stream of flyers: the invasion of Belgium was announced to the city like a shower of confetti on a summer breeze. Hats and handkerchiefs formed a choppy sea above the heads of the crowd, whilst the happy peel of Church bells rang out through the streets and squares. Flags appeared, all at once and in a blaze of colour, as if a conjurer had swept his hand across the city, adorning flagpoles and shop awnings, draping lanterns and fluttering from balconies. In restaurants and even on the streets outside couples danced the latest craze, a lively tango, whilst cabaret artists led the crowds in song. It was carnival time in the city.

Herr von Steindorf eventually found refuge from the noise

and the crowds in the Hotel Adlon, where he recovered his equilibrium over white asparagus, wild boar and a rich Burgundy, although he worried it might, under the circumstances, be considered an unpatriotic choice of wine. It certainly improved his mood and he decided that as the war escalated around him, at the earliest opportunity he would make peace at home.

When he left the restaurant, the city's celebrations had turned towards more nocturnal pursuits. The clubs and casinos were starting to fill and Berlin's *Unterwelt* had come out to play; but he ignored the best enticements of the exuberant girls and beautiful boys who worked along Unter den Linden, and found instead a hansom cab to take him back home. Katarina had long been asleep when he returned there at midnight, which was also the hour that England entered the war.

The Chamber was now out of session for the four months that had been deemed sufficient to prosecute the war, and the Prussian Siege Law of 1851 invoked. The outcry from Interior Minister Friedrich von Loebell that Germany would take on the character of a military dictatorship was casually dismissed, yet with mobilisation civil rights were suspended, and the newly created OHL, the *Oberste Heeresleitung* – the Supreme Army Command – quickly assumed control of civilian life in Germany.

Under the skilful eyes of the Military Telegraph Section of the German General Staff, the Schlieffen Plan was rapidly discharged. In less than eighteen days, orders were issued to more than three million men, and the 600,000 horses that such an army required were requisitioned and assembled at depots. Bakers, blacksmiths, cobblers and cooks; indeed a whole raft of artisans were called upon to support the vast divisions that thundered towards the frontiers, the majority west across the Rhine bridges, and a few east to the Rominten Forests, beyond the Prussian plains. Kaiser Wilhelm had stood in the August sunshine in Potsdam and declared to departing troops, 'You will be home before the leaves have fallen.'

However, the much-vaunted Schlieffen Plan had failed, utterly. Floundering on the surprise resistance of Belgium and the unexpectedly rapid advance of the Russian army through the swamps and forests of East Prussia, the German war machine had finally derailed on the blood-soaked fields of the Marne in France. Instead of the 'decisive victory' that had been assured by the end of week six in the precise plans of General Schlieffen, the German army found itself in chaos and retreating in the east, and entrenched, facing defeat, in the west.

Censorship quickly cast its shadow over the rest of the nation. Victories were loudly proclaimed, but the defeat against Russia's General Rennenkampf and the brutal invasion of East Prussia that followed went unreported, as did the unprecedented losses at the Battle of the Marne. The demand for ammunition had been completely underestimated, and on both fronts as supplies ran low, casualties ran high. Battle hospitals were ill equipped and unprepared for the horrific injuries suffered by wars' first ever victims of high explosives and shrapnel shells. The death toll so alarmed the Chancellor that he subsequently forbade the posting of casualty lists in towns and held back the volume of names from newspapers, fearing their impact on the public's morale. From November onwards journalists were banned from all battle areas, the press subsequently being solely permitted to print bulletins that the army had issued. At home, with news only of glorious victories, the German public thought that the war was nearly won.

Following his enforced withdrawal from the Reichstag, and being too old for conscription, Herr von Steindorf had returned full time to practising law. Outwardly, his life with Katarina amongst the upper echelons of Berlin society continued much as before, with visits to the *Volkstheater*, elegant dinners at Horcher's Restaurant, and English Tea – now hastily renamed Afternoon Tea – at the Hotel Esplanade on Sundays. Inwardly, he felt by turns dismayed, alarmed, and ashamed.

A hotbed of self-interest politics was thriving. Having never envisaged a prolonged conflict or the munitions demanded by enormous battles such as the Somme, Loos and Verdun, the OHL soon realised an urgent need for increasing armament production. With its large industrial base, which grew ever larger as the war progressed, Berlin was soon boomtown for the factory owner. For a minority, this was clearly going to be a 'good war'.

However, for the majority, and contrary to public pronouncements, life was growing increasingly strained. The blockade of German ports by the British Navy was starting to impact severely on vital supplies, and ration cards had been introduced for many essential goods, spiralling prices and fuelling a thriving blackmarket. In finance and in politics, the nation polarised. Whilst Kaiser Wilhelm, now safely installed at *Schloss Koblenz*, demonstrated his solidarity with the public by abstaining from hunting and dining off the silver field service of Frederick the Great, starvation stalked the slums. Social tensions stirred dangerously in the food queues and soup kitchens, where the harsh reality of constant shortages meant that rumours of a knuckle of ham inspired more interest than the fall of Belgrade. Here, resentments grew in line with the hunger, and demonstrators soon took to the streets of Berlin.

Katarina struggled with the disruptions to domestic life. Of course, their wealth meant that they were not bound by the restrictions that rationing placed on meat and cheese or bread and eggs, but the prices were ridiculous, and even on the blackmarket they were becoming increasingly difficult to source. Frau Braun, who, encouraged by inducements of a share in the spoils, had taken the initiative to embark on fortnightly 'hamster tours' to the countryside, where she could stock up on provisions by buying directly from trusted farmers, or visiting the well stocked estates of family and friends. However, in Berlin, supplies of fresh rolls and bakery products were scarce at any price, and '*Krieg Brot*', war bread – with the flour replaced by potatoes or even sawdust – began to appear on their dinning room table.

Further culinary tribulations arose when circumstances conspired to send Katarina on her first ever visit to a butcher's shop. The household was already feeling the strain of staff shortages. Two of its members had been lost to conscription, Annette had been sent home to Pomerania to convalesce after contracting a severe case of smallpox, and cook had taken the day off to collect her son – who was recuperating from injuries sustained in the battle for Artois – from a clinic in Thüringerwald. Then Frau Braun, who had gone to the country for supplies, telegraphed to say that the train for her return journey had been requisitioned by the army, detaining her for a further day.

For the first time in her life, Katarina faced a day without servants. Nonetheless, food was needed for the evening meal, and despite her burgeoning pregnancy, she was determined that she would manage alone. But Katarina, brought up to entertain and be entertained in the grand salons of Prussian society, was ill-equipped to face the turmoil of food queues or the subtleties of ration negotiations.

She had walked with a friend in the *Tiergarten*, and then, still in the same ornate empire tunic, matching white skirt and wide brimmed straw hat, she headed alone to a butcher's she had seen on one of the streets close to the *Gendarmenmarkt*. It was mid-afternoon, and although the shop was closing at four, the queue still remained quite long. Katarina, who had never previously waited in line, entered the shop, bypassed the other women, and instinctively presented herself at the counter. But this was the wrong time and the wrong place to display her social status, and the butcher, whose sympathies lay with the tired and hungry women who were his regular customers, brusquely sent her to the back of the queue. She would never before have imagined that a shop could smell so bad. The odour from carcasses and blood congealing in such quantities had been beyond the scope of anything she had previously experienced.

For the hour that she waited, Katarina had to fight the urge to retch, all the while being jostled and tripped and the target for a constant stream of hostile remarks. Feeling both hurt and extremely embarrassed, she almost crumbled and fled. Only her natural obstinacy kept her in line, and, eventually, she reached the head of the queue. She showed her ration book as requested, but was informed by the butcher that her monthly allowance was already used up. Sneering laughter had ignited the snaking queue. Katarina struggled to keep her composure, using every effort of self-will to maintain a calm and unruffled exterior, but inside she felt completely crushed.

The butcher, a chubby man with calculating eyes, an ostentatious moustache and a life lived in envy of money, sensed there was sport to be had with this society innocent and the weary women who waited in line.

'I'll do you a favour love,' he told the whole shop loudly, like a showman warming up for his act. 'Can't offer you much, seeing as your ration book's full,' he gibed, 'But I've got some fresh "roof rabbit", just in today, and seeing as you've waited so long I'd be happy to help out.'

The other women all laughed, colluding in this joke, but it was lost on Katarina who, utterly demeaned, had to fight back her tears; not that anyone would have noticed, such was her act of insouciance.

'Thank you, I'll take it,' she replied curtly to the butcher, not keen to question him further. He fetched a string wrapped package from the storeroom behind the shop, and she took it gratefully. Relieved, she paid quickly and left.

She returned home shaken and exhausted by the whole episode, but proud that she had stood her ground and certain that her husband would at least be grateful for all the effort she had gone to.

'Gustav!' she said, beaming at him around the study door, 'I've just been to the butchers for our supper. I could only get roof rabbit – I think they must be ones caught here in the city. I've had a peek through the wrapping and it's still got fur on it, so I'll need you to skin it for me.'

To her dismay, he merely looked shocked. 'Roof rabbit!' he exclaimed incredulously, his copper flecked eyes reflecting true revulsion. 'I'd rather go hungry – I could never eat such meat.' She looked at him blankly. '*Liebchen*,' he said gently, stretching a hand out to beckon her towards him. '"Roof rabbit" is slang. You've bought a dead cat.'

Wilting into her husband's lap whilst he wrapped a comforting arm around her, the tears that Katarina had held back for so long then came, a torrent of humiliation, frustration and fear. The days when her wealth and status brought her unquestioning respect and privilege had ended, and hostilities encroached closer to home than she had ever realised.

By then, Herr von Steindorf could see quite clearly the two wars being played out before the world. One suffered by millions in the trenches and forests and mountains and slums, amongst mud and wire and snow and poverty; the other fought out by a few, whose battle arenas were the palaces and parliaments across the continent. Here, as ice clinked against crystal, the struggle for territorial, ideological and financial ambitions carelessly sacrificed the blood of a generation.

Having never pursued power or money for its own sake, Herr von Steindorf had often been underestimated by those around him, and dismissed as an affable, but insubstantial man. As a lawyer he had been happy to accept clients that associates had turned away simply because they lacked the means to pay well, and his disinterest in profiteering from wartime enterprises was seen by many as a weakness, not a strength. But he had learnt early from his father, a hero of the Prussian military but sadistic bully at home, to not live his life hostage to the opinions of others. His father had never understood his sensitive, scholarly son, considering his devotion to books and passion for playing the 'cello unmanly. Horsemanship and marksmanship were the skills that showed what a man was made of, that could win wars and build a great nation or simply feed a family, his father would shout when Gustav baulked at a high hedge when riding or a clear shot out hunting. Once, he had endured a beating from his father rather than shoot dead a stag. Later on, when Gustav had announced that he would study and then practise law and not follow in his family's military footsteps, his father had left him in no doubt that he considered his place at the prestigious *Friedrich-Wilhelm-Universität* a disappointment, a sign of cowardice even, for a man's duty, so his father had asserted, was foremost to his country. From out of it all, he had learned not only to despise bigotry and distrust the military, but also to be circumspect about his abilities and ambitions.

Previously, this had held him back and he had missed out on opportunities to find a more prominent position in the Reichstag, but at last his unassuming manner was a valuable asset, as others believed, quite wrongly, that his quiet demeanour meant that they could bend him to their will. So, whilst former Reichstag colleagues and associates, scrambling amongst the scattered fragments of power, had come to lobby his support or get legal or political advice, he had been able to amass a wealth of information that he hoped, in time, would serve a higher purpose than the mere pursuit of profit.

From the reams of documents that had been brought before him, he had assessed quite accurately the gulf between propaganda and reality. Indeed, as reported, there had been significant gains by Generals Ludendorff and von Hindenburg at Tannenberg, Galicia and across Poland and Serbia, and the Allies had suffered a terrible rout in the Dardanelles. However, there had been no decisive victories for Germany, and trench warfare had subsumed the Western Front into a static 1,200-mile killing ground. For all the declarations about 'Assured Victory', Chancellor Hollweg and the OHL had not been able to find a viable end to the nightmare; or, more accurately, an end to suit their own agenda, as anything less than a 'victor's peace' would precipitate their own downfall. Out of industrial strength and political weakness, the war lumbered on.

At home, Herr von Steindorf gently stroked Katarina's expanding belly and marvelled at their private good fortune. After all these childless years, and long since he had given up the hope of parenthood, she one day changed his world forever with the simple words, 'I'm pregnant.'

Katarina had never looked more beautiful or more vibrant. Not for her the sickness and fatigue that many suffer with pregnancy, as in every way she grew, an innate longing now finally fulfilled. And with a widening waistline she had been happy to exchange her coquettish parade through Berlin society, for the solitary pleasure of a palette of paint.

Yet, watching his wife's body swell with new life as the hot summer months turned into crisp autumn days, had only added to the poignancy as von Steindorf grasped the toll of loss around him. Certainly in Germany, few realised that across Europe in little more than a year the fighting had already cost the lives of five million young men. Five million brutal, bloody, unnecessary deaths.

For some the end came quickly with a sniper's bullet or a shell that in an instant turned a man's body to dust, although Germany's own hideous invention, the dense yellow-green clouds of compressed chlorine gas, was probably feared the most. First used against the English at Ypres, it had come back to haunt her own troops, blinding its victims, and then slowly drowning them in the yellow froth of their decomposing lungs. Not even morphine could touch their pain as they begged for respite in death.

However, behind the closed doors of power, the truth of the

war was carefully concealed from the press and the people alike. Herr von Steindorf, angry and frustrated in equal measures that any pleas for peace went unheard beyond the wall of secrecy built by the OHL, waited for an opportunity to make his knowledge public.

Each week brought a new visitor to either his office, club or home. From the military right Admiral von Tirpitz, and from the radical left Karl Liebknecht and Rosa Luxemburg; from the Centre Party Matthias Erzberger, and from the Social Democrats Friedrich Ebert; from industry the head of GEC Walther Rathenau, and from the Berlin *Universität* the pacifist and renowned physicist Albert Einstein. They all came, papers and petitions in hand. Whilst Herr von Steindorf politely listened to each one, to only a few he gave advice. His parting words were the same to them all, 'This war must be ended, whatever the cost.'

Then, during the early days of November, Herr von Steindorf received a visitor who, within an hour of his arrival, caused him to make the move from passive opposer of the war, to active dissident.

The von Steindorf's had spent a quiet evening alone at home, and, after a modest dinner of baked trout and preserved pears, Katarina had retired early to bed; it was after all late in her confinement, and by then she tired easily. Not expecting any visitors, Herr von Steindorf had returned to his study to work. However, after only ten or so minutes, Frau Braun knocked on the door.

'There's a visitor for you sir,' she announced politely, though Herr Steindorf thought she looked rather exhausted, and perhaps even a trifle annoyed at having being disturbed after an already long day. 'It's a young man. He's refused to give his name, but he seems well mannered and he's smartly dressed in a cavalry officer's uniform. Anyway, he says he wishes to deliver a private letter to you, but will only do so in person. He says it's extremely urgent. He seems an honest sort so I've allowed him in, which I hope you think was the right thing to do. He's now waiting in the downstairs drawing room, although I can send him away, if you'd prefer.'

Obviously curious about his intriguing guest, Herr von Steindorf immediately went down to meet him. His visitor was indeed as Frau Braun had described, although she had not added that he wore an Iron Cross, First Class, and was also an invalid having lost an arm, probably in battle, he thought, judging by the silver *Verwundetenabzeichen* with oak leaves pinned just beneath it, the badge of honour awarded to those severely wounded in combat. Herr von Steindorf sized up the young man. He looked shockingly thin for his height, his face and remaining hand chapped and battered and scabbed, his mouth weighed down by too much responsibility and his cerulean eyes stripped of all innocence. Yet, beneath the war-ravaged exterior, Herr von Steindorf sensed an innate integrity and felt comfortable enough about allowing him to stay.

'Good even Herr von Steindorf, my name is Otto Graf von Duisburg,' he began solemnly when they were alone. 'Please excuse the rudeness of my uninvited appearance here tonight, but I am here as a friend of your nephew Marcus. We studied at Military School and served together in the same regiment. He particularly asked me to give this to you,' he said, handing Herr von Steindorf the letter that he brought from Marcus. 'It is perhaps best that as few people as possible know that we have met, which is why I have come to your home and not your office.'

The young soldier had come to Berlin for one night only on official army business, and, having arrived in the city less than an hour before, was in a hurry as he was expected to report to the Officer's barracks at the earliest moment. Herr von Steindorf took the letter from Graf von Duisburg, noting the somewhat unsteady handwriting, and sat down in the umber leather armchair, where the light from the Chinese lacquered lamp was best for reading.

MY DEAR UNCLE GUSTAV – It sadly seems so long since I last saw you and Aunt Katarina in Königsberg. How much has changed since, and not I fear, for the better.

I am sure Father will have informed you that I was transferred East with my cavalry regiment to the Carpathian Mountains, to reinforce the Austrian Divisions that are fighting here. However, you are probably not aware of how the situation has deteriorated, and now is utterly desperate. Whatever you might read in the press, the Hapsburg Empire is crumbling, and rapidly. Their army has run out of basic winter equipment; supplies of artillery and food are at a minimum, and their cavalry has been forced to dismount, having lost horses in such vast numbers that they can no longer be replaced. We share all our resources, but this has drained our own Divisions to such an extent that we ourselves are no longer an effective fighting force, and though we struggle on, side by side, hungry and without gloves or hats and sometimes without even rifles, our situation against the Russians is hopeless, as they are well dug in, heavily equipped and control the higher mountain passes.

A desolate fog descended with the autumn and has since remained, and as winter now encroaches the snow deepens daily. Madness claws at the men's minds as the conditions get worse; daylight brings the predictable terrors of artillery and rifle, but night is arguably worse, with the prospect of freezing to death, or worse, being eaten alive by the wolves, which attack us all as we sleep. Not a day or night passes without several of the men committing suicide – I suppose it can be their only relief from the horror of it all.

I write you all this, not to seek your pity or praise, but in the hope that perhaps you, out of all the people that I know and trust, are able to prevent more of our men from being sent here to face certain death in these mountains. I am hopeful that, God willing, the loss of so many lives has served some greater purpose.

Affectionately as always, your nephew,

MARCUS VON STEINDORF

For a while the two men had sat together by the fading fire in a sombre silence. Then, his face pale, his heart skewered with foreboding, but his eyes a level gaze with his young guest, Herr von Steindorf had asked, 'And how long after Marcus wrote this letter did he kill himself?'

'That night, Sir,' Graf von Duisburg replied quietly. 'I am very sorry at your loss, but if it is of any comfort, his death was no act of cowardice – Marcus had contracted tetanus. He had been lightly injured by shrapnel the previous week, and they had run out of all medical supplies to inoculate the men or even properly clean and dress the wound. He was very ill when he wrote to you and his death was by that stage inevitable; he merely hastened events.' He paused, and then took some papers and another envelope out from his battered brown document case. 'I also have a letter that Marcus wrote for his parents, if you would please kindly forward it to them.'

Herr von Steindorf nodded, knowing that his nephew must have suffered terribly to have chosen to end his life in this way. His mind sifted through memories of the shy, gentle, child with thoughtful mahogany brown eyes, whom he had watched grow into a kind and accomplished young man.

'You might also be interested in seeing these papers,' Graf von Duisburg had added, almost casually, as he brought out the confidential report and accompanying letter he had come to Berlin to deliver to the OHL the following morning, which he handed, without explanation, to Herr von Steindorf.

45

HERR KOMMANDANT – We now urgently seek yet more support and reinforcements, all of which will require authorisation by you in Berlin. Our supply lines have succumbed to crisis and collapsed. As this interminable war struggles towards its second winter, conditions in the Carpathians could not be worse. Candidly, we face decimation. It is no exaggeration to declare that hundreds of our men freeze to death daily; to date our losses already exceed more than 800,000. Without God's deliverance, we cannot hold the line for much longer; your help is essential.

COLONEL HOFFMAN

Attached to the letter was a long list of supplies that the Colonel now urgently sought: wheat, flour, potatoes, meat; boots, gloves, trench-coats, hats; horses, hay, shells and rifles. The list went on and on in great detail and for three pages, but of course, more than anything else, new recruits were needed: 100,000 additional men.

Men reduced to a commodity, alongside potatoes and socks on a list. It augmented all the loathing of military ethics that had weighed down on Herr von Steindorf since childhood. With the pain of Marcus' death coiled tightly around his heart, he felt a sharp kick of anger as he looked down the list: 100,000 men, most barely more than boys, whose life expectancy the Colonel knew would, along that sixty-mile stretch of the Eastern front, be a dismal five weeks.

'There is something that I would very much like to discuss with you,' Graf von Duisburg continued tentatively, for he was acutely aware of the trust that he placed in Herr von Steindorf by even having the conversation with him. 'From what I see and hear, it seems that few civilians have any notion about the realities of this war. Away from the front, only some understand how the nature of war has changed forever. The battlegrounds and strategies of old are now obsolete, but the tactics still employed to disastrous effect. Modern technology has created a faceless enemy with artillery and gas and aerial bombing that can efficiently kill from a distance of many miles. War has never had such a voracious appetite, and yet daily more men, lured by the promise of a "glorious victory", are sent to stand defenceless against a storm of steel, to fight a war with no aims and no chance of victory. Newspapers – naturally, as the government controls them – print nothing of these matters. It is imperative that a halt be brought to this shameful deceit. I have an idea that will hopefully redress the balance of truth – but I will need your help to accomplish it.'

Graff von Duisburg had certainly attracted his host's full attention, and they talked though the young man's plans against the dying light of the drawing room fire. By ten, it had been imperative that Graf von Duisburg leave and report to the army barracks, but by then Herr von Steindorf was already resolved about exactly what had to be done.

*　　*　　*

The crowded streets had been left far behind. Herr von Steindorf was now near to his home, and here, north of the river Spree where the city was quiet and clear, his footsteps echoed through the silent shadows. A pale slice of winter's moon hung low in the night's sky. Many men would die tonight under this same, thin moon, cold and lonely in the trenches of France, or like Marcus, on the bleak mountains in Austria. But for Herr von Steindorf, comfortably wrapped in a calf-length overcoat and heading for the warmth of his Berlin home, this was a time to celebrate life and leave for a while all thoughts of the war. He had finally become a father. Little more than an hour ago, Katarina had given birth.

For longer than even Herr von Steindorf had realised, he had yearned for this day, hiding his desire behind the neutral façade that he wore so well, but was now slipping fast. Instinct demanded that he be with his wife and new daughter Renata, and he raced, urgently, the last steps across the cobbled street to his home.

Katarina, elated and exhausted in equal measures, lay cocooned in an opal eiderdown quilt on their bed. She still felt sore from the contractions and had been slightly torn during the birth, but otherwise it had been an uncomplicated delivery, overseen at home by a brusque but efficient midwife, who now attended to the baby, and her assistant who busied herself with Renata.

Enveloping Katarina in the tightest embrace, Herr von Steindorf sat down on the bed beside her. They stayed together like this, wrapped in each other and a gentle silence, until finally the midwife brought in Renata, freshly washed and swathed in soft cotton and a warm woollen blanket, and placed his daughter in his arms for the very first time. Herr von Steindorf had never before held a newborn child, and marvelled at her tiny, perfect fingers, and beautiful, delicate features. She had her mother's eyes, pale green like peridot gemstones, and a shock of black hair that he carefully stroked.

He loved her at once. A sharp piercing love, forceful and unexpected, that shifted forever his emotional axis. Love had previously run a tranquil course through his life. He adored Katarina and was devoted to his mother, but Renata changed everything, and he ached with tenderness as she etched her indelible mark across his heart. In a quiet corner of Berlin, while Europe suffered and struggled under the vast shadow of the war's destruction, Herr von Steindorf had found the penumbra of hope.

2

SCHRECKLICHKEIT
Oil and acrylic on canvas
252cm x 206cm

Berlin, Germany. November 15th, 1995.

Rain and the rush hour imposed their time on Ellie's journey, and she arrived even later than she had intended at the *Kunsthalle*. 'Where the bloody hell have you been?' said Justin by way of a greeting, although he sounded hurt, not angry, anxiety cross-hatched across his face. 'I really needed you here,' he rasped, the words seemingly scraping his throat as he spoke.

'I'm really sorry, I just lost track of time,' mumbled Ellie weakly, in response. Then, aiming for a casual pitch, she asked, 'Are they here yet?'

Justin simply shook his head. He didn't need to enquire – she was obviously referring to their mother and grandmother.

Peering through the foyer doorway whilst unwrapping wintry layers in soft washed shades, Ellie realised that the Germans had lived up to their renowned punctuality. Berlin's *Bürger-meister* had already arrived, as had the Federal Minister for *Kultur*, and the *Kunsthalle* was awash with journalists and art world grandees who all wanted to meet the conspicuously absent artist. One hundred pairs of impatient eyes glanced expectantly towards the entrance. Ellie's stomach, perched on a high trapeze of adrenaline, leapt and then fell.

The evening was the culmination of Justin's work for the past twenty months and a crucial moment in not only her career, but also his own. At first the idea for the exhibition, 'Germany: the

Twentieth Century', had seemed an audacious suggestion to Ellie, a clever marketing tool designed to enter the world's most buoyant art market and sell her work. When her brother had first mentioned it over a greasy spoon lunch during an endless drab winter, she never imagined that it would come together. But he'd had a strategy formed for the project already, and quickly set up a meeting with the Cultural Attaché at the German Embassy in London to launch the idea.

'You'll never convince them to go for it,' she'd said, dipping crispy bacon into the aureolin yolk of an egg.

'Of course they will – the exhibition's exactly what's needed in Germany at the moment,' Justin replied confidently, spreading HP sauce over his double sausage butty. 'And Berlin's the obvious venue. The politicians there are desperate to demonstrate how great the city is now that it's the capital again, and you're the best placed artist to front it all – German enough so that your work can be a credible voice for the country, but at the same time a foreigner so they can distance themselves from it if it turns out to be a disaster. Why wouldn't they go for it?'

'But why an exhibition of my work, when they've got enough home grown artists of their own?' she'd asked, doubtful as ever of any success. 'And why art in any case? Why not something else on a larger scale, wait until the conversion of the Reichstag's been completed and then promote all of the city's new and historic buildings? Or local industry, or put on a music festival? The city has such a broad spectrum of genres and they could appeal to a much wider audience by doing that. Won't they think we're being a bit presumptuous to imagine that my art could be a voice for Germany?'

Rain had been falling in sharp angles on the city streets outside, whilst inside the steam from cups of coffee and conversations turned the café windows translucent, cocooning them indoors.

'There's a growing trend for corporations to align themselves with artists,' Justin answered whilst biting into his butty, but carrying on regardless. 'It's considered cool and contemporary and inclusive. Think of the banks and industrial giants who now sponsor major art events and galleries – they're all basically dull brands that are using art to change their image. In effect it's just carefully targeted high-end advertising, and Deutsche Bank has really led the way in this field so it's an established business model in Germany already. Well, this is the same sort of thing. Let's face it: it's about the most effective, low cost, PR exercise the Germans could make at the moment. It'll get press coverage the world over, but cost them peanuts – compared to other events – and it sends out all the right messages, most importantly that Germany acknowledges its mistakes from the past, but now with reunification is looking for a fresh start.'

He pushed his plate to the side of the table, lit up another cigarette, and opened his briefcase to bring out an armful of literature: a couple of books, one on German Art and the other titled *Modern German History*; a document pouch with articles from the *Herald Tribune, Stern Magazine* and the *Washington Post*; museum brochures and pamphlets from the German Tourist Board – all his research to demonstrate why Berlin would be the perfect venue for such an exhibition.

'Look,' he said, 'Listen to this article: "The city, when history has allowed, has long been a magnet for artists, composers and writers. By the beginning of the twentieth century it was already home to three opera houses, numerous theatres and renowned orchestras, and the cluster of museums by the river Spree had grown sufficiently large to rename the area Museums Island. However, in the division of the city at the end of World War II, these museums had fallen into Russian control leaving West Berlin severed from its acclaimed Arts heritage." '

He ordered fresh coffee for them both and then continued with his animated explanation. The Cold War years had seen two main areas of growth across the city – espionage, and the

Arts. Gradually, as both the East and West governments that controlled Berlin had come to realise the value of culture as a tool for propaganda, they had invested increasing amounts in events and institutions, from the Berlin Philharmonic Orchestra to the Berlin Film Festival and show piece galleries, so that when eventually the Wall had come down the reunited city had a combined inheritance of seventeen well stocked museums. These, it was hoped, held the key to a new identity; out of its troubled past, Berlin would become the City of Museums.

However, rather than the indifferent response Ellie had predicted at the German Embassy, the Cultural Attaché agreed that the exhibition would fit in well with the planned arts programme for Berlin, which was certainly bold and broad reaching. And so, from Justin's vague notion for a low-key wine and cheese rent-a-crowd event, the show had evolved into a cultural and spiritual watershed for the capital, and even Justin now hoped that its success would reach beyond sales figures and column inches.

Christo, the Bulgarian artist, dramatically led the way forward earlier in '95 when he had 'wrapped' the Reichstag in a million square feet of silver covered fabric, prior to the building's renovation and re-emergence as the Bundestag, and now, in the intimate setting of the Berliner *Moderne Kunsthalle*, Ellie's exhibition was presented as a brave confrontation of Germany's tumultuous century. Although of course, it wasn't.

There had been no ambitious intellectual agenda in the creating of her work, no grand plan to chronicle history, no erudite analysis of events. The paintings told her emotional journey, nothing more: she had simply painted.

It was Justin who had talked them up and sold them as social and political commentary, who had seen how their own lives had been shaped by Germany's history and how the parallel events reflected in her paintings. It was Justin who by deft salesmanship and promotion had transformed her from Ellie Tyler, unknown amateur painter, into Eleanor von Steindorf, renowned artist, and had changed both of their lives.

*   *   *

'We'd better go,' he said briskly, gesturing towards the waiting guests in the *Kunsthalle*. 'Meet and greet – before they all go home.' And they both stepped forward into the room.

This was the first time that Ellie had seen all of the paintings assembled and on display together, and, even though they had not been painted to be viewed as a group, their colour and form moved with fluency around the room. Some she hadn't seen in years, they had long been sold and were now here on loan from the new owners' private collections. A couple had been borrowed back from a museum in California, while the others, they hoped, would be sold on from the exhibition.

The simple, clean lines of the *Kunsthalle* provided the perfect contrast to the strong colours that Ellie employed in her work, muted light shimmered around the edge of the room through a border of opaque floor tiles, and – apart from three slate topped tables, each decorated with a row of single white lilies in stem glass vases – there was nothing to distract the viewer from the paintings.

Ellie had stayed away from the exhibition earlier on in the day, worried that she would make a nuisance of herself. Experience had taught her that she would most probably end up arguing with Justin over the placing of every picture, or the depth of the halogen lighting, or the shade of taupe on the suede block mounts, or any of the other details which she knew he invariably chose much better than she did, but out of anxiety she would inevitably find quite wrong. Consequently, as she finally looked around the gallery, she did so with fresh eyes. The paintings, she thought, were good, and the fact that she could even acknowledge their merit was something of a personal triumph: Ellie was, at last, comfortable with all that she had achieved. Success had certainly

53

not come overnight to her, and, in fact, for a very long time it had seemed an improbable goal.

London, England. Thursday 7th April 1977.

The first Thursday of the month was not only the last day of the spring school term, but also Ellie Tyler's seventeenth birthday. However, apart from a sketchpad from her brother, a card with £10 enclosed that her father had sent from Derbyshire, book vouchers from her maternal grandmother – she received these routinely and rather ungratefully each Christmas and birthday – and a strawberry flavoured Mary Quant lip-gloss from her school friend Lisa, the day was ignored by everyone else. Her mother, Sabina, had still been asleep and had left nothing out for Ellie before she headed off for school that morning, and when she got back home in the afternoon – at her mother's insistence, because given the choice Ellie would have made plans to be out with her friends – Sabina told Ellie, with a note of victory skewered through the words, that Ellie's birthday 'had been cancelled'.

There was no party, no cake, no celebration at all, in fact just the opposite: in the morning Ellie was thrown out of school, and that evening, as a result, she was thrown out of home. 'Happy Bloody Birthday', she said bitterly to herself as she hurriedly packed to leave for the final time.

At least, she conceded, the charade of her education, and of her family life, was finally over. She knew that she probably shouldn't have been surprised by either of those things, because they had both been a long time coming. Nevertheless, her stomach felt serrated with shock.

Ellie had wanted to get away for ages, but this enforced exile felt too soon. For some reason, naivety or arrogance she wasn't sure which, she had always assumed that when she left home it would be a decision that she made at her own convenience, and not one that was thrust upon her. Apart from having neither plans nor money – not her main concern as she knew that she could always find sanctuary with her friend Lisa's family – she was really anxious about walking away from Justin.

There were two and half years between them, and they had always been close. He was a sweet natured baby and then a small boy with an easy smile, endless blond curls and gentle blue eyes. From the outset Ellie adored him, and he returned his sister's affection with steadfast loyalty. As she sifted through her possessions, making hasty decisions about what to take, she felt that she was committing a terrible betrayal by abandoning him so abruptly. Her worry was not so much that he would miss her, but that at times he was genuinely frightened of their mother. And, unfortunately, she knew that he had every reason to feel that way. Their mother had always been especially brutal with Justin, although she was never sure why. There was no obvious reason why he deserved it, but it seemed that he was forever stained with a spectrum of bruises or a wound that was scabbed and sore.

Ellie could understand, to an extent, why their mother fought and argued with her. Since their father had left them Ellie had become increasing bold about challenging her mother's drunken and deranged behaviour. In the same way that she'd watched her father so many times, she would empty her mother's gin bottles down the sink when she found them, and over the years that had led to some bitter arguments between the two of them. It was a cycle that they endured together with depressing regularity, at least from Ellie's point of view.

Perhaps inevitably, Sabina had grown more adept at hiding alcohol around the house, and Ellie was forced to adapt to her mother's increasing connivance. It was not uncommon for her to find gin decanted into used bottles of fruit squash and secreted behind the various infrequently used cleaning products beneath the kitchen sink, or concealed between the bundles of un-ironed laundry that languished for months in the airing cupboard, or even stashed inside a lavatory cistern. Regardless of the possible consequences, Ellie poured it away all the same. And when their mother started on them, Ellie would try and grab Justin by the hand and leave the house for long enough so that their mother would have probably calmed down, or better still fallen asleep, by the time that they'd got back. Quite often after their mother slept off the alcohol she would have – perhaps rather conveniently – entirely forgotten all the preceding rage.

Later on, once Ellie had caught up with her mother in height, an instinctive slap in retaliation had proved to them both that Ellie no longer had any qualms about protecting herself.

But Justin, she knew, was just the opposite. He was conciliatory and uncomplaining, always trying to placate their mother or looking for reasons to excuse her behaviour, and he had never once come close to even shoving her, let alone striking her. Yet in spite of this, for some reason he still bore the brunt of their mother's temper, and Ellie feared that if she were not living at home and around at least some of the time to distract and dilute her anger, then God knows what would happen to him. He would certainly struggle to cope with her on his own, much as he believed that in his own passive way he dealt with her better than his sister. But Ellie had come home often enough to find him nursing some fresh wound in the aftermath of yet another one of their mother's outbursts, to know that his words were no match for her temper.

The family had been slowly eroding away for years, although the cracks between them, corroded into chasms by alcohol, had always, beyond their home, been carefully concealed. They would whitewash over everything, pretending to themselves, as much as to others, that the problems weren't there.

For many years they had explained their father's absence by telling people that he was temporarily helping out on his family's farm in Derbyshire, and by implying that he was frequently still with them in Ealing. But he wasn't. Their parents had separated, and their father had long since left home for good. And as for their mother – they certainly never went even near to the truth with her.

'She's not well,' they would say when they needed an excuse for her non-appearance at a particular event. If pressed, they would get more inventive. 'She's got a migraine,' they'd lie, or backache, or something else that sounded more acceptable, because the reality, that she was an alcoholic and drunk, was too humiliating for them all to admit to.

And for as long as Ellie could remember, they had kept a united front: all told the same lies, all kept the same secrets, although she was not sure why. On the rare occasions that she genuinely considered the matter – and generally it was a subject that she tried to avoid – Ellie surmised that they were simply too embarrassed by the truth, or that they blamed themselves for her drinking, or that the reality was just too difficult to face. After all, if you admit to a problem, you then have no excuse to ignore it.

So, throughout most of their childhood, whilst it had slowly dissolved their family life, their mother's drinking, and all its ugly consequences, had remained their unpleasant and untouchable secret. It was something that Ellie had never, ever, talked about outside her home, and even amongst themselves it was a subject that they usually discussed in euphemisms. As a result, if Ellie arrived back home and Justin said, 'Mother's ill,' she knew that their mother was drunk. They would hide her hangover beneath the words, 'She's tired,' and the harsh reality of her nasty, violent streak was described with innocuous expressions such as, 'She got a bit overwrought.' Of course, it didn't change the reality of the terror that they lived with, but at least it lent it some small degree of emotional distance.

Ellie realised that they had learned from their father to lie in this way. He had always spoken about their mother like that when they were very young, glossing over her drunkenness with the phrase, 'She's having an episode,' which in his mind added an aura of medical respectability to the depressing actuality.

At heart their father was an open and artless man, and her behaviour must have seemed an enigma to him. Most probably he was trying to protect his children, preserve their innocence amidst all the chaos around them, or maybe he was simply being a loyal husband. Ellie knew that for a long time he had loved his wife deeply, and wouldn't tolerate a bad word said against her. He had told his children often enough, and with genuine affection, how for weeks he had watched their mother across the crowded floor at the Hammersmith Palais before finding the courage to ask her to dance. Finally, as the band struck up the opening bars of 'Swingin' Shepherd Blues', he asked her to join him on the dance floor, and had hardly been able to believe his luck when she readily agreed to do so. Tall and angular, with pale skin and intense umber eyes, he'd thought that she looked like a fair haired version of Katherine Hepburn. He was mesmerised by her from first glance. She was striking looking, he'd always said, which Ellie thought was probably true. It was her mother's individuality and eclectic style that caught her father's attention, and it didn't surprise him when he later learned that she had studied for a while at the Chelsea School of Art. Unlike all the other girls in their layers of net petticoats, bright circle skirts and taffeta dresses, Sabina had no concern for fashion. He felt more comfortable with her less contrived approach to clothes. The shy farmer's son, better looking than he had ever realised with his sepia hair and open face, new to the capital from the rural north and still more comfortable in corduroy or tweed than the more vibrant fashions of the city, had always felt he had two left feet when it came to dancing. Recently graduated from Durham University and in his first job as a junior surveyor, it was all a long way from the students' and Young Farmers' dances that he had been used to. But somehow under Sabina's direction, he was soon able to master the Jitterbug and Cha–Cha and suddenly he was having more fun than ever before.

For several months their courtship had been confined to the dance halls of the capital, with Ted Heath's Orchestra or the Humphrey Lyttelton Band unaware of their role as chaperone to the pair. It was only later, when their new-found intimacy left Sabina unexpectedly pregnant, that their hastily arranged marriage exposed how, beyond the mirage of their relationship on the dance floor and a shared love of swing and big band music, they really knew very little of each other. Parenthood then amplified the uncomfortable distance between those differences.

When Ellie and Justin were still small children, usually after their mother had behaved vilely or violently or both, their father would take them somewhere quiet within the house or outside in the garden to comfort them with soothing words and a soft embrace.

'Of course she loves you,' he would tell them, with forced cheerfulness and strained, unhappy eyes. 'Of course she cares for you. It's just that she suffered so much when she was younger and saw such terrible things during the war in Germany where she was born, that she sometimes forgets how to show it.' But in the end that excuse wore thin for someone as innately un-complicated as their father. He knew that whatever his wife had gone through, it was no justification for how she behaved with their children. Or perhaps he just felt guilty. Ellie could clearly recall several occasions when her mother, her stare fierce and goading, had snarled at her father how pregnancy had trapped her into a marriage that she had never wanted. And if she said that in front of her children, Ellie could only imagine what she hurled at him when they were alone.

Looking back, Ellie conceived how her father had probably hoped his love for his wife would suffice for the two of them. He'd probably once hoped that it might even be reciprocated. Sadly, that dream gradually become a delusion, until, tragically, he realised that he was lying to himself. An alcoholic makes liars of everyone around them if they allow it, and unfortunately, they all did.

Ellie could never be entirely certain at what point in her childhood she realised that life in her household was so different to most others. But by the time that she'd finished primary school, she had learned that the quality of their daily lives was dictated by the quantity of alcohol that their mother consumed. Each day she played Russian roulette with their family life using shots of gin instead of bullets, although the end result was just the same: a few shots and they'd probably all be okay, but if she took too many then someone would inevitably end up getting hurt.

Sabina's precarious temper became the punctuation of their family life, shaping and marking their household and childhood. In the Art Room at the children's school, there was a poster of Picasso's *Guernica*, and the terror it depicted reminded Ellie not of war, but of her home life. There were so many nights when she was kept awake by the angry crescendo of her mother's shouting, imprisoned by anxiety and cowardice in the dark of her room. All too often her dreams were shattered by the sound of smashing plates and breaking glass that told of yet more broken promises, and her parents' voices – her father's exasperated cries counterpoint to her mother's discordant rant – coiled tightly around her, leaving her choked with fear. The words, 'Stop it Sabina, for God's sake just stop it!' or something similar, rang through their house like the chorus from some corrupted lullaby. But her father's pleading was always in vain, he could not stop her, much as he tried; and much as he begged her, she would not stop.

As Ellie grew older the fights between her parents seemed to get much worse. Or maybe she just grew more aware of them, and the anger in their house that constantly threatened to asphyxiate them all. Certainly, it became increasingly hard for her to remain uninvolved, until, eventually, she found the courage to go down and try and stop their fighting. She never did, of course, in fact, if ever she did try to come between them, either her father would simply insist that she left the room, or her mother would turn on her instead.

Then one evening, far enough into a damp and dull January that any Christmas cheer had long been forgotten, and the still short winter days had further dulled the family's spirits, her parents' fighting had became so fierce that she truly thought one of them might end up dead.

Like many of the very worst storms, this one between her parents had come upon them out of nowhere. They'd had a calm few months, and even Christmas had passed without the friction and dramas that in their household were as much of a tradition as a tree and the turkey. It had been one of the occasional periods that over the years the family had enjoyed, when for a short time – a few days, or weeks, or even several months if they were lucky – Sabina managed to give up drinking. For good, of course. Each time she always said it was for good. Only on this occasion she really had stopped drinking for quite a while, and as the days turned into weeks and then stretched into months, they all begun to relax and believe that her drunken days were over. But sadly her sobriety did not last, and instead their lives became very much worse.

That afternoon, Ellie and Justin stood for almost an hour beneath the heavy, gun metal sky, waiting for their mother to collect them from school. A sharp north-east wind scraped at their cheeks and gloveless hands all the while, leaving their chapped skin as raw as their nerves. The minutes dragged endlessly on and the last of the light ebbed away into the on-coming night, but still she had not shown up. From bitter experience, they could both sense the battalion of clouds gathering sternly on their family horizon.

The walk home with their mother meant more to her, than to her children. By then, they had long got used to going to and from school on their own, but she'd come to the school to collect them each day since she'd last stopped drinking. It was supposed to be her way of showing them, that sober, she could be the perfect parent.

Eventually, as the street lights flickered into life all around, and defeated by the cold, they gave up their wait and began the short walk back home on their own. They avoided each other's eyes and any conversation. Ellie felt angry and anxious in equal measures; Justin only felt anxious.

Their pace slowed with every step closer to their home. As they approached the house they could see the Murano glass lamp shining out through the half drawn maroon curtains, indicating that someone was probably inside the house. Ellie rung the doorbell, but, ominously, it went unanswered. The signs were growing that their mother was probably 'unwell'. Reluctantly, they both walked around the house and let themselves in through the creaking back door, still hoping that their worst fears and intuition would be proved wrong.

The kitchen appeared much the same as they'd left it that morning, apart from feeling both freezing and damp. The house was heated by a temperamental and noisy boiler which needed replacing, but until that time came it required re-igniting at least once a day. Its carapace clung to the wall, conspicuously silent. Cluttered across the beige Formica table were the remnants of their breakfast. A half empty bottle of milk and a Cornflakes packet. A jar with barnacles of sugar stuck to the sides. Their used spoons and bowls encrusted with dried out flakes and a pool of curdling milk at the bottom. But unlike the morning when they had left for school, the room smelt nauseous and Ellie thought that she might retch as she breathed in the air.

Wearily, they both walked through the room, past the sink that was now splattered with congealing sick and across the small gloomy hallway where a spider plant perched menacingly on a too small table.

Cautiously, they peered around the half-open door of the

sitting room. Spread out before them was the confirmation of all their qualms: their mother slumped on the sofa, wrapped, tramp-like, in her olive green candlewick bedspread, with a haze of stale smoke hanging in layers above her. She had her eyes scrunched shut and her mouth agape and the debris of a day's binge all around her: an overflowing ashtray, a crumpled cigarette packet – and an empty bottle of gin. There was cold buttered toast on a plate beside her that had not been touched and looked shrivelled and hard.

Justin looked expectantly at his sister for a decision as to whether they should wake her up or leave her alone. Suddenly, he looked so much younger to Ellie than his actual age: not ten, but a frightened very small boy. Anxiously, her mind flitted between the options – both had their drawbacks – but after a moment she walked quietly across the room and gently shook her mother's arm to try and rouse her. She was wearing her quilted floral dressing gown, and Ellie wondered whether she had got dressed into her clothes at all that day.

'Where've you been?' Sabina mumbled through sour breath, peering up at her children with glazed half-opened eyes. The words were spiked with annoyance and loosely strung together.

Ellie seethed. Obviously her mother was too drunk to remember that her children went to school most days, or even notice that they were wearing their uniforms. However, she thought it would be wise to quash those feelings.

'We've just got back from school,' she managed carefully. 'You look a bit tired, why don't we leave you in peace?' She added, now keen to quickly retreat from the room and leave her mother alone to go back to sleep.

Naively, Ellie hoped that her mother might sleep off the alcohol before her father got home. She knew that there'd be hell all around if her father came back and found his wife and the house in the state they were both in. The thought of yet another argument between her parents filled her with dread, and so she resigned herself to the job of purging the house of the stench of stale smoke and spirits and sick. She felt somewhat overwhelmed by the task ahead of her, but even more terrified of the alternative.

Forlornly, the children returned to the kitchen, Justin looking so pale and stricken that Ellie had to suppress her urge to utter profanities.

'I'll make you a jam sandwich and some orange squash,' said Ellie with a strained smile, trying her best to distract her brother. Hurriedly, she prepared him the snack that he ate slowly and in silence whilst she laboured to coax the boiler back into life. Then, trying to maintain some semblance of normality, she sent Justin upstairs to start on his homework so that downstairs she could begin to erase the evidence of her mother's excesses.

Quietly, Ellie went back into the sitting room and pulled up the sash frames on the windows – apparently asleep again, her mother ignored her. Ellie removed the ashtray, cigarette packets, and the gin bottle – which she carefully hid at the bottom of the dustbin so that her father wouldn't spot it. She got out a brush and pan to sweep up the scattered ash and discarded butts, and then sprayed the room with furniture polish to disguise the acrid odour. Hoping that her mother would have the sense to change out of her nightclothes before her father got home, Ellie brought down her mother's navy Crimplene trousers and russet mohair sweater – both were worn out and rather shapeless, but then so were most of her clothes – which she left beside her on the floor. Finally, she lowered the open window so that only a small draught of air flowed through the room. She turned off the light, and shut the door behind her so that her mother could sober up a bit before her father arrived home. The kitchen was much harder to clean and took much longer to sort out: not the bowls and spoons from breakfast, but the fetid, vomit blocked sink.

By the time her father had got back at about half past six, the house smelt quite fresh and looked fairly tidy, or at least much as it usually did. Ellie had planned to keep silent about the matter, and had instructed Justin to do so too.

Unfortunately, she hadn't cleared up around her mother as well as she'd assumed: she missed another bottle of gin that her mother had hidden elsewhere in the sitting room. When her father had gone in there to see her, she'd drunk most of that as well.

There were a hushed few seconds before their father erupted. Normally he was a quiet, gentle man, but this was one too many an occasion when Sabina had broken her promise to him – to them all – and he could not deal with the misery of her drinking yet again.

'You fucking bitch!' he'd yelled.

Terrified, Ellie raced upstairs, three steps at a time, to hide with Justin in his room. They sat together on the floor in silence, their backs pressed up against the door to keep it shut, and listened to their parents tearing their lives apart.

The row quickly combusted, with insults and objects hurled around the room and at each other. The initial thwack of a slap across skin swiftly escalated into the frenzied sound of someone slamming into a wall. There followed grunts of pain and shrieks of fury accompanying a crescendo of clattering furniture scattered. The mantelpiece mirror shattered and the fight culminated in one of their parents being knocked so hard into the door that Ellie and Justin heard the distinctive crack of splintering wood as either their mother or father hit the panel. It was then that Ellie decided to call the police.

Leaving Justin sobbing into his tightly clasped knees, she crept timorously down to the hallway and picked up the phone. Within minutes a patrol car arrived, and the family's secret battles were announced to the world by the relentless glare of its flitting blue light and the shriek of its siren through the still of the night.

For what seemed like ages, two officers pounded furiously on the front door and hollered at them to open up. By then Ellie had cowardly escaped back upstairs to rejoin Justin and avoid the confrontation, terrified of the consequences of what she'd set in motion.

'You're so bloody stupid, Ellie,' Justin had bawled. 'Why did you do that? You've made it ten times worse now.'

All the while, their parents shouting had continued uninterrupted and the front door remained unanswered. Eventually, there was silence from the police. Ellie imagined that they'd gone away. Then suddenly, from the back of the house, there was a blast of noise as the police kicked in the kitchen door and stormed through to the sitting room.

Before a word had been said, their father, the presumed aggressor, had been pinned against the wall with a truncheon held to his head to keep him in line. They'd eased up on him when they noticed white flakes of paint from the cracked door panel stuck to his head, a bruise unfurling over his cheek, and blood streaks through his dishevelled hair. He, they soon realised, was the only one injured, whilst Sabina, for all the noise that she was making, was simply drunk. But it seemed like hours before they finally left the house, and only after they took statements from them all and Sabina was ordered for a summons at the Magistrate's Court.

She never forgave her daughter for calling the police, accusing her of being disloyal to the family by getting strangers involved in their private lives. More truthfully, though she never admitted it, she was embarrassed by it all and frightened of the possible repercussions.

The Magistrates hearing was a week later, and it was a sombre time for them all, although, mercifully, for once all the arguments between them stopped. Evidently, their parents must have put on a good show of solidarity because no charges were pressed against their mother, though when they returned home from Court they'd barely spoke a word to either their children or each other, and Ellie had thought they both looked grey and harsh, like the February sky that day.

Within a month their father had left the house. He returned to Derbyshire and the family farm which his brother Peter had run since both their parents had died, working with him whilst he looked around for another job as a surveyor in Matlock or Ashbourne or any of the other towns nearby. He promised that they would all join him up there very soon and make a fresh start as a family, away from the problems that had sullied their lives in London.

In Ealing, Ellie and Justin's spirits lifted with the promise of a new life to come. For a while there was a clear sense of excitement about the house, mixed also with relief at the end to the bitter hostilities between their mother and father. However, all too soon their mother just changed adversaries and instead of their father, she picked fights with them.

Somehow the move to Derbyshire kept being put off. For at least a year, Ellie nagged her mother about when they'd move, but whenever she asked there was always some new reason to postpone their plans. They were waiting for the school year to end. Her father had not been able to find a new job and was still on the farm where there was not enough space for them all to stay. It was the wrong time to sell up in London.

In truth, Ellie was never sure that her father ever put that much effort into looking for another job, as he seemed quite happy working with his brother on the farm. Her hopes for them all joining him had been raised the following year when he'd moved off the farm – though he continued to work there – and into a gritstone cottage that he rented in Winster, a small shale-edged village in a broad valley nearby. However, it became quite apparent on their subsequent visit, that whilst full of rural charm, with a beamed kitchen and living room downstairs, with only two small bedrooms and a tiny bathroom upstairs it would be a struggle for all four of them to live there permanently. And it had taken a while, but eventually Ellie realised that the move was not going to happen, and they would never again all live together as a family.

It was difficult for Ellie to maintain a relationship with her father at a distance, and she increasingly missed him. There were occasional phone calls, although these were hard to orchestrate as she had to synchronise their timing so that her mother was out of the house when her father was inside his cottage; and there were infrequent visits to stay with him which invariably sparked a spate of jealous tantrums from her mother. But whilst Justin and Ellie felt lost – and bored – in the landscape without the sights and smells of city life when they did go to Derbyshire, their father seemed so much more at ease amongst the iridescent patchwork of walled fields and limestone outcrops stretched out in all directions around him. He appeared perfectly content with the simplicity of dropping off hay and salt licks, dipping and shearing sheep, tending ewes and lambs or trimming capping stones and shoring up walls, or driving the flock to summer pastures high on the White Peak.

For the first couple of years after his departure, their father made the effort to come home for Christmas and Easter and for all of their birthdays. But they were tense visits that inevitably fuelled a torrential drinking spree from their mother and dissolved any illusions they may have held about being a happy family, even for a single day. Justin and Ellie were always thrilled to see him, but would later pay for those hours of happiness with weeks of wrath from their mother. They had been too young and tactless to conceal their delight at seeing their father, and that only highlighted the hostility between them and their mother. Eventually, Ellie realised that her mother was probably envious of the affection they gave him; it was something she so obviously missed out on from them.

Soon the gaps between their father's visits extended even further, until finally, when their mother served divorce papers on him, they stopped altogether.

Without their father around at all, the floodgate on their mother's drinking burst open completely. It soon felt as if they were mopping up after her every day. Coffee, gin, vomit, urine; they just got used to clearing it up; because, if they didn't, then their mother would certainly never have bothered.

Ellie and Justin muddled through as best they could. They bought food if their mother gave them money, or trawled through the remnants of the kitchen cupboards and freezer, or scrounged off friends, if she didn't. In time, Ellie had grown more resourceful, selling the alcohol she found to her friends and not pouring it all away. It at least put money in her pocket for records and clothes and make-up, and food if it were absolutely necessary. Occasionally, she and Justin tidied up when the house became desperate, and even washed their clothes when they ran out of clean things to wear. Their mother did little beyond sleep, drink or shout.

Justin buried himself in his schooling and books throughout all the turmoil, finding it a comforting refuge from reality; but Ellie soon gave up. She could not see the point of it any more, and, in any case, she felt too worn down by all the problems at home to concentrate in the classroom. Then what began one day as a need to escape the unbearable pressures of school and home for a few hours, soon become a daily habit.

It didn't take long for Ellie to master the art of truancy. Nonchalantly appearing for registration at school each morning, she would then leave the building and head to Ealing station, from where she would fare dodge her way into central London. En route, she would change the more obvious items of clothing that marked her out as a school kid on the loose, and add a few extra years to her face with layers of make-up. In the late afternoon she would simply reverse the process and head back home, where her mother – who by that time of the day would already be well on the way to alcoholic oblivion – would never question her about her day.

The freedom she found in a day exploring the city was worth any punishment threatened or metered out. If the weather was good, lying stretched out in a park seemed a better place to be than the science lab, whilst on cold and rainy days, wandering around a department store or endlessly and aimlessly criss-crossing the city by tube held more excitement than any class-room ever could. But best of all, when she was on her own, there was no one threatening or shouting at her.

So, for several terms that became the pattern of Ellie's daily life, and, beyond marking a detention against her name – which she was never at school to attend – there was nothing that her teachers could do to deter her. Of course the school sent regular letters to her mother, but they remained unopened in various piles of neglected correspondence that were scattered throughout the house until Ellie eventually found, and then destroyed, them. Even she conceded that the school were probably right to expel her; no one could keep her there for the day any more. Besides, it had been a long time since she had learned a thing. Her few low grades at 'O' levels were, she felt, more of an embarrassment than an achievement; and art – the only subject that she had always loved and in which she had triumphed – her mother had insisted she drop, saying that she clearly didn't have the talent to take it forward as a career. Ellie hoped that the school would argue her cause, but, despite several pleas to various teachers, she was not aware that they ever did. Feeling defeated and undermined, she hated school from then on. Her form teacher's advice to instead work harder on her academic subjects left her feeling furious.

Work harder. You must work harder. She'd had those words flung at her so often over the years, in both the stern and exasperated tones of her teachers at school, and the fierce, angry voice of her mother at home, that they'd became like the worn down heel of shoe – an annoyance, but one that she'd learned to live with. Only, she found it just so damn hard to work at all when she had her mother's face inches from her own, red with alcohol and loathing, screaming at her; or go to school and concentrate, knowing that she and Justin had left her at home crouched like a dog, throwing up all over the floor. And how interested in her French homework did anyone expect her to be, she thought bitterly, if she'd just been slashed by her mother with a belt, or kicked down the stairs, or had witnessed her mother scythe Justin's head with the heel of a stiletto shoe. Not that anyone besides Lisa, and maybe a few other friends, ever believed her; certainly no one who might have been able to help.

On one occasion, Ellie plucked up the courage to talk to her teacher, hoping that somehow she could intervene on Justin's and her behalf. But the teacher had merely got cross and told her that she was being a 'wicked' girl for making up such preposterous stories.

Another time, after their mother had grabbed a log from the fire store and cut Justin's skull so deeply that their doctor had to come to the house and give him stitches – Sabina having artfully explained away the injury with a fictitious account of a fall from a tree, and Justin, ever the peacemaker, stoically complicit with the lie – Ellie had gone to his surgery later that day and told him the truth. She pleaded with him to help them, to at least tell their mother to stop the beatings. However, he had looked her directly in the eye and told her that her mother needed their help, and not more problems.

After that, Ellie had felt that there were few people she could trust. They might not have believed the words, but surely, she thought, the deep cuts and bruises like splattered rainbows that defiled their bodies and faces, too large and raw to be dismissed as normal on a child and renewed with brutal regularity, were information enough?

It must have been around then that Ellie gave up on school completely. She had few friends there – the tribulations that she'd endured set her far apart from her peers – no respect for the teachers who had ignored her various pleas for help, and she'd lost all interest in learning. There was not much to miss, she'd thought, and, perhaps naively, she imagined that no one there would miss her either. But that was obviously not the case, as she found out to her cost on that last day of term.

As usual, Ellie turned up for class registration at the beginning of the school day with the intention of walking straight out after that. However, the Headmistress was standing beside her form teacher and asked Ellie to accompany her to her study. Expecting the usual mild interrogation or patronising lecture about wasting the opportunity that an education provided, Ellie was instead handed a copy of a letter that the Headmistress had sent to her mother the previous day. She glanced across the page with wry detachment.

DEAR MR AND MRS TYLER – I regret to inform you that your daughter Eleanor will not be accepted back at Ealing Secondary Modern after the Easter Holidays. Her teachers, the School Governors and I, all feel that there is no point in trying to educate a pupil who so clearly has no interest in continuing her studies.

Our records show that during this Spring Term Eleanor has attended school for a full day on only nine occasions. It is a great shame that all our efforts to discuss this matter with you, and thus avoid such radical measures, have been previously ignored.

Eleanor is a bright girl who could have achieved much in her last year here. However, it is a sad truth that any chance of success in the forthcoming 'A' level exams is now out of her reach, and her behaviour, which sets such a poor example to our other pupils, can no longer be ignored.

Yours faithfully,

MRS M. FULLER MA

It didn't worry Ellie unduly in any way. After all, she had managed to intercept every other letter that had previously been sent home from the school, and she was pretty confident that she could do the same with this one, and then ride out the summer term in the same way that she had bluffed her way through that far. Obviously she didn't expect to pass her 'A' levels, but she hoped that at least she could avoid any decisions about her future until after the summer was over, which at that moment seemed a long way off.

Unfortunately, her mother, in a rare moment of efficiency – or more than likely looking for birthday money enclosed in her cards – had opened up all that day's mail. Ellie's run of luck as a truant was finally over, as amongst the cards addressed to her, and final reminders of bills sent to her mother, was the letter of expulsion from the school.

Her mother, never shy of a gin bottle at the best of times, met her at the front door, alcohol and anger seeping from every pore. She was drunk. Obviously and obnoxiously drunk, and Ellie knew from experience that it must have taken more than one bottle to fuel that level of fury.

She had just walked into the hallway when her mother hit her hard across the face, and, caught off guard, her head slammed against the wall. Ellie's bag fell to the floor spilling its contents around their feet. Slumped against the wall, winded and struggling to catch her breath, she felt numb with shock and pain. Justin rushed out of the kitchen, his eyes red and swollen from crying, and he came as best he could to her defence.

'Stop it Mother!' he pleaded, trying to pull Ellie away from their mother. 'Please stop it!' The words, sadly, were a lost plea for calm. 'Leave her alone! It's her birthday,' he added, as if that was going to change a thing.

'Stay out of this!' their mother raged at her demented worst. Instinctively recoiling, Justin fled up the stairs.

Still slightly dazed and disoriented, Ellie was bending down to pick up her bag and belongings when her mother unleashed her anger with an alcohol induced fervour. She tried hard not to listen, tried hard to pretend that she did not feel the pain, but if she was honest, she felt that she was collapsing under an avalanche of kicks and punches and words.

'You ungrateful little bitch,' Sabina screeched whilst grabbing a fistful of Ellie's hair and yanking it sharply from the roots, pulling her head up towards her own. Then, she spat in her daughter's face. Spittle and gin trickled slowly down the skin on her cheek.

'After all the sacrifices I've made, I can't believe that you let me down like this,' she yelled, the words stuck together with alcohol and falling like acid rain.

Down on the floor, Ellie saw her mother bend back her leg. Anticipating the kick that was obviously heading in her direction, she curled to the side so that her mother's foot just glanced against Ellie's hipbone and smashed instead into the skirting board. Sabina swore loudly. She must have hurt herself quite badly, and Ellie seized the opportunity to escape the situation. Youth and sobriety were on her side so she rolled away and scrambled quickly to her feet, inadvertently knocking over the hall table and sending the potted spider plant crashing to the floor. A blockade of overturned table legs, books and clothes from her bag, and her mother amidst it all – her feet splattered with soil and the splayed out spider plant – prevented an escape back outside, so Ellie took the stairs up, two at a time, desperate to gain some distance between the two of them.

'Get out of my house now and don't ever come back!' Sabina hurled the words after her daughter, bitterness seeping through into every syllable.

Ellie knew better than to argue with her mother when she was like this, fuelled by both loathing and liquor, so she kept on going, hoping that if she could get to her room, lock the door and stay out of her way, then her mother might eventually calm down. However, as Ellie reached the top of the staircase, the clatter of the hall table across the floor was an ominous prelude to the thump of her feet coming up just behind her. She made it into her room but before she could shut herself in they were both wrestling with the door that finally, with a shove from her mother, leapt inwards and allowed her in.

In a moment Sabina was at her daughter's desk, and with one movement she had swept her arm across it and sent everything crashing to the floor. From the doorway Ellie watched with horror as her art pads and books, make-up and coloured inks, tumbled in a heap onto the carpet. Turning quickly to her left, her mother was soon by Ellie's cupboard and reaching inside, scooping out armfuls of jumpers and jeans and skirts and scarves which she sent in arc through the air, a rainbow of colour that fell to the floor. She then started to rip at whatever was closest to hand, her eyes shot with excitement as she tore through the things that she knew her daughter loved the most.

She had already broken Ellie's favourite necklace, a delicate enamel daisy chain that her father had sent her the previous Christmas, and was reaching for her paintbrushes and charcoals, when Ellie vowed that this would be the last ever fight that her mother picked with her. For years she had been shoved around – verbally, emotionally, and physically – by her mother. She had been ridiculed by her in front of relatives and teachers and friends, and mostly for the simple reason that her mother had consumed too much alcohol. But Ellie had had enough. Her mother was not going to break her possessions – or her – any more.

Adrenaline heightened Ellie's resolve and kick-started her reflexes which had been dulled by the knock to her head. Accompanied by the sound of her art brushes being snapped in half, Ellie leapt at her mother from behind, locking her arms against her side, and then shoved her, writhing and shrieking, towards the doorway and out of her room.

Quickly, Ellie closed the door and turned the key. For a while her mother hammered and hollered outside her room, demanding to be let in, but Ellie focused on her plans and just shut out the noise which trailed off eventually when her mother stomped back down the corridor.

Hurriedly, Ellie grabbed a holdall and a few plastic bags and stuffed into them whatever she thought would be useful and light and easy to carry. The few birthday presents that she had been given earlier on went in first along with bits of make-up that she picked up off the floor, then her sketchpad, brushes, charcoals and paints, and finally some sweaters and her favourite flared jeans, a hand-knitted scarf, her pink platform boots, and her moss green corduroy coat from Carnaby Street.

She left her bedroom as it was after the fight, strewn with the debris of her seventeen years and endless unhappy memories, closing the door, without a shred of regret, on her childhood.

When she went to his room to say goodbye, Justin was crouched on the floor beside his bed, whimpering like a wounded animal between gasps for breath. His hair was plastered wildly across his scalp, and his face flushed vermillion by tears. Seeing him like that hurt Ellie more than anything else that night.

'Please don't go!' Justin begged, each word a struggle through shudders. 'She'll have calmed down by the morning.'

'She's told me to leave the house, Justin,' replied Ellie softly. 'She's wrecked my room.'

'But she'll have forgotten all about it by tomorrow,' he spluttered back.

'I'm really sorry, Justin, I just can't take this any more – I've got to go,' she said wearily. 'Come with me,' she added after a pause. 'I'll look after you – I'll get something sorted out. Or you could always go up to Dad's.'

'That wouldn't work out. I'd be made to come back here, and it'd be even worse when I got back,' said Justin, flatly, rubbing his sleeve across his tear soaked face. He was right, Ellie knew, their father had explained that often enough.

When their parents had eventually decided to proceed with a divorce, they had fought a protracted custody battle, which their father ultimately lost. Their mother, sober that day and smartly dressed before the Judge, had argued that Ellie and Justin were better off staying with her rather than changing homes and schools and leaving their friends behind. And of course, because she didn't work, whilst their father did, she could look after them both that much better – or so she claimed, rather convincingly. The Judge had been on her side all the way, though no one had ever asked Justin or Ellie what they would have preferred. And because of the distance between their father and them, the Judge ordered that they be allowed only one week with him every holiday. Just three visits a year. Their mother was horribly smug when she came home that day. The worst part about it, Ellie knew, was that her mother didn't really care if *she* had the children, just so long as her ex-husband did not. She had fought the whole case out of spite. Whenever Ellie and Justin stayed with their father they pleaded to see him more; but he was adamant that he had to respect the Court Order. He realised that they would end up seeing even less of each other if they went against it.

'I promise I'll be there for you,' said Ellie to Justin, hoping to at least stop him crying. 'I'll come to the school and meet you there as often as I can – but if I'm not there when you come out, don't wait,' she added, then hugged him briefly and turned to leave before he noticed her tears.

As she walked downstairs Ellie heard the television on in the sitting room. She paused and looked in through the door, which was slightly ajar. Her mother was turned away from her, slumped down in the cigarette scarred armchair watching the BBC Nine O'Clock News. Ellie was not certain that she heard her as she didn't look up, or turn around.

For a moment she stood in the doorway, taking in the stench of smoke and stale alcohol and listening to the news while she reflected about going in to say goodbye.

'The wave of terror, the so-called "*Schrecklichkeit*", continues in Germany with the killing today of Siegfried Buback, the Chief Federal Prosecutor. The Red Army Faction has claimed responsibility.'

Hearing the item made Ellie realise how little of Germany's history she knew, despite the fact that her mother had been born there. They had never talked about its past, just as they had never talked about hers. What she understood of the country was held in a few names and words that were overburdened with emotion: Hitler, death camps and The Berlin Wall; Baader-Meinhof and the Red Army Faction. Amongst it all, there seemed nothing to be proud of.

Watching her mother watch the television, Ellie realised that she had no words – either of anger or of affection – left to say to her; she just felt numb. She walked on, and then out of the house. They never even said goodbye.

A chill wind flicked through the pale green shoots of budding spring leaves as Ellie left the house. She pulled out her coat from one of the plastic bags and shrugged her arms and body inside it. She intended to walk over to Lisa's house and ask if she could spend the night there, though at that moment she didn't really care where she went. It was just a relief to leave so much behind: the rage, the fear, the pain. Everything, except, of course, for Justin.

3

SEPARATION
Oil and pastel on canvas
222cm x 285cm.

Berlin, Germany. November 15th 1995

Ellie appreciated that she would have to 'work the crowd'. Over the years Justin had lectured her endlessly on the importance of good public relations, the value of Ellie von Steindorf, the brand, and the commercial realities of the modern, media led art market. He often suggested headline grabbing ideas for her to exploit; but for her celebrity was something to be endured, not enjoyed. During the days when she worked in the box office and then on the paint-frames backstage at the Theatre Royal, she had always been grateful to remain out of the spotlight and away from the glare of the public gaze. With embarrassment, she remembered the evening of her first ever exhibition when she had spent more time hiding away in a nervous bundle, than mixing with the guests. Gradually, she learnt to quell her fears, but even after so many years it was still an effort, not a pleasure, to be at the centre of attention from so many people.

Fortunately, Justin was always quick to sift out all but the most essential individuals that she needed to speak to. 'Remember this is a business event not a social gathering, so no time wasting with friends or family at the *Kunsthalle*,' he'd insisted, back in London, when they were preparing for the evening. 'If they come, they'll have to accept that first and foremost we've got to focus on clients and critics.'

He politely yet firmly ensured that she divided her time

between the Bonn and Berlin officials, the staff from the Cultural Attaché's office in London, and previous and potential buyers.

*   *   *

As much as Ellie was an 'accidental' artist, Justin was her 'accidental' agent. For years she hadn't seen him – no one in the family had, and their communication during all that time had been limited to the occasional phone call down some crackling long-distance line or a postcard or letter bringing greetings but little news.

Aged just eighteen, a few weeks after their father's funeral, Justin had left England abruptly. It had been the bleakest of days, despite the shimmering sky and powder paint colours that the summer sun provided. Blasted by the heat and baking beneath their formal black clothes during the long graveside service, their sweat had mingled with their tears and they had both finished the day exhausted, feeling as if they had buried a part of their heart in their father's grave and had the rest of it ripped apart by their mother.

Within weeks Justin left the country and then travelled incessantly, destination unknown, searching for something, anything, that would piece together his fractured life. And then one April, mid-morning on a Sunday just days before her birthday, he had appeared on her doorstep after a seven-year absence, unannounced, unemployed and out of funds. Until she saw him with his backpacker's tan, sun bleached curls and crumpled clothes, straight off a flight into Heathrow, she hadn't realised just how much she had missed him.

'Justin!' she'd shrieked excitedly, and then flung her arms around him. 'What a brilliant surprise. I can't believe you're here – come on in.'

Curious at all the commotion, Joanna, her small daughter, joined her in the hallway and peered curiously up at the uncle she had not yet met. Justin returned Joanna's look with an equally quizzical stare, as Ellie's letter to him announcing her birth had never caught up with his travels. She invited him in, made the appropriate introductions, and over numerous cups of coffee they had slowly caught up. Conscious of the young ears eagerly taking in every syllable, their conversation had flitted lightly across the broad horizons of Justin's travels and the narrower ones that Ellie and Joanna inhabited at home. Clearly, the allure of adventure had finally lost its appeal, for behind Justin's glamorous tan and golden streaks, an umbra of anxiety still darkened his eyes. He had picked grapes in France and olives in Greece, spent months in a rum induced haze in the Caicos Islands and then on a meditative quest in an Ashram in India, in between working sheep farms in New Zealand and crewing charter boats just about everywhere. But, he realised, the time had come for him to stop, standstill, and finally vanquish the past. That much at least, he had learnt from his travels. He didn't say that he was lonely, but Ellie heard it anyway, caught between the words.

Eventually, the novelty of having a visitor wore off for Joanna and she slipped away back to her room.

'Shit Ellie – I can't believe you've got a kid!' he said in a hushed yet excited voice when Joanna was out of earshot. Ellie's shrugged shoulders and opened hands gestured, 'It happens!'

'Who, and where, is the father?' he asked, still in the same whispered voice.

'He's someone I met at work – an actor – but we split up when he left to work in America. He doesn't know about Jo – I only found out I was pregnant just before he went away, and there was never really the right opportunity to tell him. We're not in touch.'

Justin looked slightly taken aback at that, but continued, 'How the *fuck* did mother react?' And then, having avoided the question for so many years, in a more sombre voice he added, 'And how is she these days?'

'She'd been practically passed out for several days when I told her about Jo,' Ellie replied in what she hoped was a matter-of-fact tone, recalling the squalor of the depressing few days she'd spent with her at the time. 'It barely registered – she'd been on a real bender and wasn't really interested. We hardly see her these days. She's much as ever, I guess. Well, actually sometimes she's much worse. She can get seriously close the edge at times but unless there's a real emergency, I just stay away. You know, I'm busy enough with work and Jo . . . I just don't have the time or energy for all her dramas.'

Justin sighed, and then went over to take out a new packet of cigarettes from a duty-free carton in his rucksack. 'Well, you look amazing,' he said, lighting up and clearly wanting to change the subject. 'And so grown up. You actually got your own place and it's half decent. And a kid, bloody hell Ellie . . . . and you look so happy,' he added, somewhat wistfully, only emphasising her impression that he was anything but.

'Thank you,' she replied. 'It's a bit hectic at times, but we're managing. And Jo's so sweet, she never makes a fuss. After all the hours she spends in nursery she's still so easy going, and we make the most of the time we do have together. I don't want her to go through what we did – I just want her to be happy.'

The poignancy of that thought had weighed down upon them both. Justin lit up another cigarette and Ellie stared in silence at her empty coffee cup, shocked at how quickly their childhood could still crash tumbling into their present day lives.

'You must be starving,' Ellie said, trying to change the subject. 'How about a sandwich? All I've got is some ham and some Dairylea, and bread obviously, oh, and there's some white wine that's already open in the fridge.'

'That sounds great.'

Later, after they'd eaten, he asked somewhat nervously, 'Would it be alright if I stayed a while? It won't be for long – a week or two at most, and then I'll be off again.'

'Of course you can,' Ellie replied, excited by the prospect.

'We're a bit tight for space, but you can have the sitting room sofa bed for as long as you like.'

He unpacked his few possessions from a battered black rucksack. Thick jumpers and thin T-shirts, worn in jeans and washed out shorts – there was not much more, but it was all that he possessed.

Carving out a corner from the tiny apartment in a rundown road of Maida Vale, Justin slotted easily in with their everyday lives. He was naturally more tidy and organised than Ellie, his few belongings kept neatly stacked beneath a corner table, and the sofa bed thoughtfully folded away before she was up and dressed each morning.

Between the demands of long hours at the theatre and those of Joanna, both Justin's company and help had certainly been welcome. Piles of ironing slowly ebbed away; cupboards were cleared, cleaned and sorted; a broken washer on the bathroom tap was finally fixed, and the garden carefully weeded then seeded with larkspur, cornflowers and sweet peas. When not at school, Joanna spent more time at home and not with the child minder, and they'd eaten freshly cooked food and not out of the freezer. And as Justin's tan had begun to fade, so did the impasted pain across his eyes.

Justin's stay of a week or two became a month or two, and after that neither of them had mentioned him leaving again, although for a long time Ellie thought that he might be off again at a moment's notice. But he hung around and then announced, having spent the day sorting through the canvas filled cupboards, that he would sell her paintings.

'I don't know why you're wasting your talents working backstage for a pittance,' he'd said one evening, stirring lemon and cream into strands of spaghetti. Then, pointing a sauce tipped spatula to the paintings he had leaned up against the wall, he'd added, 'I think you could live off those. They're as good as any paintings I've seen for sale. If not better. I've no idea what an art critic would make of them, but I'm sure there's a market for them.'

'What, Portobello maybe?'

'I'm serious, they're expressive, and those colours are so bold and energetic. I mean I can't really tell what the hell is going on in it, but it's still really powerful. I'm moved by it. Leave the theatre and just work on your paintings.'

'Good idea. And I suppose that the mortgage will just pay for itself.'

'But you'll be doing what you enjoy. And, you can work around Jo's schooling so you'll see more of her. El, I need something to do, I'm going stir crazy sitting around the house doing the bloody ironing all day. I need a challenge – not to mention the money.'

Ellie had almost laughed at the idea, but realised that Justin was serious. 'They'll never sell,' she replied, convinced she was right, but her mind a pendulum between the exciting thought of more time with her daughter and days at an easel, and bills still unpaid.

'Then you've nothing to lose by letting me try,' he added with a rare bright smile, and then pierced the cork of a Chilean carmenere to toast the idea.

For as long as Ellie could remember the canvas had been her catharsis, a place where she could safely heal her emotional wounds with years of turmoil emerging as slashes of colour across her paintings. As much as she had grown to love her oils and brushes, and secretly aspired to success as an artist, she had never imagined that she would make the shift from passionate amateur to acclaimed professional. But, she realised, Justin was clearly right when he said that she had nothing to lose by letting him try; though with a mortgage to pay and now three mouths to feed, she had thought that she would wait awhile until she left the Theatre.

There were endless false starts, missed opportunities and blunt rejections. Justin sold a couple of paintings, cheaply, to friends, and a local restaurant was surprisingly successful at selling Ellie's work off its walls. But, frustratingly, the gallery boys had shown little interest. The art world had, to a large extent, moved towards photography, video and technical installations. Paintings, oils especially, apart from the stratospheric prices achieved by auction houses for the idols of Impressionism, were not in demand. Galleries were looking for an assured return when the costs of an exhibition could run into thousands of pounds. An unknown artist, they kept repeating, was simply too risky an investment. And, although there had been a long tradition of using established artists as designers for the stage, from Graham Sutherland to Marc Chagall and Pablo Picasso and more recently Howard Hodgkin and David Hockney, there were few examples of the opposite path, from backstage to gallery, having previously been taken, and they seemed unwilling to take that route with Ellie.

But at least with all the meetings and all the talk Justin had learnt a lot about the art market. He had soon grasped that many prominent artists relied as much on a high profile as obvious ability. Flamboyant ideas that attracted attention in the press, whether good or bad it didn't seem to matter, could give an artist, even of questionable talent, a commercial edge that at the time Ellie was certainly lacking. For Ellie to achieve the success and acclaim that Justin aspired to on her behalf, he realised he would have to 'sell' her as much as her paintings, and so eventually he'd decided that if he couldn't find an established gallery to take her on as a client, then he would establish – albeit temporarily – a gallery just for her.

In the run up to Christmas he found a closed down shoe shop on the King's Road close to Sloane Square, and, via the estate agent's placard, contacted the owner and convinced him – with the enticement of the useful publicity that the event would bring him – to let them have free use of the premises for a week whilst they remained empty. With that in place, a local wine merchant was persuaded to provide free wine for the opening night, journalists from the *Evening Standard* and *Time Out* magazine were sent invitations, and every friend, acquaintance or contact, however tenuous, was coaxed to come along for a viewing. And so, from such inglorious beginnings, began Justin's transformation from directionless drifter to successful art agent and businessman, and Ellie's metamorphosis from unknown stagehand to solo exhibitor.

*　　*　　*

Gradually, they made their way round the *Kunsthalle*, the whole room a slow waltz. People moved in clusters stopping briefly for a greeting here, or to pause by a painting or to reach for the stem of a glass of champagne. Ellie was trying hard to give her full attention to everyone she spoke to, to let them know she appreciated that they'd come, and their support, and their compliments. And all the time she passed a glance around the roomful of faces, looking out for either their mother or grandmother, whilst beside her, with one hand a fist crammed into the corner of his charcoal jacket pocket, and the other a series of sharp angles clenched around a champagne glass, Justin, she could tell, was starting to panic. Not that anyone else would notice, he was too well practised at hiding emotions. But Ellie could hear the silences stretch between each sentence, and see the shadows fall across his face.

Usually small talk smoothed by champagne came easily to Justin, who had learnt to excel at the business of selling. The shy boy from her childhood and unassuming young man who'd appeared at her flat just a few years before was almost imperceptible beneath the successful façade and the Savile Row suits that he now wore so well. As usual, women of all ages vied for his attention. Yet tonight as he worked the room he connected with no one, and looked lost on the tide of conversation that swelled around the room and threatened, it seemed, to pull him under at any moment.

Of course, it didn't help that he had burnt through the better part of an eighth and then indulged in a white line to counteract it just before the show had opened, or that for the first time in almost fifteen years there was a real possibility that he would see their mother, Sabina, the woman who had torn his emotions to shreds, and then left him to pick up the pieces.

London, England. February 1946.

The cold morning and clouds that hung grey and angry in the air outside, reflected accurately Sabina's mood. She was sitting silent and still on her new school trunk in the hallway of her new home in the quiet north London suburb of Finchley.

She sat silent and still in a way quite unnatural for a child of her age, but much of the past year had been spent like this, so she sat, resigned, wrapped in grief. After hours, days, and weeks at a time, hiding from the Russians in the forests and farms of Saxony, then later waiting endlessly with other refugees in the school that served as an American internment camp, and the village halls that the Red Cross had requisitioned across Germany, her body slumped naturally, submitting to an uncertain future.

The happy childhood that was once her life in Dresden was long gone. Almost everything that she had loved from that time had been lost. Her father, brother, paternal grandparents and great-uncle were all dead. Her home, and those of all her neighbours, had been burnt down; indeed the entire city had been reduced to a pile of ash and rubble by bombing.

Every familiar and loved possession from her childhood had been destroyed: the mahogany clock, whose chime had always been a comforting accompaniment to their daily lives; the photograph of her father, newly graduated as a doctor and as handsome as any screen idol, which she had kissed each night since his death; every toy that she had ever enjoyed with her brother, and all the books and items of clothing that she had ever cherished, were now gone.

Her friends were either dead or had been left behind, some of them with injuries so frightening that she worried how they now coped with charred limbs and scarred skin and lungs that had been stripped raw so that every breath had become a bout with pain, just as she wondered how they had fared against the inevitable terrors inflicted on them by the invading Russian Red Army. And the woman who had once been her loving mother Renata, was, although still physically alive, now emotionally dead. She had only just turned eight years old, yet any last remaining shreds of innocence hung tenuously to her being.

Sabina sat gravely watching the constant activity of her maternal grandparents, Gustav and Katarina von Steindorf, who were new to her also, making the last minute preparations for her departure to her new school. She had arrived with her mother in England just a few weeks before, and once again, to her dismay, Sabina found herself being shunted on to yet another unknown destination. However, on this occasion she would be travelling alone by train and miles away to the middle of the English countryside.

It had been decided by her mother and grandparents, although without any discussion with Sabina, that she would start at the boarding school after the half-term break of the Lent term. Until then, she had not heard of the expression boarding school, but from the description her grandparents had given her, the prospect of it filled her with dread. The few difficult hours of schooling she had received each morning at the Johannstadt Kindergarten in Dresden had been bad enough. There, she had struggled with letters and words that had never made sense to her in the way that they seemed to for other children, and when her education had been brought to a halt by the bombing of the city almost exactly one year before, it had been something of a relief to her to no longer have to endure her time in the classroom

In the intervening months she had certainly not missed her lessons, and had done little more than glance at the pictures in the few books that had been provided for children in the Red Cross centres she stayed in. Now, the thought of whole days in a classroom, toiling in a language that she little understood, when previously she had barely managed lessons in her own language, filled her with dread. Had she believed in a God she would have prayed for divine intervention to prevent her departure. However, she had long lost faith in the existence of any benevolent spiritual power, so instead she silently cursed her mother for sending her away.

Katarina, talking incessantly to no one in particular, was fretting over shirts and shoes and mismatched socks and a skirt that she declared was quite the wrong colour. Previously, before her family had been torn apart in Dresden, she had enjoyed the indulgence of pretty fabrics and colourful clothes and small smart shoes, but now Sabina felt quite scornful that anyone would find such things of the slightest importance. After being obliged to wear clothes stripped from a corpse directly in front of her, where the only concern had been if lice roamed the seams, the colour and cut of an item of clothing now seemed trivial indeed. Ever since, she had thought that anyone who coveted beautiful clothing was worthy of little more than contempt; she had seen how the wrong garment could cost you your life, and doubted that she would ever again find any pleasure in an item of clothing or footwear. Whilst hiding in the Spreewald forest after they had fled from Dresden, she witnessed a woman shot dead just a few feet away from her, picked out between the trees by a Russian sniper because of the blazing crimson of the coat that she wore. But worse by far, when she had been so close to Joachim during the firestorm in Dresden, she had seen that the delicate balance between life and death could be dictated by the seemingly innocent choice of footwear.

'So many items, from clothing coupons? It's quite ridiculous,' Katarina muttered to anyone who would listen. It seemed to Sabina as if her grandmother always found something to complain about. 'At home we never needed a uniform to go to school, and our lives were so much simpler. Did anyone ever learn anything more because they wore a uniform? I think not. All this work, all these labels, and all of it so much money!' The School Uniform List had certainly been nothing but problems for Katarina, nothing but problems.

Sabina was a very lucky little girl. She knew this because *Großmutter* Katarina told her this constantly. She found this very confusing because she thought that being lucky would mean being happy, but she could not remember when she had last felt happy, so she thought it very unlikely that she really was as lucky as *Großmutter* Katarina told her. What Sabina felt most of all was not luck, but a hole inside her, gapping and raw, the size and shape of her father and brother.

She could barely remember her father now, no photographs remained of him, and the years since his death, crammed with turmoil, had almost erased his image from Sabina's memory, although occasionally, her mind recaptured a glimpse of his smile and the dimples it carved, or his cerulean blue eyes, or his rough chin at the end of the day when he had come to kiss her good-night. But if her father was an ache that gnawed incessantly at her heart, then Joachim, her brother, was a pain that slashed across her soul.

During the few years that he had lived, Joachim had filled her world. May had been cold and wet in '41, the year of his birth, like the rest of that spring. Yet the morning of Renata's con-finement had dawned with a glorious soft turquoise sky that hinted at coming warmth, and, finally, after months of needling rain and grasping winds, the changing of the seasons. Overnight, the city was transformed into a depiction of Oskar Kokoscka's *Dresden Neustadt*. The Saxon elms that lined the streets were bursting with fresh spring leaves, bluebells had bloomed, and forget-me-nots spilled pools of pale blue down over window boxes. For the first time winter coats were gladly cast aside as the strong, bright sun spread a shimmering new palate over Dresden, and when Renata had arrived by ambulance at the Bauhaus inspired Johannstadt *Frauenklinik*, it was generally agreed that it all augured well for the birth of a child. Later that day, and much to the consternation of the stern midwife, Dr Sebastian Lange had arrived to assist in the delivery of his child. The infant, a beautiful and serene boy, was named Joachim. Sabina, then a three-year-old cacophony of light ochre curls, had been captivated by her baby brother from his birth.

Despite the realities of war deprivations, Dresden, with its beautiful Baroque architecture, had remained an idyllic city in many ways untouched and in some even improved by the war. Petrol rationing had virtually cleared the streets of cars while the buses and trams ran a greatly reduced service, creating a pedestrian's paradise amongst the cobbled streets and shaded squares and the graceful gardens of the Brühl Terrace. Locals joked that Churchill had an aunt who lived in the city and that had spared it from being a target for Allied bombing raids. And so Dresden, with its elegant spires and domes strung out along the vine-clad hills of the Elbe, had, compared to Berlin and the Rhineland which were already under frequent and brutal air attack, remained a quiet backwater in the process of the war.

For Sabina, it was a happy carefree time, unaware as she was of the horrors that had swept through the nation since Adolf Hitler, the extremist but undoubtedly popular leader of the National Party, had stormed to power. She knew nothing of the *Schrecklichkeit* that had forced her family to escape from their home in Berlin, leaving her mother in Dresden and sending her maternal grandparents even further afield to London.

The swastikas that hung throughout the city and either chilled or cheered the hearts of the Dresden residents, were meaningless adornments to such a young child. The Gottfried Semper Synagogue, burnt out during the Kristallnacht Pogroms, and the *Aktions* inflicted on the city's Jewish community prior to arrest and possible brutal detention or even deportation, went unseen by her child's eye. For Sabina, these were innocent days as the war had little impact on her world: there was love in her home, sufficient for her to eat despite the escalating shortages of foods, and, for the moment, her family remained intact in Dresden.

Now etched in sepia in a recess of her mind, their time spent together had flowed with ease and happiness. During the first of the few summers that they had all four enjoyed together, on the rare occasions that her father Sebastian was not on duty at the hospital, her parents would make the most of the hot, sunny days and load up a pram with the children, what passed for a picnic in such times of rationing – perhaps rye bread and radishes or chopped herring roll mops and gingerbread biscuits for a treat – a sketch pad for Renata, and fishing rods for Sebastian to entice the local carp. They would then head through the quiet, shimmering streets, down to the banks of the river which coursed through the heart of the city. Finding shade under a chestnut tree close to the cattails and reeds, *Mutti* would sketch, whilst Sabina, just old enough to help tend to Joachim, rocked him in his pram until he slept, or lay with him on a rug whilst he gurgled at her with delight. In the evening, if *Vatti* had been lucky on the river, there would be fried fish for supper.

That winter, or maybe the next – her memories of him, like the lost pieces of a long forgotten puzzle, were scattered and frayed – *Vatti* had taken her to skate on the small lake that each winter froze over in the city's main park, the Großer Garten. They had left home early without *Mutti* or Joachim, who must have been too young to join them, and she had sat astride *Vatti's* shoulders as he walked through the muted, snow-covered streets. Years later she could still picture the patchwork sky of pale coral clouds on a cobalt blue background stretched over the city sky-line, and the trees thick with hoar frost glistening silver all around them, and could almost feel the cold prick the skin on her cheeks and hear the crunch of snow beneath her father's feet. And occasionally, just occasionally, she could even recall the feeling of pure contentment that she had felt at that moment, secure in her father's presence.

The Großer Garten had been completely empty, and in the crisp, morning air, sunlight picked out diamond flecks across the snow. Only the sounds of small red squirrels performing an acrobatic search for frosted rosehips and blackbirds snacking on ivy seeds, syncopated the swoops of their skates on the ice. It was the only occasion she could recall that they had spent time alone, and she stored the memory carefully away and never shared it, afraid perhaps that what was so precious to her, would be to another, just trivial.

As the spring days stretched into the summer of '42, she had watched Joachim clown tumble his way towards walking, great whoops of delight punctuating each inevitable fall, and later, when he had stammered into speech, she was there, coaxing his va, va, va's into *Vatti*, and mu, mu, mu's into *Mutti*. But he had always laughed more than he had spoken, and for this she had loved him, even though he was clearly *Mutti's* favourite and often she lived in the eclipse of his smile. Sabina's last memory of them all four together as a family was Joachim's second birthday, another May day with perfect spring weather, when he had raced gleefully around the sitting room furniture clutching his much prized present of a wooden motor car painted Prussian blue, unconcerned with the special treats of cinnamon cake and poppy seed crescents that weeks of saved ration coupons had managed to supply. And when *Vatti* had died that autumn, so horribly, so unfairly, somehow Joachim, who was too young to understand fully the reality of the loss, had got them both through the bleak months that followed, distracting them with his still irrepressible laughter and joy.

*   *   *

Herr von Steindorf, looking tired and showing all of his seventy-three years, stood leaning on his walking stick by the front door of the family house in Finchley. 'Sabina,' he called to her gently, 'We must leave for the station now so that you don't miss the school train. It's time to say goodbye to your *Mutti*.'

She went dutifully upstairs to her mother's bedroom, desperately hoping for a reprieve from the enforced separation. But it did not come and Renata, who lay pale and hollow eyed on her bed, seemed strangely detached about letting her go.

'It'll be fun there *Liebchen*. You'll make lots of new friends. We'll visit all the time and if you really don't like it, you can always come home. It doesn't have to be forever,' said Renata, flatly.

Sensing the insincerity behind these words, Sabina failed to find a reply and instead fleetingly kissed her mother's cheek. She tried hard to offer her something of a smile, but, as she turned to leave, her young, angry eyes revealed all the betrayal of innocence that her child's heart had already endured.

She left the house in silence, barely managing to look at *Groß-mutter* Katarina and as she shook her hand goodbye, any words of farewell choked in her throat. *Großmutter* Katarina was so cross with her sullen ingratitude and lack of manners: didn't the child realise all the hard work and expense that had gone into organising her place at boarding school?

Großvater von Steindorf had ordered a taxi to take them from Finchley to the mainline station at Marylebone, but at every stop along the way, each queue of cars or red traffic light or pedestrian crossing, the evident turmoil in his granddaughter's eyes brought him close to telling the driver to just turn around and take them both back home.

'I think that you'll be much happier at boarding school, *Liebchen*,' said Herr von Steindorf, his words barely more than a whisper. He felt so torn about sending her off, and knew that he was attempting to reconcile himself as much as Sabina to the separation. He wished with all his heart that there was some viable alternative; however, after innumerable hours thinking through all the options, it seemed the best possible solution. Perhaps not for Sabina, but certainly for his own wife and daughter to whom he also had to give due consideration.

Renata, if he was honest, was now his greatest concern. The relief he had felt when he received his daughter's letter through the International Red Cross the previous September, had been immense. Throughout the war years mail between England and Germany had been entirely cut off, and they had been unable to correspond at all. Katarina had struggled badly with the lack of communication, whilst Herr von Steindorf, ever the pragmatist, had not worried unduly about his daughter whilst Dresden remained at a distance from the conflict. But for the seven long months following the destruction of Dresden in February, until he received her letter, he had been worn down by the burden of not knowing whether Renata had survived either the Allied bombing raids, or the ensuing Russian invasion. He frantically pursued every contact he could think off in his attempts to find out if she had somehow withstood all the conflicts. But the more information he received, the more pessimistic he became. It truly seemed like a miracle to him when Renata's letter arrived, albeit a badly tainted one bringing as it did the terrible news of both Sebastian and Joachim's death. Even though he had never known of his grandson's existence, it pained him to think that his daughter had suffered so much grief. At the time of writing, Renata and Sabina were staying in a former school that the Red Cross had requisitioned for *Bombengeschädigte* – the bombed out homeless – on the outskirts of Bremen, a German city then under British command. From that moment he campaigned tirelessly through the International Red Cross, pulling every string and exerting every pressure that he was able to, to expedite his daughter's emigration to England. However, nothing prepared him for the shocking state he found her in when he finally met her at Waterloo Station, shortly after the New Year in 1946. His own daughter, and he had not been able to recognise her at all. Physically and mentally, she had been all but destroyed.

He had been looking out for an elegant auburn haired woman who had recently turned thirty, and, without giving them a second glance, he had walked straight past the elderly, grey haired woman with broken teeth and the rather grubby looking child beside her, whom he mistakenly assumed to be her grandchild.

'*Vatti! Vatti*' Renata called out to him as he was walking away. He turned around, surprised to hear the German words being spoken, but still not aware that they were directed at him. '*Vatti, es ist mir*,' she said, softly, tears clearly welling up in her sad, glazed eyes.

He finally discerned something of his daughter in the woman's frail voice, and knew that it was Renata. The beautiful, vibrant young woman he said goodbye to a little over eleven years before in Berlin, had been reduced to a broken old woman in the intervening years.

*   *   *

In the back of the taxi, *Großvater* von Steindorf gently squeezed Sabina's hand. She managed a small smile, although the gesture made her realise how rarely she had physical contact with other people. *Mutti* had not hugged her once since the bombing, and *Großmutter* Katarina had only ever shaken her hand. Only *Großvater* von Steindorf would ever stroke her cheek or ruffle her curls or wrap his arms around her. The comfort of *Vatti's* bear hugs and rolling about with Joachim seemed a lifetime ago – which of course, in a way, they were.

'It must seem very difficult at the moment,' Herr von Steindorf continued. 'But we can't look after you so easily at home. Your mother's still so unwell, and *Großmutter* Katarina and I are now too old to take care of you properly. This way, at least you'll now have people of your own age to play with each day.'

Sabina listened numbly, silently watching the Finchley Road unfold outside the taxi window, and wondered why she had to go away. It was certainly true that *Mutti* was still not at all well. Since their arrival in England, apart from the occasional walk in the garden on warmer days, her mother had hardly stepped out from her parent's house and spent most days in bed with the curtains drawn shut. Sometimes she appeared like a wraith in the dining room and joined them for a meal, but usually she took them alone in her room on a tray, if she bothered to eat at all. Frequently the tray reappeared later outside her door with the food untouched. The von Steindorf's doctor called regularly at the house to see her. Each time, Sabina watched him come and go. Pressed up against the landing banisters, she could hear the concerned tone of the doctor's conversation with her grand-parents after he had examined her mother, although not the contents. Of course, no one had thought to mention these matters to Sabina; it was only from the pained expression in her grand-parents' eyes after each visit that she was able to gauge the state of her mother's health. And part of her anxiety about going away was that *Mutti* might be so ill that she too, like Joachim and *Vatti*, might die.

As the taxi edged along St John's Wood Road and the final few streets towards Marylebone Station, Sabina edged ever closer to *Großvater* von Steindorf hoping to carve out a sanctuary within the curve of his arms. Her mind was frantically searching for words to change his mind, flitting between ideas like a trapped bird desperate to escape. But none came that were suitable. Against the tribulations that she had already endured being sent off to boarding school was as nothing, and she knew that any protests against it would seem trivial indeed. By the time they drew up outside the station she had retreated emotionally, a habit she had long ago acquired when the world became a dangerous or difficult place. Herr von Steindorf walked her across the station concourse to the teacher waiting at the ticket barrier to escort the children to school, where Sabina, locked inside her own little world, looked straight ahead and barely nodded to say goodbye.

Boarding school was a bleak, dreary Hall in a quiet Home Counties corner where Sabina felt marooned in the countryside without friends or family or any of the distractions that city life had once offered in Dresden. At best, the other girls ignored her. With their easy smiles and neatly ribboned hair they had no desire to have as a friend the strange foreign child whose odd behaviour and Teutonic accent marked her out as the disparate refugee. At worst, this was excuse enough for them all to make her life there hell. Each day was a fight against the searing and particular loneliness that only comes from isolation within a crowd.

Sabina was an easy target for those who sought one. Her grief-rimmed eyes and pale face, excavated by months of hunger, seemed too old for her child's body and beside the other girls she looked tarnished and worn as if the smoke from the Dresden fires, or the dirt from the forests and farms where she had lived for months, had never completely washed off.

She followed her grandfather's advice and pretended to be Swiss, a plausible, less complicated identity to carry, and one, as he pointed out, that was not without some grain of truth as *Großmutter* Katarina had entered England on a Swiss obtained passport.

As Sabina's English improved, she wove herself a brand new past that was glamorous and happy and everything that hers was not. But she was not artful enough to carry the lie and sensing her lack of sincerity, the other girls loathed her even more. She longed for friendship, affection ideally, even scraps of attention would have done, but her attempts to assimilate were always clumsy and failed. Whatever she wished for, Sabina would neither fit in nor find common ground.

In every way her life was too different. Whilst other girls brandished their status with tales of a war hero father – either dead or alive – Sabina sat tight lipped, feeling unable to mention her own father's name or even share his memory. An English school, she imagined, would be an unlikely venue to find an audience receptive to the idea of the good German. No one had ever explained to her fully the circumstances of her father's death, but it had certainly never been described to her as a *Heldentod*, the hero's death much revered by the Ministry of Propaganda that gave a veneer of glory to a victim of war. She remembered clearly the whispered conversations and awkward glances from other people back in Germany, and felt that in some way there was an element of shame attached to his death. Although Mutti had told her firmly, the words sharpened by bitterness, to never believe, no matter what she heard, that her father had been anything other than very brave, that there'd never been a more honourable man.

Her mother too, set her apart from the other girls. On the rare occasions that *Mutti* came to the school, Sabina felt the double edges of embarrassment and guilt. Embarrassment at her mother's appearance: and guilt that she felt the embarrassment. While the other mothers who came to the school looked fresh and elegant in Sabina's eyes, her own looked austere and dowdy in comparison. Grief and trauma were indelibly etched across *Mutti*'s face, and her once gloriously auburn hair had quickly withered to a sombre grey in the aftermath of Joachim's death. All this had added at least an additional decade to her actual age. But worst of all, thought Sabina, she made no effort to conceal the livid scar, still the shocking vermilion of hot running lava, that pulled her skin taut across her left hand, now a useless, ugly, embarrassing claw. Sabina still winced every time she looked at it. Previously, in Germany, especially during the last months that they had lived there, severe injuries had been so commonplace that they went un-remarked. Now though, away from the war and amongst people who most likely had not lived through an air attack and certainly never faced the realities of an invading army, her mother – as one of Sabina's classmates so cruelly taunted her given the nature of her injury, but much to the amusement of the other girls – 'stood out like a sore thumb'.

Terms passed at school with steady if dull predictability, the winters blasted by ruthless winds, the summers torpid and stifling. And although in time Sabina grew used to the grey, gothic building, with its dark wooden panelling and linoleum corridors, the dormitory windows kept permanently open and the rhythms and smells of boarding school life, she never got used to the solitude.

She could count on cold meat with boiled potatoes on Mondays; games, whatever the weather, be it hockey, rounders, netball or tennis on Tuesdays and Thursdays; heads scrubbed with Cold Tar Soap in icy water on Wednesdays, a four-inch bath on Saturday and Chapel twice on Sundays. But she could never count on a single friend.

Whenever lessons, sport or prayers or meals were over, Sabina would watch from the side of the dorm or the edge of the play-ground while the other girls played their games. She was never asked to join in with the skipping ropes and the rhymes that they chanted as they raced around, she never traded in cards or swapped sweets from her tuck or played conker fights in the autumn, and if ever they played at hide or seek they would trick her into hiding, and then leave her unfound for hours.

Großvater von Steindorf's regular Sunday visits, when for a few short hours he relieved her loneliness over pots of tea or lemonade and buttered scones or chocolate madeleines, were all that she looked forward to. *Großvater* von Steindorf, with his kind eyes and gentle voice, somehow kept her going.

However, eventually and inevitably, the fact and fantasy of her existence collided and a playground game begun innocently enough by the other girls, ended in an ugly explosion of Sabina's emotions and a contemptuous classmate pinned to the ground being pummelled. That was the first of many occasions when her anger would be clearly displayed by another person's blood.

With expulsion threatened, *Großvater* von Steindorf, ever the politician, interceded, and her place at the school was saved. However, her strange behaviour had already earned her the dubious accolade of 'The Naziest Girl in the School', although the bitter irony, which was lost on the other girls, was that amongst them all probably no one had suffered more directly from the Nazis, than Sabina.

As terms at school became increasingly difficult, Sabina's holidays dragged slowly by in a dull routine. Whilst *Mutti* remained remote and silent, *Großmutter* Katarina more than filled that silence with her oft voiced litany of her struggle with life in reduced circumstances in a strange country. Around the house, Sabina was called upon to perform the duties that *Groß-mutter* Katarina had previously expected of her servants back in Berlin. Her waking hours were filled with endless and exhausting chores. Brushing carpets and dusting furniture. Washing laundry and hanging it out. Ironing umpteen shirts and huge linen sheets. Peeling vegetables, laying the table and washing up after meals. And if by some rare chance none of that was required, there was always the darning of stockings and socks and smalls to be done. Her memories of family life from before the war sometimes seemed like a cruel trick of the mind.

Sadly *Großvater* von Steindorf, though always loving and warm, was often absent as, even in exile, German politics pre-occupied him much as before. Herr von Steindorf had high hopes that he and other political refugees would be allowed to participate in the resurrection of a German democracy. Their country, bankrupt and in ruins, lay occupied and ruled from Berlin by the *Kommandatura*, the Military Government of its former enemies: France, England, America and Russia. But the four powers, having carved up a post-war Germany early in 1945 at the Yalta Conference, rapidly found that with the end of hostilities their agendas had changed, their ideologies were at odds, and there were no policies on which they could reach agreement. Separation of the country had come to look increasingly inevitable.

Herr von Steindorf was eager for an opportunity to return to Berlin. He was anxious to consult with former colleagues and perhaps guide or advise them, and also to make decisions about their home and his office, which they had left behind. He knew that his hopes for a renewed democracy after more than a decade of Hitler's dictatorship looked fragile indeed, and that both their house, which had been reduced to rubble after a heavy bombing raid in 1943, and his office, now lay inaccessible in Berlin's Soviet occupied sector. Nevertheless, he felt compelled to at least try and address these situations.

Leading communists had been sent to Berlin from Moscow to initiate reforms in the Soviet zone. From the start, they demonstrated clearly that dissent would not be tolerated from either the local population, or the three other ruling powers. Alliances and enemies changed quickly as the chill of the Cold War swept across Europe.

Stalin, who controlled at least half of the country, demanded harsh reparations from the Germans, dismantling entire factories from their zone of occupation and transporting them, along with all the food grown in this agricultural heartland, back to Russia. Cut off from its farms' supplies and facing starvation, the rest of Germany turned to the West for help. In response, planes from Britain and America, which had previously brought bombs, now formed an airlift bringing wheat and potatoes and corn.

At home, Sabina listened from behind closed doors to her grandmother's endless talk of loss and blame and frustration. *Großmutter* Katarina, tired of the constant struggle and angry at her husband's intentions to remain involved in events in their former homeland, turned on him yet again.

'Do you not think that the time has come to stay out of politics, Gustav? Can't you for once put your family first? Look at the suffering which we've had to endure, and all of it caused by your meddling in affairs that were best left alone,' she sniped, reverting to her well-stocked verbal armoury.

'I rather think that Herr Hitler caused us more harm than I ever did,' he replied automatically. The argument was all too familiar ground for him.

'Look at us now, refugees, with hardly a penny to our name – and to think of the life we once had.' Katarina's voice was weighed down with resentment at the decline in their circumstances, both socially and financially. The advantages that they had both enjoyed in Germany were long gone, and beyond a small circle of exiles they had made few friends since their arrival in England. 'If you had stayed a lawyer and kept out of the limelight we could have quietly survived the war and then continued our lives much as before. But now we have nothing – not even respect. No one has any regard for a refugee.'

'You're naïve Katarina, to think it would have been that easy for us had we remained in Germany,' replied Herr von Steindorf, his voice now edged with irritation. 'Even if we *had* stayed, if I *had* stuck to law, we might have all been killed. It's ridiculous to speculate – I would certainly at some point during the war have been conscripted into the *Volksstrum* Army, and God knows what you would have had to endure left on your own once the Russians took over the capital. Just look at what they did to Renata. Did you never think that perhaps you were spared the same fate – or worse even – by our coming here? Or we might even have starved to death or succumbed to typhus and cholera, just as so many others did. And how much is now still standing of Berlin? Our house, we know, is in ruins, and let's face it we would have probably died along with Frau Braun had we stayed. Renata managed to salvage my old leather armchair and the Chinese lacquered lamp, but that was about it. Far too much was destroyed in that raid and we would have most likely been too. It's now a pile of rubble, as is half the country. Indeed, the half where our home once stood has lost one dictator, only to have him replaced by another. Do you *really* think that by staying we would have achieved a better outcome?'

Katarina knew in heart that her husband's words were true, but pride would not allow her to concede on the subject. For a while a fractious silence hung in the room eventually broken by another voice, a hollow monotone that was barely audible, 'But Papa, if you had stayed in Berlin and not left the country we would never have gone to Dresden.'

Sabina recognised her mother's voice through the shut door. This was unusual; Renata hardly ever entered her parents' conversations, let alone their arguments. Then she added bitterly, 'And if we had stayed in Berlin I would had never met Sebastian, and I would never have gone through the pain of losing both my husband and son.'

'But *Liebchen*,' replied Herr von Steindorf, obviously hurt by his daughter's words and now hoping to find some small appeasement. 'At least, if nothing else, you now have Sabina. If we had all remained in Berlin, you wouldn't even have her. Please try to look for the good in the situation.'

However, Renata's reply shocked both her mother and her father, though not Sabina who, unbeknown to them all, heard the whole conversation as she sat alone on the floor behind the closed sitting room door.

'Look for the good in the situation!' She snapped back at her father. 'I wish I'd never met Sebastian or had Joachim because then I wouldn't have to live with their loss. It's not true that time heals all wounds. There's not an hour that passes that I don't grieve for them both. Not a night goes by without reliving their deaths, or worse, in my dreams they're still alive – because then when I wake up, I have to mourn them yet again. Sometimes I feel demented with grief and having Sabina makes none of that better.'

And Sabina, listening in silence in the hallway outside, felt in her heart the painful truth of her mother's words.

*　　*　　*

In time Renata found work in the local library and with it a degree of equilibrium amongst the tranquil, ordered rooms where her remoteness went unremarked. She felt comfortable with the code of silence that was a necessary part of the job. Without conversation there was no need to explain her German accent or her deformed left hand, less chance of awkward questions from colleagues or small talk with the public. Sorting the books became her sanctuary, a safe, easy exercise that dulled the pain of her daylight hours.

After work, and overtime to stretch the day out if she was lucky, Renata rode the bus the short distance back home where she dined quietly with her parents before retreating to her room with a book. Occasionally, she joined a group of acquaintances for an evening of bridge and sandwiches and silence. It was a small, unexciting life she knew, but that suited her just fine.

However, Sabina's return at the end of each term changed all that every time. Sabina took her back to people and places and feelings that Renata would rather have kept at a distance. She saw her dead husband reflected in her daughter's face and grieved him yet again. She saw her dead son in her ochre curls and endured the loss of her favourite child once more. It was a loss that brought both anger and blame and a private cold war of attrition. It was also a loss from which neither mother nor daughter arguably ever recovered.

Later on, Sabina found escape in illicit forays with stolen shillings to the Swiss Cottage Picture House where Gene Kelly and James Dean provided exciting, if brief, companionship, or the Electric Ballroom in Leicester Square where the loud music would drown out, for a while at least, the past. There would be terrible trouble when she returned home, she knew, but, compared to what she had already endured, it always seemed of little consequence. In any case, she deserved it all, she felt. Every harsh word, every slap, and every thwack of a ruler across the back of her hand or her thigh: it was all deserved.

Sabina tried ever harder to find distractions to forget the devastation that she had lived through, to find something, anything, that would numb the pain inside. Cigarettes achieved that for a while, and stolen sherry from the sideboard decanter certainly helped as well. But before long she discovered other, less obvious routes to emotional oblivion: the binging then vomiting of food; the heady flirtation with death as time and again she delicately drew a sharp blade across her wrists, like an artist hatching at a scraperboard, then watched her blood drip slowly into a towel.

Despite it all, each night in her sleep the Lancasters came back to bomb her, and the firestorm raged once more in her dreams. Yet again she was choked with smoke and flailing from the heat, and frantically searching all around for her brother; until, inevitably, she woke with a start. And then, drenched in sweat, she remembered: she had let his hand slip, and in the chaos of the separation, whilst she had thought she would vomit up her own heart with the horror of it all, she had watched Joachim die.

4

Sturm
Oil on canvas
144cm x 115cm

Berlin, Germany. November 15th, 1995.

'There's a good chance she won't be here,' said Ellie, quietly to Justin, between a brief pause on their orbit around the *Kunsthalle*. He looked at her blankly, his thoughts adrift elsewhere. 'Mother,' she continued, knowing that all his anxiety about the evening was bound up in his feelings about her. 'It's quite likely that she's not come to Berlin and even if she has, that she won't show up tonight.' He nodded his head slowly, doubt daubed across his brow. 'I haven't spoken to either mother or Grandma since Sunday,' she added. 'Told them both to meet us here – that way everyone's going to be on their best behaviour. We've not spoken since. It's been a frantic week. I've had a million things to organise for the girls before coming away, not to mention Grandma's birthday party on Sunday. The phone's not stopped ringing. I've honestly no idea if either of them has even left London.'

Hope skimmed across his eyes as they flitted like moths around the room in search of their mother. He'd heard often enough how unreliable she could be, the countless times that visits had been cancelled or re-arranged – their mother had an endless litany of medical conditions on which she could call for excuses – or simply forgotten in a fug of alcohol. There was every possibility, without the need to fabricate reassurances for Justin, that neither of them had come.

In fact, Grandma had never actually told Ellie that she would be coming. She only ever acknowledged receipt her tickets and hotel confirmation, but, despite some protracted phone calls whilst they'd meandered around the subject and Ellie subtly tried to pin her down, she had deftly managed to avoid any discussion of her decision. Although Ellie had known all along that their grandmother, born and raised and then chased from Berlin, had always vowed that she would never return there.

*   *   *

Renata had little regard for either Germany, or Germans. If ever a conversation even glanced in that direction, you could see her eyes darken and the furrows deepen in her craquelure face. It was unpredictable what her response would be, either a splattering of sharp words or an uncomfortable silence, which was possibly worse, whilst the past poured out and gnawed on her mind. 'Bloody Germans, let them all go to hell,' Ellie had heard her utter more than once, her voice still as thickly Teutonic as the day she'd left Germany. And Ellie, or whoever else was there, would look embarrassed and turn away whilst she fought the temptation to say, 'But, Grandma, you're German yourself!' Although she never did, of course. During their childhood they had seen little of their grandmother, and their infrequent visits to see her were never much fun. She was constantly critical of their mother, although the reverse was certainly true, and much as Ellie had secretly agreed with a lot of what her grandmother said – especially about her mother's drinking and the way she treated, or rather mistreated, both their father and her children – she loathed listening to yet more arguments: they had enough of those at home.

So, despite their grandmother living not far from them in Finchley, they had visited her only once or maybe twice a year, until even those few visits stopped altogether after their father left home. Much later, with hindsight, Ellie came to realise that it was probably her father who had kept the uneasy peace between them, and without him there to act as their buffer, the snipping had become too hazardous a war zone for them all to enter.

Even as a young child, Ellie had been struck by the gulf of difference between her mother and grandmother, as there was no obvious link between the two of them. Physically they were so unalike, the way they dressed was completely different – her mother dressed chaotically in an unsuccessful riot of colour, unconcerned whether the clothes she wore were even clean or not, whilst her grandmother was always smart, if somewhat sombre – and their way of living was also vastly disparate.

Renata lived on her own in the house in Finchley which had belonged to her parents, Gustav and Katarina von Steindorf, who were by then both dead. It was plainly furnished in cold earth tones, a rather impersonal space devoid of family photographs and the general clutter of everyday life. Whilst always meticulously tidy, the house had a melancholy air. Since retiring, her days had followed a rigid pattern: there were allotted times for shopping and cleaning, and even for reading – her books, as befitted a former librarian, were carefully collated along rows of shelving – and listening to records from her classical collection. The contrast to her daughter's shambolic family life in Ealing could not have been greater.

When Ellie and Justin had been very young, it had felt like a duty, not a pleasure, for them to visit their grandmother. She had demanded manners from them which they had never been taught, and which they'd struggled to find. Any meal that they shared had been accompanied by her exasperated *tut tut tuts*, and a running commentary on their social shortcomings: napkins ignored (they never used them in their own home where their stained, frayed and unmatched collection languished forgotten deep inside a kitchen drawer, so they never thought to use them at her house); an elbow on the table; drinks slurped from cups; cutlery inelegantly clutched. They tried their best to behave in what they thought was an appropriate manner when they were around her, but each time they invariably came up short. It had been all too easy for both children to dismiss their grandmother as a difficult old woman who was hard to please.

In addition, to their young ears, her English seemed clumsy, even strangely comical: long, stilted sentences delivered in a sad, stark voice. Sometimes she would speak to them in German, which perplexed them even more as she knew that they had never been taught the language. And, occasionally, inexplicably to them, she would call Justin 'Joachim' which always left him feeling quite unnerved. But as a child, for Ellie the most disturbing thing about her grandmother was her forearm and left hand, which were puce stained and frighteningly disfigured, with the skin between her clawed fingers like dried droplets off a melted candle. Looking back, she remembered with shame that as a young girl she'd found it truly repugnant.

Renata was never excessively difficult with either of her grand-children – she never shouted at them or argued in the way that she did with their mother – yet she had never seemed especially pleased to see them. It somehow felt to them as though they were an unwelcome intrusion on her well ordered life. Justin, especially, seemed to make her anxious. Ellie had noticed that their grandmother could barely look at him, and, that when she did, the suffering that she carried around her, which even as a young child she could clearly see, seemed to rub raw her old emotional wounds.

Ellie knew that her grandmother had had a terrible war, not that they ever discussed such things. On the contrary, in their home any talk of war, or of their family history in Germany, was completely *verboten*. It was only much later on, when she had her own daughter Joanna and rekindled her relationship with her grandmother, that they slowly grew much closer. Gradually, Ellie had collected some fragments from her grandmother's life together; laying in the sombre background, before adding the more delicate details to her life's canvas from an overheard conversation here, or an unguarded comment there. However, a large part of the picture had still remained blank, and was only finally filled in when Ellie subsequently changed her working name to von Steindorf. Had she known the upset she was about to cause, she would have done things differently.

It had been Justin's idea to change her name, and one that she had been happy to agree to. 'Ellie Tyler', he'd decided after the indifferent response that gallery owners and directors had initially shown him, was too pedestrian. It held no glamour, no sense of excitement. It seemed that to set her apart, something altogether more exotic was called for.

They scoured books on art with the thought of 'adopting' a name, leafed through *Roget's Thesaurus* looking for a word that held the right ambience, and poured over telephone directories in the hope of finding a suitable pseudonym. But none of the words or names seemed to feel quite right.

From the start, Ellie had insisted that she would keep at least some part of her name, because while she could see the rationale behind re-branding her image, she wanted to retain a sense of her own identity. For weeks they had pitched back and forth a hundred and one ideas: Ellie Picasso – how illustrious! Titian Tyler – and she'd dye her hair flame-red! However, for all the fanciful suggestions, nothing workable came to mind.

'Have you noticed how we usually imagine a person is that much more interesting when they have a foreign name?' Justin had remarked one day, raising his head from the glitz and gossip of a Sunday tabloid. Then, turning the page to Ellie and pointing to a picture of Justin de Villeneuve, the famed photographer, he'd asked, 'We're both called Justin, but when you add the surname who sounds more exciting – him or me?'

'Well, him of course. But that's not because he *sounds* more "exciting", he *is* more "exciting" – he used to go out with Twiggy. In any case it's a bad example, I don't think that's his real name,' she'd added, more concerned with mixing raw umber and Brunswick green pigments as a colour wash for the set design drawings that she was working on.

'Exactly, that only proves my point,' Justin had replied, stretching his legs out and sinking deeper into the sofa. 'He chose a fancy foreign name to create an image for himself. Well, you're – we're – half-German, we don't even need to make that bit up, that's already our identity. We should market you as a German artist – most critics and curators think that the only exciting paintings around at the moment are coming out of Germany. I can't remember where, but I read an article in which an art dealer said that it's all those decades of gore and angst reflected on the canvas that gives their paintings an edge. Oh, that's brilliant. That's the angle I should take with your work – we say that they're a reflection of Germany's history,' he'd added, little realising how astute that decision would prove to be.

'It's something to think about,' she said, vaguely, her mind now preoccupied with keeping her lively young daughter away from the drawing board and the pen and ink sketches that needed to be finished for the following day.

'But it's a bloody good idea,' Justin answered, scooping Joanna up and onto the sofa as she raced noisily past him. 'What was mother's maiden name? It would give you more credibility if we used a family name.'

Ellie dipped a card in the colour to check the tone whilst she thought for a moment. 'Lange,' she said, finally. 'Grandma's name is Renata Lange – so that was mother's maiden name.'

'It's not German enough – that name could come from just about anywhere. What about Grandma's maiden name?'

'I'm not sure – I don't think anyone's ever told me,' she'd replied. 'I know I met Grandma's parents on a few occasions when I was very small, but I don't remember much about them. Her father was a politician when they lived in Germany – a lawyer too – but something happened sometime in the '30s and he'd had to escape the country. That's why they ended up here. He wasn't Jewish, so it wasn't that. Who knows? All I remember is that he and his wife – our great-grandmother – seemed incredibly old and slightly intimidating, although in hindsight that was probably just how their heavy accents and old-fashioned ways seemed to a very small child. I think Grandma said that her father had been unwell for a very long time and died from some sort of complications due to that, then his wife died a short time after – you see that a lot with couples who've been together forever, don't you? Anyway, I'm not sure that I ever knew their names – I called them *Oma* and *Papi* if I remember – but after they died we never really spoke about them that much.'

But later, when the day was almost over and she was carefully cleaning her sable brushes, Ellie had remembered a newspaper clipping announcing the death of Grandma's father which she had found amongst a pile of papers at their mother's house. Curious to know more about their great-grandfather, she had taken it away to keep herself. Confident that she still had the piece, she searched it out from a box of mementos that she stored beneath her bed.

The cutting had by then turned a dark butter yellow, but the details, still clear across the crinkled paper, were headed: Gustav von Steindorf, 1879–1964.

It was a name that echoed faintly in her memory. Over the years Ellie recalled having heard it from time to time. Of course, she had always heard him referred to as 'your great-grandfather', so she'd never really absorbed the fact that von Steindorf was actually her own family name. For a day or two she had tried on the name in her head, repeating it over and over to see how it felt, and writing it out to see how it appeared on the page. It certainly held all the qualities that they were both looking for, and, most importantly, the name von Steindorf felt comfortable to her.

'That's the one!' Justin had said, full of excitement a few days later, when she'd shown him the newspaper cutting. 'Ellie von

Steindorf, that sounds the part. No, we'll use your full name, Eleanor. Yes, Eleanor von Steindorf – perfect.'

From then on, that became her working name. Suddenly, doors opened and the right people in the industry began to take notice, and she received her first invitation to be exhibited at a major gallery.

Expecting that their grandmother would be flattered by the gesture, Ellie and Justin were quite unprepared for the outpouring when they showed her the brochure with Ellie's work displayed using the name von Steindorf. For a few moments their grandmother had just looked at it, turning it over and over between her right hand and her left, disfigured one. And then, before half a lifetime's tightly restrained emotion erupted, she muttered for a while in German – her mouth buckling, her face pumice grey – although all that Ellie and Justin could understand from amongst the words, was the name that she kept repeating: von Steindorf.

Berlin, Germany. June 30th 1934.

'Herr von Steindorf! Herr von Steindorf!'

Up in her third floor bedroom, Renata woke with a start and sat up, out of breath and close to panic, as if escaping from a very bad dream. Unfortunately, it was only when she awoke that the nightmare actually began.

She knew instinctively from the aggressive tone of the voices in the street below that these were people not in trouble, but looking for it. Her heart rapped frantically against her ribs like a Morse code SOS.

'Von Steindorf! Von Steindorf!' The shouting at the front door continued, but louder this time; the hammering fists became more insistent.

Renata had no idea how long she had been asleep nor any feel for the hour, for her room was still completely dark with no hint of daylight behind the curtains, although it hardly mattered as she was now fully awake, alert to every sound that filtered up to her room.

'Von Steindorf! *Öffnen Sie die Tur auf!*' The man's harsh voice was as persistent as ever, but now accompanied by the crescendo banging on the front door. Renata realised that wooden batons had replaced the fists first used.

From the bedroom directly below she could hear her parents muffled voices, whilst from above, the sound of footsteps stumbling in the staffs' attic rooms, then the creaking of an upstairs door before someone hurried down the servants' staircase to attend to the disturbance at the front door.

Renata slipped out from beneath her gold satin covered eider-down quilt and edged as quietly as possible towards her bedroom door, absurdly conscious of her every move and the slightest sound that she made: the snap of a floorboard beneath the Venetian red carpet; a click in her anklebone. She opened the door a thumbs width to hear more, although it was hard to make anything out from amongst the crossfire of words between Frau Braun, the elderly housekeeper, and the two or more unknown male voices that she contended with in the entrance hall below. Evidently, Frau Braun's protestations were in vain, and it was not long before Renata could hear the ominous sound of boots clanking on marble, then a rumble of feet up the house's main staircase.

The men – Renata was unable to see whether they wore the uniform of the *Sturmabteilung* Brownshirts, or if they were dressed in the distinctive black leather trench coats that the Gestapo favoured – had not proceeded far, when, accompanied by skirls of protest from her mother, the door to her parents' bedroom opened and her father's sonorous voice brought a halt to all activity in the house, '*Ich komme sofort.*'

For a moment there was silence from the men on the stairway and in the entrance hall below, and then Herr von Steindorf, already immaculately dressed in a charcoal grey suit and making the final adjustments to his distinctive carmine and silver silk striped tie, walked calmly downstairs to face the intruders.

With her door now slightly further ajar, Renata could clearly hear the graven tones of an unseen officer placing her father under arrest, then a clatter of boots leaving the house and descending the outside steps. A car door slammed; an engine started.

Renata, desperate to have some parting communication with Papa – offer him a reassuring wave or blow him a surreptitious kiss from her hand – ran to her bedroom window and thrust open the sash frame. In the gleam of the house lights that had now been switched on, she saw a black Mercedes clearly branded with a Swastika in the street below, but all she could catch of her father as the departing car eased away through the quiet fore-dawn, was the silver grey hair on the back of his head. Probably less than ten minutes had passed since the first fist had knocked on the door.

Renata slumped to the floor, close to a faint, struggling through gasps to breathe. Tears spilled down over her cheeks and dripped unchecked into the carpet. She wrapped herself into a tightly curled ball, and lay there, utterly bereft, clenching her legs until her knuckles turned white from fear and the cool night air spilled in at the still open window. She hardly noticed, her senses being too choked by the question of when, if ever, she would see her father again. Eventually the sobbing eased, but a fearful headache, thumping like soldier's boots across her temples, soon replaced this, as if kicking in the reality of what had just happened.

Renata was shocked by her own naivety. She had ignored all the signs that events might lead to this and dismissed her father's warnings that the country was in such crisis. Till now, she had thought that talk of unwarranted arrests and beatings and men who just disappeared was exaggerated by both Papa and the press, and in any case, it was something that only happened to other people – militant extremists perhaps, looking for trouble, and Jews who stood up against the Nazis or had simply been in the wrong place at the wrong time – but not people like Papa, a famous lawyer, a politician renowned for his commitment to social reform and respected for his long held agenda of peace.

There had been, she knew, escalation in street violence for the past year and a half since Hitler had been appointed Chancellor. Conflicts between Nazi members and their Communist Red Front opponents had become increasing bloody and frequent both in Berlin and other major cities. Even Renata had been alarmed by accounts of these that she had heard. But in truth these events had always seemed far removed from her own comfortable circumstances, and she had never imagined that they might actually intrude on it. Now she realised how foolish she had been.

Papa had always tried to open her eyes to the problems around her, had shown her endless articles that he thought she should read to gain a broader understanding of political matters: the leader column in the pacifist *Die Weltbühne* until it was banned and the inflammatory anti-Semitic *Der Stürmer*, or on occasions his own articles which had been published in the *Berliner Tageblatt*, or the ridiculous outpourings in Göbbel's weekly newspaper *Der Angriff* that always managed to particularly irritate him, although she had never actually bothered to read it, for she could not imagine that anyone would take the strange looking man seriously. Almost daily, Papa had tuned into the wireless for her to hear the news, and he had dominated mealtimes at home with his troubled thoughts on the demise of democracy, which as a lawyer troubled him deeply.

'We are now living under a dictatorship where the law counts for nothing,' he would tell them all gravely. 'There is no telling what evil can flourish in times when people can be arbitrarily imprisoned without a warrant or trial.'

Yet, Renata had somehow felt detached from it all, for her life continued much as before and she remained sheltered from the harsher realities around her. Political affairs, she felt, were some-thing that pertained to other people only, were some abstract philosophy that had little impact on her own life. She could see no link between herself and the pyres of 'Un-German' books set ablaze by the Nazis the previous year on Berlin's *Opernplatz*, or a Jewish Professor expelled from the *Friedrich-Wilhelm-Universität*, or a newspaper banned and its editor imprisoned.

There had been problems in the Reichstag, and indeed in Berlin and Germany, for as long as Renata could remember. It seemed that for all of her life she had listened to Papa preach his politics and voice his fears of the nation's decline. He would preach to her, to her mother, to any guests who came to the house, or to their hosts if they were out visiting friends – even the servants. Now, she realised, she had never really listened, she had merely sat quietly whilst his words washed over her, her thoughts gossamer light and elsewhere. Her thoughts would be about her horse, Knödel, a fat piebald that she endlessly adored, or the jazz that she played when her parents went out, a dance at a house by the Wannsee shores and nights to come at the latest café, or the new dress from Paris that she longed to show off. She had floated through life as gay and free as a champagne bubble, where her father's politics had certainly been a serious thought too far.

It was not that she didn't respect Papa, quite the contrary. In fact, she had always appreciated that he was clearly the most exceptional of men. She had been told by so many people how he had steered a fragile democracy through the civil unrest that a bankrupt Germany faced after the signing of the Armistice and the Treaty of Versailles, and of his efforts for reform in the newly established Weimar Republic. It was just that she usually found all his rhetoric rather dull. Depressing, even. Over the years she had learnt to feign interest at his endless talk. There was always some or other crisis that held his attention, whether the foreign debt consequent to the huge reparation demands, or the shifting coalitions and the never ending elections, re-elections and changes in leadership that had widened the cracks in the Weimar Republic until it had finally fallen apart. She hadn't even tried to keep up with all the complicated political manoeuvrings that in little over four years had brought the country Chancellors Bruning, von Papen, von Schleicher and now Hitler. However, the course of compromise, which Herr von Steindorf had always believed to be the root of social and political stability, had eventually been exhausted by spiralling inflation, the deepening depression and rising unemployment, by the escalating violence of the National Socialists and the rise in anti-Semitic hostilities – Jewish shops were increasingly vandalised and their owners arbitrarily beaten – and by a myriad conflicting forces that Herr von Steindorf had been unable to mitigate against.

Yet until now, Papa's lecturing that the political extremism which had replaced the democratic ideals of Weimar Germany was a danger to the whole of society – to European stability even – had seemed a remote idea to Renata. But clearly, as his own arrest had just proved, the country was, as he had said for so long now, careering towards cataclysmic events.

*　　*　　*

Renata had no idea how long she had lain on the floor by the window, although it must have been quite a while as the night had ebbed away and left the sky the oyster grey of a dull early morning, when Frau Braun knocked at her still open door.

'Your mother has asked that you join her in ten minutes time for breakfast in the dining room. Until then she will be busy on the telephone in your father's study, and has asked that she not be disturbed.'

Roused from her thoughts Renata only then realised how cold she had become, her feet numb and blushed blue, her legs and arms stung with goose pimples.

'Alright, I'll be there for breakfast,' she answered wearily.

She dressed mechanically, without first taking a bath as was her custom, merely reaching for the nearest clothes in her closet, a polka dot shirt in raw sienna and a matching skirt with accordion pleats. She neither washed her face, nor brushed her hair. Uncaring, she went downstairs to join her mother.

From the flat grey sky a light rain smudged the windowpanes in slow staccato beats. On the dining room sideboard Frau Braun had laid out yoghurts and fruits and soft boiled eggs that would never be eaten. Katarina was seated at the table already, her silver cigarette case and an ashtray in front of her, a shrunken, uncharacteristically dowdy figure, huddled beneath cirrus wisps of smoke.

Renata crumpled into a chair beside her mother and stumbled through a dozen questions, her voice small and anxious, whilst Katarina tried to placate her with appropriately soothing platitudes, although, having spent most of the morning since her husband's arrest ringing around his friends for advice and help, she felt more fearful for his safety than before she had picked up the telephone. She hoped, if possible, to spare her daughter the facts and further worry.

Facts, however, were blurred with rumour; the obvious summation from all she had been told was that Hitler had ordered a purge of alleged plotters against the Nazi administration. The targets were wide ranging and, from what Katarina could make out, seemed strangely disparate and indiscriminate. But that of course, had become a hallmark of Adolf Hitler's Germany.

She had heard from two separate people that senior SA leaders in Munich had been executed by an SS unit led by Hitler himself. More alarmingly, she was told that here in Berlin, Vice-chancellor von Papen, whom Herr von Steindorf had long known but also long disliked, and who just two weeks ago had delivered a harsh speech against the Nazi regime at Marburg *Universität*, was now under house arrest. Furthermore, SS officers had stormed von Papen's offices at the Vice-Chancellery building, shooting dead some of his staff and arresting the others.

Katarina was not entirely certain how her husband fitted into this equation of events. The only common denominator between them all seemed to be a voice of dissent against the Nazi regime. Certainly, Herr von Steindorf had never had dealings with the SA, and, beyond the Reichstag, he had never had a social, working, or even an advisory relationship with von Papen. However, she knew that since the previous July, when the Nazi Party had been declared the only legal political party in Germany, numerous non-Party politicians and lawyers who had defended political activists and trade union members, had been arrested. Her husband fell into both of these categories.

To compound matters, only recently Herr von Steindorf had made a vehement protest to the Reichstag and to Herr Sahm, Berlin's Mayor, over the detention and internment of Herr Theo Hirsch, a prominent Jewish lawyer in Berlin who had mentored him during his first tenure out of law school. Any, or all of this, thought Katarina, might have provoked her husband's own arrest.

Katarina relayed none of this to her daughter. Instead, she tried hard to make light of the situation as she answered Renata's endless questions, 'Of course Papa will be home soon – in a matter of hours most likely,' she said with considerably more confidence than she felt. She kept to the truth when she replied that he was most probably being questioned because he had always been such an outspoken critic of the National Socialists, but intentionally lied when she answered, 'No, they wouldn't dare harm Papa in any way – he's too well known, and even Adolf Hitler knows when to draw the line!'

Eventually, Renata's questions fell away into silence, and the two of them sat hunched unhappily together, each slowly sipping the now cold coffee whilst Renata tore strips of a breakfast roll into ever smaller pieces, none of which she ate. Her mother, unusually, failed to notice this rare lapse in table manners.

Hours later, lying on her bed bored and ignored and impatient for news of her father, Renata realised that in all the confusion of the day, she had forgotten that she had arranged to meet her friend, Lore Bernstein, at a café in the *Tiergarten* where they were to have had ices before heading to watch *Ein Lied Für Dich* at the pictures. She had remembered too late to reach her by telephone as by then Lore would have already left her house in Grunewald, and she knew that her friend would be cross. But the prospect of Lore in a grumpy mood was by then the least of her worries.

The house had settled into an uneasy silence. The staff were anxious not to intrude on the family's suffering and were keeping themselves quietly occupied out of sight, and Katarina, having retreated to the study after breakfast, had not emerged from there since.

Renata picked up a book and made every effort to read it, but she struggled to keep her eyes on the page or her mind on the words. Giving up eventually, she left her room and wandered upstairs to the painting studio which her mother had created out of the former nursery.

Art and painting had become her mother's passion, fed by the capital's thriving Modernist movement, the Expressionists in particular, and her canvases, oils mainly, were neatly stacked around the room in various stages of progress. Katarina had never trained formally, nonetheless her work was thoughtfully composed and boldly executed and she had even exhibited in Herwarth Walden's renowned gallery, *Der Sturm*, which had long championed Europe's most acclaimed avant-garde artists. She always worked alone and in silence, drawing her inspiration from the broad strokes and vibrant shades that lit up the canvases she so admired of Marc and Chagall and Kandinsky. When she was finished for the day, Renata would join her upstairs for instruction on the tools and techniques of painting and drawing. This, she hoped, was some compensation for Renata's abandoned plans to begin the preliminary course at the Bauhaus after she had finished her *Abitur* exams. The previous year the Art School, too radical for the stringent dictates of the day, had finally succumbed to pressure and closed.

Choosing a small scraperboard and a sharp knife-blade cutter that Renata thought best suited her mood, she sat quietly at the workbench beneath the large dormer window and chiselled her anguish into a *s'graffito* sketch whilst she waited for news of her father. She certainly knew better than to disrespect the strict house rule that she was never to enter or even knock on the study door whilst it was closed.

Inside her husband's study, Katarina was suffering the most traumatic day of her life. With every hour the news, and with it her husband's chances of a safe return, was getting worse. Further SA men had been executed in Munich, clearly without trial, and whilst Katarina was not especially upset by this news *per se*, for she had little sympathy with those party members whom she generally regarded as undisciplined thugs in uniform, what alarmed her most about the situation was the unbridled violence that martial law engendered, and the possible consequences that that might hold for her husband.

The telephone rang yet again. It was her husband's old friend and retired General, Kurt von Duisburg. '*Guten Morgen*, Frau von Steindorf,' he began. 'I am most sorry to hear the news concerning your husband. I am ringing because I have information that I think might be important for you to know. Earlier this morning SS officers stormed the home of the former the Chancellor, General von Schleicher, and he was executed where they found him.' Katarina's felt sick to her stomach as she listened. 'I strongly recommend that you leave your house at once,' continued the General. 'I truly don't wish to alarm you, but your own life could be in danger as well, as it is rumoured that the SS officers have also shot dead von Schleicher's young wife. You must get out of the house immediately,' he urged her. 'Leave now. Don't bother to pack anything; just go. To a friend's or somewhere public – but somewhere that's busy. I would invite you here, but I'm not confident that my own situation is that secure, it's highly likely that I have my own enemies within the SS. You must not be naïve about this – if your husband has been interned, then you could be in as much in danger as he is. Listen, there are some things that I must attend to now, but I'll meet you at three this afternoon in the Tea Garden at the Hotel Adlon and we'll take stock of things then. Bring your daughter, have lunch with her in the main dining room, and I'll join you both later. You'll be safe there. Even if the SS find you, they won't touch you – they prefer to do their worst unseen. Too many foreign journalists and diplomats use the Adlon as their watering hole so at the moment it's probably the safest place in Berlin.'

When the call ended, Katarina's hand was trembling so violently that she barely managed to replace the receiver in its cradle. Her mind was reeling from the unknown terror of her husband's fate, to the horror of the von Schleichers' alleged murder. Certainly, if a former Chancellor and his young wife were not exempt from Nazi savagery, than nobody was.

She went to her husband's drinks cabinet, poured herself a deep glass of Chartreuse, then sat back down to drink it and think through the ramifications of the last conversation. General von Duisburg was certainly right, Katarina realised: she and Renata should get away from the house at once.

She called up to Renata on the house telephone, '*Liebchen*, we've got to go out for the day,' she said as lightly as possible, trying to sound a lot calmer than she felt. 'So smarten up a little, because we're off to see someone who's going to help Papa. We're meeting him at the Hotel Adlon, so we might as well have lunch there – it'll cheer us both up! I'll see you downstairs in about five minutes.' She put the telephone down quickly – she was not yet ready to deal with any more questions from her daughter.

Katarina had no idea what danger the next hours or even days would bring her family, but she was now certain that she would not sit passively at home and let their fate be decided by other people. Before she left her husband's study, she opened the lock on his safe and removed two thickly rolled wads of Reichsmark from the pile that was stored inside.

Knowing that being better groomed would help her feel more confident about confronting the world, she went upstairs to her dressing room. Without even having to look in a mirror, she knew that with all the stress of the morning and tears that she had shed, she looked awful. Considerable gloss would have to be added to her lacklustre appearance.

There was no time to change completely, but some deft changes to her dress would at least draw attention away from her forlorn looking face. The stockings she was wearing had seen better days but would have to do, and the cotton dress in a dull camel colour was not what she would normally choose to wear to the Adlon, but after slipping on a magenta silk jacket, a string of pearls and some higher heels, there was once again a glimmer of her usual luminescence. A soft brown pencil added an arch to her eyebrows, and a coral lipstick much needed colour to her face. It was then time to go.

Within the hour Katarina and Renata were glancing, unenthusiastically, through the menu in the Hotel Adlon dining room having left word with Frau Braun of their intended destination, should, miraculously, her husband arrive back at the house. It was just after one o'clock and the restaurant was rapidly filling with the city's diplomatic elite, and, much to Katarina's consternation, a surprising number of men in Nazi uniform.

The room was abuzz with chatter. Like a hornet's nest, thought Katarina nervously, and she felt uncomfortably placed at the heart of it all, braced for a sting that she felt could strike at any time. Conscious of the many heads that turned in their direction, especially the Nazi officers clearly in celebratory mood drinking champagne from large saucer glasses only two tables away, and the familiar faces amongst the other guests who would probably have known of her husband's arrest, she managed somehow to feign an equanimity that she certainly did not feel, and ordered generously for them both from the *Mittagessen* menu. They ate a vegetable broth, a dish of pork and prunes with parsley buttered potatoes and then a goat's cheese savoury, and whilst Katarina made every effort to ignore the other diners in the room and to distract her daughter from the day's events, she felt raw from the whispers of gossip that rippled around them.

With their meal ended – and eaten more heartily than either of them had expected – Katarina was only too eager for them to retire from the turned ears and curious stares in the dining room and to wait over coffee in the Tea Garden for General von Duisburg. She was pleased to see that there were few guests scattered around the tables amongst the sentinels of potted palms, so a private conversation would at least be a possibility. In the far corner a solemn looking pianist in an oversized suit played a leaden waltz that weighed down her mood even more.

At three o'clock precisely, General von Duisburg entered the Tea Garden and approached the von Steindorf women who were seated at a round linen covered table by the open French doors. He looked pale, hollowed eyed and preoccupied, and much older than Katarina had remembered him: a remnant of the revered General that he had once been. She knew at once that he brought more bad news.

'*Gnädigen Frauen,*' he greeted them formally with a half bow from the waist, and then took Katarina's outstretched hand which he raised to his lips and skimmed with a kiss.

Katarina offered the General a seat at the table and coffee from the pot that she had already ordered. Wasting no time on trivialities, the General continued on from where their conversation had been left off earlier that day. Renata, who scarcely knew of the day's events beyond her father's arrest, sat there aghast.

'I have found out that your husband has been taken to *Oranien-burg*, the prisoner camp just north of Berlin,' he began gravely. 'But beyond that, I have no news of him. There have been many more murders by the SS today, including all of von Papen's staff at the Vice-Chancellery building, although I believe that von Papen himself is still alive but under house arrest. The former head of the Conservative Party and most of the leaders amongst the local SA have been shot as well.' He paused to light a cigarette for Katarina – there was a slight but nonetheless perceptible tremor in his hands – and then one for himself, before he continued. 'Most of this information came to me from Monsieur Francois-Poncet the French Ambassador to Berlin, whom I have known for a good many years. I have asked him to meet us here. He has a lot of contacts, and I think that perhaps there may be some way in which he is able to help you.'

Renata, who had grown more ashen by the minute since the General's arrival, looked to her mother for some reassurance, but Katarina was at a loss for words and felt quite numb with all of this news. It seemed a faint hope that her husband could have survived such a day of ruthless barbarity.

'I am most grateful for your thoughtfulness, General von Duisburg,' said Katarina, choosing her words carefully. 'But why would the French Ambassador have any interest in our safety, and indeed, why are you helping us when clearly you have so much to preoccupy yourself with at the moment?'

The General looked at her a little surprised, but realised that if she did not understand his own indebtedness to her husband, then, under the circumstances, of course she must be feeling cautious. He drank some more coffee and sat forward in his chair to keep his voice low, confidential.

'Monsieur Francois-Poncet, I agree, owes you nothing, but he is coming here at my request. There is no authority in this country that a German citizen can turn to for protection at this time, so you must realise, and please take this point most seriously, that your only chance to find help right now, is from outside of Germany. Chancellor Hitler is anxious to prove his worth amongst European leaders and will, to a certain extent, bow to pressure from other countries – England and France especially. My acquaintances at the British Embassy are slight, but I've known Monsieur Francois-Poncet for long enough that I know I can trust him, which is why I've asked him to come here. Believe me, he is as alarmed as any liberal-minded German by events that he sees here and is only too pleased if he can bring diplomatic pressure to bear on this government. As for my own motives in helping you today – they are very simple – I most certainly owe my son's life to your husband.' He held her eyes in a steady gaze as spoke these words, and she knew that they came from the heart, although from her puzzled expression it was clear she had little idea of the facts of the matter.

'During the War, my son Otto went to your house to meet your husband,' he continued, his tone noticeably proud when he spoke of his son. 'They had not met before, but Otto had been serving with the same cavalry regiment as your husband's nephew – I never knew him, but if I remember correctly his name was Marcus – and my son delivered some letters that he had written to your husband shortly before his death. I knew none of this at the time; in fact, it was long after the war had ended before Otto even mentioned the matter to me. I was serving on the Western front near Arras when all this happened, not a General yet, but heading there, and we hardly saw each other throughout the War – but in any case, he didn't want to compromise my own position.'

There was a slight lull in the conversation. The General looked lost in his memories and Katarina, puzzled by his recollections, leaned forward to catch his attention again. 'I'm sorry General von Duisburg,' she said tentatively, 'I'm sure that your son did come to our house just as you've told me. I remember that we received some correspondence from Marcus after his death, and

I certainly recall how upset my husband was with the whole matter, but I don't understand how he saved your son's life.'

'Well, Otto didn't just deliver Marcus's letters that night, he also asked for your husband's help. He'd been severely wounded on the Eastern Front – in fact he'd lost an arm – so he'd been transferred to the army headquarters in Vienna, and an administrative position. One of his first assignments was to deliver some documents to the army headquarters here in Berlin – they were highly sensitive, so they didn't entrust them to the post. It was a long, slow, journey and he always was a curious child, so naturally he found the time to open the sealed envelopes and read the papers that he was carrying. And what papers! These were frank reports that on the one hand spelled out precisely the hopelessness of fighting in the Carpathian mountains – they'd completely run out of weapons and ammunition and medical supplies, and on average, the men were dead within five weeks of arriving there – and on the other hand, asked for tens of thousands of reinforcements. Otto was an angry young man who had just watched his best friend die and couldn't believe the futility of it all – it seemed obvious to him that with winter approaching a strategic withdrawal off the mountains, at least until the spring, would have been more appropriate. So, with time *on* his hands, and these papers *in* his hands, by the time he'd arrived in Berlin he'd formed a plan. But he needed help from someone completely trustworthy, who, even if they didn't want to get involved, would at least not report him to the authorities – which is where your husband came in. Otto had all these documents which would seriously embarrass both the army and the government if they were made public, and it was his original plan to just leak them to a newspaper. But your husband could see the limitations of that idea. He knew precisely the extent of newspaper censorship. So, he took Otto's idea in a different direction and had flyers made up using the most inflammatory parts of the papers they had. He then had them distributed as widely as possible, all over Berlin and some other cities too – Frankfurt, Hamburg, Hanover, Bremen, Leipzig – perhaps elsewhere as well, although I forget the specifics of it all now. It was like a bomb going off – opened people's eyes to the war's realities. The government lost a lot of support, which it never regained.'

'I remember vaguely that my husband was very preoccupied with getting some papers printed,' Katarina recalled thoughtfully, 'although he never told me the details. I remember more clearly the outcry when those flyers were distributed. It caused rioting in parts of the city and started a wave of anti-war demonstrations. I just never realised how my husband was involved,' Katarina said, adding a surprised smile. 'But I was heavily pregnant with Renata at the time, and then busy with her as a new-born baby and more concerned with staying away from any armed uprisings – walking past the city's soup kitchens was chaos enough for me. However, that doesn't explain how my husband saved your son's life.'

'Otto's plan was very much a rough cut, a young man's reaction to the senseless savagery he'd seen as a soldier. As I said, Otto's idea had been to approach the papers, but it was your husband who enlarged upon it and thought through the ramifications for my son. Getting the flyers printed was a fairly simple matter for your husband, he had the right contacts – he knew newspaper owners with printing presses and appropriately placed politics – and getting them distributed was only a matter of spreading enough Marks amongst hungry youngsters looking for some easy money, and there were plenty of those around at the time. Most importantly, he realised that unless they were very careful, than it would have been only too obvious who had leaked the information, and that would have meant a Court-Martial and certain death for my son. But your husband knew that as a civilian – and as a former politician with a high profile – the repercussions would not be particularly severe if he publicly took the blame for leaking those documents, and that way my son would never fall under suspicion. He went to great lengths to get inside the office where Otto was delivering the documents and then blatantly "steal" them himself. Of course your husband was put under a great deal of pressure when he stood up for his "crime", and later, after the war when Otto introduced me to him, he told me that there had been threats of charges being brought against him for theft, but in the end, they never amounted to anything.'

Both Katarina and Renata sat quietly, amazed by what General von Duisburg had just revealed to them. It all rang true for Katarina, and explained so much to her that before she had never understood, in particular, her husband's distinct metamorphosis after Marcus' death.

Katarina poured them all more coffee and they sat in the summer breeze that billowed out the damask drapes besides them, waiting for the French Ambassador on whom they had all placed such high expectations.

Monsieur Francois-Poncet arrived looking crisply laundered in a plaid shirt of mint green and pale pumpkin orange, white flannel trousers, a dark blue jacket and a toned in tie. Katarina could not help but notice what a colourful contrast he made to the usual sombre suited Berliner, or the increasingly common sight of black-clad Nazi soldiers.

General von Duisburg introduced the two women to the French Ambassador. '*Enchanté* Madame,' he said to Katarina, his voice filled with a vibrancy that Katarina realised had long since withered in most German men. 'It is most certainly a pleasure; I have had the honour of meeting your husband previously.' He turned and greeted Renata, and then sat down with them at the last remaining available chair.

'This is a sad day for Germany, indeed for any country that values freedom,' he said, his voice soft yet serious. 'None of us can begin to understand how these events have begun, or indeed where they will end. What is most important now, is to ensure all of your safety. Madame, Mademoiselle,' he addressed the two von Steindorf women, 'I would strongly recommend that you take rooms here until we have further news of your husband. And you will come with me,' he said, turning his attention to the General, as if the matter were already settled. 'You can stay at my Embassy until we can see which way events are turning. At least you'll have diplomatic protection there, and the not inconsiderable distraction of our wine cellar,' he added, hoping to lighten the sombre mood.

'I am most grateful for you very generous offer, Ambassador,' replied the General. 'However, I have been a soldier all of my life and I've never fought shy of facing an enemy, so I must decline it.'

The conversation did not run on much from that point. Monsieur Francois-Poncet repeated his offer to General von Duisburg, who again declined, and then it was time for the General to leave.

'There is much that I must attend to,' he said wearily, suddenly looking extremely old. 'I'll be in touch with you all very soon,' he murmured in a tired voice, before shaking their hands and walking languidly away.

They never heard from him again. Later, as dusk stripped the last strands of light from the dull summer sky, General von Duisburg was shot in the back as he climbed down from the taxi that had taken him back to his town house.

Before Monsieur Francois-Poncet had left the Adlon that afternoon, Katarina had joined him as he walked across the hotel's inner courtyard towards the main lobby and the foyer doors.

'Do you think,' she began discreetly, seizing the few moments of total privacy before they stepped back inside the hotel building, 'That the *Obersturmbahnführer* at Oranienburg might appreciate some bottles of cognac or a good crate of wine sent with my best compliments? Would it perhaps help him realise that it's no longer necessary to detain my husband – if, of course, he is still alive? I have the means with me to purchase some gifts, if you think it appropriate.'

Monsieur Francois-Poncet admired her audacious spirit and accepted the roll of Reichsmark that she tentatively pressed into his hand, reassuring her that he would make further inquiries and initiate the most practicable plan.

'Here's my office number,' he said, offering her his card. Call me at any time, and of course I can be here in moments if necessary, our Embassy is almost opposite the Adlon, just across the Pariser Platz. I will, *bien sur*, be in touch just as soon as I have any news.'

Katarina followed Monsieur Francois-Poncet's advice and at once took a suite of rooms at the Hotel Adlon. It gave her some comfort to think that she had the French Ambassador, with all his diplomatic authority behind him, just yards away from where they were staying. She then called the house – sadly, although perhaps predictably, there was no word from her husband – and arranged for Frau Braun to bring over some fresh clothes and a few personal possessions. There was no more that the women could do, but wait. From the set of decanters laid out in their suite on a walnut bureau, Katarina poured herself a generous finger of whiskey which she drank in a bracing gulp, then sank exhausted onto the green-gold brocade sofa.

They filled the rest of that day playing card games in the suite's *terre-verte* sitting room, before ordering up a light supper of pickled herrings and beetroots and a chilled Ruhr Riesling, and then drawing a bath each and retiring early to their bedrooms for the night.

Neither of them slept well, and in the early hours the SS officers came knocking again in Renata's dreams. She sat up with the same bolt of shock as the night before, but this time, thankfully, there was only silence and then a long, restless wait until the dawn.

Renata was up and dressed with the cerise tinted sunrise, but there was nothing to do and nowhere to go as her mother had decided that they should avoid the attention that they drew in the public rooms, and remain upstairs in their suite. In any case, she felt wretchedly tired and lethargic, and in no mood to dress up to face the world.

Their rooms up on the fourth floor were at least spacious and lavishly furnished, and their sitting room, with its silk lined walls, opened out onto a small balcony with fabulous views that stretched from the *Tiergarten* behind the *Brandenburger Tor*, across the Pariser Platz and then down along Unter den Linden. High above the square in the fresh early air, Renata watched the city emerge into the bright morning light whilst she waited for her mother to wake. She followed with envy the movement of couples who meandered in and out of the Adlon, of men in smart suits walking briskly to offices and Embassies around the square, and nannies pushing prams and cajoling children towards the park. She would never again have the nonchalance that all these people appeared to have: in a little over twenty-four hours she had come to realise the transience of life.

The day unfolded slowly, and hotter with each passing hour. The cloudless sky, a pale manganese blue, darkened by degrees into a deep shimmering noon without a wisp of wind. Across the square the shadows quickly shortened.

Katarina had finally woken at eleven but with a terrible head-ache, so she remained in bed propped up against pillows drinking strong black coffee and scouring, unsuccessfully, the *Berliner Tageblatt* for news of her husband. Just before lunchtime, Monsieur Francois-Poncet sent over a hand written note delivering the sad news of General von Duisburg's death. Katarina closed the curtains in her bedroom and lay back stricken on her bed, the pillows and sheets damp with her tears and fearful perspiration.

By mid-afternoon a haze had settled over the city, and their rooms, even with the balcony doors and all the windows open, were stifling. Below, in the Pairiser Platz, pedestrians slowed their pace to a stroll and birds retreated to trees for some shade. Renata longed to wander over to the *Tiergarten* where the air would be fresher, but knew that would be quite out of the question, so to cool down she ordered mint leaves with crushed ice and lemonade to be brought up to the suite, and then mixed these together with a dash of brandy from the crystal decanter. She had abandoned her game of solitaire and the book she had begun – her mind was too tired and troubled and skidded carelessly across the words – and sat alone in the sitting room, certain that she would go insane with the strain of the wait.

Evening eventually came with lavender skies slowly fading into an indigo night. Still, there was no news of Herr von Steindorf. Renata, worn out from two difficult nights and days, finally fell into a deep dreamless sleep. Katarina clutched her pillow and stared blankly at the dark walls for hours.

The following day passed in much the same way, although Katarina did get out of her bed and suffered the interminable hours anxiously pacing the suite whilst Renata slumped, melting, across the sofa, or stared numbly out over the heat drenched city, the scene reminiscent to her of Ernst Kirchner's painting, *Brandenburger Tor, 1929*. By then, they neither had an appetite for food or games or even conversation. Occasionally, they cast an accusing glance at the telephone as though it was purposely withholding good news from them. None, however, came.

Late in the afternoon, Katarina put a call through to Monsieur François-Poncet. However, he was away from the Embassy at the time and had left her no word. She replaced the receiver and lit yet another cigarette and poured out a generous measure of brandy. Renata knew better than to question her mother about the call. In any case, all the answers she sought were there in her mother's forlorn frown and each weary inhalation of smoke from her umpteenth cigarette of the day.

Slowly, the day ebbed away, although the heat remained, heavy and oppressive, bringing gathering clouds and growls of thunder and a nauseous headache for Renata. A summer storm provided their evening's entertainment and something of a distraction. Angry lashes of lightening illuminated the city spectacularly, and an hour of heavy rain at last cooled the sultry air and brought a breeze to their rooms so they at least slept better that night.

Just after eight the following morning, Katarina was startled from her sleep by the ringing telephone beside her bed, and the hotel operator asking to put a call through.

'*Bonjour Madame, ici c'est Monsieur François-Poncet.*' She recognised the French Ambassador's voice immediately, after the operator had put him on line. 'Please excuse the hour of this telephone call, however, I have very good news! You are very astute, Madame, the *Obersturmbahnführer* at Oranienburg does indeed have an appreciation of fine French cognacs and American cigarettes, and after reconsidering the matter, he now realises that there is no longer any need to detain your husband further. So, I am pleased to inform you that my chauffeur has just left with my assistant to collect him. Hopefully, they will be returning to the Embassy within an hour or so. I shall walk over to meet you at the Adlon at nine, and then bring you back here to meet him.'

The suite was soon a vortex of elation. Maids appeared to press clothes and clean shoes, while a waiter brought in a procession of trays bearing a breakfast to suit the celebratory mood: fresh, strong coffee and squeezed fruit juices; soft baked *Brötchen* and small sweet pastries; glazed spiced hams and slices of cheese and endless dishes of eggs in all guises. Katarina and Renata relished the feast whilst they bathed and then dressed and coifed.

Sitting with Monsieur François-Poncet in the drawing room of the French Embassy a short while later, the two women looked radiant, unrecognisable from the anguished figures who had stalked the suite in the Adlon during the previous few days.

Thoughtfully, Monsieur François-Poncet had ordered up

from the cellars a bottle of Perrier-Jouet Champagne, and as that cooled in a silver ice bucket and they waited for the imminent return of Herr von Steindorf, they heard how his release had been secured using a combination of diplomatic threats and entreaties, and *cadeaux* purchased with the Reichsmarks that Katarina had given him.

'And how did you get these gifts to the *Obersturmbahnführer?*' Katarina asked, wondering if the Ambassador had gone there in person.

'Well,' Monsieur François-Poncet began, as a droll look washed across his face. 'I thought I would embellish your idea a little with one of my own, and so, and I hope Madame will forgive me for using your money in such a way, but it occurred to me that the *Obersturmbahnführer* might also enjoy the company of a particularly charming French lady who, shall we say – entertains – in the finest circles here in Berlin, and I sent her over with all the gifts that we purchased, to meet with the *Obersturmbahnführer.*'

Renata was utterly shocked by this bold admission and was fully expecting her mother to admonish the Ambassador in some way, so her surprise was even greater when instead Katarina let out a throaty laugh. She could not remember when she had last seen her mother look so happy.

A brisk knock at the door turned all their heads with anticipation at Herr von Steindorf's return. Indeed, it was Monsieur François-Poncet's secretary, announcing that he had arrived at the Embassy and asking if he should be brought in to the drawing room. However, from her fretful tone and harried face, they sensed that something was very much amiss. The jovial mood amongst them all turned sombre in an instant. They waited in silence for Herr von Steindorf to enter the room.

Presently, with a member of staff supporting him on either side, a routed, bloodied figure, with eyes and mouth and cheeks so cut that the flattened nose went unremarked amongst the scabbed and swollen contours of the face, and clasping an arm that was obviously broken, limped painfully into the room. And if it hadn't been for the crumpled carmine and silver silk striped tie that was loosely knotted around his neck, Katarina would never have recognised that in the ruins of this man, was her husband.

5

ISOLATION
Oil on Canvas
79cm x 68cm

Berlin, Germany. November 15th 1995.

A soft voice greeted Ellie from behind, '*Ein schönen guten Abend, Frau Eleanor von Steindorf?*'

Recognising the slightly frail yet playful tone, Ellie turned around. Her grandmother had come after all. Ellie had never seen her grandmother so elegantly dressed, glamorous even, powdered and perfumed in a damson-coloured suit with a peach silk blouse, and a diamond broach she inherited from her mother. Her hair was styled quite differently too, her grey curls cut much shorter and loosely blow-dried rather than rigidly set. Ellie recognised that in her own quiet way, her grandmother seemed determined to make something of a triumphal return to the country she had left torn and bleeding almost fifty years before; and from the picture of grace and composure that she saw before her, her grandmother had certainly succeeded.

'Grandma you've come!' said Ellie, embracing her. 'I'm so glad. You look fantastic, by the way. Thank you so much for making the effort to come – I know it can't have been easy.'

'I am very glad to be here, and so proud of you,' she replied, smiling. 'I wouldn't have missed it for the world. I have lived through most of the twentieth century and been witness to many of the tumultuous events of Germany's history during that time, so I feel a strong attachment to the message that you and Justin are giving out to the world with this exhibition. I wanted very much to see it for myself.'

*   *   *

Renata had travelled infrequently, and never overseas, after arriving in England at the beginning of January in 1946. She had occasionally accompanied her father on day trips to visit her daughter Sabina at boarding school, but these, she felt, had never been a success. Whilst Sabina would always be thrilled to see her grandfather, Herr von Steindorf, she had been sullen and withdrawn with Renata. It was bad enough to have to endure the sniggering and pointing that her presence provoked from the other girls, but to be snubbed by her own daughter was a humiliation too far. Especially as it was such a momentous exertion for her to get there. Renata had always returned from these outings feeling by turns angry and exhausted. In the end, she had stopped the visits altogether.

In truth, although she had never admitted this to anyone, she felt a deep surge of panic whenever she went anywhere new or even thought about doing so for that matter.

For Renata, travel had lost all its romantic appeal on the day she had been forced from the burning ruins of Dresden and sent on the precarious path of the refugee. It held still strong memories of terrors, cruelties and violations that she had never be able to talk about, but which still leapt out at her in her dreams or crept up on her during the day, stealing her away into a silent desperation, a tableau vivant of Munch's *Scream*. For the eleven months until she had met her father at Waterloo Station she had often had no idea where she and Sabina would be or sleep that night, let alone the following day. For a long time they had rarely changed their clothing and had always slept fully dressed, ready to take flight at a moment's notice if needed. They had slept everywhere from the forest floor to a makeshift camp erected by the army on the outskirts of Dresden, and around firesides along country roads and on billiard tables in deserted hotels where every available inch of carpet was occupied by other similarly displaced people on the move. To sleep in a barn or stable or even on hay bales spread out on a farm cart, acquired the semblance of a treat. A disused holiday cottage that they had made use of in the Spreewald for a few weeks in the early spring had certainly been a luxury. Later, after a surprisingly uneventful surrender to the American army near Braunschweig, requisitioned schools and village halls had been an oasis of comfort and calm. Everywhere they went seemed to be strewn with the detritus of destitute lives: litter, old newspapers and empty tin cans; abandoned trunks and rucksacks and clothes hampers with their rifled contents scattered all around; mirrors and paintings and discarded canteens of cutlery and formerly treasured pieces of porcelain; endless pony traps with broken axles, and legions of prams which had been cast aside when they had lost a wheel. Often, there were children crying all on their own, whether orphaned or just separated from their family it was impossible to tell. Mostly, Renata ignored them; she barely had the energy to keep an eye on Sabina, let alone anyone else's child. Often, they were left retching by the stench of animal carcases rotting by the side of the road in the summer sun. They tried their best to ignore the whimpering of horses, collapsed from starvation and exhaustion, slowly dying amongst this anguish. Several times they had come across burnt out clusters of tanks, military staff cars and trucks with the charred remains of their soldiers either still inside or beside the vehicles, and also groups of dead civilians who appeared to have been shot. By then, she had become so immune to death that she passed by or even stepped over a corpse as if it were a fallen tree. A week of a frantic, but ultimately futile search through the still burning Dresden rubble, amidst bodies too numerous to even count, for some trace of Joachim's body or any sign of Herr and Frau Lange or Katarina's brother, had ensured that.

After her arrival in England, there were days when merely leaving her bedroom at the house in Finchley had induced a tightness across Renata's chest and a fight for breath such that she wondered if she were suffering a heart attack, or simply losing her mind. There were nights when she lay awake shaking and in pain reliving the time when she had almost burnt to death one night, and then almost frozen to death the following one. There were nights when she lay asleep, shaking and in pain, reliving the time when drunken Russian soldiers had stumbled into the Spreewald barn where they had been sheltering, and raped her along with the other three women in their group.

Sometimes in her dreams she fought back. She got hold off the bottle one of them had smashed into her mouth and then held with the jagged edges to her neck like a blade, forcing her to submit. In her dream the bottle became *her* weapon, and time and again she thrust it like a dagger deep into her attackers until she had left them for dead. Those were the good nights, although she still woke feeling ravaged from such dreams. On the bad ones her dreams simply repeated the depravities as they had actually happened. The solders coming into the red-bricked and weathered beamed barn, drunk but not so intoxicated that they didn't know how to control the situation. Waking the women with a lantern shone in their faces, a shove of their rifle butts to their stomachs, and a kick to their thighs or buttocks. They'd reeked of alcohol and sweat and urine. They knew that any farm building, be it a storage area, a cattle shed or a pig sty, would have refugees sleeping there every night. They knew that the women would be asleep and exhausted and too weak to put up any real form of resistance. They knew that the women were most probably travelling without men to protect them and very likely had children asleep in the upstairs of the hayloft. In broken German, one of them had threatened, 'If you wake up your little darlings we'll sort them out as well.' They had clearly done this before. Resigned to her fate, Renata thought to herself, 'I won't make a sound. Go ahead, fuck me and leave. Just stay away from my daughter or I promise I *will* kill you, somehow. This is as nothing compared with losing Sebastian and watching Joachim burn to death before my eyes so you're not really the all powerful so called men that you think you are.' It would hurt she knew, but she'd already given birth to two children so the pain they inflicted would probably not be that great. She could just lie there and endure the sordid act, and in their state it probably wouldn't last that long in any case. The soldier standing by her had unbuttoned his flies then wrapped his mouth around the bottle that he was drinking from indicating that this was what he expected her to repeat on him. Her stomach lurched. This, she couldn't do. This was such an intimate act and she knew that she wouldn't be able to detach herself so easily from performing fellatio on the soldier, as to conceding to his violation of her. '*Komm Frau!*' he'd demanded. Instinctively, she'd shaken her head in disagreement. His response was to smash the bottle hard into her mouth and hold the cut glass to her neck which he held there all the while he raped her. Her only consolation was that the agony from her knocked out and broken teeth was so great that she barely noticed the other pain that he inflicted upon her.

After that, there was no safe place she felt: death and brutality could come at any time and in any place. The thought of a trip to Bedfordshire, or central London, or even the greengrocer's nearby in Finchley High Street, could provoke lengthy episodes of nausea and sweats and shaking fits. They could engulf her at any time, leaving her feeling trapped and isolated and unable to communicate with the rest of the world.

Her parents had been keen for her to begin treatment with their dentist in Upper Wimpole Street – her mother Katarina was far more concerned about the appearance of her broken and missing front teeth than she was herself – but it had taken months before she was able to attend even the preliminary appointment. Time and again her parents had been forced to cancel the appointment, as the very thought of it had left Renata paralysed with dread. Ultimately, increasing pain in one of her teeth had convinced her to visit the dentist, but to hide her extreme anxiety about journeying alone she had used the excuse of her poor English to persuade her father to accompany her. Nonetheless, each subsequent journey to see the dentist over the following few months was a harrowing ordeal that at times left her speechless and fighting for breath.

Eventually, when some of her emotional strength had finally returned, she began to make the occasional excursion for pleasure. She visited some of the London museums with her parents, attended a series of chamber music concerts at the Wigmore Hall with them, and also an art exhibition at the Royal Academy in Piccadilly with a colleague from work. But even these events had required a great deal of cajoling from both of her parents to persuade her to go.

And once, all four of the family had spent a week together at a small hotel on the Isle of Wight, where they had gravely gone through the motions of participating in a summer holiday together. Sadly, the week had been more fraught than relaxing, with Katarina ever keen to point out how the resort compared unfavourably to the elegant shores of the Baltic coast. Secretly, Renata was rather delighted by this, as her mother was clearly in no hurry to repeat the adventure.

Since her arrival in England, aside from these irregular excursions, which had more or less ceased after her parents' deaths, she had seldom ventured beyond a few roads close to her home in Finchley and the library where she had once worked. She felt comfortable having her life of books and bridge contained in that small, safe world. Her more recent visits into central London, to see Ellie's work at two different shows, had required a great deal of coaxing from both her grandchildren. The journey back to Germany must have made demands on Renata in so many ways; all the same, she seemed quite happy to be there, and maybe even pleased that she was finally confronting – and possibly even conquering – those long cast shadows.

She put a hand to Ellie's shoulder and they kissed on the cheeks. Then she turned to Justin and with her breath catching slightly, she reached out to hold him tightly whilst scattering a flurry of German words all around him.

Locked in her embrace and blushing slightly, Justin succumbed to her affection.

'Thank you for coming, Grandma,' he said warmly.

Much paint had dried on the canvas since the argument they had had after Ellie began using the name von Steindorf. At the time they'd expected their grandmother to be flattered, not furious, that they had chosen her name. However, until the subject had dulled a little, it had been simpler for Ellie and Justin to stay away.

Instead, Ellie had kept in touch with her by post. Initially with just birthday and Christmas cards and photos of Joanna, and then as she progressed as an artist with clippings from papers or postcards from towns where she was exhibiting. Firstly, in York and Bath, and then the following year there were exhibitions in Edinburgh and Dublin and Oslo. Finally, after that, Renata had called with an olive branch invitation for her grandchildren to come to her house for afternoon tea.

In hindsight, Ellie realised they should have been more sensitive in adopting her name, knowing as they did her reluctance to exhume the past. But it had taken a while for her to understand that every utterance of her grandmother's family name, took her back to a past that she had no wish to visit. Nevertheless, it certainly proved to be a turning point in Ellie's career, for finally, many years after she was first seduced by the alchemy of colour on canvas at the Theatre Royal, and long since her initial attempt with oils at an easel, her career as an artist began to move forward.

London, England. September 1981.

Days had quickly stretched into weeks, each begun by Ellie with the intention that she would make a start with her painting but ending with yet more excuses as to why she hadn't.

Work was somewhat chaotic and exhausting. The run of *The Best Little Whorehouse in Texas* had finished unexpectedly early in the middle of August, leaving a wake of anxiety in Drury Lane whilst the Stoll Moss management made decisions on how to breach the gap until the next known bookings the following year. It was an anxious time for them all. Eventually, it was decided that the Theatre would remain dark – except for the Royal Variety Performance, which was already booked and almost sold out for November – until *An Audience With Dame Edna* opened at the beginning of February. During that time it was agreed that a skeleton staff would remain in non-essential roles in Drury Lane, while all the others would be transferred to other Stoll Moss theatres around London. Fortunately for all the staff, there would be no redundancies. Ellie, who didn't feel up to facing any more changes, volunteered to stay behind and help June, the box office Manager, keep the front of house ticking over.

Aside from all the challenges and changes at work, Ellie was still feeling emotionally frail after her father's funeral up in Derbyshire a few months before, and Justin's sudden departure less than a week later. She was certainly far from ready to face the solitude and soul searching that work at a canvas would impose, so the spoils of art supplies from her trip to 'L. Cornelissen & Son' had remained untouched.

Finally, on the last Sunday of the month, a dull day when there was no work at the Theatre to distract her from her loneliness and a brisk wind that declared the end of the summer and discouraged all thoughts of going outside, Ellie felt the time had come to pick up her brushes. Paul, the Assistant Scenic Artist at the Theatre Royal, whose tall wiry frame was kept so thin by the enthusiasm and energy that he put into his painting, had lent Ellie a collapsible wooden easel that he'd years before consigned to his attic. Eventually, with the back and each leg groaning arthritically at the long forgotten movement, and the top opening to become perfectly flat so that the palette could be laid across it, she coaxed it upright and into place.

From out of the first bag she retrieved one of the canvas panels that she'd bought to work on. It was fairly small, only 8″ x 10″, the cloth inexpensive hemp with a large grain weave that was pre-stretched and with little give, and already oil primed so it required no further time-consuming preparation. It seemed an un-ambitious place to start. Even then, Ellie was eager to work on large scale canvases – probably inspired by the ones that she saw each day backstage – but that was what all the artists at the theatre had advised her to begin on, and with various Fine Arts degrees from the Royal College of Art, the Slade School of Art and other top colleges, and then years as working professionals between them, she knew she was lucky to get their advice.

Next, Ellie laid out the few tubes of oils that she had finally bought. From amongst the endless exotic names it had been hard to choose which colours to buy, as each of the dozens on offer in 'L. Cornelissen & Son' held its own allure. Red seduced with Carmine and Cadmium Scarlet, Venetian Red and Alizarin Crimson and many shades besides, while blue darkened by the subtlest degrees from the palest Cerulean Blue through Cobalt to Winsor, French Ultramarine and then Prussian Blue. The yellows stretched from a light Naples Yellow via Lemon Chrome and Indian ochre to Raw Sienna, whilst green began with a pale Emerald than ripened into a rich Sap before mellowing to a muted dark Olive.

'You really don't need many colours,' Paul had said, emphatically. He'd been painstakingly marking out precise twelve-inch gaps along the edges of a new scroll of canvas, and used the ruler in his hand like a baton to emphasise his point.

'Rubens painted with a maximum of five colours, and Titian said that it was possible to be a great painter using only three colours!'

Ellie had been on her lunch break and had taken her sandwiches backstage to the paint frames, to spend the time watching the artists at work. They had come to accept that she would just turn up and quietly watch them, and over time they had reached an unspoken agreement whereby either before or after her shift in the box office, and even during it whilst the Theatre was dark and they were exceptionally quiet there, that she would help out as an additional studio assistant. She ran errands to 'Brodie and Middleton' just a few doors down in Drury Lane, or to 'Cornelissen's & Sons' which was a short walk away, or was simply on hand to help Paul mix the powdered paints and the fixing agents. Finally, Ellie felt that she'd found her niche at work.

Little by little, she learnt the differences between size powder, emulsion glaze, animal glues and shellac, the various solvents that were needed to clean the myriad brushes, sponges and rollers that were used, and the different methods of preparing the colour dyes and aniline treatment. It was work that required attention to detail and patience – both qualities that she'd always struggled to find – but she was grateful for the opportunity, and for the unexpected calm she found within herself when she was immersed in it all.

The paint frames were one of the few departments where all members of staff had remained even though the Theatre was dark. With three giant wooden easels, the largest in the country stretching some fifty feet into the vaulted ceiling, the artists who worked on the vast scrolls of canvas were sought after for their expertise in creating hand-painted backcloths by theatres and opera houses the world over. At the time, one of the paint frames was taken up with a canvas for *La Scala* in Milan, while the others were assigned for the sets of Drury Lane's new production of Gilbert and Sullivan's *The Pirates of Penzance*, that was due to open the following May.

Paul was working on the preparatory stage of this process, carefully plotting out the grid for the backcloth with precise marks along the edges. Ellie had offered to help him stretch chalk rubbed string between these points to complete the grid, when it would then be ready for painting. First, the Scenic Artist would block in the colour, square by square, a scaled-up version of the set design drawings, before the Master Artist would embellish the final details to create the finished look.

'And always, always buy the best quality pigments that you can afford,' he'd continued, sitting back on his heals as he finished measuring out one side of the canvas.

Lacking Titan's austere resolve, in the end, when Ellie had finally chosen which oils to buy, she had settled on a limited pure colour palette which amounted to a warm and cool version of each primary, as well as viridian, Payne's Grey, Titanium White and ochre. Ten tubes in total. However, to begin with, she'd decided she would work with just three, white included. This, so she'd been told, would be the best way to learn about each of the oils' differing qualities – which apparently varied enormously – and to a large extent determined the way that an artist worked. Each colour had its own particular softness, opacity or transparency and, most importantly, specific drying rate. All these characteristics had to be absorbed by any aspiring artist, before then advancing to the much harder challenge of mixing colours and oils with a binding medium.

'That's how most students start out at Art College,' Paul had told her in response to her lack of enthusiasm at this slow paced start. 'You've got to get to grips with the basics and really learn the craft; otherwise you'll never progress beyond a certain point. Bring in the canvas when it's finished – I want to see how you get on,' he added. Ellie hoped that her efforts would do justice to his good advice.

Under Paul's instruction, she began to work on her initial composition using a soft pencil on paper. It had been a simple design, the standard fare of the novice painter: a plain ceramic jug. Taking advantage of the quiet hours whilst the phones rang infrequently in the box office, Ellie drew the jug endless times over many days. Gradually, she had learned every nuance of its shape – the slope of its spout, the tilt of its handle, the arc of its side – until eventually she felt assured enough of its every curve and line that she could begin the brushwork without either drawing or under-painting.

'Confidence,' Paul had said to her at some stage, 'is the key to all painting. If you hesitate with your brushwork it shows on the canvas as weakness. So whatever you paint, do it with conviction.' It was advice that Ellie would always try and live up to.

A mahogany palette that had lain unused and unclaimed on a shelf in the paint rooms was dusted off, and by general consent lent to her as well. Traditionally, a dark wooden palette was used by artists to stop light reflecting on the canvas, and along the top of the one that she was borrowing she squeezed out some French Ultramarine and Cadmium Deep Yellow, and then across the middle a large amount of the Titanium White. The remaining palette space would be used for colour mixing. From the second bag she brought out the brand new brushes, a combination of soft hairs and hard, bristles and blenders, round points, filberts and flats. At last, Ellie ready to paint.

She thought that she'd begin using a no 4 flat bristle brush to paint in the blue; it would naturally be quite stiff and enhance the rougher finish that she expected from her first attempt at painting. For the yellow, she would use a softer round point. Dipping it cautiously into the warm swirls of colour and then the white paint, Ellie mixed the two quickly together on the palette before applying the paint directly to the canvas in short, choppy strokes. Gradually, she became more confident about adding less or more white to vary the tone of the blue or the yellow, or intensifying the colour by layering extra paint directly from the tube onto the brush and even the canvas. And as the colours slowly changed their shade they took her thoughts to different places, bringing back long forgotten memories like snapshots from an album; and much as she tried to erase them, with each dip of the brush into paint, they kept on coming back.

Mixing the deep blue and the luminous yellow brought back the perfect skies and brilliant sunlight from the day of her father's funeral, and all her grief still as disabling and raw as when she stood by his graveside. Once again she was struggling to pour a handful of earth onto his coffin, and shredded by anger at her mother's awful behaviour that day, and the notion of why she had even bothered to come at all when by then they'd been acrimoniously divorced for years. Justin had been by Ellie's side throughout the day, ashen and disconsolate over their father's sudden death and numb with incomprehension at their mother's bitter words. And then within a week of their father's funeral, whilst Ellie had still felt lost in a fug of grief and bruised by their mother's savage outburst after the service, Justin had packed up his possessions and left the country to hitch across the continents. Ellie had never felt so alone or emotionally adrift.

At the time of their father's death, she and Justin had been living together in Sudbury Hill for about two years. He'd left their family home in Ealing just as soon as he'd turned sixteen, shortly after he had taken his 'O' Levels. The house they shared was due for demolition but had been lent to them by the property developer who owned it. Their father had done surveying work for him when he'd still lived in London, and made the arrangements on their behalf. The situation suited both the developer, who preferred to have the building occupied in order to keep squatters out, and the two of them, as it was rent free and they were both living on a limited budget. The house was just about habitable, although there was no heating or phone and most of its contents had been stripped, carpets and curtains included. All that remained were a few items which the previous occupants thought worthless, and had left behind. Nonetheless, it was theirs to call home until planning permission was granted to develop the site into a block of flats. Throughout their time there, especially after Ellie's romance of the moment had ended, she'd come to rely on her brother's company more than she cared to admit.

On the morning when he'd left, Ellie came down to grab breakfast before heading to the Theatre and found Justin sitting on the wooden packing crate that they used as a table, a bulging rucksack at his feet. He was clearly waiting for his sister, passing the time with a cup of coffee and a cigarette. He didn't look up. Normally, he would have been long gone for work by then, so she was very surprised to see him there.

'Taking a few days off?' she asked.

'I've handed in my notice,' he replied by way of an explanation. He looked neither excited nor regretful at this move – they both knew that his job as a postal clerk at the local sorting office had never been more than a weekly wage to him. They had never discussed it, but it was obvious to Ellie that had circumstances been different at home he would certainly have stayed on at school to take 'A' Levels, and then aimed for University. He was naturally bright and devoured books at a rapid pace. She felt quite angry that their appalling home life had robbed him off that opportunity, though she had never voiced that opinion to Justin.

'Have you got something else in mind?' she continued.

'I'm taking a ferry to Guernsey tonight,' he said, his fingers nervously drumming the side of the crate.

'But you'll be back soon?' she said, with uncertainly creeping into her voice.

'I don't think so. It's the height of the tourist season over there at the moment, and one of the guys at work – his aunt owns a guesthouse on the island – says she's always looking for staff and even if she isn't, she'll know plenty of other people who are.'

'Well, I guess I'll see you at the end of the summer then?' Ellie added, after an awkward pause.

'I don't think so,' he'd said quietly. 'It's a short crossing from there to France, and I'm thinking about working on the grape harvest which starts in September – there's good money to be made at the vineyards. After that, I'm not sure. Maybe I'll head down to Greece, then Turkey and probably India. Nothing's definite, but I doubt I'll be back for Christmas,' he muttered quietly, while slowly stubbing out his cigarette and pushing the ash around with the still smoking butt. His eyes were fixed firmly on the ashtray to avoid his sister's.

Ellie flicked the switch on the kettle to bring it back up to the boil, numb with shock. She couldn't believe how much he'd already planned out, and without having mentioned a word of it to her before. They had barely buried their father and the thought of letting go of her brother for God knows how long, was a hard punch to take. Clearly, there was nothing that she could say to stop him; her brother would soon turn eighteen and was free to do as he liked, and she was his sister and not his parent. Besides, Ellie knew how abandoned he'd felt when she left home and he'd been stuck on his own with their mother in Ealing. She had tried her best to look out for him, though she wondered whether he'd appreciated the fact. Even when she'd been desperate herself, and each day had felt like she was stumbling through some Daliesque landscape with all the familiar landmarks of family and home life surreally distorted or stripped away, she'd gone back regularly to see him, to make sure that he was alright and that the situation with their mother hadn't deteriorated too much. During term-times they had generally met up at his school, and then hurriedly caught up whilst Ellie walked him most of the way back home. In the holidays they got together in cafés or at friends' houses or at the park. It had always been snatched time, and never particularly relaxed. They would be constantly keeping an eye out for their mother; they both knew that Justin would see the worst side of their mother's temper if she'd found out that he'd seen his sister. Ellie also always made sure that he knew how to find her, in case the worst happened at home, and, for whatever reason, he had to leave suddenly. Wherever she was staying, which at times had variously included Lisa's home, other friends' sofas and floors, a garden conservatory and a room in a Shirland Road squat, Ellie had always made it quite clear to him that he could just turn up at any time, unannounced, and she would look after him.

Yet despite her best efforts at that time, which in reality had amounted to little more than stolen moments most weeks, she had watched the colour quickly drain from her brother. Within a few weeks of her departure his spirit began to noticeably dull. After some months he looked extremely drained. Eventually, when he had moved into Sudbury Hill with his sister, his essence seemed to have been entirely stripped away.

'I've got to get away,' he'd said, echoing the words that Ellie had spoken to him all those years before. 'My life's crap here. Now that Dad's dead I don't feel that I've got any family any more – apart from you, of course,' he added hastily. 'I know we didn't visit him that often, but I just can't get my head around the fact that I'll never see him again or that he's not there at the end of the phone or a train ride away. And apart from Mother, who I've no interest in seeing whatsoever, who else is there?'

'Grandma? Your friends from school?''

'I've pretty much lost touch with all of them. And as for Grandma, apart from the funeral, I don't remember when I last saw her. She's not exactly a bundle of laughs when we do – I hate the way she always stares at me, and it freaks me out the way she talks to me in German when she knows I don't speak the language. I hate my job, I can't get a girlfriend, and we're living in a shit-hole. I don't see what I'm hanging around for.'

Ellie could understand his frustrations and had realised that in many ways his life really wasn't that great, but, selfishly, she still didn't want him to go. She stirred her coffee in silence and sat down opposite him at the table. She had no idea what to say. If she begged him to stay there was always a chance that he might change his mind, at least for a while. But she also realised that he would soon resent her for doing that. Having left home even younger, Ellie had hardly been able to use his age as an argument to dissuade him, so she dismissed that idea as well.

'It won't be long before we can get a proper place of our own,' she eventually said, picking up on a conversation they'd had the previous week on the train back from Derbyshire. 'Things will be much easier then,' she added, trying to sound reassuring.

Before they'd left Winster, their Uncle Peter had taken them to one side and explained that their father's will named them both as the main beneficiaries. Beyond a small life insurance policy there was little to his estate, he'd explained. The house in Ealing had been signed over to their mother as part of the divorce settlement, and the cottage he'd moved into in Winster was rented, not bought. However, with that in mind their father had taken out the insurance policy, and their uncle could see no reason why it would not be paid out quite quickly. Their father had never mentioned any of this to either of them, and it had taken a while for the fact that they were soon to receive an inheritance to sink in. Along the slow journey back to St Pancras, Ellie had suggested to Justin that if there was sufficient, they lump the money together and move out of the house in Sudbury Hill and into a place of their own. They knew that they would have to move from the house at some stage, they'd been fore-warned by the developer that it would probably be by the following spring, but if they could avoid another winter in a house without heating or hot water, then so much the better.

Justin, still sitting on the wooden packing crate, toyed with the cigarette packet, passing it back and forth between each hand as if he were playing with a pack of cards. 'Ellie, this house is just a small sum in the whole equation,' he'd replied eventually. 'And moving out won't make that much difference to my life. Sure, Dad's money will come in useful, but there's not going to be enough to buy a place outright and I don't even want to think about getting tied down with a mortgage at the moment. I don't want a job or a house or even a relationship that requires any real thought or commitment. I want to be free of all that crap and just clear out my head.'

At that point Ellie conceded there was little she could do but to wish him well, ask him to keep in touch and if possible organise a *poste restante* somewhere along the way. He'd then got up to head off. They hugged briefly, awkwardly, their bodies out of sync, and she kissed him on the cheek as they said goodbye.

By then Ellie had been running late to get to the Theatre for ten. She'd quickly dressed into some old skinny jeans and a Patti Smith T-shirt, spiked her recently short cropped hair and made some toast that she never ate, realising only after she'd made it that she'd lost any appetite. She then left and hurried to the tube to take the Piccadilly Line into work.

The house had seemed unbearably quiet in the weeks following Justin's departure. Ellie stayed out as much as possible doing anything rather than go home alone. Even a visit to the launderette had seemed like an easier option than facing the empty rooms at the house.

During the week Ellie worked overtime whenever she could. Ironically, bookings for *Best Little Whorehouse* had increased as soon as it was announced that it was shortly to close, so for a while they were busier than ever in the box office. At other times she just hung out backstage with the artists at the paint frames, or within the hub of gossip and endless activity that swirled around the wardrobe department. After work, Ellie would meander over to the pubs they all went to, usually the Nell of Old Drury or The Opera Tavern, where there'd always be a known face and a conversation to join in with. And of course, royalists or not, they all made the most of the party spirit as London ground to a halt in celebration of Prince Charles' marriage to Lady Diana at the end of July.

Sundays were always the hardest to endure, Ellie felt, without the distractions of the Theatre or even the flimsiest of love affairs to while away the hours. She had to force herself up and out of the house, to escape the loneliness. Sometimes she spent long periods of solitude immersed in Monet's immense *Water Lilies* at the National Gallery, or simply wandered alone through the city along the Embankment, past the Knightsbridge stores or the Camden stalls, and around the familiar labyrinth of Covent Garden streets. It all passed the time and numbed her emotions. Ellie had come to realise that if she were busy or tired or surrounded by people, she could almost forget how unhappy she actually felt. Walking into 'L. Cornelissen & Son' to buy the brushes and oils had been the first time her spirits had lifted since Justin's sudden departure.

Slowly, stroke by staccato stroke, the small canvas that Ellie was working on became covered with paint, until by the end of the afternoon she had completed her first painting, *alla prima*: all in one go. She left it for a couple of weeks to become touch dry, and then, nervously, took it into work.

To her relief, Paul was full of praise for her fledgling talent and had plenty of advice for her next painting. He soon had her progressing onto other subjects and more complex techniques – glazing, scumbling, applying impastoed paint with both a brush and a knife – but most importantly, the whole process evolved into a much needed catharsis as the magma of her emotions erupted onto the canvas.

Memories that haunted each colour, and even each medium or implement of art, were exorcised by the process of painting. Gradually, as Ellie's volume of work increased, the anger inside her subsided. Bit by bit, vivid primaries and tangerine orange no longer routinely reminded her of wax crayons and being five years old once again, so bewitched with those small, bright sticks and a colouring book that she could ignore the horror of her mother yet again passed out on the sitting room sofa, leaving her two small children hungry and unsupervised until their father's return home. Charcoal eventually lost its ability to take her back to her teenage years; a time spent anxiously hiding from her warring family sublimating her fear into stark, black streaks. And in time, she could pick up a paint brush without becoming hostage to the memory of her mother maliciously snapping her small collection of fine art brushes before then throwing Ellie out of her home. Art had become her emotional alchemy.

It was mid-October before Ellie finally heard from Justin, when he sent her a postcard from Chateau de Pizay, a turreted dream of castle close to Macon in the Beaujolais region of France. 'Hi Ellie, Enjoying the grapes! Think of me if you drink some of the Beaujolais Nouveau. Justin x,' was the brief message, but she was glad to have heard from him all the same.

Christmas then loomed before her and for many weeks she dreaded it, imagining that without her father around, with whom she'd spent the last few Christmases up at his cottage in Derbyshire, and being out of touch with the rest of her family, it would be a lonely time. She sent cards to her grandmother and Uncle Peter, but nothing to her mother. They had not been in contact since her father's funeral.

But then, having feared the worst, each night through December developed into a party backstage at one of the nearby theatres, which then transferred, after a wine-fuelled invitation from Ellie at some point that month, to her house for Christmas Day. Word spread quickly of a party which could get as out of hand as the guests could manage because the venue was soon to be demolished. Claire, who'd been the Stage Manager on *Best Little Whorehouse* but who was now somewhat under-utilised at the Cambridge Theatre, became the event's organiser, drawing up lists of food and drink and other essentials – candles, crackers, disposable cutlery, plates and napkins, glasses, corkscrews, coal and firelighters – and assigning duties to every known guest.

Early in the day on Christmas morning, two set decorators, fresh from a raid on the props department, arrived to transform the stripped rooms into a winter wonderland. From out of the Theatre van they brought armfuls of decorations, a trestle table and a cloth to cover it, an assortment of chairs and an array of ornate candlesticks. Lush pine boughs soon followed, and an avalanche of stage snow packed in large polythene bags and garlands dripping with holly and ivy. Claire appeared a short time later with her Deputy and Assistant Stage Manager, and commandeered the two working gas rings and the ageing oven in the kitchen. Ellie watched the proceedings in awe, having had her offer to help cheerfully declined. Soon the house warmed to the sweet wintry scent of cinnamon mulled wine, and by lunchtime Claire had conjured up a feast that was spread along the moss coloured scrim draped over the trestle table. Guests were by then arriving with mince pies and ripe cheeses, and boxes of chocolate and bottles of wine to add to it all. A fire had been coaxed out of the disused sitting room fireplace, and playing in front of it, courtesy of the double bass player, clarinettist and trumpeter from the orchestra pit, was a live jazz band. Against her every expectation, Ellie had a very happy Christmas.

The party also served as a grand finale for the old house, because soon after, at the beginning of March, as Ellie moved out, the bulldozers moved in to clear the plot. By then, she was in the fortunate position of having her share of her father's inheritance, and had enough money for the deposit on a small flat in a quiet but rundown road in Maida Vale. The rooms were far from large, and the kitchen and bathroom did justice to the estate agent's description of compact, but there was a second bedroom which could be rented out to help pay the mortgage. Most importantly, the sitting room was south facing with French doors that opened out onto the flat's own small, walled garden, gilding the room, even on the gloomiest of days, with light.

In that room Ellie really began to make progress with her painting, and by the early spring when the daffodils splattered cadmium yellow around her garden like a vibrant backcloth to her sitting room studio, she had stopped working with a limited colour palette on simple pictures of still life objects, and had progressed to a full spectrum of colours and more complex compositions.

Ellie flirted with the differing styles of artists that she admired, reproducing the circles scattered across a Miro canvas, dripping paint on to an unstretched canvas laid over the floor in homage to the Action Art of Jackson Pollock, and exploring subtle gradients of colour as Rothko had. Then her flirting took on an entirely different hue in the middle of May when *The Pirates of Penzance* swept, swashbuckling, onto the Drury Lane stage.

'Stay away from the actors,' was the blunt warning Ellie received on her very first day at the Theatre. Imparting this jaded advice was Sonia, who had never let a cheerful thought stand in the way of a cynical one. 'They're all trouble,' Sonia added, peering at Ellie over her black-rimmed glasses whilst tallying ticket stubs like a bank clerk counting notes. Sonia was one of the eight staff who ran the box office, and was teaching Ellie how to reconcile the attendance slips that the ushers had collected from each ticket at the previous night's show, with the box office records. 'Especially the good looking ones,' she'd gone on, warming to her theme. 'Remember, it's their job to make make-believe believable, and they have to change the role that they play so many times, they forget who they actually are. And you can never have a proper conversation with an actor – you never know if they're just repeating lines that they've learnt from a play. But worst of all, they're snobs – by the time they make it to the West End they think of us as front of house drones and themselves as the queens, which often as not they are, of course! They forget that just a few years before they were starving students at the RADA, and then had to schlep through the provinces or even start off as strippers just to beg for an Equity card. If it's a casual fling you're after, that's fine, but you won't see them for dust once their contract here has run out.'

Sonia's words held all the scorn of someone who had worked in the theatre for over thirty years and who had probably seen as much drama backstage as on it. Judging from her words Ellie imagined that she had been very hurt by some of it at some time herself, but as the newcomer to the box office she hadn't feel it her place to probe any further. It was a job that she'd been lucky to get and was keen to keep. The Theatre Royal, Drury Lane, with its grand tradition as the world's oldest working theatre, was by far the most exciting place that she had ever worked in, and she was anxious to make a good impression. Finally, after living pretty much hand to mouth since leaving school and home – waiting tables, working market stalls, drawing the dole – Ellie had a regular weekly wage packet and with it, she hoped, a bit of an easier life. To begin with, at least, Sonia's advice about dating actors had been easy to follow. At the time Ellie was seeing a barman she had worked with in her previous job at a restaurant. It had been a light romance and that had suited them both until the gossamer threads that had held them together slowly unravelled, and they drifted apart.

Watching the shows was the fantastic perk of the job that was understandably envied by others. Ellie always made every effort to get to know the shows well, using the excuse, as if one were needed, that it helped her to sell more tickets. Generally, she would see a show in rehearsals, standing in at the back of the auditorium. Since she had worked there she had been lucky enough to catch Carol Channing in the dazzling revival of *Hello Dolly!*, Denis Quilley and Sheila Hancock the following year when they starred in the magnificently staged and darkly humorous *Sweeney Todd*, and after that *The Best Little Whorehouse In Texas* which opened for business, to the apparent shock of West End audiences. And then, after the Theatre had been dark all through the winter, Ellie enjoyed *An Evening's Intercourse with Dame Edna*, followed by *An Audience with the Not The Nine O'clock News* team. *The Pirates of Penzance* were then gathering on the Theatre's horizon, with the show's opening night scheduled for the last week in May.

After the long weeks of technical rehearsals that had been necessary to perfect the manoeuvring of the show's centrepiece, a large scale Pirate Ship, the production was in the final days of dress rehearsals with the director, Wilford Leach, doing full run-throughs in costume with both the cast and the under-studies, when Ellie entered the auditorium at the back of the Dress Circle. By then, when an unknown actor strode forward on the Pirates' Ship with such vitality that even at the rear of the Theatre his presence set her heart racing and turned her mouth dry, Sonia's words of warning about actors had conveniently long slipped her mind.

The actor was understudy to Michael Praed who was playing Frederick, the young, handsome hero of the show. He looked uncannily like Michael, Ellie thought, with the same wavy brown hair and doe-eyed grace that softened the impact of his sculpted body, but it was his smile really, that lit up his light umber eyes and the whole auditorium, which held her attention every moment he was up there on stage.

Ellie had no idea who he was, of course, as all the focus in the box office and all the publicity material was on the stars of the show – Tim Curry, George Cole, Pamela Stevenson and Michael Praed – and all the understudies were unknown actors to her. But after that, she thought about him constantly: his voice, his face, how he moved on stage. It all made for pleasant reveries, especially when the box office was particularly quiet. Without wanting to draw attention to the matter, but determined to find out who he was, Ellie waited until the programmes arrived later that week in time for the preview performances. Pouncing on a copy at the earliest opportunity, she flicked through the pages until she found his headshot printed amongst the company members. Finally, she could put the name Milo Phelps to his face. And printed beneath his black and white photo was a brief resume of his acting career: 'Milo was born in Bedfordshire and trained at the Central School of Speech and Drama. Since then, he has appeared as Joseph in a European Tour of *Joseph and the Amazing Technicolour Dreamcoat*; as Diesel in a production of *West Side Story* in Cheltenham, and he has featured in several TV commercials. *Pirates of Penzance* is Milo's first West End musical.'

Knowing his name was one thing, but unless their paths crossed by chance, Ellie realised that it would be hard for her to meet him without igniting a fuse of gossip that would snake from the front of house along 'The Run', and then around the all the rooms backstage. Under different circumstances, it might have been easier to forget about him, to dismiss her feelings as a trivial infatuation, but they were working together – albeit in different areas of the theatre but nonetheless under the same roof – and her thoughts as she went through the routine of her day refused to settle on box office business, and kept racing back to Milo instead.

Soon, all Ellie's activities seemed to take her backstage. At the time she anticipated him most likely to arrive, she would find some thin excuse to loiter by the Stage Door. Later on, she would dawdle near the actors' dressing rooms, and whenever possible in the wardrobe department where the actors most often milled around. She volunteered to work the late shift and finish at nine, simply so she could head for a drink where the cast would most likely go after the show.

And then, having run spurious errands all over the theatre for the three or so weeks since the show had opened, and lingered until closing time at all of the obvious drinking haunts that the actors frequented – but without so much as a distant glimpse of him – Milo stepped in behind Ellie late on a balmy June afternoon, while she queued for a sandwich at an Italian deli during the break between the Saturday matinee and the evening performance.

He looked slightly slimmer out of costume, and even taller, dressed in a crumpled Clash T-shirt and battered black jeans, though his athletic frame and performer's deportment managed to make the clothes look chic not shabby, as they would have done on a less honed physique. Ellie blushed as he clearly caught sight of her staring at him. For a moment she thought about stepping out of the queue and leaving the shop, but the words *carpe diem* echoed between thoughts of quietly slipping away. Then the heavy set woman behind the counter forestalled her exit by taking her order, and she realised that she was in as good a place as any to flirt. In a hasty bid to gain a few extra moments by his side at the counter, Ellie asked for her sandwich to be toasted and ordered a citron pressé that she knew required freshly squeezed lemons.

'You were really good as Frederick,' she said, half-turning towards him and smiling, her eyes a steady gaze with his.

He looked slightly puzzled as he had not yet played the role to the public. 'Thank you,' he replied somewhat shyly, his voice mellifluous and gentle.

'I work in the box office – I saw you in dress rehearsal,' Ellie explained.

The hesitant look left his face and he returned my smile. 'Oh, I haven't seen you around the Theatre. But I guess you stay front of house, mainly.'

'I go backstage occasionally,' she said evenly, managing to suppress a wry smile, but thought, if only you knew.

By then, Ellie's food and drink were ready and she had to move a few paces to pay at the end of the counter, but with every step she was aware of his subtle stare on her. Emboldened by this, she decided to take things just a little further.

'And if I see you at work, should I call you Frederick the

Second?' she said coyly, having no intention of letting him know that she'd already made the effort to find out his name.

'Milo,' he replied laughing.

'Bye Milo,' she said softly and slowly, and then turned around and left the shop quickly without so much as a backward glance.

Yes! Ellie thought to herself; and within a week they were lovers.

6

PERDITION
Oil on canvas
363cm x 254cm

Berlin, Germany. November 15th 1995.

Renata's arrival at the *Kunsthalle* elicited a noticeable change in Justin, and for the first time in days he smiled.

'I never thought you'd actually come,' he said to her.

'I wasn't going to, of course,' she replied cheerfully, still clasping her grandson's arms. 'But then I began to think, what good reasons do I really have for not accepting the invitation?'

'And did you have any?'

'That was the thing – none. All my excuses were – well just that, excuses. And not good ones either, I've outgrown their use. In a few days I'm going to turn eighty, and I think it's time for me to be a little less frightened of everything.'

'Grandma, that's fantastic,' said Ellie.

'Well, you're our most honoured guest,' said Justin lightly. 'We probably owe this all to you,' he continued, sweeping his hand around the room. 'You've been the inspiration behind so much of it. I'm really glad you're here.'

As he gradually unwrapped himself from his grandmother's arms, the carved lines of worry slowly erased from Justin's face.

*   *   *

Justin's anxieties about meeting his mother again had drawn ever darkening shade over his life during the past few weeks, leaving his nights sleepless and his spirit subdued. The two of them had not spoken since his father's funeral, some fourteen years before. But unlike his grandmother, who had always made it clear that she would be happy to see her daughter if she ever stopped drinking, Justin had remained emphatic that nothing would change his feelings about seeing his mother again, as, even sober, he just didn't trust her behaviour.

'I wouldn't mind seeing her if it was merely a case of walking on eggshells around her, but I won't walk across a bloody mine-field to be with her,' was his frequent refrain. Besides the un-predictability of her nature, he felt he could never forgive all the betrayals she had inflicted upon their family over the years. Ellie thought it not unconnected that he had never dated anyone for more than a few weeks, and that the first sign of any emotional intimacy with a woman, would, invariably, also be the last.

On the Monday of the week prior to the exhibition, Justin had turned up at her house in a bleak mood for a working lunch to discuss the final details for the *Kunsthalle* opening. The evening before, Ellie had a Bonfire Party that grew from a small gathering for Joanna and Millie's closest friends, to large party for both sets of their classmates and many of their parents as well. It had been a cloudless night, crisp enough to justify mulling wine with damsons, bay leaves and Demerara sugar, the after affects of which had slowed her down all morning. She had made a half-hearted attempt to clear up the pumpkin coloured paper cups and plates that were scattered throughout the house, and clean what seemed to be her entire collection of pots and pans and baking trays. But despite these efforts, the house had been still in disarray when Justin arrived.

'It's bloody freezing out there,' he said, crossly, in lieu of a greeting when Ellie let him in. The mellow tones from the November sun had certainly bellied a sharp autumnal chill, but he had dressed a season adrift with clear attention to style, not Celsius, without a coat or even a jumper, wearing a thin summer jacket and lightweight trousers. Sensing her brother's black-hued mood, she had quelled her sibling's instinct to score points with some sharp quip, and instead just concurred with his comment.

He headed immediately downstairs to the kitchen. Following a few paces behind, Ellie noticed the newly formed folds of fabric gathering in his jacket against his rapidly thinning frame. In a clatter, his briefcase and portfolio landed on the counter, and he'd rubbed his hands together whilst blowing across them to warm them up. He then walked over to her wine rack and began inspecting the labels on a selection of bottles before helping himself to a Chateau Leoville Barton that she thought probably deserved a grander occasion, though, too tired and hungover to argue, she said nothing. He poured them both a glass, lit a cigarette and then sat down at the kitchen table to begin sifting through a file with all the details for the upcoming exhibition.

'I'm leaving for Berlin on Thursday,' he began. 'I need to be there to make sure that all the paintings clear customs smoothly. I know that the *Kunsthalle* have co-ordinated all the freight and pro-forma invoices for each painting, but I want to be on site just in case there're any problems – we don't want any empty spaces on the walls.'

Ellie nodded in agreement. They had been through enough dramas in the past with unaccompanied paintings being held up in customs, or even lost in transit, to know that the transport of art across borders rarely ran smoothly.

'And we've got to make a decision now on which invitation to accept after the Exhibition, and then decline the others, ideally by the end of today. People are going to start getting pissed off if we don't give them an answer soon. I think the Cultural Attaché's invitation to dinner is probably the one to go for as he set it all up for us in the first place, although *The Sunday Times* journalist needs to be kept sweet as well. She's talking about doing a feature in the magazine, and that's serious exposure. What d'you think?' he asked, and then gulped at his wine while he looked at Ellie for a response.

'I really don't mind,' she replied. 'I hardly know any of the people involved because you've dealt with them all along. It's up to you who we should spend the time with. We could always book something ourselves and then invite all those different people, that way no one feels left out. Just bear in mind that we might have to bring mother and Grandma along as well.'

'There's absolutely no way mother is coming. It's a business meeting, not an AA meeting,' he snapped back. 'And in any case, whilst I'll just about tolerate her being at the exhibition, I'm not going to spend any more time with her than that.'

'I'm not saying we have to, but if things go well amongst us all at the *Kunsthalle*, we might want to include them later on. It's ages since you've seen her and you've changed an awful lot in that time – you might feel very different about it all when you see her. I just think we should leave our options open.'

'I might have changed, but my feelings haven't. After all the crap she put us through she can go to hell as far as I'm concerned. I don't believe she's changed, I don't believe she ever will, and I still get upset just thinking about it.'

By then, Justin was visibly angry, and a palpable tension swirled uneasily around them and filled the room.

'It's not good to drag all that anger around,' Ellie had said, eventually. 'It's time to let it go; can't you see how it's still damaging your life? You've never let anyone get remotely close to you because at some level you think all the women you meet will turn out to be just like her. Not everyone's like that; you've just never let anyone get close enough for you to see that for yourself. You've got to resolve this somehow, or you'll never have a relationship of any meaning. Reconcile things with mother, not for her sake, but for yours. You're so much stronger now, she won't be able to hurt you any more – I promise,' Ellie added with a note of optimism in her voice that she was not actually feeling.

'My thoughts have always been that she won't be able to hurt me any more if I never see her again,' he replied bitterly, pain spilling over his face, concealing his handsome features beneath anguished furrows. 'You've no idea what it was like living with her when you were gone,' he'd continued, approaching the words slowly, cautiously, as if they were stepping-stones across a deluge of emotions. He'd taken out and lit yet another cigarette even though he'd barely put out the last. 'She was worse than ever – a complete monster. It was bearable – just about – when there were all of us at home, we could protect each other, and there was someone else around to help defuse things if she got too far out of control. But first Dad left, which really pissed her off – as you know – and then you, and that just compounded the situation. I had to face all of her fury on my own, every day – it was a fucking nightmare. She was drinking more than ever, a bottle of gin a day, minimum, often more – a bottle or two of wine as well – so that she'd be vile in the morning with a hangover, and then a vicious drunk later on.' As he paused and inhaled deeply on his cigarette, Ellie noticed for the first time that an ochre stain had formed across his fingers. He exhaled the smoke with a heavy sigh a moment later. 'Nothing I ever did was right, or good enough in her eyes, but I was naïve enough back then to think that you could reason with a drunk, when of course there's no rhyme or reason to anything they say or do. Whatever I did or said was wrong and in her eyes justification for her to hit me. You know I never even took my French 'O' Level because on the morning of the main written paper she smashed my head against a wall so hard that it gave me concussion. I don't even remember what the argument was about – there was rarely any logic to it all. Often, it was just some imagined wrong, something I was accused of having done or said that was entirely made up, or a completely disproportionate reaction to something that I had done, but not in the "right" way – the washing not hung up to her liking, or a bed not properly made, which considering how she generally did none of those things herself, was fucked up to say the least. And if I said even one word to defend myself that could set her off some days, on others saying nothing would make her madder still. I never said that much to you because I couldn't see what difference it would make – there was nothing you could have done to change the situation, and I thought the same went for Dad – it wasn't as if she'd have listened to you or him or anyone else, for that matter. I survived. That's the only way to describe that part of my life – survival.' His voice had become much quieter, and Ellie could see the pain it caused him to vocalise his thoughts. 'In some ways I wish I'd found the courage to stand up for myself and fight back, but there was always a part of my conscience that told me that hitting a woman, and in particular hitting my mother, was wrong. I just couldn't do it. Looking back, I realise I should have either gone to the police – God knows she would be arrested or sectioned if she did those things to a child today, although I'm not sure they would have paid much attention to me in those days – or I should have just left and gone to stay with Dad, but at the time I really thought I was stuck there with no way out. There were several times when I seriously thought about . . . ' But his voice at that point fell away, leaving the rest unsaid.

Ellie poured them both another glass of red wine, only rather larger this time. For a while they sat silently, ignoring the reheated lasagne that had become almost cold and the tired looking salad left over from the night before, both lost in the dark memories that their mother still roamed: doors slamming, the smell of vomit and overflowing ashtrays, the arguments with their father, with them; their mother drunk at the school gate, shouting 'Fuck off!' to the teachers or other parents if they interfered; her insults and the constant stream of criticism that she levelled at them.

Words had always been her most potent weapon, more wounding than any cuts she'd inflicted with shoes or belts or whatever else had been close to hand. Her tongue had stripped them of their childhood and left shadows of pain which were still too sore for Justin to examine, and continued to tear through so much of his life.

However, by then Ellie had already sent their mother a plane ticket and an invitation to the *Kunsthalle*, though, as she'd pointed out to Justin, the power now lay with them. They were no longer the children she could once abuse; they were both now successful, independent adults, and the control, if she came to Berlin, would lie with them.

'You won't be on your own this time, and if she does come – and she's never shown much interest in my work before, so she'll probably not bother – you'll have me to back you up and hopefully Grandma as well,' she'd added, striving to find some reassurance for her brother, but in fact more doubtful than ever that she had done the right thing by inviting their mother.

*   *   *

Against this background, when their grandmother arrived, elegant and composed at the *Kunsthalle*, Ellie was delighted to see that Justin was ignoring his own previous instructions – *that friends, and especially family, would have to wait till later* – and looked more comfortable in her company than Ellie had ever seen him before.

'And how was the journey?' he asked. 'What was the Channel Tunnel like? You're the first person I know who's travelled through it.'

'It was very exciting. The train was not so quick getting to Dover, but once we left Calais it was unbelievably fast. How things have changed in the fifty years since I left mainland Europe. Everything was in ruins then. Rubble everywhere; absolute desolation. And the last time I travelled through Europe was on a Red Cross train repatriating German refugee children who'd been evacuated to Austria. I didn't have the correct papers for the train, or to cross from the American zone where we were staying at the end of the war, into the British zone where I wanted to be. That was in August 1945. There were no other civilian trains running at the time, only freight trains. But I had heard that these Red Cross trains stopped not so far from us in Hanover, on their way to Bremen, and I was determined for us to get on one. The American officer in charge was very kind, very polite, "No problem Mam," he said, when I explained in my very poor English that I was trying to join my parents in London, and that it would be so much easier to organise if I was living within the British Zone. "There's space in the luggage van if you don't mind the floor," he told us. We certainly didn't. We had trekked for such a distance at the end of the war that to be travelling whilst sitting down seemed a luxury for us. It was crammed with other people too, all of us desperate to somehow get somewhere else. He let us share the bread and sausages and cheese left over after mealtimes, and at night we put candles in mugs and all sang the Viennese songs that the refugee children had been taught.'

Listening to Renata, Ellie realised how proud she felt of her grandmother for coming, and for the obstacles, on so many levels, that she had managed to surmount to get there.

Dresden, Germany. October 1943.

With one arm clasped around Joachim, who was curled up half asleep against her shoulder, and a letter that she had just picked up from the foyer clasped between her teeth, Renata unlocked the front door to their apartment with her free hand and then led Sabina inside, through the unlit entrance hall and into the murk of the sitting room. She let Joachim slip gently out of her arms and onto the sofa where he slowly unfurled, rubbing his eyes and yawning. She took the letter out of her mouth and placed it on the side table. It was clearly from Sebastian, but she would read it later on in bed when she could savour his words. Her first priority was to draw down all the blackout curtains before she turned on the lights and attended to the children. The blackout regulations were very strict, and people were routinely imprisoned over even one illuminated window.

With the blackout in place and the Chinese lacquered lamp switched on, Renata removed her soft felt hat, dislodging a fine mist of icy droplets that had formed on the wave of hair which fanned out beneath the turned-up rim. The apartment was hardly warmer than the wintry night outside. Clearly, the heating had not come on that evening; escalating coal shortages meant that the building's heating was increasingly restricted. Shivering slightly, Renata walked from the sitting room through to the bathroom where she grabbed a towel that she quickly tousled through her damp auburn hair. With one movement, she then scrapped it all back off her face and twisted it round into a ragged bun at the nape of her neck. Hurriedly, she then pinned it into place with a small cluster of grips. The last thing she needed was a cold or indeed anything more serious, so even though it was long past the children's bedtime and Renata intended to only wash their hands, teeth and faces and quickly change them into their nightclothes, she nevertheless still took the time to cursorily dry off her hair before ministering to Sabina and Joachim.

The three of them had returned home unexpectedly late through the first bloom of hoarfrost after high tea with Sebastian's parents. Joachim and Sabina were now tired and fractious, both with her and each other. Renata was truly grateful for the kindness shown by her in-laws, Herr and Frau Lange, who each week invited her to bring the children and take afternoon coffee at their airy apartment overlooking the tree lined gardens of the Dürerplatz. They were always made to feel most welcome, and for Renata it was undoubtedly the culinary highlight of her ration coupon existence. Real ground coffee, which was scarcely available in the shops even if one had the required ration card to attain it, or a staggering two hundred marks a pound on the black-market and as such a luxury Renata could never herself afford, and a homemade cake baked with real butter and seasonal fruit – rare treats indeed – would later inevitably be followed by entreaties to stay for high tea. Frau Lange would always have a fresh soup prepared and wheat or rye bread, *würst* or sometimes smoked herrings and even a cheese. Dishes that displayed either scrimping in private to save up enough coupons, or severe penalties risked to buy such foodstuffs illegally; though that was a question Renata had never found the nerve to ask of her in-laws. Today, much to Renata's embarrassment (for she had forgotten entirely and had arrived empty handed), it was Herr Lange's birthday.

'I'm so sorry,' she'd said to them both, and offered her father-in-law a kiss in compensation. He was a tall man, slightly stooped from his years as the organ master at the famous Kreuzschule choir school where Sebastian had also been a chorister, and with slightly wild silver hair as Beethoven was always depicted in paintings.

'Don't worry *Liebchen*, what do I need more presents for at my age?' Herr Lange had responded graciously. 'We're just pleased that the three of you can be with us today.'

'Go and kiss your *Opi, Kinder*,' Renata had said to Sabina and Joachim. 'A big special birthday kiss and hug!'

Needing no further encouragement, the children had both ran energetically towards their grandfather. Despite the circumstances, Frau Lange, with her customary flair, had prepared quite a celebration. 'Come Renata, sit down,' Frau Lange had said, gesturing to the dove grey and gold brocade armchair, with a view out over the city skyline and the garden square below. 'I have some coffee already prepared, and plum cake with whipped cream that we will say is *Opi*'s birthday cake so we can all sing Happy Birthday to him!'

Frau Lange had a natural elegance from her neat bob to her petite, slender frame, and dimples in her cheeks when she smiled. Renata knew from photos in silver frames around their apartment that she had been a most attractive young woman. She had been a piano teacher all her life, and after she served them all some of the plum cake she sat down at their Bösendorfer baby grand piano and led the singing for her husband's birthday.

'You must stay for an early supper,' Frau Lange stated as if the matter were already settled.

'That would be lovely,' Renata replied, grateful for what she was certain would be a rather more exciting meal than any she would have prepared for herself.

On that account, she was right. A fruit wine accompanied the pork escalope sautéed in butter that Frau Lange had served with beetroots and carrots baked in a horseradish sauce, all such long missed luxuries that at the end of the meal she readily succumbed to the offer of a brandy which she lingered over.

Finally, Renata bundled Sabina and Joachim back into their coats and hats and gloves, and they walked around the square to wait for a bus or tram at the Travel Booth. After a frustrating wait she went over to the barrel shaped duty policeman inside and enquired, 'When is the next bus or tram due to arrive?'

'Tonight there will be no more buses or trams running for at least two hours,' he replied abruptly.

'Then would you please issue me a permit for a taxi, since public transport is so delayed?' she asked with studied politeness, weary of his brusque manner. This was the usual procedure that civilians were advised to follow since fuel and staff shortages had made bus and tram services ever less reliable.

'There will be no taxis running at all this night,' he answered, dismissively.

Silently swearing, Renata resigned herself to the long walk home. She was aware that the last glow of twilight would soon turn to night and the expected full moon would not rise till much later. She was unsuitably dressed for both the walk and the weather, but further delays would only compound her problems as the temperature seemed just about to plummet. Fortunately, she kept a thick knitted blanket in the base of the pram which she tucked around the children, cocooning them together beneath the small arched hood. The walk home seemed endless, and a few times she had taken a wrong turn, disorientated by the damp mist that lurked unexpectedly around corners and the dark streets left unlit as an air raid precaution, and with all the windows blacked out in the houses. By the time she eventually reached the front door of their apartment block, having slipped in her patent heals on the frozen pavement and once skidded on an empty chestnut shell concealed amongst a cluster of fallen leaves, she was certainly regretting the indulgence of the drawn out brandy and not having had the foresight to leave a little earlier.

Renata's hair was now dry and she sighed as she took a last glance in the oval mirror that hung above the bathroom sink. Sometimes she struggled to recognise as her own the gaunt cheeks and dull eyes that seemed to have shrunk from a vibrant peridot to withered olive.

The war was now into its fourth year and with no end in sight. Each week, it seemed, brought the sorry news of yet another friend or family member killed either in action or in a bombing raid. On the Eastern Front alone, the campaign had claimed the life of at least one family member amongst virtually everyone that she knew.

However, the past several weeks since Sebastian had been deployed to the *Konzentrationslager* at Buchenwald near Weimar had been especially tough, and had taken their toll on Renata. For, regardless that he was there to work and not as a prisoner, the very thought of him being in a concentration camp brought back all the horror of the time her father had been detained in Oranienburg: terrible memories that now stalked her days and seized her dreams. Subsequent to her husband's unexpected departure, she frequently woke in the dead of night with a terrible sense of foreboding.

Naively, they had both imagined that Sebastian's work as a

doctor would keep him in Dresden. In private they had often discussed how their own small family might avoid the harsher realities of the war. Sebastian's orders, issued via the chief of staff at the Friedrichstadt *Krankenhaus* after an edict from the General Wehrmacht Office in Berlin, had come as a complete shock to them both, but had been impossible to evade. He was within the age range of conscription, fit, and his work as a doctor deemed essential for the war effort. He briefly tried to argue his case to remain in Dresden with the head of the hospital, citing the city's shortage of trained medical staff with so many doctors and nurses having been transferred to field hospitals on the battlefronts, but he had been curtly rebuffed. The need to develop a vaccine for typhus was deemed a priority at the highest levels in Berlin. The disease was cutting a swathe through sections of the army and labour camps that were vital to the production of essential war supplies. Orders were given to the Waffen SS to create the Division for Typhus and Virus Research, and as a great deal of progress on this research had been made already at Buchenwald, facilities that were already established there were being expanded to accommodate the new directive. However, additional medically trained professionals were needed to expedite the process, and as Sebastian specialised in treating infectious diseases, the head of the hospital had considered that he was the best man for the post. With that decision there had been no further room for discussion. If Sebastian had disobeyed the order he would have faced certain arrest and imprisonment: possibly even in Buchenwald.

He bid farewell to his tearful wife and children just forty-eight hours later. Both Renata and Sebastian were in deep shock at the turn of events, for not only were they distraught to be separated from each other, but also frightened by the reports emerging from Buchenwald. Since Renata had seen first-hand the results of what occurred in these *Konzentrationslager*, they were under no illusion that these accounts were in all likelihood true. Their only solace in the situation was their belief that as a doctor,

Sebastian's contribution to the war was at least being directed into the saving of lives, and not to the slaying.

That had been almost ten weeks before, at the beginning of August, and since then he had not been allowed back home on leave. To begin with, they had corresponded frequently, but as Sebastian had been required to sign a pledge of secrecy when he entered the camp, even the slightest mention of life – or more particularly death – at Buchenwald, or his work there, was without fail suppressed beneath the censor's thick blue stripes. Knowing that their correspondence came under such scrutiny had taken the pleasure out of any personal intimacies that they put to paper, and their letters soon dwindled and shortened. Subsequently, they mostly wrote about the children or inconsequential family news, or the weather or other innocuous trivia from their daily lives. Although hidden within Sebastian's apparently mundane subject matter, Renata sensed a growing subtext of desperation and horror. Nevertheless, she still welcomed any letter that her husband had sent her, and looked forward to opening the one she had just received when she went to bed.

From the living room came the sound of over-tired children. Howls from one, and indignant shrieks from the other. Renata went quickly through to intervene and hopefully dispatch them both hurriedly to bed. At moments such as these she greatly missed Sebastian's help. Where she would resort to shouting at the children, Sebastian would subtly distract them until their squabbling ceased and they had calmed down completely. Unfortunately, it was a tactic that she had never managed to master, and she snapped at Sabina who had clearly just snatched her brother's much loved Steiff bear.

On her own, Renata found the demands of a toddler and a small child an enormous strain. At least Joachim now slept through the night, though he still rose early each morning hungry for her breast milk. Nonetheless, she felt constantly tired and rightly estimated that for years she had struggled against a crescendo of weariness. Moreover, Sabina's behaviour was becoming ever more difficult, and the wilfulness that was to be expected in a child of her age seemed suddenly excessively amplified. Renata recognised that this was most probably because she missed her father so much, but it added to her lassitude just the same. To her dismay, Renata had almost come to dread the early evenings when her levels of energy and patience with the children were at their lowest ebb, and they were at their most tired and demanding.

'Come on Joachim, let's be quick and get you to sleep,' she said, briefly fluttering a flannel over his hands and face in lieu of a wash. 'Now let's get those teeth brushed too!' she added, trying to sound enthusiastic about the metallic tasting cleaning powder that now substituted for toothpaste. She quickly changed him into his navy checked pyjamas before giving him a brief feed and nestling him under his thick feather eiderdown.

Next, Renata hurried through the process of getting Sabina to bed, hastily exchanging her cinnabar wool cardigan and smocked pinafore dress for a brushed cotton nightdress, and then watching while she gave her teeth a cursory clean.

'Now bedtime,' she said efficiently, as she followed her out of the bathroom.

'What story are you going to read to me *Mutti*?' asked Sabina.

'It's too late for one Sabina, you know that.'

'But you always read to me. You promised when *Vatti* went away that you would read to me instead of him. You promised me, and you promised *Vatti* as well!' she shouted angrily.

It was true that she had taken over Sebastian's ritual of reading Sabina a bedtime story, and she felt somewhat guilty about breaking this promise; however, exhaustion had claimed her last reserves of the day.

'Come to my bed with a book when you wake, and I'll read you twice as much then,' she pledged as she exited from the bedroom.

Utterly fatigued, Renata went through to the sitting room.

Her own childhood had been populated by a governess, house-keeper and cleaners and cooks, so nothing had prepared her for her current existence. She had been taught how to check if a table were laid correctly, but, other than giving orders to the kitchen staff, not how to prepare any food to put on that table. Her mother's sole culinary advice had been to ensure that the cook prepared pastry on a damask tablecloth and rolled it until it was sufficiently fine for the pattern of the cloth to be seen clearly beneath it. Unfortunately, she now had neither the staff to make the pastry, nor the knowledge to make it herself. In any case, rationing was now so severe that even the most capable of cooks felt challenged. Each day seemed a relentless struggle against the tide of domestic chores, the laborious necessity of queuing for food, and caring for the children. Under different circumstances she would at least have had a cleaner, but there were simply no available household staff: all woman under the age of forty-five and without children had been called up for labour duty, and any over that age who worked as domestic help were generally already in long held positions. Yet, of all her tribulations, the lonely evenings, after the children had fallen asleep and without Sebastian's company, were the hardest to endure.

Glancing at her watch, Renata walked purposefully towards the bookshelves. Across the rows of shelving, an assortment of framed photographs and paintings were artfully propped against the books. She moved to one side the Kokoschka inspired land-scape of Dresden's skyline that her mother had painted before she left for London, then turned on the wireless that the painting was placed in front off to screen. The last act of Wagner's *Die Meistersinger* brought life to the room, but Renata turned down the volume and carefully tuned the multi-frequency band, stopping when she heard the now familiar chime of a deep ringing bell. A cursory glance would have dismissed it as the basic single-frequency *Volksempfänger* found in most German homes, and designed to jam out all stations other than official Party broadcasts by the *Großdeutscher Rundfunk* from Berlin. However, its almost identical casing housed a more sophisticated radio that could receive the signal from the BBC in England. Renata slumped into the umber leather armchair beside the bookcase, knowing that when the chimes stopped she would have to concentrate hard on the announcement, and weave the difficult English words into some discernable meaning.

Listening to the news from London had become a nightly ritual, even though all foreign transmissions were officially prohibited. Renata knew that there were severe penalties for the 'moral traitors' who breached these strict laws: eight years imprisonment at the very least, though the death sentence was on occasion arbitrarily imposed. Nevertheless, since her mother had left the country and she had stepped out of the shadow of her famous father's name after acquiring a new one with her marriage, she felt considerably less conspicuous with the authorities. In general, they focused their attentions on the Jewish population rather than those classified as Aryan, as she was. The broadcast gave her a sense of connection to her parents who were, so far as she knew, still living in London. Moreover, it was a chance to glean some fragments of truth about the war, although, frustratingly, much of the bulletin slipped through the gaps in her grasp of English.

It was a habit that she could trace back to her teenage years, when her father had sat down with her each day to listen to the news. At that time she had barely paid any attention to the broadcasts, feigning interest only for the sake of her father's approval. However, after his arrest and brutal beating in Oranienburg, her outlook had changed completely, and subsequently she avidly absorbed every available piece of information from newspapers or the radio. That had been more than nine years before, and all the dire predictions that her father had made back then had, unbelievably, been overshadowed entirely by actual events.

*   *   *

Herr von Steindorf had left Berlin just as soon as his wellbeing allowed after his release from the Oranienburg *Konzentrationslager*. The need for his immediate exile from Germany, until the excesses of Hitler's Nazism had been quelled, had been agreed by all those around him. But as his absence was assumed to be only a temporary one, it was never discussed whether or not Katarina and Renata should accompany him.

From Oranienburg, it had been a slow road to recovery for Herr von Steindorf. The French Ambassador, Monsieur Francois-Poncet, who orchestrated his deliverance and brought him to his Embassy, had been adamant that Herr von Steindorf remain there throughout his convalescence, as only in a foreign Embassy could his safety be guaranteed by diplomatic immunity. This had not only extended to summoning a surgeon and his nurse to the Embassy to set Herr von Steindorf's broken arm and stitch up the deep lacerations cross hatched across his swollen face and battered body, but also to inviting both Katarina and Renata to remain there as his guests as well. Not only were they comforted to be at Herr von Steindorf's side until he was sufficiently fit to travel, but they were also grateful to be sheltered from the aftershocks of what the press had quickly labelled the 'Rohm Revolt', and which continued to reverberate dangerously around the capital, trailing a wake of unlawful violence.

Slowly, during the sweltering weeks of July and August, as the city simmered beneath the threat of civil war and Chancellor Hitler achieved a *coup d'etat* when he assumed the title of Führer on Hindenburg's death, the bloody wreck of a man that had been delivered almost lifeless to the French Embassy was carefully coaxed back to health. Whilst Katarina took over the responsibility of nursing her husband, replacing warm compresses with ice-cooled ones, changing the dressings on his wounds when required or soothing un-dressed lesions with liniment oil, Renata assumed a vigil beside her father, reading to him or cajoling him through crossword puzzles on the days when he did not tire too quickly.

His face had been so badly beaten that the limpet like scabs around his lips cracked painfully if he tried to bite, or even chew his food. As a result, for the first few weeks his meals were all pureed, and in turns they had fed him, mouthful by painful mouthful, until eating normally once more no longer caused him fresh bleeding. Renata had to fight back her tears when it was her turn to feed her father: it upset her so much to see him suffer in this way. Both mornings and evenings Katarina had bathed the few uninjured parts of his body, and daily changed his bedding, bringing him at least some small degree of comfort from the sweltering heat that clung so oppressively to the city. Throughout it all, she never once complained that she'd missed her annual retreat to the Baltic coast.

As the summer progressed, Herr von Steindorf spent most afternoons beneath the shade of the linden trees in the Embassy garden, drinking coffee and scrutinizing as many newspapers as could be brought to him; in particular any foreign press that had not yet been banned. Disseminating the lies from the propaganda left his spirit waning as his body slowly recovered. When his strength allowed, he had private, frank discussions with Monsieur Francois-Poncet about their shared fear of the rise of Nazism, and the reality of his experience within Oranienburg. With his own family he remained conspicuously silent about his ordeal, wishing to spare them the details of the abuse he had seen and suffered. Renata regularly sat by his side, happy to keep him company. Occasionally, her friend Lore Bernstein came into the city centre to meet her and they ventured out from the Embassy for a brief walk together, though they never went far. Berlin-Mitte, they both felt, now had a distinctly aggressive edge to it and whilst they felt safe within the confines of the *Pariser Platz*, many of the once glamorous window displays along Unter den Linden were now defaced with yellow placards brandishing anti-Semitic slogans, and an increasing level of armed SA guards stood menacingly in shop doorways, or chatted raucously in groups that provocatively blocked the pavements. Even a visit to a café in the *Tiergarten* to eat cherry ice-cream and find reprieve from the excessive humidity, had been tainted by the prevalent slogan '*Jüde Verrecke*' – destruction to Jews – hurled maliciously at them in response to Lore's distinctive Judaic features, by the toothless hurdy-gurdy player who churned out music-hall melodies on the path nearby.

Gradually, the swellings on Herr von Steindorf had subsided, the wounds scabbed and then ebbed away to marbled scars whilst the angry bruises blazed iridescent before dimming and eventually disappearing. As September's breeze beneath clear azure skies brought a lift to all their spirits, the Embassy doctor pronounced his arm to be finally mended. By then, all the paper formalities of exit and entry visas and a valid passport had been completed, so within days he had bid a poignant farewell to his wife and daughter in the Ambassador's drawing room, then seized the opportunity to leave the country relatively discreetly by accompanying a diplomatic delegation from the Embassy that was taking the night train from Berlin to Paris.

The following day, Katarina and Renata returned from the cloistered atmosphere of the French Embassy to their family home in a dark mood, although they at least felt relief that Herr von Steindorf had been able to get out of Germany and was now out of danger. Moreover, they both took solace from their staunch belief that he would be away for a few months at most. Surely, they had reasoned, the depths of political turmoil had already been reached and the situation must improve sometime soon.

In Paris, Herr von Steindorf installed himself at the Hotel Ansonia where an ever growing group of exiled German nationals were congregating. He decided to remain there and await the result of the forthcoming Saar referendum, determining the future of the territory which for the past fifteen years since the Treaty of Versailles had been under the League of Nations administration. The ballot would be a clear gauge of Hitler's popularity; and a vote against Germany would probably precipitate his political demise. Depending upon its outcome, Herr von Steindorf would decide his next course of action. However, the plebiscite produced a surprising ninety per cent vote in favour of the region's return to Germany, a result which Goebbels was quick to proclaim as a victory for National Socialism. Any doubts of Hitler's overwhelming support amongst the majority of the people were dispelled, and with that his continued domination was assured. Clearly, in light of Hitler's Saar triumph, there would be no imminent return to Germany for Herr von Steindorf.

From Paris, he journeyed to London where he felt his contacts with other exiled Social Democrats were better, as was his command of the language. Herr von Steindorf found rooms to rent in a red bricked mansion house behind Marble Arch, and concentrated his energies on rousing diplomatic opposition to the Nazi regime from the British government. In time, he had secured meetings with amongst others Sir John Simon, the British Foreign Secretary, and Lord Privy Seal, Antony Eden, at the Foreign Office in Whitehall. His agenda was two-fold: to give a witness account of the atrocities carried out by the Nazi regime and urge the British government to ease immigration controls for German nationals into Commonwealth countries; and to warn them of the true extent of Germany's ambitious and secretive re-armament programme. Inevitably, as his efforts to find support in London intensified, in Berlin, Katarina and Renata came under increasing scrutiny from the German authorities. Their home was put under constant surveillance by the Gestapo. Every package arrived opened and examined, and all letters, especially those from Herr von Steindorf, even though cautiously written to appease the censor, were delivered barely legible for the thick blue lines. They scarcely used the telephone any more, mindful of the click they heard each time they picked up the handset which warned them that it was tapped. Both the women were followed and frequently harassed when they left the house. And with all of these intrusions on their lives State sanctioned, there were no avenues of recourse for the women whatsoever. Even a letter bemoaning their circumstances to Herr von Steindorf would be pointless and potentially dangerous; it would never make it past the censor's desk, and might possibly get them both arrested.

Feeling increasingly isolated and under mounting pressure, Katarina began to make discreet enquiries about the possibility of them joining Herr von Steindorf in England. Unfortunately, it had become a far more complex matter than she had ever imagined, and every avenue of investigation seemed to lead to a dead end. Britain had ceased issuing tourist visas to German nationals, as so many simply remained in the country with no intention of returning home. New policy meant that they could only go there if they formally applied to emigrate. However, that would necessitate raising 15,000M which the British government demanded as surety from immigrants. She simply did not have access to that amount in cash. There were substantial assets of course, the family house and also stocks and bonds, but these were all held in her husband's name and she would not be able to conclude any transactions on his behalf: regulations demanded that that would have to be done by him in person. She was outraged to discover that even if they were able to liquidate their possessions, they would be obliged to pay 25% of that amount in Reich Flight Property Tax when they left the country.

But shortly after having abandoned the idea of leaving Berlin as impracticable, an attempt to make economies caused Katarina to immediately reverse that decision. After taking coffee with a friend at a fashionable *Konditorei* on the Kurfürstendamm, Katarina dropped in on a haberdashery just a few doors away in a search for a more *au courant* trim to update her slouch Fedora hat, rather than visit her milliner and buy a new one. Whilst she was browsing amongst the feather plumes and organza bows, SA troops began to rampage along the elegant avenue targeting all the shops marked out by posters as Jewish owned premises. In a matter of seconds the shouting, screaming and cacophony of destruction was upon them. There was no time to make a hasty retreat. Stormtroopers were smashing in the windows of the haberdashery, showering everyone confined within the compact space of the shop, with a stream of potentially lethal shards of glass. Instinctively, Katarina and the other customers backed deeper into the room, away from the windows. A piercing scream filled the shop and Katarina was shocked to realise that it was she who was making the noise. She had always imagined she would maintain a calm façade in such circumstances, and was embarrassed by her lack of composure. One of the other quick thinking customers began pulling rolls of fabric part way out from the storage shelves along wall, and Katarina followed suit with a third stranger, although she realised that her hands were trembling so badly that her efforts to help were of little effect. However, before long they had fashioned an effective shield out of the bolts of cloth. The shop keeper and his assistant had meanwhile crouched down low behind the counter. When the shop front had been completely destroyed, two SA men stormed inside wielding clubs and shouting at all those within, while a third stood in the doorway barring both entry and exit. Up against the chromatic fabric wall, Katarina felt on the verge of tears as she realised she had lost control of her bladder. She had never before felt such fear or humiliation.

The uniformed hooligans now directed their abuse at the shopkeeper and his young assistant, who Katarina judged to be his daughter, and began to smash the glass-topped counter housing a display of decorative buttons and buckles which separated them from the intruders. A fountain of glass splinters exploded through the shop. The pale-faced assistant trapped behind the counter shrieked in pain, cupping her check which had obviously been cut by flying glass. Katarina could feel the woman beside her trembling, and glancing at her profile she noticed that she was silently sobbing, a course of tears trailing down her face. Katarina resolved that if she ever got out of the shop alive, she would leave Berlin immediately: she could no longer withstand the strain of life in the city. Her brother Magnus, who lived in Dresden, would have to, for the time being at least, take both her and Renata in.

After what seemed an age, but in reality was a few minutes only, Katarina managed to escape unharmed from the haberdasher's, slipping out whilst the storm troopers were distracted with their efforts to completely vandalise the shop. The two youths inside, who by then had delivered some sharp blows to the shopkeeper and had slapped and kicked his assistant, called to their accomplice on guard in the doorway to help them finish off within so that they could then move on to other premises. The man turned slowly around and sauntered in, whistling, obviously enjoying his outing of the day. He cockily greeted Katarina and the two other women pinned up against the fabric bolts, and then breezed up to the till which he deftly opened with a well practised thwack from his truncheon. Then, whilst he was ostentatiously helping himself to the contents of the till, and the other SA men were pulling out the myriad drawers around the room and scattering the contents on the floor, Katarina had edged away from the flimsy barricade that they had constructed, and out of the shop.

By late that same evening, she had arrived with Renata and a few hastily packed suitcases in Dresden. Magnus, whom Frau Braun had telegraphed on her behalf from Berlin, was awaiting them both at the Neustadt *Bahnhof*. He wore cream flannels, a duck-egg blue shirt with a lime green sweater draped over his shoulders. He was slightly taller than his sister with the same slender frame, and auburn hair that he oiled and combed back off his forehead. His round Windsor glasses only magnified the look of anxiety in his large ochre eyes.

Renata, who had been spared the terror that her mother had endured, arrived in Dresden with a mixture of relief and apprehension, but resentment also. Whilst she understood her mother's reasons for their hasty departure from Berlin and was glad to be able to escape the shadow of violence that hung over their lives there, she was sorry to be leaving so much behind, and without even being given the chance to say farewell in person to any of her friends. Her mother had made it quite clear as they had packed their few bags, that their stay in Dresden was intended only as a temporary measure whilst they made arrangements to somehow or other join Herr von Steindorf in London. But that, Renata knew, having watched Lore Bernstein's family struggle through the interminable process of organising emigration to Palestine until their eventual departure to Haifa just after Easter earlier that year, might still take some considerable time, during which, she was in no doubt, she would be stuck at her uncle's home with little to do.

Renata had not been to Dresden for a number of years. Her mother and her Uncle Magnus were not the closest of siblings, and their visits had for the longest time been curtailed to when Magnus had combined a trip to Berlin on business, with visiting them. Now that she viewed the Saxony city through adult eyes, she thought that whilst the spires and cobbled streets clearly lent it a rococo chocolate-box charm, it was certainly, in comparison to Berlin at least, quiet and hidebound. From her first impression when her uncle fetched them from the Neustadt *Bahnhoff*, she noted the differences between the cities, which in her estimation were not at all in Dresden's favour. The few cars on the streets looked functional rather than fashionable, as they generally were in Berlin, and, as they swerved around pedestrians and passing cars, she was horrified to note that there were no traffic lights installed in the city at all. The shops appeared drab and without a great variety of goods, and the clothes stores displayed outfits several seasons out of date. Even the 'Latest Movie' that was showing at the cinema they passed, Kiepura's *Ein Lied Für Dich*, she had seen many months before in Berlin. By the minute,

Renata's conviction that she had been banished to some provincial backwater was increasing. She now had few expectations that she was in for anything other than a very dull time.

'Welcome to my home,' said Magnus, rather hesitantly, when they arrived at the front door of his apartment on the south side of the *Dürerplatz*.

Stepping inside, much to Renata's surprise, they were met with an interior as *avant-garde* as any in Berlin. The broad hallway, with its herringbone parquet flooring, was dominated by a large chrome mirror set against black and silver scalloped wallpaper and beneath a shimmering metallic ceiling. However, the biggest revelation had been in the eau-de-nil sitting room, reclining against cream silk cushions that toned in with the brocade covered sofa.

Magnus shuffled somewhat nervously into the room behind his sister and niece. An undeniably handsome man, with corn coloured hair and eyes like a summer sky, rose to meet them. He appeared not much older than Renata, and rather flamboyantly dressed in a purple velvet smoking jacket and matching pointed shoes.

'This is Fabian,' said Magnus, struggling to catch their eyes.

'I'm so pleased to meet you,' gushed Fabian, leaning in to kiss Katarina, who'd looked rather aghast, on the cheek. 'I think we should have a glass of something special to celebrate you being here!' he continued, turning to Renata.

'That's a wonderful idea,' said Magnus, feeling somewhat in need of a drink himself. 'If you show our guests to their room, Fabian, I'll mix us all a cocktail.'

Katarina and Renata were shown to a room decorated in vanilla shades that had twin beds with carved cherry wood bedsteads.

'I'm afraid you'll have to share this room. We've only got three bedrooms and Magnus and I share one, whilst Magnus uses the other as his painting studio. Make yourself at home and then come and join us for a drink.'

Katarina gave him a slightly frosty smile as he exited from their bedroom. Finally, Renata understood the undercurrent of disapproval that had run through her mother's conversations about Magnus for as long as she could remember. At least, she thought, with the company of characters like Magnus and Fabian, their stay might yet prove to be more interesting than she had first imagined.

A cocktail of *Sekt*, sugar, lemon and gin awaited them in crystal glasses on a silver tray in the sitting room.

'I'm sorry your visit has been prompted by such difficult circumstances,' said Magnus as he offered the glasses around. 'But we're glad to welcome you nonetheless. Tomorrow, we'll tour through Dresden and out to Coswig then over the Elbe Bridge – perhaps even take a trip on one of the pleasure streamers. We'll picnic in Meissen besides Schloss Albrectsburg, where the porcelain is made, and then in the evening we've been invited to a bridge party at the Lange's, our neighbours below. I've telephoned Frau Lange already, and she's inviting another lady in the building to join us, and their son Sebastian, who's just qualified as a doctor, to make up another four. It might not be as exciting as the life you're used to in Berlin, but let's make the most of the situation and at least enjoy ourselves.'

*　　*　　*

In the unheated Dresden sitting room, the chimes of Big Ben gave way to the precise intonation of the BBC broadcaster. Listening intently, Renata thought that the newsreader was announcing Italy's declaration of war on Germany. Her spirits soared with the news. She could not be entirely certain for her English was far from good, but the item took up much of the programme, which indicated to her that it was a matter of some importance, and many of the key words she had now heard numerous times and felt confident that she understood. Certainly if true, and contrary to all the propaganda in German broadcasts and broadsheets, the military was in retreat or defeat on at least two important fronts. As the transmission continued, her mind wandered, as it usually did, to her parents in London. She imagined, hopefully, her parents listening to the very same broadcast in the small flat that they had rented in an area to the north of city called Hampstead. The thought gave her a good deal of comfort. She held on to this image, because in truth she had no idea where the two of them were now: the last letter that she had received from them arrived towards the end of August in '39, but as soon as war was declared between Britain and Germany, all forms of communication between the two countries ceased altogether. At best, she determined, they were still comfortably installed at their Hampstead lodgings, where they had happily settled. The local heath reminded them in many ways of Berlin's *Tiergarten*, although of course there were endless other options which often toyed with Renata's imagination. It was very likely they had been obliged to move; landlords, they had written, seemed unwilling to give foreign nationals long leases, and the current address which Renata had for them was the last of several she had received since her father's arrival in England. A strong possibility also, was that they had been interned, for Renata knew that in many countries during wartime it was common practise that enemy aliens residing there would be arrested and housed in prisoner-of-war camps. Indeed, she had once met a Bremen man who had spent the previous war captive in the stables of a racecourse near Oxford in England. Obviously, the very worst prospect for Renata was that her parents were already dead.

Renata made a conscious effort to escape the thought, standing abruptly and promptly turning off the wireless. She frequently worried about her parents' health, in particular her father's, mindful of his still fragile condition when she had last seen him nine years before as they had bade farewell in Berlin. Sadly, the image of her father that came to her whenever she thought about him was the memory of the bloody and battered man who had arrived, half alive, at the French Embassy. She often wondered whether he had ever really fully recovered from his beatings in Oranienburg.

She restored her mother's oil painting to its regular vantage point propped in front of the wireless, plumped up the coral velvet cushion on the armchair she had just occupied, picked up Sebastian's letter, turned off the light and then left the sitting room.

Sabina and Joachim were sleeping peacefully when she looked around their bedroom door en route to the bathroom to prepare for bed. It grieved her that her parents had never met the children, for Sabina had been born after her mother had already left the country to join Herr von Steindorf in London, but they had no idea even of Joachim's existence as he had been conceived after the war had begun, when the postal service between England and Germany had already been suspended. Of course, her father had never even met Sebastian, and she longed for the day when the whole awful business of the war would be over and finally they could all meet up as a family.

Renata went through to her bedroom, which, being north facing and without heat for the day, was glacial. Ideally, she would have had a hot bath to warm up, but it had been months since there had been more than a basin full of hot water available for each apartment. Shivering, she pulled down the black out on the window and then turned on the light before reaching up to pull out an extra merino wool blanket from the top shelf of the mahogany armoire. She was looking forward to finally reading Sebastian's letter. Hurriedly, Renata got into bed to change out of her clothes within the relative warmth of the covers. She even managed to laugh quietly at herself, imagining how amused Sebastian would have been to see her struggling to remove her pencil tight skirt beneath the bed clothes. But, as she slowly untied the bowed top of her silk cream blouse and undid the buttons down over her breasts, she thought how Sebastian's laughter would, at that point, have turned to lust. Immediately, she felt aroused. It was, she realised, the first time since Sebastian's departure that had she felt the desire for intimacy, and she realised how much she missed the passion that they had always shared as a couple. Sebastian was always keen to undress her when they made love, as if carefully unwrapping a precious gift: buttons would be lingered over; a bow leisurely untied; a dress or skirt slowly eased away from her body until her lingerie was revealed below. Ideally, her heeled shoes would be kept on, for a while at least, over her silk stockinged feet. He loved her to wear sensuous undergarments in soft fabrics, and she in turn responded to that desire in him.

Uncertainly, she ran her hands lightly over the silk of her blouse, feeling with unexpected pleasure the curve of her breast below. The delicate stroke across her nipples sent a surge of excitement through her body, and she leaned back on her bed to savour the sensation. Slowly, she ran her fingers from her breasts, over her soft stomach and down to the satin of her lingerie. Stroking herself gently through the wisp of material, she realised that she had never beforehand touched her body in this way; it was, she decided, exquisitely erotic. She wondered how Sebastian would react if he were watching her now, and thought excitedly how she would put that point to the test the next time that they met. Meanwhile, imagining that her hands were his, she slipped her fingers beneath the satin hem of her French knickers, and as her mind replayed past intimacies that they had shared together, she found the private pleasure that she had missed for so many weeks.

Afterwards, she lay thinking that whilst the experience gave a certain sense of satisfaction, it only emphasised the elements that were missing: Sebastian's smooth skin entwined around her own; his aroma that always heightened her arousal; but most of all, the singular element that above all others she missed the most but could not emulate – his kiss. He had once left a postcard of

Gustav Kilmt's famous painting, *Der Kuss*, on her pillow. On the back of the card, a beautiful reproduction of the shimmering couple sharing a kiss, he had written, 'This reminds me of us'. She had kept the card, in a drawer, and occasionally traced a finger across the golden figures and concurred with Sebastian's sentiment.

With a sigh she reached over to open his letter. She was surprised when she opened the letter to see that there were no blue stripes of censor's ink across the main body of text, so she could read it in its entirety. None of Sebastian's previous letters had passed by the censor unscathed, and this in itself unnerved her slightly. Also, she could tell from the handwriting that it had been written in haste, and that sense of urgency from Sebastian now rubbed off onto Renata. Her antenna for the worst was on full alert as she began reading the letter:

MY DARLING RENATA – Please forgive the brevity of this letter. Everything that I love is you and the children. Realise that you are the best of life I have known. Do many fun things with Sabina and Joachim. I think of you always. Take them to skate in the *Großer Garten*. I remember so much laughter in our house. On sunny days fly a kite with the children in the meadows by the Elbe. Never forget our love. I shall love you all forever. Send my kisses to the children. Hug them often. Every kiss from you I cherish. Remember that the purpose of life is to love. Endeavour always to find happiness.

With the deepest gratitude for the love we have shared,

SEBASTIAN, xxx.

Renata struggled to breathe. Her husband's letter was like no other he had previously written. The short sentences and unusual syntax were completely at odds to his normal writing style, and there was a poignancy to each phrase that alarmed her. She read and re-read the letter, trying to finesse out a layer of meaning that her instinct told her was there. Finally she saw it: the first letters of each sentence when joined together spelt out a word. It was simple code now that she thought of it, but subtle enough to slip past a censor. She picked out the letters: P–E–R–D–I–T–I–O–N–I–S–H–E–R–E; then she picked out the words: PERDITION IS HERE.

Renata's heart was now racing fast. Sebastian would not have gone to such lengths unless there was a matter of some importance to convey. Yet, the dichotomy of it all perplexed her, for here was a letter expressing both his deep love for her and the children, but also damnation and eternal ruin. Perdition Is Here. Where, she wondered – within their family? She doubted that: every sentence of the letter proclaimed just the opposite. He must mean at Buchenwald. She could not fathom whether the letter was a warning or statement, or maybe even both. Was he telling her in some bizarre way that he thought their marriage was over? That hardly seemed possible, although there was certainly a feeling of saying farewell and looking to the past, especially with the use of the past tense in the last sentence. Why had he not written instead, 'With the deepest gratitude for the love that we share'?

Renata ran endless interpretations of the letter through her head, but, despite the many declarations of his love for her, never arrived at sanguine conclusion. Eventually, she fell into a sleep that brought her no respite from her troubled thoughts.

She was woken just after first light by Joachim's small body burrowing under her quilt to find the comfort of her breast. She enjoyed a cuddle with her son whilst he sucked enthusiastically at her milk, and she mulled over the day ahead. They had few plans arranged, and she decided that she would sit down early on and write a careful letter in response to Sebastian's. She knew that she would have little peace until she had found out that all was well with her husband.

Her answer to that question came much soon than she had expected, and before she had even put pen to paper. At eight in the morning precisely, a sharp knock at the front door of their apartment interrupted their last few mouthfuls of breakfast. Renata's heart began to race, almost uncontrollably. They were not expecting any visitors, and certainly no one they knew would make an unarranged social call at such an hour. She smiled bravely at the children and, with her thoughts spinning in a thousand directions, went to open the door.

A rosy cheeked boy, not more than fifteen, stood outside the front door dressed in Hitler Youth uniform. Unsmiling, he raised his arm in salute and said earnestly, 'Heil Hitler'. He looked expectantly at Renata for her own 'Heil Hitler' in response, which, when she remembered a few seconds later, she half-heartedly gave. He then handed her a sealed telegram, and, having performed his duty, turned around and ran off.

She saw the Buchenwald stamp at once and tore open the envelope, her hands trembling in fearful anticipation, her head screaming: Let it be good news, please God; but her heart telling her otherwise.

The telegram had been signed off by an *Obersturmbahnführer*: this could only be bad news she knew. Her heart and instincts had, unfortunately, been right. The message was brutally perfunctory, 'Sebastian Lange deceased this morning October 19th 1943. Letter follows.'

Renata could barely breathe. She collapsed in a sobbing bundle in the doorway. Sebastian had been right; Perdition Is Here. He had obviously known he was about to die – in what way, she had no way of knowing yet – but in his last, hasty lament to wife and children, he had defiantly damned his executioner.

7

AMELIORATION
Oil and mixed media
150 cm x 300 cm

Berlin, Germany. November 15th 1995.

'Why don't you take Grandma around and show her some of the paintings,' Ellie suggested to Justin. 'And maybe introduce her to some of the people we're going to dinner with later? I'll circulate by myself, and catch up with you both later.'

Justin seemed quite pleased to be offered this diversion, and, finding a glass of champagne that he offered to their grandmother, he led her towards the paintings. Herr Backheuer, the tall art correspondent from *Stern* magazine with wolf-grey hair and a Schnauzer's moustache, spotted his chance, and, notebook out, stepped in towards Ellie to fill the void.

Then suddenly, whilst she laboured under Herr Backheuer's journalistic attentions – *Do you think that Art has a function in politics?* 'I think that the function of Art is to elicit a response from the viewer. Sometimes that's emotional, sometimes intellectual, and occasionally it's both. Any resonance that I create with an audience I consider a success.' But this exhibition is a commentary on the politics of Germany's twentieth century: after all, that is the title! So which is more important to you with this exhibition, the paintings or the politics? 'The title is "Germany: the Twentieth Century", and my paintings are a reflection of the events of that time, but I'm not making any political judgements with my work,' – the couple to their left stepped aside, revealing an old woman who was glowering coldly at Ellie from toad like eyes.

Unkempt and dishevelled, her appearance was so at odds with all the other guests that for a moment she wondered who the woman was and what she was doing at the opening party.

'So you think that your paintings reflect actual events? Actual events!' the woman flared at her, stepping closer.

With a sinking feeling, Ellie slowly reconciled the unfamiliar face of the woman before her, with the all too familiar voice. Her mother had come after all. She was barely recognisable. Ellie struggled to assimilate just how much she had aged during the eighteen months since they had last met.

Her mother's tired, thin and frayed appearance struck alarm bells within her. It usually acted as an accurate barometer of her alcohol consumption of late, and the signs were not good – the puffy, unmade-up eyes bruised with fatigue, the carmine lipstick dragged unsteadily over her crumpled mouth, and the burgundy stain running rampant across her nose and sagging cheeks – in fact, every indication was of a body in crisis. In addition, a severe haircut had robbed her mother of her enviable curls, and its former soft sandy colour had faded completely so it appeared drab and unruly, like a worn out scouring pad. She certainly appeared all of, if not more than, her fifty-seven years. And drunk. A pungent mix of stale smoke, alcohol, and too much perfume – lily of the valley, which was meant to mask the rest, but never did – hung over her. Ellie's memory was hijacked by those odours which she remembered so well from her youth. The seventeen unhappy years of her childhood, with all its accompanying fears and sadness, avalanched back down upon her. For a moment Ellie floundered between the past and the present, barely able to breathe. She was still conscious of her surroundings and the need to maintain a semblance of calm, but at this moment even a fixed smile required an enormous effort. She focused on regaining her breath, until, gradually, a degree of strength and equilibrium had returned. With that came the feeling of resentment: her mother had assured her, utterly, that if she came, she would not drink.

As her anger gathered momentum, a difficult silence hung between them while Ellie considered whether to respond to her mother's comments, simply ignore them, or ask her to leave.

But, before she had made up her mind, her mother started again, 'This is ridiculous. A pretentious ego-trip. How can you possibly comment on these things?' she slurred even louder. 'What do you know of Germany? Of what we went through? And the twentieth century – you've hardly seen it! Your paintings, your daubs of paint – you can't turn those events into pretty pictures and make the past a better place. It's an insult to us who lived through those times . . . the things I saw won't disappear with a lick of paint.'

Obviously, without Ellie realising, her mother had been listening to Herr Backheuer and herself. The temptation to really give her mother a piece of her mind screamed through her thoughts as bold as a Lichtenstein painting. Instead, she bit down on her lower lip to hold back the words. The most high-profile exhibition of her career was not the time or place to try and win an argument with a woman who was drunk. Her mother looked furious; Herr Backheuer wrote notes with raised eyebrows and interest. This was not the meeting that Ellie had planned in her head – her mother was quarrelling with her before they'd even said hello.

Faces turned, necks craned, and people stared. Her mother's raised voice was attracting unwelcome attention. The journalists scattered around the room viewed the feud with a buzzard's eye for carrion, whilst the other guests began to look uncomfortable. Such rancour appeared out of place at an art exhibition, and, as both the artist and as her daughter, Ellie was feeling increasingly embarrassed. Somehow, she had to either appease her mother, or get her to leave as quickly – and quietly – as possible.

'It's so good to see you!' Ellie managed more brightly than she felt, having decided to simply ignore her mother's comments. She was also acutely aware that for the worst of reasons she was the centre of attention. 'I'm so glad you've come!' she added, perhaps rather theatrically, as she was feeling anything but glad. Bending awkwardly towards her mother in greeting, Ellie was again hit by the acrid odour around her. Instinctively, she pulled away from her in revulsion, so they never actually touched. As the repugnance washed away, shame and guilt and sadness swept in to take its place. Deep within, she felt consumed by sorrow that she could not bear to get close enough to her mother to give her a simple, single kiss.

Recalling Justin's 'What the fuck for?' response when she had told him she wanted their mother to come, Ellie was beginning to think the same herself. She wondered why she had ever imagined that on this occasion things would turn out differently between them. Invariably, their encounters always turned out badly, with Ellie either close to tears or anger or both. Suddenly, she felt very foolish. All along she had been worried that by inviting their mother she was setting Justin up for an emotional fall; but it had turned out to be Ellie herself who was reeling. She had always thought that her attempts to repair their damaged relationship demonstrated her strength. It was slowly dawning on her that perhaps it takes a greater will to simply stay away from someone who is invariably destructive to your life. And her mother certainly qualified on that account. Nothing positive ever emerged from Ellie's dealings with her mother. Somehow, even the briefest encounter left Ellie feeling bruised.

She recalled their last meeting, on the morning of her birthday the previous year. Even though there had been no raised voices or any argument, she had felt demeaned. Her mother had phoned with an invitation for her to collect her present and Ellie drove over to her mother's house, not with high expectations, but with some degree of excitement nonetheless. Both the house and her mother were in their habitual state of disarray and faintly redolent of alcohol, though under the circumstances Ellie decided that was something best ignored. Her mother offered her coffee; black as there was no milk in the house. She was given her unwrapped gift, a jacket which her mother explained she had bought in a sale, worn a few times, and no longer wanted. Aggrieved, Ellie had wondered why her mother imagined that the old fashioned floral print would suit her any better or even fit her for that matter, as they were at least two clothes sizes apart. Had her mother been short of money she wouldn't have minded, but inheritance and divorce had provided her with funds to spare. Ellie was speechless, stubbornly refusing to go through any ritual display of gratitude. The 'present', she thought, epitomised her mother's feeling for her: the incessant thoughtlessness; the lack of care. In truth, what it really revealed was the lack of love. Hastily, she made her excuses to leave and they parted beneath the clamour of a brutal silence.

For many months that was how things remained between them, and Ellie felt quite comfortable with that as the *status quo*. Neither of them bothered to pick up the phone or send a letter or note to the other. Joanna and Millie's birthdays both came and went without even a card from their grandmother – not that they noticed, she had been an infrequent feature of their young lives – and Christmas passed in just the same way. Ellie ignored her mother's birthday when it came around in January, as happened conversely in April. And if it hadn't been for a whisper of loss that occasionally echoed around Ellie's thoughts, she would never have felt her absence.

It wasn't that Ellie missed her mother's company: what she missed was the relationship they could have had if things had been different. Or, she imagined, if her mother had at least just stopped drinking.

Slowly, as the long, dry summer stretched deep into September, Ellie had changed her mind. By the time she and Justin were compiling the guest list for the *Kunsthalle*, any thoughts that she could alter her mother's behaviour – stop her drinking sprees, small hope, or her constant criticism, or, heaven forbid, elicit some small scrap affection – had long been abandoned. But she wanted, even if subsequently they were then to remain estranged, for their parting to at least be peaceful; for the anger that had shadowed their every separation over the years, to be absent. With that hope in mind, Ellie had sent her mother the invitation to Berlin.

'I appreciate you coming here tonight,' said Ellie, determined to regain control of her feelings and thereby the situation. Journalists at her side, armed with notebooks, also heightened her awareness of the needed to at least appear to be polite.

'I'm exhausted,' her mother answered tersely. 'I had a terrible journey,' she added, the words noticeably sliding together as she stumbled through the problems she had faced to get to the *Kunsthalle*. 'The airport bus was very slow – there were road works on the M4 so I almost missed the check-in. The cabin staff were so rude – it took forever to get served. Then I had to wait ages for a taxi and when I got to the hotel the receptionist didn't speak a bloody word of English and it took forever to get checked in and up to my room.'

'Well, I'm sorry you've had a difficult time, but now that you're here can I show you around?' enquired Ellie, a shade of impatience brushed over the sentence.

'I need to sit down for a while, is there a chair anywhere? I can't see any chairs,' her mother blurted. 'Surely you don't expect people to stand around all night?'

In fact, her mother didn't look at all well. Although whether that was due to the tiring journey, or the by then obvious over-indulgence of duty-free drink on the plane and from the hotel mini-bar, Ellie couldn't be sure. Either way, she was furious that once again her mother was avoiding actually viewing her work. In all the years that Ellie had painted, her mother had come to only two or possibly three of her exhibitions, and had always left without giving more than a cursory look at her work. Inevitably, her mother would either be in a hurry to get elsewhere, or she would feel 'unwell' and have to leave. It was the same if Ellie gave her brochures or articles about her art. Without looking, her mother would put them aside with the promise that she would read them later, although it was always obvious to Ellie that she never did.

'The benches were taken out to create more space,' replied Ellie, making a strenuous effort to sound affable. 'But I know there are some chairs in the cloakroom. I could fetch one here for you if you like, or would you prefer to sit out there for a while? I could come and see you in a few minutes after I've circulated a bit more in here.'

Her mother nodded, turned, and then elbowed her way towards the foyer without another word. Ellie watched her shabby figure disappear from sight, a kaleidoscope of tension grinding roughly around her head. Within a minute, thankfully, there were other people beside her, more questions to be answered, and more small talk to be made – all of which were a welcome distraction.

The British contingent talked excitedly about Norman Foster's winning design for the Bundestag, whilst the East and West Germans kept slightly apart: the Berlin Wall might have been successfully dismantled, but the aptly described 'Wall in the Head' still clearly remained.

London, England. November 1989.

Ellie's shift on the paint frames finished at six in the evening. She had organised herself so that the paints she had used were stored away and her brushes were already cleaned and drying. For once, she was ready to leave on time. Promptly, she headed around to the dressing room area where she knew everyone well enough that they allowed her to shower and change. Generally, she would head off directly from the Theatre to collect Joanna from the childminder. If ever Ellie went out socially straight from work, it was usually to one of the pubs close by, either *The Opera Tavern* or the *Nell of Old Drury*, in which case she would stay in her old 'painting' clothes that more than made do for her work as assistant Scenic Artist. Consequently, her rarely seen efforts to dress to impress drew a mix of good hearted banter, mild questioning, and, at times, even heavy interrogation. However, this was one occasion when Ellie knew better than to succumb to the gossip mongers of the Theatre.

'Can we watch the evening news?' she asked, pointing to the television in the corner of the dressing room.

'Do we have to?' protested Amber, the willowy assistant make-up artist with hair dyed to match her name, who was styling a wig ahead of the performance. 'I'm watching *Hollyoaks*."

'What's *Hollyoaks*?' Ellie replied.

'Crikey Ellie, it's the new show on Channel 4. Keep up!'

'That's what I'm trying to do, by watching the news.'

This was not simply a tactic to divert their attention away from her: she was genuinely interested in the news. Europe, potentially the world, was teetering on the brink of a seismic political shift. Events across Eastern Bloc countries and between East and West Germany were changing, week by week, and at times even day by day. Borders that had remained closed for many years were suddenly and unexpectedly opening up, and protesters were gathering where previously they would have faced certain arrest. A revolution seemed to be unfolding, more rapidly than anyone would have predicted, and, thankfully, more peacefully.

Amber obligingly switched channels, and they watched, trans-fixed, a lengthy news bulletin of the vast crowds of demonstrators gathered in Berlin's *Alexanderplatz*. When it ended, the room was hive of speculation over how events would subsequently unfold. It seemed too audacious to even hope that democracy might finally come to East Germany. Ellie had a strong urge to call her grandmother and discuss it all with her, but, for the moment, that would have to wait. Unusually, Ellie had other more personal matters to address elsewhere that evening.

As she dried and then curled her hair – having invested in recklessly extravagant highlights just a few days before – plundered the senior make-up artist's extensive palette of pencils and powders and blushers and brushes, and then changed into a new soft coral wrap skirt with a matching silk shirt, Ellie kept telling herself that this was not a date, but an important and serious meeting. And yet despite all that, for all sorts of reasons, Ellie still wanted to look her best.

When she left the Theatre Royal, the foyer was rapidly filling with the excited faces and chatter of an expectant audience, and a swarm of taxis were pulling up with yet more people all eager to see the recently opened and critically acclaimed *Miss Saigon*. It was a dry and mild November night and as Ellie had arranged to meet up at Rules, the renowned restaurant just a few streets away, she resisted the temptation to jump into one of the taxis and chose instead to walk. After chasing and rehearsing strands of conversation in her head all day, she thought that a few minutes of fresh air and solitude would help her gather her thoughts one final time.

Ellie was the first to arrive at Rules, and went to sit amidst the burnished wood and gilt mirrors of the Cocktail Bar. Too flustered to peruse the drinks menu, she simply ordered a gin and tonic to assuage her unease. It had taken her years – six to be precise – to finally face up to the conversation that she was about to have, and, now that the moment had come, she felt raw with anxiety and guilt. To add to her confusion, those feelings were also tinged with relief, and even a touch of excitement. Some Dutch courage was definitely called for. One way or another, the evening was likely to be very emotional.

Milo and the drink arrived at Ellie's side at the same time. Awkwardly, aware that her body was suddenly a tremble of nerves, she stood up to greet him and they kissed on both cheeks. His presence hit her just as it always had: with a sharp jolt before they even touched. She would have been happy to lean closer and become enfolded within his embrace, but, reminding herself that she had a serious matter to raise with Milo, she stepped back.

'You look fantastic,' he said with obvious delight. To her embarrassment, she felt herself blush.

'You're looking really well too,' she replied truthfully, trying not to sound too gushing.

They both sat down and she took a quick sip from her drink while Milo ordered an Old Fashioned from the menu of traditional cocktails. During the seven years since they had dated, Milo had acquired an air of assurance that was very alluring. He had filled out too, in the most of attractive of ways. It was a struggle for Ellie not to sit and simply gaze at him. Memories of their time together came back in a flood, and she had a strong urge to reach out to hold his hand, which, with an effort, she resisted.

'I'm so glad we ran into each other again last week,' he said, raising his glass. 'Let's drink to destiny, kismet, call it what you will!'

To Ellie, it certainly felt as if the previous week fate had brought them side by side again in the queue at the same sandwich bar where they had met some seven years before. Initially, they had both been slightly shy, obviously aware that an element of nostalgia had brought them back to that place, and probably slightly self-conscious as to what that revealed to the other about those feelings. In Ellie's case, she was still working at the Theatre Royal, Drury Lane, but there were endless other cafes and delicatessens that she could choose from in and around the myriad streets of Covent Garden, and it was certainly true – though she would never have admitted it to anyone – that when she went there it was always because she had Milo on her mind. It had been something of a shock to actually see him there, right in front her, and of course her first thought was, 'Shit, I should have at least put on some mascara today.' Afterwards, Ellie couldn't remember who had spoken first, or much of what had been said, although she did recall the unmistakable frisson that followed a brief kiss on the check when they first said a self-conscious 'hello'. But all else as they stood there and ordered their lunch, was a collision of thought in her head and a charge of emotion to her stomach.

In her fantasy reunion, which, given the tie between them she knew was almost inevitable at some point, she had always imagined herself to be poised and elegant. But there in the queue, having rushed out from the paint frames in her old worn-out jeans, paint smeared sweatshirt and scrapped back hair, she thought she was possibly the least glamorous looking woman in London. Not that Milo seemed to notice, or if he did it he was too polite to mention it. Or, perhaps just possibly, it didn't actually bother him that much. Nevertheless, Ellie was mortified that on their first meeting after being estranged from each other for so long, and in light of their history together, he should see her like that.

'What brings you to Covent Garden?' she'd asked.

'I've got an appointment with a casting agent on the Strand,' he'd said, 'I thought I'd grab a sandwich first.'

'What's the part?'

'Chris Keller in Arthur Miller's *All My Sons* – do you know the play?'

Ellie shook her head to show that she didn't.

'It's about a family shadowed by the actions of the father during the war. I'm up for the part of one of the sons – the disillusioned war hero returning home.' He'd glanced at his watch, and then added, 'I haven't got much time, but would you like to sit down and eat with me?'

Ellie had intended to get her sandwiches as a take-away order, and vanity and anxiety almost prevailed, but, drawn as ever to Milo, she resisted the urge to make her excuses, grab her lunch and go. 'Sure, that would be great,' she'd answered, smiling at him.

They sat down opposite each other at one of the red leather covered booths and a waiter appeared to take their order. Whatever childish considerations Ellie had about her appearance, they were insignificant in comparison to the conversation that she knew she had long owed to Milo. Clearly, a hurried lunch was not the right time for such a talk, and the café certainly not the right place, but it would at least be a useful opportunity to resume communications between the two of them.

'What are you up to now, still at the Drury Lane?'

'Yeah, I'm still working there. No longer in the Box Office though, but backstage on the paint frames. I'm now an assistant Scenic Artist.'

'That's brilliant. I guess that would explain the Jackson Pollock look you've got going on,' he said with a gentle laugh, gesturing to the splatters of paint in her hair and on her hands and clothes. 'I remember that you were really into your art when we first met – you'd set up a home studio.'

'Still got it – in fact I'm really keen to become a full time artist. My brother's selling some of my work – but not quite enough to give up the day job, just yet.'

'That's really exciting – on both counts. I know how sought after the positions on the frames are, how did you get the gig?'

'Pester power. I just kept turning up and made myself invaluable so that when the job of studio assistant came up they knew that what I lacked in experience I made up for with enthusiasm. I did that for three years and then got the promotion – just a couple of months ago, in fact. I'm really enjoying it – it really is art on a grand scale. And how about you? How was *The Truly Wilde* tour?' It was a hard question for Ellie to ask, as the tour had clouded their relationship so much.

'Really good, thank you,' he replied, perhaps a little wistfully. 'The US is a fun place. The tour went well and on the back of that I got a part in TV show, and then a few film roles as well. Nothing major, but steady work nonetheless, and in this business you've got to be grateful for that. But I enjoy being on-stage more than anything else, which is why I'm back in London. I can't believe we ran into each other – I must admit that I came here because it reminded me of you, but I never imagined I'd actually see you.' He glanced at his watch, and then added, 'Listen, I'd love to talk more, but I've really got to go.'

Aware that she had to seize the moment and ask if they could meet again, Ellie was glad when Milo continued, 'I'd love to catch up properly – would you like to meet again sometime?'

'I'd like that very much,' she replied, tying to sound casual about the matter.

They exchanged phone numbers on paper napkins, and then Milo had to leave. Ellie was aware that neither of them had enquired of the other about their private life, but she'd noted that his wedding finger was absent of a ring.

True to his word, he called a few days later and suggested that they meet up for dinner.

'Let's meet for an early supper at Rules, then I can come straight from work – my treat,' Ellie offered.

Milo had sounded rather surprised at the gesture, but Ellie was adamant. Having considered the matter for the past several days, she'd decided that the intimate surroundings of an elegant restaurant might soften the blow of the news she intended to deliver; and if he were there as her guest.

And so they sat surrounded by the gilt framed pictures in the bar at Rules, toasted destiny for bringing them back together, and then looked through menu. Or at least Ellie went through the motions, though in truth her head was a whirl of thoughts elsewhere. Too distracted to make even the simplest of decisions, she simply repeated Milo's choice when the waiter came to take their order.

'I'm really glad that we bumped into each other,' she said, in what she hoped was a serious, yet gentle tone. Ellie planned to delay the discussion no longer. She feared that if she procrastinated in the slightest, it would be too easy to let the evening slip away and avoid the topic altogether. Also, that way if Milo, perhaps justifiably, got angry and wanted to leave, then it would be easier for them to walk out from the bar, rather than get up and go from a dining table. 'There's something that I really should have said to you seven years ago when we stopped seeing each other,' she continued. 'It's actually been something I've wanted to tell you for a while now, but kept putting off – for reasons that, with hindsight, now seem unimportant.' Ellie was talking quite slowly, trying to compensate for her instinct to race through her thoughts and words, and attempting to soften the forthcoming announcement with an apologetic tone.

He looked at her with a slightly quizzical expression, as he could probably tell from her tenor that this was not some trivial matter, but something rather serious.

'When you left the Theatre Royal to go to the States, I was pregnant,' Ellie managed more calmly than she had feared. Clearly uncertain where this was leading, Milo said nothing, but quickly crossed his arms and legs in an automatic gesture of defensive.

'I was pregnant,' she continued, 'and then gave birth in August 1983 to our daughter, who I called Joanna. And before you ask, of course she's yours, or we wouldn't even be having this discussion . . . .I'm sorry, I don't mean to sound so defensive'.

An intense unease settled over them and quashed all conversation. Finally, a waiter enquiring whether they wished to go through to their table, rescued them from their silent impasse. Ellie looked at Milo for an answer, wondering if he wanted to stay and resume the conversation, or to leave.

'Let's go and eat,' he said simply, his voice barely more than a whisper.

Taking their seats, they avoided each others and the waiters' eyes whilst potted Dorset crab was placed before them and a glass from a bottle of Puiy Fume poured out. After the waiters had ebbed away, they both focused on their food, the chimes of their cutlery only highlighting the strained silence between them.

'I cannot for the life of me imagine why you never told me this before,' said Milo eventually, but in such a quiet and measured way that Ellie could not tell if he was hurt or angry, or resorting to a line from some past performance.

'I found out that I was pregnant on the same day that you were offered the part of Jack Worthing in *The Importance of Being Earnest*,' she replied, talking to his plate as she could not look up to his face. 'You probably don't remember, but we had arranged to meet early that evening in *The Old Nell*. We had about half an hour to grab a bite together after I'd finished for the day in the Box Office, and before you were due backstage to get ready for the evening performance of *Pirates*. I'd gone to my doctor that morning and he'd confirmed my pregnancy. I planned to tell you in the pub that evening, but then you burst in, so full of excitement about being offered the role, and quite frankly I was in shock. I knew that if you took the part it was a year's contract to tour the States. And while I understood that it was a fabulous break for your career, it still felt quite painful for me that you seemed so blasé about leaving me for so long.' Ellie paused for a moment, caught up in the hurt she had felt that day, and took a gulp of wine. Her crab, she noticed, had hardly been touched. 'Anyway,' she carried on, with a sigh, 'that evening was obviously not the right moment to share my news, and after that I thought that I would wait and see if you did actually sign the contract to tour or not, as I didn't want my pregnancy to sway your decision either way. Then, after you'd accepted the part you were in such a whirl for the next few weeks until you left, and the right moment just never seemed to come.'

'But don't you think I had a right to know,' said Milo, slightly more forcefully this time. 'It might have swayed my decision: but so what? I would have lived with the consequences of whatever decision *I* made. Acting parts come around all the time, but I can never get back those lost years with my daughter. You robbed me off the opportunity to at least make that my own choice.'

Silence rolled back in on them. They both barely moved. Ellie was conscious of him clutching the stem of his wine glass, his other hand a tight fist on the table; but she couldn't look up to catch his eye. There was laughter all around them, the clink of cutlery on fine china, the top and bass notes of animated conversations, and a stream of waiters around the room. Set apart from all that, Ellie and Milo sat paralysed within their own private drama.

'I wasn't even certain if I would carry on with the pregnancy at that stage,' she eventually continued. 'In fact, I thought it more probable that I wouldn't. Everything was stacked against it, really. I know that we'd had a great time for the six months that we had dated, but we hardly made any big commitments to each other – we hadn't moved in together or even got particularly involved with each others' lives, apart from that one time I met your parents. And you'd never met any of my family. You were auditioning for a part which would take you away for a year, so I thought things between us were more or less over in any case.'

'I gave you no indication that my accepting the role meant that I wanted to end the relationship – in fact just the opposite.' Milo sounded cross now, although his voice was far from raised. 'If I remember I tried everything to persuade to you that our relationship could survive the separation. I don't recall saying one thing that would have given you the impression that by me going on tour meant I wanted to break up with you. I remember trying very hard to persuade you to join me every couple of months wherever I was at the time, and saying that if we planned it well we could see much of the States together, and both get a lot out of the experience together. It was you who decided that our relationship couldn't survive the distance and separation, and it was you who ended it.'

He was right in everything that he'd just said, Ellie knew. Obviously, he had taken the part, and, after a strained few weeks between them during which they had seen less and less of each other, and every exchange had been tinged with exasperation, they had met for lunch just a few days before his departure. He had repeated what he'd already said so many times: that whilst he loved her very much it was a great opportunity for his career, and despite all that she had previously said, he still hoped that they would find a way to make their relationship survive the separation. Probably less than reasonably, her hormonal fug being her only valid defence, Ellie made it clear she thought they should simply make a clean break. They parted that day, tersely, without even a kiss on the cheek or a hug. A few days later, after his departure, Ellie made an appointment to see her doctor. Her intention had been to end the pregnancy, though when the moment arrived she simply could not go through with the procedure. One way or another, she decided, she would manage on her own.

'It's not much of an excuse,' began Ellie, 'but I was quite young, quite frightened, and I felt totally alone. My father had died the previous year, I wasn't talking to my mum, my brother was off travelling God knows where, and my boyfriend of only six months was going away for the next twelve months. I didn't want you to think I was trapping you into a relationship that you didn't want – I'd heard my mum throw that line at my dad their entire marriage after she got pregnant with me, so I'd seen first hand how destructive that situation can be – or holding you back in your career. I could see that it was a big deal for you to get a contract like that, and had learnt enough about acting to know that a full year's work with a prestigious touring company was a big break for any actor – I thought that ultimately you would resent me like hell if I stopped you going.'

'And it never occurred to you that I might resent you like hell for having stopped me from seeing my daughter for the past six and a half years.' Beneath the quiet voice, there was an evident fury to Milo's words. They felt like a slap in the face, but Ellie realised that it was probably no less than she deserved.

'I'm truly sorry,' she managed eventually. 'For a while, after Joanna had been born, I had every intention of writing to you via your agent and letting you know. But to begin with I was either so busy or so exhausted that I never got around to it, and then when I returned to work it was even worse, a constant juggle of work and a small baby and never enough sleep. Writing a difficult letter like that was something all too easy to keep putting off. Then after a while I just felt ashamed. And the longer I left it, the harder it became. Sometimes I even thought that I'd wait until Joanna was old enough to ask about seeing you, and then help her get in touch with you herself if she wanted to. And then we ran into each other last week, and I took that to be a sign that this was something that I had to do right now.'

Their half-empty plates – a reflection of their feelings, not the food – had been cleared away, and a flurry of waiters were pouring out Haut Brion and bringing them game pie and endless permutations of vegetables. It all provided a welcome pause in the conversation for them both to catch up with their thoughts.

'Does my daughter even know about me, or are you with someone else now who she regards as a father figure?' he asked dispassionately, when they were alone once more.

'She knows that you're her father, and there's no one else except my brother who takes a paternal role in her life.'

'Does she ever ask about me?'

'From time to time as she's got older she's made the odd comment, or asked about you – but only since she started school and noticed that most of the other children live with both parents. I've answered her questions, as and when they've come up, as simply and directly as is appropriate for a young child.'

Milo looked at Ellie with a solemn expression, for what seemed like an age. She barely managed to return his stare.

Finally, with his face and tone softening, he asked, 'Do you think that she might want to meet me?'

'Of course she would,' replied Ellie, relieved.

His face lightened, the worry lines easily erased. 'Then I would very like very much to meet her.'

Suddenly, Milo was a cascade of questions. When was Joanna's birthday, what was her colouring, who did she look like, did she enjoy school and have many friends? In her relief at his gentle acceptance, Ellie gushed out the answers. Soon she brought out her wallet and was proudly offering him the photos she kept inside it, of Joanna from over the years. He studied these all intently, and seemed genuinely moved as he noted the changes from cherubic infant, to impatient toddler struggling to stay still for the camera, to young child with a shy smile in her first school uniform.

Hostilities over, they were at last able to enjoy their food. Soon, the game pie and vegetables were dispatched, and after that they lingered over plum crumble and homemade vanilla ice-cream, Milo all the while keen to catch up on his daughter's young life. By the time coffee arrived, it seemed the most natural thing in the world for them to be making arrangements for Milo to come to the house the following Saturday and meet his daughter. Ellie felt both relieved and delighted: after all, he could have so easily turned his back on them both, and walked away forever.

Outside the restaurant as they prepared to go their separate ways, Milo took her in his arms and hugged her tight. 'Thank you so much,' he said tenderly.

'What for?'

'For telling me about Joanna. It was very brave of you – it would have been so easy to have kept on avoiding telling me.'

He kissed her on the cheek, and, having said their goodbyes, his parting words were, 'See you on Saturday at three!'

Half expecting a phone call from Milo to cancel the plan, Ellie waited until Friday evening to let Joanna know that her father was coming to meet her the following afternoon. As predicted, she was like a clown full of excitement, a barrister with her questioning, and a fashion stylist over her plans for what to wear. Ellie responded by withholding sugar, keeping her answers honest but brief, and assisting her in putting together what she eventually deemed to be her most appropriate outfit.

In the morning Ellie decided to take Joanna for a swim to distract and calm her down. They then had a light lunch that in their anticipation they could barely eat, after which Joanna changed and waited for her father to arrive, her attention divided between *The Aristocats* video and the front door.

Promptly, at three, Milo arrived carrying a distinctive red and gold Hamley's bag. Joanna, who had succumbed to a rare moment of shyness, was soon coaxed out from behind Ellie's legs by the gift, and before long was back to her more exuberant self when she found the Cabbage Patch Doll inside. It wasn't long before she was proudly showing her father the collection of toys in her bedroom, and rearranging them all so that the new addition would have pride of place. Ellie made a tactful retreat to the kitchen to give them some time alone together. Against a background accompaniment of their chatting, Ellie made them all a much needed pot of tea.

Milo stayed for an improvised early supper and then left at around six, having made plans to repeat the visit the following week. The flat seemed suddenly empty and quiet after he had gone, despite Joanna's loquaciousness about her father and the afternoon.

Milo's visits soon became a regular feature of their weekends. Depending on his work commitments and Joanna's social life, he would come over on either Saturday or Sunday afternoon. Generally, he came just after lunch and took Joanna out, either to the park if the day was sunny, or at least dry, or the cinema or a swimming pool, if there was rain. On their return, they would all sit together whilst Joanna ate an early supper.

It wasn't long before Joanna found new ways of enticing her

father to stay longer, though he never appeared to need that much persuading.

'I bet you can make the bubbliest bath ever Daddy!' she challenged him, asking him to stay for bath time.

'You bet!' he replied, beaming. 'I can blow more bubbles than a humpback whale!' At which they both burst out laughing.

'You're an actor Daddy; you'll be the best bedtime storyteller in the world!' she later announced with an endearing conviction whilst presenting him with a choice of books to read from. He lapped up all the attention. Finally, to persuade him to put her to bed, though no persuasion was really needed, she declared solemnly, 'Teddy wants you to tuck us in for the night Daddy'.

'And teddy shall not be disappointed!' he replied with as much enthusiasm as if he were on a West End stage. In his daughter, Milo had found his most adoring of audiences.

Without planning or discussion, Ellie and Milo got into the habit of carrying on with their conversation after Joanna had been put to bed for the night. Quite naturally, a bottle of wine would be opened and perhaps later on a take-away ordered, and, increasingly, the talk was not just of Joanna, but of their own lives as well. And often as not, before they had even noticed, it was late and the evening had slipped away. It became increasingly hard for Ellie to kiss his cheek and not his lips whenever he left at the end of his visit.

At the end of Joanna's school term, Milo joined Ellie and Justin when they went to see her cast as a Shepherd in the school nativity play. Afterwards, they all celebrated the success of the expanding acting dynasty with a visit to the local pizzeria. At the end of the evening, when they came to say goodbye, Milo, at last, kissed Ellie purposefully on the lips.

As Christmas approached, Ellie invited him to join them on the day for the festivities, but he had long agreed to be with his own family. By way of a compromise, he asked if he could come over in the afternoon, after he had finished his lunch with them.

In case he felt it was too much, too soon, Ellie forewarned him that her grandmother would be with them as well.

Milo arrived mid-afternoon on Christmas Day, laden with small gifts for them all and of course a much larger one for Joanna. Tellingly, thought Ellie, he had also brought a present for Joanna from his parents. She hadn't previously asked whether he had told them about their new found granddaughter, but, from the gifts they'd sent, he evidently had.

As the street lamps flickered on and the evening closed in, they all put on coats and scarves and hats and gloves and headed through the tree lined avenues down to the Grand Union Canal which ribboned through Little Venice nearby. Along the waterside where they walked, the brightly painted barges and houseboats were decked with tiny Christmas trees and a sprinkling of shiny decorations, which cast prisms of bright light onto the grand cream stucco villas lining either side of the darkening streets. Renata and Justin strolled a few steps ahead while Joanna walked between Ellie and Milo, determinedly clutching a hand of both parents, her voice an aria of chatter and her skipping feet an accompanying clatter. Ellie knew that not many miles away, most probably at their old family home in Ealing, her own mother was very likely alone and miserable, but she quickly jostled that thought to one side. For that moment she felt all the joy for life of the couple in Chagall's *Promenade* and a sense of peace that had so often seemed elusive.

Returning to the flat with flushed cheeks and blowing cold spouts of air, they all warmed up with hot chocolate and sherry and mince pies. Soon after, Justin drove their grandmother back to Finchley, and Milo and Ellie put Joanna to bed. And then without discussion they headed to the sitting room, where they curled up on the sofa in each other's arms and searched the television channels for some easy entertainment. Later on, it seemed perfectly natural when Milo stayed for the night, and then every one after that.

8

MAELSTROM
Oil on canvas
330cm x 300cm

Berlin, Germany. November 15th 1995.

In contrast to the champagne and conversation that effervesced around the *Kunsthalle's* main gallery, outside in the cloakroom any pretence at social graces had been cast aside. Another row within Ellie's family had just erupted.

Alerted by a keen eyed waitress who had discovered the two of them arguing, Ellie's mother and grandmother were shouting savagely when she got to them. Sabina's slurred words sloshed around Renata's indignation, whilst their angry faces were reflected myriad times by the mirrors about the room. Ellie felt completely engulfed in the fray. Yet again, her mother seemed determined to establish a higher place in the family hierarchy of suffering, though Ellie wondered why that were an argument anyone would wish to win.

'You couldn't wait to see the back of me. You just shoved me into that hell-hole of a school and never visited. You haven't got any idea how painful it was for me; you were as dead to me as father was, I was . . . I was an orphan. They nearly killed me for being a German, and you didn't even try to protect me. After Joachim died . . . '

'Yes, you lost your father,' Grandma interrupted, quickly cutting off any mention of Joachim, as their arguments always escalated out of control when they ventured into his memory. 'I still miss him greatly, and he was a very special man. But so was your husband. He was kind, moral and a good father. Did you appreciate any of those qualities? Not a bit. Instead you squandered them and drove him away. I lost my husband because those same qualities cost him his life.'

Ellie's hope that by meeting in a public place both her mother and grandmother would at least feign a veneer of grace, had fast faded. Obviously, her presumption that she would be able to orchestrate the reunion more carefully had been naïve.

Where the argument between the two of them had begun, she had no idea, but her mother had certainly looked pleached with spite when she arrived at the exhibition, and her grandmother had never been one to humour her daughter's darker moods or tolerate any drunken behaviour. Although Ellie had no recollection of the two of them ever being together without a disagreement ensuing – she recalled as a child always hiding away, either outside in the greenhouse or upstairs in the attic to escape from their rows – she had trusted them to come to Berlin in a more conciliatory mood. Her intention had been for the exhibition to provide them with an occasion to be reunited as a family in a peaceful way, and not to be used as an opportunity for the settling of old scores.

Her mother and grandmother had seen each other infrequently over the years. Ellie had not been with the two of them together since her father's funeral, when her mother, already drunk on her arrival at the service, had scraped barbed wire comments along the line of mourners around his grave. Withered with grief and the glare of the summer sun, no one had said a thing. Later, when everyone had proceeded from the Church in Winster and gathered at her uncle's farmhouse, they were equally mute when stoked up on sherry she'd hacked at his memory with her ice-pick tongue. No corner of their marriage had been safe from her that day, until, mercifully, their uncle had called for a taxi to just take her away. Afterwards, their grandmother had made it very clear that aside from unavoidable occasions such as funerals, until she was certain of her daughter's sobriety, she wanted as little to do with her as possible.

From then on her mother's life and drinking spiralled out of control. None of the family had any desire to stay in touch with her, she had few friends, and no work or hobbies that Ellie was aware of. She relied on alcohol to fill the void.

Ellie's first indication of how bad her mother's life had become was a message left for her at the theatre by her mother's neighbour, Mr Colman. 'Your mother's not well, please give me a call,' it stated simply, alongside his number. Ellie remembered him from her childhood as a rather forbidding old man with an unruly beard and a disapproving knot between his overgrown eyebrows. Nonetheless, she appreciated that he'd made the effort to track her down and help her family.

With a sigh, she had dialled the number. 'Er, Mr Colman, it's Ellie Tyler here. You left a message for me to call you.'

'Ah yes,' he'd replied with a note of disapproval in his voice. 'I'm afraid there's a problem with your mother. I've been asked by the doctor to get in touch with someone in your family. Without some help, she's clearly not going to last much longer on her own.' There had been an accusatory tone to his words, though whether these had been directed at Ellie, or her mother, or her family in general, she wasn't certain. 'You were the only family member I knew how to contact – your mother once told me you worked at the theatre – which is why I called you,' he'd continued. 'Anyway, she's in quite a state. Been drinking for days from the look of things. The house is in a hell of a mess, and she's just the same. I knew she was at home as I saw lights go on off now and then, but milk bottles were gathering in increasing quantities outside her door so I realised that something was up. She didn't answer the door, so I let myself in with a spare key she'd given me, and eventually found her in her bedroom. She was incoherent, so obviously I called the doctor. But he only confirmed what I thought, that she wasn't ill, just intoxicated.

"Beyond prescribing aspirin and sleep, there's nothing I can do for her medically," is what he said. He asked me to try and get her some help, and says he'll return tomorrow.'

Ellie had felt utterly humiliated by the conversation. However, despite that, and all her former fury, she'd said resignedly, 'I'll get there as soon as I can. Thank you for everything you've done.'

'Oh, and bring some food,' Mr Colman had added. 'There's absolutely nothing for her to eat in the fridge or cupboards: I checked. And I'll leave the key I've got under the dustbin by the back door, so you can let yourself in.'

She'd called her childminder and made arrangements to pick Joanna up much later, obtained permission to leave work early, and then took the Central Line out to Ealing. At the corner shop just past the station she bought a selection of tinned soups, a fresh loaf of bread, a carton of eggs and a packet of cheese.

Returning to the house after such a long absence, Ellie felt somewhat unnerved. Stepping inside, time seemed to suddenly slip away. All at once she was back in a life that she had managed to leave at the back of her mind, and almost convince herself that it had simply been a very bad dream. With a sinking feeling, she returned to that reality.

A brooding silence was her only greeting. Ellie hadn't been into the family home since her mother had thrown her out on her seventeenth birthday. It appeared depressingly unaltered. Briefly, she peered in at all the rooms on the ground floor before reluctantly going upstairs. The house was filthy, the stale air a malodorous mix of cigarettes and alcohol and vomit. Nothing appeared to have changed since her childhood. As expected, her mother was asleep upstairs in her bedroom, a thin, washed-out figure huddled beneath unwashed sheets. Ellie struggled against feelings of sadness and anger that she had striven so hard to escape for so long.

Once again, Ellie found herself searching the house for bottles of alcohol. It was an all too familiar process, although at least Ellie knew from experience where to look. In fact, there really wasn't much hidden around the house: just a small bottle of gin and some cheap cans of beer. She poured them away. Clearly her mother had consumed whatever else she'd bought, as there were endless empty bottles of Bacardi, gin, brandy and wine, plus discarded cans of lager and cider strewn about in nearly every room. Ellie felt thoroughly depressed by it all.

Despite her annoyance, Ellie nonetheless gathered the empty bottles and cans and assembled them into more or less orderly lines beside the back door. Then, she scrubbed out a saucepan from the pile of dirty crockery stacked up in the sink, warmed some soup on the fat splattered hob, and took it up to her mother. Dazed and barely coherent when Ellie woke her, she appeared unaware that she was talking to her daughter. Ellie hovered beside her whilst she consumed soup in uncertain sips. After that, Ellie dashed off a note saying she'd return in the morning, and left to pick up Joanna.

Grudgingly, Ellie took the following two days off work to watch over her mother. She made sure that her mother ate some food and abstained from alcohol. She took away the empty bottles and cans and made a cursory attempt at sorting the house out and stocking up the kitchen. She felt part gaoler, part nurse and part cleaner, and resented it all.

To begin with, her mother was mostly silent, apparently unaware of Ellie's presence. But by the afternoon of Ellie's second full day there, she was considerably more alert and appeared pleased to see her daughter. She was full of contrition. She had no idea how she had let things go so far. Of course she would make weekly visits to the doctor's surgery, and she'd agreed that it would be a positive step if she joined her local Alcoholics Anonymous group. Finally, shortly before Ellie had left that day, she'd told her mother about her daughter Joanna. She would let Sabina meet Joanna, Ellie had made quite clear, when her life was back on a sober track.

At that point her mother did try hard to make changes to her life, although it was hardly a smooth progression forward. For a long time she managed to stop drinking, she attended AA, and the weekly visits to the doctor eventually became a monthly check-up. Ellie would phone her on Sundays and perhaps take Joanna to visit her every few weeks; but sadly, each time that she thought she could take her mother's sobriety for granted, that trust was rewarded with first a drunken spree, then the traumas that went with her withdrawal from alcohol, and then another round of detoxification. Afterwards, inevitably, her mother would once again promise abstinence. A predictable pattern emerged. Between bouts of drinking her mother would come back into Ellie's life for brief and emotionally bruising periods – which were motivated mostly by guilt on her behalf – and then out again for long absences that generally felt something of a relief.

Absurdly, reflected Ellie, she had actually believed her mother's promise that she wouldn't drink if she came to Berlin. Ellie had imagined that the chance for her mother to finally make amends with both her mother and her son, would be incentive enough to keep her off alcohol.

Obviously, Ellie realised, she'd been wrong. Caught up in the maelstrom that swirled between her mother and grandmother in the *Kunsthalle* cloakroom, Ellie knew that having created the problem in the first place by inviting them both, it was her responsibility to try and resolve it.

Her main concern, apart from separating the two of them, was to keep journalists and Justin away from them both. An argument within the family was the very nightmare that he had wished to avoid. Thankfully, the waitress who'd been astute enough to find her, offered to stand as sentinel outside the cloakroom until the quagmire inside had been quelled. But as ever with the animosity between her mother and grandmother, that seemed a long way off.

Dresden, Germany. February 15th, 1945.

When at last Sabina opened her eyes, she had no idea how long the stranger had been shaking her shoulders. '*Nimmt ein bißchen Wasser, Kind!*' An old woman with a kind but strained face was coaxing her with warm water that she offered in a chipped enamel cup. Sabina slowly sat up, then emptied the cup with quick, noisy gulps, whilst the woman called to her mother, somewhat impatiently, '*Wacht auf! Setzen Sie aus!*'

There were tiny movements through her mother's frail body, the slight turn of an ankle; an almost imperceptible flicker of an eyelid. Just enough to show that she was still alive. The woman prised her up to a sitting position taking care to avoid the charred skin and swollen left hand and the blistered forearm, the now all too familiar results of terrible burns. She remained impervious to Renata's incoherent protests, and, after refilling the cup from the milk churn she carried, she placed it against Renata's scabbed mouth and forced her to drink the water.

The woman had neither the time nor energy left for pleasantries. Beyond waking survivors and warming them with a drink of heated water, she knew that for the moment there was little more that she could do for them.

Unwittingly, she had been witness to the apocalypse that had been Dresden's destruction. It had begun midway through the Shrove Tuesday evening, when, from her smallholding close to the forests on the hills just north of the city, she had been alerted by an ominous rumble of aircraft engines passing overhead. The sound of planes in such close proximity was an occurrence infrequent enough to warrant her attention and concern. Hastily grabbing her heavy fern green loden coat which she slipped on over her nightdress and dressing gown, she stepped into her heavy outdoor boots and scrambled outside across the icy ground. Even though it was dark, she wondered whether she would be somehow able to spot if the planes were either Luftwaffe, and therefore not a threat to her, or enemy aircraft en-route else-where, please God, and not bound for Dresden. Green marker flares dropped over the city a short time after brought the answer to that particular question. They were soon followed by almost a thousand white magnesium parachute flares, or 'Christmas trees' as they were commonly referred to, which descended like ghostly apparitions from the aircraft, illuminating the wintry city below in an eerie silvery beauty. Suddenly red target flares burst open showering a crimson glow over the distant buildings. It was a benign and colourful prelude that belied the onset of slaughter that was shortly to follow.

She was expecting some form of defence of the city to begin, as surely it must, but no search lights were switched on, no anti-aircraft gunners began firing, and no German fighters appeared in the skies to bring deliverance. She was not to know that just a few weeks before the little flak that had lain mostly unused in the city for much of the war, had been dismantled and shipped away to areas deemed more at risk. Now, in her hour of need, Dresden lay entirely abandoned and unguarded by her rightful protectors.

Almost immediately, the careful choreography of close formation bombing began. By then she had been joined by the Silesian family of *Flüchtlinge* – refugees – who had been billeted on her farm since the end of January, and together they watched as the two hundred and forty four Lancasters flew in wave after relentless wave over the city, fanned out at increasing angles on an arc across the target area, and released their loads of high-explosive bombs and incendiary sticks. Then, lightened by several thousand pounds, the planes surged upwards and curved gracefully away to the south to begin the long, arduous, haul back home.

Aghast at the spectacle, it was nevertheless hard not to be mesmerised by it. Flecks of light gilded the landscape as the exploding bombs ignited the buildings below, emitting a dia-phanous haze along the city skyline. Soon, the fires rippled out-wards and began to merge together, emblazing a vivid amber web through the winding streets and an angry red aura all above, whilst throwing vast plumes of charcoal clouds to the surrounding skies. It was both devastating and fascinating to watch.

Eventually, she returned inside, feeling not only cold but also rather uncomfortable at being an audience to the destruction of so much, and the self-evident death of so many. A little after midnight, emotionally exhausted by all she had witnessed, she finally fell asleep and was thus spared the horror of watching a second wave of Lancaster bombers, twice as numerous as the first, which descended on Dresden from the south in the early hours of the morning.

Shortly before dawn, after a fitful few hours of sleep, she awoke and ventured outside again to see the city submerged beneath a sea of fire with an impenetrable wall of smoke and dust and debris rising up for more than a mile into the skies above. It was Ash Wednesday in Dresden.

By then, a few people had appeared on her frost bound fields, some on foot, others atop horse-drawn carts, and she directed them to her courtyard with its barns and outbuildings. Only a minority of them, at least from a brief glance, appeared especially injured, though amongst them they clearly displayed a broad spectrum of deep shock, from mute misery to hysteria, from all they had witnessed. These were the fortunate early escapees who had fled ahead of the maelstrom.

Throughout the morning, whilst their numbers and the severity of their injuries steadily increased, she felt able to deal with the influx. But after midday, when the third air raid within twelve hours struck the city, her small half-timbered house and few outbuildings had been rapidly overrun in the exodus that ensued, and had soon come to resemble a chaotic battlefield dressing station. Instinctively, those able attended to the wounded in whatever way possible. Before long, every available space within the farmhouse brimmed with the injured and the dispossessed, many of whom, it quickly became apparent, had not eaten in a very long while. Within hours her meagre supplies of potatoes, swedes and carrots, cannily withheld from the quota of produce demanded from farmers and carefully stored between layers of straw and soil in the hens' barn beneath the roosting shelves, had been eaten uncooked. By that stage she had offered these willingly, resigned to the fact that the end of her days on the farm seemed imminent, one way or another: either in the wake of another wave of bombing which by now she most certainly did not rule out, or by evacuation ahead of the advancing Red Army who were now only a matter of hours away and their invasion of Saxony seemingly inevitable.

Through all the rest of that day, and, excepting a few stolen moments of sleep during the night that followed, she had tended to those most in need. To begin with, she had cleaned and dressed their wounds using her limited supplies of soap and bandages, improvising with torn bedding and clothes and lace tablecloths, but those had fairly rapidly run out. From then on, she put her efforts into making those suffering as comfortable as possible, which by then, given the constraints of her situation, amounted to little more than a kind word or a drink of water. Towards dawn, and despite her exhaustion, she had put on her Loden coat and wrapped a thick teal coloured headscarf across her face to muffle the ash in the air, and headed outside to search for survivors. Fire illuminated the sky with blood red swathes amongst towering clouds of smoke and debris, like an Old Testament depiction of Hell.

Ice across puddles snapped beneath her feet as she ventured along pathways. Soon, she arrived at the forest that bordered onto her farmland. As she had imagined there were endless people who had been out all night. Some had gone there believing a forest to be the safest place if the bombers returned, as no enemy would waste their weapons on such a low value target. Others had escaped from the city as far as the forest, but with their serious injuries had got no further. From all that she had been told and in view of the harsh frost that had gnawed at the land the previous night, she was afraid of what she would find. Shockingly, it was worse than anything she had envisioned, the numbers overwhelming, the tragedy harrowing.

Mothers clung, bereft, to the cold corpses of tiny children. Children sat distraught beside the body of a dead mother. Survivors of all ages struggled with cuts or torn limbs, skin shredded by shards of glass, faces battered and bruised, eyes lost beneath swellings, and bodies oozing secretions from crimson burns. Some coughed incessantly, their lungs clogged or scarred by smoke inhaled in the inferno, whilst others wretched a blackened trickle of vomit. Many wandered alone in mute misery, either separated from their family by the chaos of the past two days, or most probably, the sole survivor.

As quickly as possible, she had returned to her farm and organised a group of the stronger *Bombengeschädigt* – those disposed by bombing – to help her, heating water in an urn over an open fire, and then distributing it from milk churns to as many survivors as possible.

'*Erstmal die Eltern und Kleiner,*' she told her improvised group of volunteers, realising the need to concentrate on the very old and the very young in the first place, as they were the most at risk from hypothermia, although in reality it was whomever they stumbled upon, waking and warming them from the winter's night air. All too often they had come too late, and now their corpses, blackened by frost, grimaced out across the forest floor. Happily, here was one who had been easy to wake, this tiny, frightened, scrap of a girl with a halo of corn coloured curls, she would be alright, the old woman thought, although the chances for the woman who lay beside her, whom she assumed to be her mother, looked slight.

Sound drifted down through the deep layers of Renata's sleep. Someone seemed to be calling her, although the words were lost across the chasm of her consciousness. She had no interest in the voice that called to her; she wanted only to be left alone. But the

voice was calling her again, more urgently this time, and movement pulled her up through her sleep to a slumped sitting
position. Against her frozen lips the slight warmth of the cup felt
comforting, and she opened her parched mouth instinctively.
She sipped slowly at the water, almost reluctantly, as if uncertain
whether she did in fact wish to surface from the cold. She paused
between sips: between life and death.

There had been a peace in her sleep, and death would have
come with ease, would have been a relief, an escape from pain.
The pain in her body, especially her hand; and the pain in her
heart. But from the edge of life she could see her daughter Sabina
beside her, fragile as a *Meissen* figurine, and now the desire for
death sent ripples of guilt across her thoughts, so she drank more
forcefully, and by the time she had reached the bottom of the
mug, that means of escape had dried up.

The old woman had already moved on when Renata muttered
a barely audible, '*Danke schön*,' through her smoke stripped
throat, although there would be many times in the years ahead
when she would ask herself if she were truly grateful that her life
had been saved.

Pain spiralled up through Sabina's right ribcage, although the
rest of her body was numb from the cold. Branches from the
frozen bracken bush that had been her bed for the night scrapped
her face as she slowly stood up, dislodging a thin frosting of ice
that sprinkled over her body. Sleep had shut down her memory,
and it took a while for Sabina to take in the reality of her strange
surroundings, and understand why, after the turmoil of the last
two days and despite the cold, the sharp air was so unexpectedly
soothing: they were no longer amidst the roar of bombing and
the deafening accompaniment to the destruction of Dresden. In
the stillness her body no longer vibrated to the shrill roar of
bomber's engines or the shocking bursts from incendiary bombs.
Jolts from crumbling buildings and falling debris no longer shot
through her being, and the fires that had ripped the air from her

lungs and threatened so many times to take her life, had been left behind.

Hunger knotted Sabina's stomach; it seemed so long since she had eaten. She remembered some kale soup eaten at *Großmutter* Lange's apartment before they had gone to the Circus Sarassani, a treat of fresh sausage earlier on, and *Frühstück* at their apartment that morning, a slice of *Lebensbrot* that she had shared with her brother Joachim and a small portion of stale cheese that had tasted awful, but Mutti had made her eat nonetheless. It all seemed such a distant memory.

She looked at Mutti huddled beside her, her pale, gaunt face smeared with smoke, dried blood daubed over her singed dark auburn hair, and her hand an open, oozing wound. Then instinctively, she glanced around for the distinctive blond curls that belonged to her brother. He was never far from her side, and must be somewhere close by to her now. But then, consumed by despair, she remembered the desolations of the previous two days.

Dresden, Germany. 13th February 1945.

Shrove Tuesday dawned with pastel coloured skies and a confection of clouds strung along the horizon of hills. After endless weeks, the dreary metallic fog that had clung to the city had finally lifted. The spring like weather bode well for the *Fasching* carnival, the much loved celebrations in the lead up to Lent.

Renata was determined to make it as happy an event as possible for the children; a pleasant distraction from the realities of war. Notwithstanding the many uncertainties that surrounded their lives and the distinctly sombre mood that subsumed the city, she would make every effort to ensure they enjoyed the carnival atmosphere and the circus later that evening. It seemed such a long time since they had had any fun together, and God knows that they all deserved it.

The evening was a surprise treat that *Großvater* and *Groß-mutter* Lange had organised to compensate the family for the

233

rather subdued celebrations of late. Firstly, the rather bleak Christmas that they had all endured a short time before, with a just a small tree from Chemnitz, two scrounged candles and a small carp to mark the occasion, followed by an equally restrained *Sylvester Abend*, and then Sabina's birthday which had been an similarly frugal affair.

Fortunately, at the beginning of February the Circus Sarrasani had been given special permission to put on a run of performances for *Fasching*, and Herr and Frau Lange had jumped at the opportunity to treat their family with tickets. They were only too aware that since Sebastian's death there had been few opportunities for the three of them to enjoy such outings together. Not only were there very few activities to indulge in, but finances were certainly a constant worry for Renata. All in all, it had been an extremely tough time for her, for not only had she had to struggle with her grief after her husband's execution in Buchenwald, but also the unwarranted humiliation that it had been printed in the section of the *Dresdner Anzeiger* where those sentenced to Capital Punishment were listed. There, along with those shot for racketeering and spreading "lies" from foreign broadcasts, Sebastian was listed as executed in Buchenwald *Konzentrationslager*, Weimar, for insubordination. However, fearing reprisals from the Gestapo, Renata felt powerless to defend his name in any way.

A few months after Sebastian's shocking death, a former colleague of his, Dr Mosell, had bravely made a point of seeking her out when he had been on leave from Buchenwald. 'Your husband's problems with those in command begun from the outset of his arrival at the camp,' he explained as they walked together away from prying ears and eyes in the *Großer Garten*. He wheezed slightly as they made their way around the water feature in front of the *Sommerpalais*. He was overweight and smoked profusely and was clearly unfit. 'You know Sebastian – he just couldn't keep his bloody mouth shut,' Dr Mosell laughed wryly, and even Renata, still raw with grief, managed a small smile at this truthful appraisal of her late husband. 'On the first day he had railed at the *Oebersturmbahnführer*, "You can't keep 10,000 men in such conditions – lice ridden, sleeping in wooden bunks without blankets and forced to collect rain water because they have no access to clean drinking water. You have to improve their living conditions." Obviously, this did not go down well with anyone in authority at Buchenwald. We had all learnt very quickly there that our status as Doctors meant very little unless we were furthering the Führer's cause.' He exhaled noisily. 'But that had nothing really to do with his subsequent sentence to death, other than he had already ruffled feathers. The real problem came when he started work on the typhus programme. They've been testing out new variations of vaccines in the camp for ages, and to put it mildly some of the methods they're using are rather crude. Well, deadly would be more accurate. They're contaminating healthy young men' – he paused with tears in his eyes, then carried on – 'not men, boys in truth: seventeen, eighteen some of these Russian prisoners. Anyway, they're contaminating them with typhus infected lice and sometimes even injecting them with vials of contaminated blood to then test out the various vaccines. And Sebastian knew, having already watched numerous young men deteriorate and die within days of being infected, that these vaccines were ineffective. He quarrelled bitterly with the Head of our department, Dr Ding. Told him he absolutely refused to participate in infecting healthy young men with a deadly virus. He argued that the experiments were completely unnecessary in any case, as a great deal of progress on other vaccines had already been made elsewhere and were now readily available and proving reliable. However, Dr Ding, who we all knew was under pressure to justify his Department's funding with a presentation at the Bacteriology Section of the Military Medical Academy in Berlin later that month, closed the debate by saying that the matter was not open for discussion, and then dismissed him from the "laboratory". Sebastian was arrested later that day. There was no trial at all, just his execution the following morning.'

It was the first and only time that Renata and Dr Mosell met. Of course, he had no evidence to back up these claims, but Renata had no reason to doubt him. However, beyond Herr and Frau Lange, who had travelled on her behalf to Buchenwald to collect Sebastian's urn, until she left Germany, she never repeated this information to anyone.

To compound her problems, Renata grappled with the constant worry over a lack of money. Having lost her right to a widow's pension because Sebastian had been found guilty of treason, she was left with the standard ration card that barely provided even a basic standard of living. With two small children to take care of it was impossible to consider most jobs on offer, but occasionally she cleaned the apartments of a few local residents in return for food coupons, and Herr and Frau Lange helped out as much as they could with food and clothes and treats for the children. The visit to the Circus Sarrasani was the most special one to date.

Sabina and Joachim were a frenzy of excitement with the thought of it all. For once, Sabina headed willingly to *Kindergarten*, unconcerned whether or not her teacher would shout yet again as she struggled with her reading. With the prospect of the famous Sarrasani acts to look forward to, especially the Lipizzaner horses and the tigers of which she had heard a great deal from friends, she could easily endure a few hours at school.

During the morning Joachim accompanied his mother whilst she cleaned for Frau Witt, a deaf old lady who carried a large ear trumpet and with whom she traded her time for food coupons. After that, they dropped in on a friend who was lending the children costumes for *Fasching*. They stayed for a short while only while Renata drunk a corn coffee with her friend, and Joachim had changed into the cowboy outfit, complete with a miniature Stetson hat, a holster and gun and a Sheriff's badge, and real leather chaps. Afterwards, they collected Sabina from *Kindergarten,* and then returned briefly to their apartment to prepare themselves for the exciting afternoon and evening ahead. Renata was pleased that the tasselled squaw dress was large enough to be worn over her daughter's ordinary clothes. She realised that later, after the sun went down on a cloudless winter day, it would be exceptionally cold. Footwear, as ever, provoked an argument with both the children who, by choice, would go barefoot if given half a chance.

'Hurry up and put your boots on, we've got a lot of fun things to get through today,' coaxed Renata.

'It's sunny. Don't need boots!' said Joachim with a sweet grin and a four-year old's logic.

'I've got my shoes on already,' added Sabina.

'No, it'll be really cold later. You need to be wearing boots. Come on, get them on.'

'My boots hurt,' Joachim protested.

Renata was well aware that he'd had them for a long time and feared that they probably were too small. Yet another purchase to make with money she didn't have, she thought wearily, and sighed. 'Let's try them on,' she said, managing a smile nonetheless.

Joachim squeezed into his boots as requested. Renata bent down and gently pressed the front of the boot. Unfortunately, Joachim was right: the boots were indeed too tight.

Despite her misgivings, she relented. 'All right, you can wear your slip on shoes. But Sabina, your boots are fine and in any case they match your outfit, so put them on and let's get going!'

Carefree in the first warm sunshine of the year, a happy little squaw and her cowboy rival skipped happily along the cobbled streets, oblivious to the growing throngs that Renata identified as refugees. She was only too aware that the Russians had been rapidly advancing from the east all year, and were only a few hours away at most. With vast movements of people through the city it was impossible to suppress the truth of the total collapse of the eastern front and the horror of the atrocities inflicted on those expelled, especially with so many Dresdeners involved in bringing them food through the National Socialist Welfare organisation, the NSV, and indeed the whole railway network in the city struggling under the pressure of transporting evacuees in one direction, and sending troops in the other.

It seemed that nothing could halt the Russians at this time. The previous week they had broken through the supposedly impregnable defences that had been constructed along the river Oder, and, since then, they had been an unstoppable force, destroying everything in their paths. Officially, German propaganda announcements pronounced that this was a planned military strategy which would allow the German army to re-group along the 'Elbe Line'. To suggest otherwise, the authorities had made clear, was a treasonable offence, though in private, amongst trusted people, Dresdeners spoke of little else. However, whilst the building of anti-tank ditches had begun in the surrounding area, it was hard to believe that these would be any more of an effective defence against the Russian offensive than those which had already been run through further east.

For more than a week now, both the *Hauptbahnhof* and the *Neustadt* station had been overrun with refugees. They arrived in their thousands by the hour, expelled from the Soviet path and now destitute, sleeping out overnight on the station platforms whilst awaiting either transport further west or re-housing in private homes, or in transit camps set up in closed down schools, or in other public buildings around the city. A stream of trekkers on foot pushing small handcarts, or the more fortunate Silesian farming families in horse drawn carts, had soon turned into a flood that coursed through the city as the days progressed. Generally they stayed for a night or two only, camping out in the squares or the *Großer Garten* while their horses took some much needed rest. There were free soups and sandwiches and even cigarettes on offer to the refugees at field kitchens set up by the NSV, and also the welcome use of washing facilities available at the stations, all of which they were grateful to partake of, before heading off to the west once again.

Slowly, Renata and the children made their way towards the long and elegant Prager Straße, where grand nineteenth century buildings housed some of the most popular shops. Winter light glossed over the city's rich yellow and ochre rococo buildings, and a flurry of snowdrops and the first flush of crocuses offered the promise of approaching spring. Decorations hung here and there in windows and groups of children played carnival games. Despite all the obstacles, a contingent of Dresden was still determined to enjoy the day. As a treat, the three of them popped into the snack bar of 'Jacobs', an exclusive city butcher, where Renata used the ration coupons she had just earned at Frau Witter's to buy sausages for the children, and a black-pudding soup for herself. After that, they strolled to the heights above Dresden, and then headed to the Dürerplatz where they popped briefly in on Uncle Magnus, who was still inconsolable following the death of his companion Fabian five months previously in the campaign in Kurland, before arriving at Herr and Frau Lange's for high tea in the late afternoon. Afterwards, they took the tram across the Elbe to Neustadt, where the Circus Sarrasani had their permanent home in the *Carolplatz*. Affectionately known as the 'Big Top', it was in fact a large solid building with extensive cellars and store rooms and stable blocks to house the many and various animals that were all part of the Sarrasani family.

It was already completely packed when they got there, with all two thousand seats filled and the aisles jammed as well. The mood was mixed. The Dresdener children were caught up in the carnival atmosphere, whilst the city's adults were more circum-spect. However, the many *Flüchtlinge* – the refugees – both children and adult, whom Trude Sarrasani the circus owner's wife had allowed in for free, were noticeably subdued.

Sitting between her brother and her mother, Sabina oscillated between gales of laughter and pangs of anxiety. Earlier, whilst she had been eating her soup with Joachim in the kitchen at her grandparent's apartment, she had overheard her mother and grandparents in the sitting room across the hall discussing the worsening crisis of the war. She was old enough to understand much of what they were saying, and as she looked around the exhausted faces of the refugees amongst the audience, she realised that they were not exaggerating when they described the difficulties that they faced.

Terrible stories were emerging from the refugees who had arrived in Dresden, she heard *Großvater* Lange tell both her mother and grandmother in a whispered conversation that she strained to overhear as she reluctantly picked at her bowl of kale soup in the kitchen with her brother, though she failed to fully grasp the meaning of all that he said. The *Gauleiter* – Party Leader - of Breslau, the mayor of the Silesian capital just a hundred miles away and a feared and fanatical Nazi, had expelled half a million of the city's civilians at a few hours notice into temperatures of -20 degrees C, and tens of thousands of women and young children had frozen to death in the snow and ice as they trudged unaided to collecting centres some twenty miles away. But the prospect that most alarmed *Großvater* Lange, from what Sabina could hear, was the inevitable and imminent invasion of the city by the Russians.

'The war is over for Germany,' he had stated emphatically, but simply voicing what they all already knew. 'Only a fool would think otherwise, and it's now only a case of when and to whom we all surrender – and just pray to God that it's not to the Russians. Renata, you must have a small bag packed and be ready to leave with the children just as soon as Gauleiter Mutschmann gives permission for the population to evacuate the city. As for us,' he paused for a moment, and took a deep breath before he continued, 'Well, we've discussed it together and decided not to leave the city – at least not voluntarily. If we joined you we would only slow you down, and even if a general evacuation is ordered, we would probably not leave either, but take our chances with fate. We're elderly, this is the only home we've known for thirty five years, and we've less to fear at our age from the Russians. But as a young woman you're in grave danger, and from some of the things I've heard even Sabina could fall prey to their depravities – it's not a situation that you can allow to happen. I've got some money which I've put aside and want you to take.' He held up the palm of his hand to stop her imminent protest. Then more slowly and softly, because he didn't want her to feel bullied into following his suggestion with all its implied dangers, 'I think you should also seriously consider destroying you identification papers, inventing some story – the most obvious would be to pretend to be a Silesian refugee – and leave Dresden immediately in any case. And then head west as quickly as possible.' He repeated it again, like a mantra, 'Get out now Renata whilst there's still a chance, and head west and surrender to the British or Americans.'

Now, as Sabina looked around the circus' seats at the forlorn faces of the refugees, she dreaded the prospect of soon becoming one herself.

A drum roll quickly distracted Sabina from her thoughts. Suddenly, the Cavallini clown troupe came tumbling into the arena or glided atop unicycles juggling batons of fire: it was George Seurat's *Circus* painting brought to life. Soon, they were tripping up over each other, throwing buckets of water and then, miraculously, precious sweets over the younger members of the audience. The lucky recipients gasped with delight, amazed at the unexpected treasure.

Eventually, the clowns slowly exited, still full of somersaults and slapstick and even more sweets. The crowd could barely contain their applause. With more fanfare, beautiful white-plumed Lipizzaner horses trotted majestically into the ring, two abreast, with dazzling showgirls atop them in top hats and sequins and silk. Sabina sat there transfixed.

The Lindströms had enraptured the audience to such an extent that a preliminary air-raid warning was ignored entirely by the audience, who in any case barely heard it above the music from the band. When Preto's Unrideable Donkey followed them, ambling noisily and uncooperatively into the arena, such was the gaiety by then that few in the auditorium had their thoughts elsewhere. The sirens sounded for a full-scale warning which the donkey answered with a loud hee-haw, and the audience roared with laughter. What an act! What droll humour and with a donkey, was the general consensus murmured among the applause. Yet suddenly the band stopped, and almost immediately an urgent voice broadcast over the *Drahtfunk*, the public announcement radio: '*Achtung! Achtung! Achtung!* Major enemy bomber forces are now approaching the city area. The dropping of bombs is to be anticipated. Make immediate use of air raid protection facilities.'

Circus attendants appeared at once in the aisles and began directing the anxious audience towards to the air raid shelters in the warren of rooms down in the basement. Afraid that little Joachim might get trampled in the fray Renata quickly picked him up, heavy as he was, and taking Sabina firmly by the hand she hurried as best she could to the cellars below. Just as she settled her children on the ground against a bank of sandbags, a chorus of whistles struck up an overture to the roar of bombs falling. An ominous crescendo climaxed in a thunderous explosion whose impact shuddered through the cellar, throwing up a fog of dust. The lights failed and the pitch black that enveloped them only heightened the sense of danger. All about people wept and prayed and sobbed in fright. Someone passed around a flask of Schnapps. Crouched down on the floor Renata clasped her children tightly into her body. Beneath them the ground shook and behind them the walls jolted, and all around the roaring growls of high explosives threatened at any moment to consume them. She heard Joachim yelp and felt Sabina wince as the impact of an exploding bomb very nearby threw them down on the ground. They lay together, huddled on the dirt floor in the darkness, every tremor like a shockwave through their bodies. Renata stroked the children's hair and gently kissed them for comfort, her own as much as theirs, until eventually the din subsided and relative quiet ensued.

Finally, the all clear sounded and a Sarrasani staff member appeared with a lantern to lead them up from the basement. Smoke from a small fire that had started in the straw and hay stall billowed around the building, so staff swiftly directed them out through the delivery doors. Renata emerged from the circus with Joachim, who was sobbing, clasped to her chest and Sabina trailing by her hand, bewildered. Only then did she notice how violently her whole body was shaking with fright.

All around was chaos. She walked around to the open square in front of the building to gain her bearings and assess the situation. A bomb had exploded on the roof of the main entrance hall and debris from that explosion was scattered across the road. Thankfully, the fire that it had started, as well as several others from incendiary devices, had been quickly put out by the circus staff. Nearby buildings had been less fortunate and suffered much more damage. Flames leapt rapaciously out of doorways and windows along the streets nearby. In the distance, across the river, the sky glowed fluorescent orange and red above the Altstadt. The noise was escalating all the while. Close by, a small Jack Russell tied up to a post howled incessantly until one of the Cavallini clowns came and rescued it, and they ran off together through the burning streets in the direction the Elbe. Still half in costume and in full make-up but with coats and scarves and winter boots hurriedly layered on top, the glamorous riders of the Lipizzaner ponies were untying the startled animals from the fences where they had been left for their safety, and leading them away from the 'big top', again towards the Elbe. Audience and staff were running in all directions. From somewhere inside the circus building came the terrified roars of frightened tigers trapped in their travelling cages. Amongst it all Renata stood dazed, uncertain what to do next. She tried to gather her thoughts and assess her best course of action, wondering what Sebastian would have decided if he had been there. She knew it was a weakness, this inability to make her mind up, but she had been fortunate that for most of her life first her father, and then Sebastian, had made decisions for her that she had always implicitly trusted. It was simply a skill that until Sebastian's death she had never really needed to learn.

Many of the buildings nearby were now blazing fiercely, and in comparison the damage to the Sarrasani seemed slight. Local residents who had fled their burning houses were gathering in the main lobby with armfuls of their most precious possessions, and she toyed with the idea of remaining there as well with the expectation that the fire brigade must surely arrive very soon. She certainly had no idea whether there were any public air raid shelters in the vicinity and indeed the city was notoriously short of them, so that was not an option open to her. However, eyeing up the billowing smoke growing in intensity around her whipped up by the strong north-westerly wind, and the mounting noise as fires took hold of the area, she thought it unwise to seek shelter in any of the basements of buildings close by. She thought back to all she had heard about the conflagrations in Hamburg, and decided at that moment to follow the many Sarrasani staff that were leading clearly terrified circus animals down to the safety of the Elbe meadows. This was, in any case, the instruction issued by the authorities who advised the Dresden residents to assemble either in the large expanse of the *Großer Garten*, or by the open fields by the Elbe. She would observe those guidelines now.

Finally, having made up her mind on a course of action, she set off there at once. She struggled as she carried Joachim and could not manage to do so for very long, especially when they had to pick their way through or over debris. However, he slowed them down even more if she made him walk. It was a dilemma for her. He was nearing four years old now, and as heavy as you would expect a boy of his age, and yet he was also frightened and tired. Renata alternated between carrying him, and encouraging him on foot as they made their way towards the Elbe.

They followed others obviously heading in the same direction, choosing a route through the widest streets where there was less likelihood of the road being entirely blocked by collapsed buildings, and kept to the middle of the road to better avoid further falling debris from either side. When roof tiles showered down from a burning building, a string of Lipizzaner horses a little way ahead, already frenzied, reared up screaming and required all the strength of the circus handlers to restrain them. At this, and the sheer bewilderment of the entire situation, Sabina burst into tears. Renata went through the motions of offering her some comfort, aware that her rote consolations of, 'everything will be fine – don't worry,' and, 'in a minute it will all be better,' were clearly nonsense. However, stupefied as she was with shock, it was the best that she could manage.

She had no choice but to slowly cajole the children along, over mounds of rubble and around vast craters that high explosive bombs had gouged out of the road, side-stepping burning window frames that had been blasted out by the force of an explosion, and away from furiously burning buildings where the walls threatened at any time to collapse.

'Please Sabina and Joachim, we must try to hurry up,' she called to them, perhaps more impatiently than she intended, but she had to almost shout just to make sure that they heard her. It felt as if she were having to pull them along, and she was all too aware that the nearer they got to the river, the more ferocious were the fires. The bombing had obviously been even more intense over this area which was closer to the heart of the city, just across the river. She glanced behind her the way they had come. It was glowing bright from the light of fires. There was no possibility of safely retracing their steps as heavy curtains of flames now hung along much of the street they had only recently passed, and the skyline above it sparked like a giant bonfire reflecting the growing inferno below. It was matter of real urgency to get to river now and they had to pick up their pace, but steadily so, as there were jagged shards of glass from blown out window panes almost everywhere, and any fall could have had serious consequences on account of those alone.

Suddenly, a huge explosion roared through a street nearby. Instinctively, they clung to each other as the vibrations struck them with a jolt. Renata imagined it was a time delayed bomb, but within moments a cacophony of eruptions all around them told her that this was the beginning of yet another air attack. There had been no new siren warning, but almost immediately a terrible din of aircraft overhead confirmed her worst fears. Sabina and Joachim were both screaming and crying, and she clasped each child close into her body, but she was beyond offering any words of comfort, feeling drained to the core herself. A short distance ahead a building collapsed in an avalanche of thunder and bricks, spewing dust and splinters of wood and sparks of fire into the street. The tremors beneath their feet almost threw them to the ground.

The air was heating rapidly, fanning gusts of wind that care-lessly tossed about billowing smoke and debris, much of which was on fire. From the crescendo of noise alone it was obvious that the fires were spreading at an astonishing rate, and it was becoming difficult just to breathe with so much ash, and ever less oxygen, in the air. They passed a house where fire had taken hold of the lower floors and they could hear, even above the roar of explosions nearby and the snarling gale, the screams of terrified people trapped in the upper floors. Knowing that there was absolutely nothing she could do to help them, Renata tried to distract the children and urge them on. For a moment she was shocked by her callous disregard for their plight, but she soon regained her focus for her own small family's survival.

Battling the wind, it took increasing strength and determination just to keep going. Some elderly people, she noticed, appeared to have given up the fight against the endless explosions and the elements and cowed in doorways awaiting the end, whatever that might be. Glancing down side streets that were a rage of fire, Renata realised that their options were rapidly running out. Ignoring the pain in her arms, she picked Joachim up again and took a resolute grip of Sabina's hand.

'It's not far to go now. We have to race,' she yelled to the children. Ahead, maybe a hundred yards or so, was the turning to the left that she had been aiming for and which took them directly down to the river meadows. *Please God let that road be passable*, she prayed in her head. Ordinarily, it would be a five minute walk to reach the river. However, by then, a few yards could take that long and each one felt like a hard won victory.

Suddenly, it was as if they were caught in a giant cauldron of fire. Behind them were only collapsed buildings and towers of flame which, whipped up by the maelstrom, engulfed everything as far back as she could see. To the left, people were emerging coughing and covered in soot from the blazing buildings, and a few doors ahead to the right, explosions, set off by drums of chemicals stored in the shop, ripped through a pharmacy. A shower of glass from the windows and myriad storage jars burst out from the shop and they narrowly escaped the potentially lethal cascade. Renata felt a surge of panic rise within her. She was ready to either collapse in tears or scream hysterically. However, she realised that if they were to have any chance of survival she had to fight both of those urges. Taking a brief look around, she realised that they could be cut off by the growing inferno at any time, but for the moment there was still a narrow path ahead where the fires had not yet taken a complete hold. Still clasping

Joachim and clutching Sabina by the hand, she scrambled along through the burning debris, buffeted with every step by the mounting gale. She gave a small sigh of relief after they passed the pharmacy without further explosions from the chemicals stored there. They had almost reached the turning to the left that she had been aiming for, when they were met by people hurrying out of the street towards them.

'There's no way through – half the street's collapsed and the road's impassable,' someone shouted at her as they crossed paths.

'Get to the nearest basement, you'll all burn out here!' another shrieked at her hysterically.

She ignored them both. It appeared that her prayers of a few minutes before had not been answered, but she would judge for herself if she thought there was a way through because she knew that there was certainly no way back, and she doubted that anyone sheltering in the basements or cellars nearby would emerge from this inferno alive.

They turned the corner, Renata still holding Joachim to her chest and Sabina by her side. The situation really did not look good, but it was not much worse than the road they had just navigated. Fire lined one side of the street, whilst the rubble from several collapsed buildings on the other side formed a deep smouldering barricade across the road. However, it was far from engulfed by fire, and not insurmountable. In any case, they had run out of all other alternatives. As they approached the mound of flaring debris, she put Joachim down on the ground, and took Sabina's hand which she had held in her own and placed it firmly around Joachim's. Realising that she would not be able to carry Joachim and at the same time climb up over the debris, she planned to climb up first and then pull the children up behind her.

'Hold onto your brother tightly,' she shouted to Sabina, fearing that he could be thrown to the ground by the gale. Hastily, she clambered onto the shifting bricks and fragments of doors and windows, hoping to avoid the shards of glass which were hard to spot amongst the rising dust, but which she just did not have time to look out for. A few feet up, she secured her footing and reached back down to pull up the children.

'Take my hand and keep hold off Joachim,' she shouted down to Sabina. 'Step up carefully, there's glass everywhere.'

Below, amidst the roar of encroaching flames, Sabina could barely hear her mother. She reached up to grab her outstretched hand and allowed herself to be pulled up, but to Sabina's horror Joachim's hand had slipped out of her own.

'Grab my hand,' she hollered to him, as the gap between them widened.

'I can't,' he screamed to her, rooted to spot on the ground below. He was reaching up to her, howling in agony, his arms flailing wildly like broken sails on a windmill. Sabina could see his socked feet sinking into the viscous tarmac, holding him hostage. The melting tarmac must have clasped his shoes and he had slipped right out of them, whereas her boots had held on to her firmly. But by then Sabina had been pulled up by her mother and was by her side, entirely out of his reach. Below, Joachim looked up at her pitifully frightened, tortured and confused.

'Why didn't you help him up with you?' she shrieked angrily at Sabina. 'I told you to hold on to him!'

'I tried,' she whimpered, partly in shock as she realised the terrible danger that she had left Joachim in, but also because it was a struggle simply to get enough oxygen to speak.

Her mother was screaming at her, consumed with anger and her mind whirled like the hurricane around them. She had tried her best to hold on to Joachim and little understood how they had ended up apart, but words entirely failed her efforts to explain any of it to her mother.

'Just carry on over the rubble,' Renata finally hollered to Sabina. 'I've got to go down and get Joachim.'

But Sabina stood frozen in horror at her culpability in Joachim's plight, and watched her mother totter unsteady back down towards her brother.

Instinctively, Renata knew that their time was running out. She could barely see the side of the street for the sheet of flames around them.

'I'll come down and help you, but start climbing up!' Renata called out to Joachim.

But still he stood, rooted to the spot, his arms reaching frantically out to his mother. Tears were now streaming down his face. It was clear to both Renata and Sabina that he was in very real danger now, the gale ripping at his clothes and the fire encroaching from behind.

'*Mutti! Mutti!*' he sobbed to her, although the words were lost on the wind. He was trying to move forward, but the more he struggled against the melting tarmac, the deeper he sank.

'Come on Joachim!' Renata yelped to her son, in panic, not comprehending why he would not step towards her.

Beneath her, some bricks shifted suddenly sweeping her off her feet. Instinctively, she reached out to grab at a fallen beam to stop herself falling, little realising how it was permeated with fire. She screamed in agony as her hand and forearm were burnt in an instant. And then she screamed in horror as she watched her son become engulfed in flame.

9

LUSTRATION

Mixed media

330cm x 330cm

Berlin, Germany. 15th November 1995.

Ellie stepped in determinedly to end the argument between her mother and grandmother.

'Please,' she said firmly, palms held up, gesturing for the shouting to stop. 'This is *not* the time or the place.'

For a moment, there was silence. They both looked at her surprised.

'Grandma,' Ellie continued quickly, before either of them had the chance to cut in, 'I'd really like you to enjoy the evening and my paintings – would you please go and rejoin Justin. We'll see you a bit later.'

Her grandmother gave her a small, almost relieved, smile. Then, without a glance at her daughter, who had already started goading her again, she walked out of the cloakroom.

'Mother, please can we – ' began Ellie, hoping to placate her somehow, but she was immediately interrupted.

'Please what?' she railed at Ellie with her hallmark glower and wild gesticulating hands. 'Please shut up and go and admire your self-important paintings next door? Please make ridiculous small talk with a bunch of strangers and pretend to the world that we're a big happy family? Please watch you swan around, the centre of attention, with everyone telling you how wonderful you are? Well, you're not going to get any of that from me. I'm sickened by it all. How dare you exploit what I went through like this and then expect me to be fawning all over you telling you how wonderful you are?'

'Mother, these paintings are really not your story,' interjected Ellie, not willing to be a total pushover. 'If they're anyone's story, they're mine. That's where they all began – with *me*, with *my* life, and with *my* emotions. It was Justin who saw how they work on other levels and the exhibition grew from there. You haven't even looked at the paintings, so you really can't say.'

'I don't need to,' she shot straight back. 'It's all here in the exhibition notes,' she snarled, opening the programme and scanning through its contents. ' "*Perdition* confronts the horror of the atrocities within the concentration camps . . . " and so on; "*Maelstrom* propels the viewer into the terror of the conflag- rations in German cities . . . " et cetera, et cetera. My life on the walls for your gain and glory, and to hell with what it puts me through. It's anything for money or the limelight with you isn't it? And if I get hurt, well so much the better. That's the way you've always been. It's always been self, self, self, without a thought for anyone else.'

The blather continued. Bursts of outrage and self-pity and resentment. Ellie bit down on her lower lip to dam her instinctive response. She had nothing to say that was worth prolonging the argument, but feared that if she walked away her mother and the rant would simply follow. To conceal her turmoil she entwined her trembling fingers behind her back. Imagining how she would paint the scene brought some sense of relief. She recalled Jackson Pollock's quotation that he did not want to *illustrate* feelings but to *express* them, and in her head she was rolling out a large canvas across the floor and then applying flat black oil in a thick impasto with splatters of cadmium red. At one point, failing to get Ellie's attention, her mother's whole body seemed to clench menacingly towards her, coiled tightly with pent-up rage. For a moment, while Ellie dispassionately considered how her mother's scarlet contorted face resembled a portrait by Francis Bacon, she seriously thought that her mother was going to hit her. Eventually, her mother backed away.

'I don't know why you bothered to invite me when I'm obviously not welcome,' Sabina snapped in an aggrieved tone. 'It's always the same with these things. I make all the effort to come and then you ignore me when I get there. I won't stay when I'm clearly not wanted.'

Sabina was fumbling over doing up the buttons on her coat, and took forever to co-ordinate each one through its respective hole. She bristled with frustration. Ellie felt embarrassed just watching, and oscillated between pitying her and despising her. Next, her mother laboured with her belt. It all seemed to take such an age that Ellie wondered whether her mother was secretly hoping that she would beg her not to leave and implore her to come and see her paintings. Ellie had done that before at other events – and to no avail – but this time she didn't make any effort to stop her, or try and persuade her to stay. By then she had already decided to abandon her objective to reconcile her mother with the rest of the family. She was also finally resigned to the fact that her mother had no interest in her, or her work.

At length, after searching around various pockets in her coat, Sabina brought out a mustard yellow crocheted hat that she pulled down low across her forehead, picked up her battered canvas tote bag which lay collapsed on the floor, and then left the cloakroom, spitting obscenities and with a slam of the door.

Utterly drained, like a squeezed out tube of paint, Ellie slumped against the wall on the cusp of tears, though from relief or sadness, she wasn't quite sure. She was grateful for a moment of silence and solitude in which she could gather her thoughts, and quell her emotions. Soon, some of the guests came in, and she took that to be her cue to rejoin the others.

Justin was standing across the foyer in the doorway to the exhibition hall, talking to a small group of people whilst waiting for Ellie. As she emerged from the cloakroom, he immediately rushed over.

'What the bloody hell just went on in there,' he asked rather loudly.

His expletive drew curious glances from the few people scattered through the foyer.

'Keep your voice down,' she said sharply, feeling too frayed to deal with the additional attention. 'Usual stuff,' she continued with a weary sigh. 'You were right – I shouldn't have invited her. Where's she now?'

'She's gone. I was keeping an eye out. She came out of the cloakroom and then immediately left the *Kunsthalle*,' he replied cheerfully, looking brighter than she'd seen him for a very long time. For that at least, Ellie was pleased.

A part of her was relieved: she really didn't need the stress that her mother's presence had created. But another part of her felt completely crushed: she had failed entirely in what she had hoped to achieve.

'Come on, let's go and find Grandma and all have a glass of champagne,' said Justin. 'This ought to be an evening of celebration as much as anything. If mother doesn't want to be a part of all this – and a part of us – that's her loss. You've tried, God knows you've tried, but for now you've just got to let it go. After all, we came here to do a job tonight.'

Managing a brief, if forced, smile, Ellie followed him back through into the viewing hall. It was apparent from the overall response that commercially and critically the exhibition was considered a success. However, for the rest of their time at the *Kunsthalle*, Ellie felt raw and miserable, the praise and accolades for her work, as nothing. Justin, by contrast, seemed like a man reprieved, and they reversed the roles that they had adopted earlier, he being animated and sociable, while Ellie retreated into herself and barely uttered a word to anyone. Their grand-mother, they observed, was a picture of composure and deep in conversation with Berlin's *Bürgermeister* on a slow, painting by painting, tour of the gallery.

Before long, most of the crowd had dispersed. The journalists had made their notes, drunk their fill and slipped out of the *Kunsthalle*, while the majority of other guests had likewise made the effort to see and be seen at the exhibition, and had now ebbed away to further engagements elsewhere in the city. The hall was all but empty again.

Their grandmother came over with a small smile on her face.

'My darling Ellie,' she began, opening out her arms to draw her to close. 'Please forgive me – I let you down in the cloakroom. I shouldn't have allowed myself to get drawn into such an argument and embarrass you like that.'

'No, Grandma, please don't apologise, it's not your fault at all,' countered Ellie, grateful for the comfort of her embrace. 'I shouldn't have invited her. I don't know why I did. It was my mistake in the first place.'

'You mustn't blame yourself. You did nothing wrong by trying to build bridges within the family.' Her grandmother's voice was soft and measured, and her hands rested gently on Ellie's arms, squeezing them occasionally to emphasise a point. 'It's not your fault that your mother doesn't want to be a part of that, but that's not something you can change. She seems to want to remain the way she is. But remember; it's a choice she's making. She could just let it go, forgive herself – and the world – and strive for some harmony in her life.' She paused for a moment to catch Ellie's eye and then continued, more lightly, 'And now I want to enjoy the rest of this evening and my grandchildren. I'm so proud of you both, and so glad I came. It really has been a momentous occasion for me. I can't thank you enough.'

'Thank you Grandma,' replied Ellie, tears welling as she leaned into her grandmother's arms once again.

Ellie felt deeply grateful for her grandmother's comments, and for those alone she thought that the evening had been worthwhile.

Of course, Ellie realised that it was not her paintings *per se* which had moved her grandmother, but the experience of returning to Germany, and to so much of her past. 'And I'm so proud of you Grandma – you've been very brave by coming here tonight,' she added. Her grandmother gently stroked her back by way of response.

They were interrupted by Justin's clear voice ringing out through the hall, announcing that the taxis taking them to a nearby restaurant had arrived. There were eleven of them heading off to dinner together, including the Director of the *Kunsthalle*, the British Cultural Attaché, and Frau Proske, a long-standing collector of Ellie's work from Düsseldorf. Their mother would have been welcome to round that figure up to twelve, had events turned out differently, as Justin had relented on her joining them all when he'd made the reservation.

They gathered at the cloakroom and collected their scarves and hats and coats and umbrellas. Shortly after, they stepped out into the sharp November night and the two cinereous Mercedes people carriers awaiting them, and then eased away from the *Moderne Kunsthalle* through the streets glistening silver after the rain of earlier on.

The roads had emptied of their rush hour chaos and they soon arrived at the restaurant in a newly restored neo-classical building along Unter den Linden. Like much of re-emerging Berlin, the restaurant was a bold modern statement of sleek minimalist chic. It had been decorated using a simple palette of gloss black floors and lacquer and leather chairs, a white ceiling and tablecloths, and the walls a rich aubergine sheen. Its clientele was equally stylish and appeared dressed in line with the décor. Ellie feared that her own winter pastels looked distinctly out of place.

They were shown to a long table with views out onto the restaurant's rear courtyard and while they took their seats the surplus setting was discreetly removed. Justin had pre-ordered the Tasting Menu for them all, which consisted of small servings of seven of the restaurant's signature dishes. Soon the aroma of autumn woods rose from a wild mushroom velouté, then lobster ravioli in a saffron sauce was followed by duck breast with pumpkin mousse, medallions of beef, lavender sorbet, a selection of cheeses from Germany's Allgau Mountains, and lastly, fresh berry compote. Gradually, as the dishes were brought before them and then slowly consumed, Ellie gained a greater distance from her earlier despondency. The evening had shown in such sharp relief the differing paths away from difficult times. Her grandmother had emerged from the past and now lived with peace, whilst her mother was still hostage to events of half a century ago. It wasn't difficult to decide whose role model it would be wise for her to follow. In spite of the debacle of her mother's attendance, Ellie was determined to enjoy the evening. After all, if her grandmother had managed to find a calm centre after all the traumas she had endured, then the petty dramas of her own life would be easy to leave behind. Finally, Ellie felt considerably lighter.

*   *   *

The following morning, as Ellie ate a late breakfast amongst the butterfly palms that rose from terracotta pots in the hotel's *Wintergarten*, she was unexpectedly joined by her grandmother.

'I want to stay on for a bit,' said Renata, out of the blue, as the waiter placed a fresh cafetière of coffee in front of her along with a basket of pastries. From past conversations, Ellie had always imagined that her grandmother would leave Berlin at the earliest opportunity. 'I want to see if I can recognise anything from before,' she continued. 'The city has been through so much during the six decades since I lived here. I want to go back to the *Tiergarten*, to the *Kurfürstendamm* and *Friedrichstraße*, maybe even the *Wannsee* – all the old places. I didn't get the chance to yesterday. And I would very much like to take both you and Justin out for lunch on my birthday – to the Adlon Hotel. I think that will be a good place to celebrate my birthday, don't you? The last time I was there was not such a happy occasion, waiting for my father to get out of a concentration camp. I am interested to see how they rebuilt the place since it was burned down at the end of the war. Finally put all those ghosts to rest.'

'I think that's a great idea,' Ellie replied enthusiastically. She had a flight booked back to London later that day, but this was clearly important to her grandmother. 'I'll call Milo – see if he can manage another few days without me.'

'Thank you, *Liebchen*,' her grandmother said simply.

'But if we stay on till Saturday, what about our plans for your birthday party on Sunday? You won't get back in time.'

'Then why don't we all fly back together on Saturday evening? That way I get to celebrate with lunch in Berlin, and then a party the next day in London – that seems an appropriate parallel to my life, I think. And I get to fly for the first time on my 80th birthday.'

'But I thought you were terrified of flying!'

'I still am – but I'm going to do it anyway,' she said and then smiled.

London, England. June 1997.

Returning home from the lows and highs that she had felt in Berlin, Ellie considered that her relationship with her mother was permanently over. Seeing her, albeit briefly, had been such a depressing and exhausting experience, that it wasn't one she was inclined to repeat.

Thankfully, back in London, Ellie's life was endlessly busy. The exhibition had elicited an avalanche of attention, and there was a deluge of letters to reply to each week and a barrage of questions from journalists most days. In addition, Christmas was by then fast approaching bringing its own whirl of activities. There were drinks parties to attend, a multitude of cards to write, and Ellie had long pledged to paint the backcloth for the pantomime at Joanna's school as well as make costumes for little Millie's nativity play. It had never occurred to her to send any gift or even a card to her mother, and, not surprisingly, they received nothing from her. By the New Year Ellie had mentally and emotionally put her mother to one side, and the old wounds had obviously healed because for the first time her absence cast no shadow at all.

Spring then brought a commission to create an installation for the atrium foyer of a Frankfurt advertising agency, rehearsals at the National Theatre for Milo, and the usual merry-go-round of Joanna and Millie's activities and increasingly hectic social life.

From there the year had unfolded rapidly, with Joanna stepping into teenage-hood in June, a visit to the Suffolk coast in July and a family holiday with both Justin and their grandmother to Sorrento in early September. Then in mid-December, much to their surprise, a Christmas card and some cash for Joanna and Millie had arrived from her mother. Ellie had ensured it was acknowledged with a thank you note from them both, but had restrained from resuming communication with her mother beyond that point.

Quite unexpectedly, her mother had again written to the girls towards the end of the following March, this time telling them how much she missed them and inviting them to come and collect some chocolate eggs on the forthcoming Easter Sunday.

It had been something of a quandary for her. While the rift between her mother and everyone else had not been kept a secret from the girls, it was not something that Ellie had particularly drawn to their attention. So in all innocence of the family politics, and having always been spared their grandmother's more difficult side, they had both been keen to go.

'What do you think?' she asked Milo. 'Should I take the girls?'

'It's your call, completely. She's your mother.'

'But they're your daughters as well. What happens if we get there and she's drunk? Her promises to remain sober mean absolutely nothing, we all know that, and even if I call ahead to check on her that isn't foolproof. Jo's now at an age where she's streetwise enough to spot a drunk when she sees one, and I don't want them to see their grandmother like that.'

'You'll know immediately if she's drunk – and if so, you just leave. But from what you've told me she probably won't even come to the door if she is – and again, you walk away. But if you want my opinion, I think that if they want the occasional contact with their grandmother, we shouldn't stand in their way. After all, she's never behaved badly towards either Jo or Millie in the past. Perhaps she'll be different with them. Perhaps this is her olive branch. I'll come with you – we'll pop in, be very polite, get the Easter eggs, and go. We just won't give her the opportunity for any arguments.'

As with the girls, Ellie had always curtailed Milo's relationship with her mother. On the infrequent occasions that they had arranged to meet up, she had learnt to always phone in advance to try and gauge her sobriety. And also to walk away if it turned out that she'd got that wrong. As a result, neither Milo nor the girls had ever been exposed to the very worst of her ugly temper. His sentiment towards family life was also very different from hers. His childhood had followed a gentle course into adulthood, and his family still came eagerly together for weddings and christenings, and to indulge at Christmas or spoil on birthdays. They lingered comfortably over winter lunches or summer barbecues, and, in spite of Milo and Ellie's inauspicious beginnings as a couple, they had made her feel so welcome, and had been thrilled at meeting Joanna, and then later when Millie had been born. Her family – or rather her mother – was unfathomable to him.

'You've never seen what she's really like,' Ellie had continued. 'Ten minutes in her company have left me distraught for days. People always imagine that I'm exaggerating, but she can be vicious. You heard what happened in Berlin.'

'But as you said at the time, it was you making the move then to try and patch things up. This time it's her. She's the one getting in touch, so perhaps she *has* finally grasped the point that she's losing out. People do stop drinking, get their act together.'

'I've been there before with her. Heard all the pledges – seen them all fall apart.'

'But it *is* different this time,' he'd emphasised. 'From what you've said, she's never made the first move before. You don't have much to lose really by giving it a go, and obviously if there's any sign of trouble we'll just leave.'

With mixed feelings, Ellie had sent her mother a short letter advising her that they would arrive at her house at around eleven. To keep the visit purposefully brief, she'd added that they could only stay for half an hour as they had previously arranged plans for the rest of the day.

On the Easter Sunday they arrived at her mother's home a few minutes late, after a chaotic start to the morning. Anxiety had kept Ellie awake for most of the night, whilst Joanna, in true teenage form, had been indignant on being roused. Millie, by contrast, was a frenzy of excitement after an early morning raid on her haul of confectionary. All in all, it was not a good combination, and it had taken forever, and most of her patience, for Ellie to coax them both out of pyjamas and into clean clothes.

It had been her first visit to the house in Ealing for almost two years, and beneath the vibrant March sky the place looked ivy-choked and exhausted. Tendrils of paint hung languidly off the window frames and the front door, a horde of weeds had invaded the front path, and the border shrubs were a tangle of neglect. Ellie rang the doorbell with a knot in her stomach and endeavoured to summon a smile to her face.

After a pause, the door was opened by her mother, who'd looked annoyed, but at least not drunk.

'Oh, you're finally here,' she said impatiently. 'Don't you think I've got better things to do than hang around for you all day?'

It was not an auspicious start.

'I'm sorry,' Ellie had muttered, bristling already. A part of her had been tempted to just turn around and leave, but in her relief to have found her mother sober, she didn't. Instead they all stepped, subdued, out of the balmy sunlight and into the gloom of the hallway. They then followed her tentatively, and in silence, to the sitting room. Milo finally managed a bright smile as a greeting, but both the girls succumbed to the strain and suddenly wilted.

For once the house had looked reasonably tidy; though stripped of much of its former clutter, the cartography of burns and stains were even more visible. Her mother appeared less haggard than before, although still far from well. A red crackle glaze maintained its blaze across her cheeks, and her gait had slowed to a lumbering crawl.

'Sit down,' she said plainly.

'We picked you some daffodils from our garden,' Joanna solemnly announced, before handing the yellow bowed flowers to her grandmother at arms length.

'That was very thoughtful. They'll brighten up this room no end,' she responded, looking genuinely pleased.

'And I made you a card,' Millie added, timidly offering her best effort at drawing bunnies and flowers and Easter eggs.

Their grandmother looked at the card and smiled.

'That's very good Millie, thank you,' she said with more affection than Ellie had anticipated. Perhaps Milo had been right, she thought; perhaps she could have a different relationship with her grandchildren than the one she had with her.

'I've prepared a tray of coffee and I'll bring the girls their Easter presents,' she told them all, as she slowly struggled out of her chair.

'Thank you,' Ellie replied, hesitant to prolong the visit, but not wishing to cause offence. 'Do you need any help?' she added. 'Jo can bring things through for you, if you want.'

Evidently reluctant to engage with her grandmother, Joanna shot her mother a severe look at this suggestion and appeared visibly relieved when it was then declined.

In her grandmother's absence, Millie tiptoed over and whispered, 'I don't like it here. It smells strange, and grandma's scary.'

'Well, if you remember, you asked to come, so now just sit quietly and be polite,' Ellie responded quietly, if impatiently.

Joanna mouthed to her mother from across the room, 'Can we go soon?' To which Ellie nodded 'yes' in reply.

Eventually, their grandmother returned with the tray laden with mugs of coffee, fruit juice for Joanna and Millie, and their gift-wrapped presents as well. Ellie was touched by her mother's effort, but wondered if it was too little too late. The gulf between them seemed too great to bridge, and the distance of time seemed to have become a distance of emotion for the girls as well. Their expectations had sadly fallen far short of the reality of seeing their grandmother.

Thankfully, Milo filled in the awkward crevices in the conversation with comments about the unseasonably warm weather and the forthcoming General Election. With coffee cups emptied, and diminishing returns on the small talk, they offered their thanks and made their excuses to leave.

'Thank you for the drinks and the girls' presents,' Ellie said in parting on the doorstep, relieved to be back out in the sunlight.

'They're growing up quickly. Let's not leave it such a long time till we see each other again,' her mother said in a hopeful tone.

'No indeed,' she responded, noncommittally. 'Have a good weekend.'

They drove away with a spectrum of relief and sadness, guilt and optimism. Ellie had no idea how – or whether – their relationship would progress from there, but she was grateful that they had at least parted peacefully.

A phone call two weeks later came as something of a shock. An unfamiliar woman's voice asked, 'Is that Ellie Tyler?'

'Yes,' she answered, imagining that it was a journalist who'd somehow got hold of her number.

'It's Caitlin Murphy here. I'm a nurse at the Ealing Hospital. I'm sorry to inform you that your mother was brought into A&E here earlier today. She's since been admitted to the gastro-enterology ward, where she's in a stable condition. We traced you via her doctor – you're listed as her next of kin.'

Suddenly, Ellie's heart was pounding furiously. 'What's happened? What's wrong?' she managed, slightly dazed.

'I'm afraid I can't give out details over the phone. All I can say is that there appear to be complications due to an ongoing medical problem. If you come in we can let you know more.'

'Right,' she answered, with a sigh, 'I'll come over.'

Ellie had been busy on the phone for most of the morning and had barely started in the studio for the day. Hastily, she put her brushes into white spirit and replaced the tops on the tubes of oils she'd been using. Then, still in her paint splattered working clothes, she left the house to drive out to Ealing.

It was a perfect, warm, spring day, and Maida Vale was in full bloom. Daffodils and narcissi flaunted the gamut of yellow from pale chalk to burnt orange, and cherry trees smudged blossom in marshmallow colours against a sky the lapis blue of Matisse's *Icarus*. Despite the brilliance of it all, Ellie felt that she too was crashing back down to earth.

Fortunately, there had been little traffic along the Westway and Uxbridge Road, and twenty minutes later she pulled into the hospital car park. Amongst the labyrinth of corridors and lifts and stairs, she eventually found the gastroenterology ward, and then the duty doctor.

'Ah, good morning,' the doctor said, looking up from her notes. Her voice was soft and mellifluous and she looked young, Ellie thought, with chestnut hair drawn up into a clasp, and pretty, delicate features. 'I'm Dr Farrow. Thank you for coming in so quickly. I'm afraid your mother collapsed in her local off-licence earlier this morning. The owner called an ambulance and they brought her here, still unconscious. They gave her a CT scan in A&E, so we know that she hasn't suffered a head injury, and also a chest x-ray, and that was fine. However, there were issues with the liver function tests which is why she's been brought up here,' she briefed Ellie before they went on the ward.

'But I saw her just a fortnight ago,' Ellie protested, struggling to take in what she'd just been told. 'She was looking so much better. I thought she'd stopped drinking.'

'Two weeks is a long time in the life of an alcoholic, I'm afraid. There's a good reason why they say take it a day at a time in AA.'

'I'm just a bit shocked by it all,' Ellie stated, pensively.

'I can understand that. But if a body is already weak from abuse it can go into decline very rapidly if someone starts drinking again,' Dr Farrow explained. 'Would you like to go in and see her?'

Ellie nodded unenthusiastically, and then, feeling embarrassed and upset, she followed the doctor to the far side of the ward. In the bed lay an old woman with her eyes shut and drips attached to a swollen vein in her hand. For a moment Ellie assumed that they had made terrible a mistake. The shrunken figure, a tattered pile beneath the sheets, and the consumed features with muscles twitching beneath the parchment thin skin, could not be her mother. Unfortunately, out of the lurid face in front of her, Ellie eventually assimilated her mother's features. It was a shocking realisation. Occasionally her mother's limbs trembled. Suddenly, she appeared to have a mild seizure, and Ellie thought that she was about to watch her own mother die.

'I think we'd better go,' Dr Farrow said quietly, guiding Ellie gently by the arm to the door. 'That's delirium tremens – the muscles going into spasm. Probably looks much worse than it is. It's quite normal in cases of alcoholic withdrawal,' she added.

They'd gone through to her office. 'She has regained consciousness, but she'll be very confused for a while. She's probably not really aware of what's going on or where she is, and she's certainly not up to any conversation. If she does talk, it most likely won't be anything coherent, though she won't know that. It looks as if she's hardly eaten for days, and in medical terms she's on the edge of starvation – also severely dehydrated. Obviously she's been drinking alcohol, but although that's a liquid it actually dehydrates the body. She'll need to be on the Pabrinex drip for at least three days. The other one is for antibiotics – she's very vulnerable to infection of the liver at the moment. I'm afraid she's in for a bit of a tough time. By this evening we anticipate she'll have a high fever – it's a normal part of the cycle of a chronic drinker withdrawing from alcohol – but it will cause intense sweating, and thereby exasperate the dehydration.' She paused, and then asked, 'Any questions?'

Ellie shook her head, overwhelmed by it all.

'Well, we don't anticipate much change in her over the next two days, so I'd come back then if I were you. You can call any time if you want to, and of course we'll call you if there are any major developments.' She smiled kindly. 'We deal with this more than you probably realise. You mustn't blame yourself.'

'Thank you. It's easy to beat yourself up over this one, think that if you'd gone that extra mile you'd somehow have sorted it out.'

'But we both know that's not the case,' she replied sympathetically.

With trepidation, Ellie phoned the Ward the next day to get an update on her mother. Dr Farrow had not been on duty and none of the other doctors were available to talk to, so she'd left a message asking for news. Eventually, a nurse rang her back with the news that her mother was stable and still in the cycle of experiencing delirium tremens. They weren't expecting much change in her condition within the next twenty-four hours, and Ellie was advised to call back or come into the hospital then.

The following afternoon Ellie returned to the hospital to see for herself how her mother was progressing. Mr Metcalfe, the Consultant Gastroenterologist who'd examined her mother, had been in the ward's office when she arrived there, and a nurse introduced the two of them. He was in his mid-fifties, tall and wiry with round, metal-rimmed glasses that emphasised his thick brows and stern eyes. He took Ellie to one side.

'It doesn't look good,' he informed her sharply. 'She has chronic upper gastrointestinal bleeding, which is presenting as occasional vomiting of blood and anal blood loss, and that means she has acute, possibly chronic, liver damage. We've done a liver ultrasound, and we're going to have to do a biopsy, but from what I've seen, I would estimate that unless your mother stops drinking entirely, she's probably got six months to live – at most.' He clearly favoured a more forthright approach than Dr Farrow.

It was difficult news for Ellie to take in.

'Thank you,' Ellie mumbled feebly to Mr Metcalfe as he turned and walked away.

One of the nurses took Ellie onto the ward to see her mother. As before, Sabina was attached to two drips and asleep. Ellie didn't stay long, and had been very glad to leave.

Wary as Ellie had been about assuming some responsibility for her mother, in the end, she felt she had little choice. She held off from telling Justin and her grandmother about this latest incident in her mother's life, knowing that it was unlikely to elicit much sympathy. But having spoken with the Consultant, she thought that they should at least know of her condition. Then, they could decide for themselves whether to get involved or not. Later that evening, she finally phoned her grandmother to fill her in.

'I'm sorry *Liebchen*,' her grandmother had said. 'I just can't feel sorry for her. As far as I'm concerned she's brought this on herself. I respect your decision to help, but I don't see what I could do even if I wanted to. I can't stand on guard duty over her for the rest of her life to stop her from drinking. Help her if you want by all means – but don't let her take you away from your own children too much, they must be your main concern.'

Justin was much the same when she'd then called him. 'Jesus, Ellie, you've got to be kidding – do I want to see her? No way. Look, do what you have to do, but count me out. I'm just not interested,' he said tersely.

Ellie understood their points of view, and also that alcoholism doesn't easily attract empathy. But, she had resolved to make the effort to be there for her mother; if not out of compassion, then out of a fear of guilt. Consequently, most weekdays, she drove out to Ealing in the early afternoon and spent an hour or so at her mother's bedside before returning to pick up Jo and Millie from school.

After ten days off alcohol and on a high calorie diet, her mother began to gain weight. The liver biopsy revealed acute Hepatitis, as expected, but it was hoped that she would be able to make sufficient progress in her recovery to be allowed home after a further four weeks. At that stage, Ellie reduced her visits to three times a week. There was only so much disruption she could impose on her own family life or her work, which, much to Justin's dismay, had more or less ground to a halt.

Some days Ellie's efforts to see Sabina had been in vain as her mother had slept the whole time. On other occasions she was plain rude: as obstreperous and obnoxious as ever. Even so, Ellie kept up the visits. She was, she knew, her mother's sole visitor.

Then, quite unexpectedly, one afternoon, when the ward was sweltering beneath an approaching summer storm and empty except for a few other patients at the far end of the room, her mother finally opened up about how her addiction had started.

'Until I started drinking, I had nightmares every night after my brother was killed,' Sabina began quietly. 'Every night I relived Joachim's death, or the other terrible things we saw, over and again in my sleep. And I'd seen some terrible things that no one should ever see. After the bombing we lived in the forest for a while, but mother was fixated about trying to find Joachim's body. Every day for at least a week we trudged into Dresden to try and find some remains of him, or any trace of my father's family who had got lost in the bombing as well. The fires were still burning, in fact the city burned for days, until it was reduced to a charred skeleton. Mother left chalk messages for them on the blackened walls, but of course we never heard a thing. We saw rubble and bodies everywhere we turned. We never did find Joachim though, or my grandparents or great-uncle, no matter how many ruins we tramped over, or how many corpses we examined. There were so many that the authorities didn't know what to do with them all. In the end the soldiers just piled up all the bodies and set fire to them as well. The smell was disgusting. The strange thing was that after a few days no one cried any more, we'd all got so immune to death. But for me it seemed to come out in my sleep when I dreamed – all the very worst of what we'd seen. Sometimes I would wake and be physically sick. And it didn't get much easier after we left Dresden either. I never knew what our plans were, they seemed to change all the time. Sometimes we trekked with other people, sometimes alone. We were hungry most days, slept rough for months and stripped corpses for clothes. And always in fear of something – either bombs, or being strafed by planes or attached by the Russians. You'd hear screams in the night and never know if someone was being attached or having a nightmare or in the death throes of typhus. In the end the cries and muffled shrieks became an inconvenience you learned to live with, just like the lice, but one that you ignored. Mother got attacked one night by the Russians – she never spoke about it, but I knew. When I came down from the hayloft one morning she'd lost most of her teeth in a fight. She was a changed woman after that. Barely spoke to anyone for ages – for years, literally. Perhaps if I'd been able to talk about it, I'd have lost some of my anxiety in that way. But I'd long stopped having conversations with my mother, and, except for her, no one's experience in England came close to any of it. I guess it all got bottled up and exploded into my dreams. But then when I discovered alcohol, it was almost like an elixir for me – the nightmares stopped if I drank enough. And then on days when I didn't drink, they came back, the same terrible, ugly nightmares – mostly Joachim's death, over and over, and each time the terrible feeling that it had been my fault, that I should have done more to save him. So it was simple really – if I carried on drinking, there were no more nightmares. Your father sent me to a psychiatrist for a while, but I could never bring myself to talk about the truth of those dreams or even Joachim's death. You see, it was hard for a German living in England to get any sympathy at all for what *we* had suffered during the war. I learnt *that* lesson well enough at boarding school. It was always, well, you started it – as if it had anything to do with my father or mother or my brother or me. We were just an ordinary family with no interest in Hitler or politics. And then they'd mention Coventry and the blitz in London, but what's the use in trading statistics? This number died during this raid or that number died in that raid, and the futile analysis of, well, there were so many military killed here and that many civilians killed there. And then you realise the truth in the saying that the death of 10,000 people is a statistic – but the death of one, a tragedy. But my tragedy, the death of my father and then of my brother, was just one among so many millions, and not very interesting for the rest of the world. I was not so strong like my mother. She coped so much better – and didn't I always hear about it! I'm sorry for you that I was not more like her.'

Ellie was crying by then, silently heaving sobs with tears rolling from her cheeks onto the hospital floor. She was crying for the senseless waste of her mother's life, a life that in many ways had ended with her brother's on the night of the Dresden bombing, and she was crying for Joachim, the much loved little boy who had never got the chance to grow up to be her uncle.

Sabina reached out and squeezed her daughter's hand, although the small gesture of comfort only increased Ellie's tears. Ellie had grown so used to the ongoing war between them that she struggled with a moment of intimacy and kindness.

Twelve days later her mother left the hospital with orders to visit to her own doctor each week, and an assurance to Ellie on her final visit to the ward that she would resume attending AA meetings. In return, Ellie promised that if her mother maintained her sobriety, she would phone her every Sunday, occasionally assist her with some shopping, and allow her to see her grand-daughters.

Ellie called her on the evening she was discharged. Earlier that day, Ellie had sent over a cleaner, a box of groceries and some cerise tipped tulips. Her mother sounded genuinely touched by her efforts and at peace with the world. For the first time, Ellie felt some sense of optimism about her mother's future.

As agreed, Ellie called her the following Sunday morning, although the phone went unanswered. She was mildly concerned, but rationalised that her mother may have gone out to buy a newspaper or some milk. An hour later, Ellie phoned again and once more there was no reply. She kept on calling at regular intervals until the early evening, but each time without success. By seven, she was really starting to worry. She was aware that her mother had few friends and little in the way of a social life, so even if she had gone somewhere for Sunday lunch, she would have been back by then.

Sunday evenings were always a busy time in their household – getting the girls to finish off their last pieces of homework, packing up school bags and sports kit and organising fresh uniform for the start of a new week at school – but instinct told Ellie that something was very much amiss with her mother.

'I've got to go over and see if she's alright,' Ellie said to Milo, when her mother's phone rang on endlessly yet again.

They'd had a busy weekend themselves. Saturday had slipped

away with music lessons and parties to attend for the girls, and on the Sunday they'd had friends over for the day. The house was in a state of chaos. Washing up multiplied in unruly piles in the kitchen; Joanna sat with hunched shoulders and endless books finishing off a geography project; and an over-tired Millie scattered cushions and clothes as she searched for mislaid Beanie Babies.

Milo looked at Ellie as if to say, you've got to be kidding, although in fact he managed a more graceful, 'Have you rung the operator to check if there's a fault?'

Her spirits leapt. She hadn't checked if there was a fault with the phone line, so perhaps her worrying had been for nothing. However, a call to the operator, and a prompt test of the line, soon ruled out that problem.

'I'll get Millie to bed and then I'm going over,' Ellie said decisively.

Milo looked displeased and Joanna muttered something about her being a drama queen, but her intuition sensed a serious problem. She hurried Millie through the process of getting to bed, and then left the house soon after.

There was heavy traffic all the way. As she'd edged slowly forward along the White City flyover the crimson sunset cast brilliant streaks across the urban skyline; but by the time she arrived in Ealing, the evening had mellowed to a muted purple subsuming her mother's house in shadow. Ellie knocked on the front door, suddenly aware that her mother might actually be quite cross that she had turned up uninvited: she always hated unexpected visitors, probably fearing that they might find her drunk. However, no one came to the door.

Peering through a gap in the sitting room curtains Elle could see that the television was on, though there was no sign of her mother. A light from somewhere in the back of the house shone into the sitting room, in the style of an Edward Hopper painting.

As on so many previous occasions, Ellie walked around to the back of the house to get in by the kitchen door. This time however, she found it locked. A light was clearly on in the room, but the blinds had been drawn so she couldn't see inside. She banged loudly on the glass panes of the door for an age, but as before she was ignored.

By then, Ellie had to fight the surge of panic she felt inside. The sense of foreboding that she felt all day, sharpened to an excruciating pain in her stomach.

Flustered, she hurried over to Mr Colman's house in the hope that he might know of her mother's whereabouts, or perhaps still have a spare key. Ellie explained the situation and he was polite and sympathetic, but unable to help on either account. Having seen lights go on and off in the last few days he had realised that she was back from hospital, though he hadn't actually seen her. There was probably some simple explanation, he said to Ellie with such enforced heartiness that it was quite apparent he didn't believe it himself. He suggested that if she were really that worried she should ask the police to gain access to the house, rather than break in herself. Ellie gratefully accepted his offer to use his phone and call the police, who agreed that it was an urgent matter.

Mr Colman administered strong, sweet tea to pass the time while they waited. It was strange, thought Ellie: she had known him for most of her life but they had barely spoken before. They made polite small talk, but her clamouring head struggled to be coherent. Thankfully, the police arrived before too long.

Without delay, the officers repeated Ellie's attempts to get her mother's attention; but these were again in vain. Between them, they agreed that one of them would remain with Ellie at the front of the house, whilst her colleague forced access at the back and then searched inside.

Waiting silently in the dark, suddenly all the sounds around them seemed amplified to Ellie. As the officer broke in, the shattering glass reverberated like a clash of symbols in a quiet piece of music, and passing cars seemed to roar rather than slide by unnoticed. In her heightened awareness, she heard the officer's every footstep, and each door opening or closing, as she listened out for clues to what was happening inside. Movement in the sitting room, than a pause of about a minute but still no voices from within the house, told its own story. It was no surprise when the young officer reappeared at the front of the house and quietly said that he regretted to inform her, that during his search of the house, he had found the body of female inside.

Ellie asked if she could go inside and see her, but the officer shook his head. First, a coroner would have to be called and then a preliminary investigation concluded. It was likely to be a long night, he explained.

In a stupor, Ellie returned to Mr Colman's house and asked if she could use his phone again. For an age she sat in silence and simply stared at the phone, unable to dial any numbers.

*   *   *

The following days passed in a dull blur for them all. Justin focused his attention on their grandmother, about whom they were both very worried. Ellie, meanwhile, was assigned to liaise with the coroner's office and organise their mother's funeral.

She searched the house in vain for instructions of her mother's wishes. Judging that she would have wanted a service that was simple and not overtly religious, Ellie instructed a firm of funeral directors to organise the broad strokes of the service and find a local minister willing to conduct it, while she filled in the details of music and casket and flowers. Their lives felt on hold as they waited for the funeral at the end of the following week. Ellie ignored her easel, Renata her food, whilst Justin drank and smoked ferociously.

Layers of vanilla and silver clouds added lustre to the June sky as Ellie and her family drove westwards for the late morning service. Justin and Renata were waiting for them besides the small fountain outside the Remembrance Hall when they arrived at the

Hanworth Crematorium. Mr Colman, his grown up daughter, Jessica, and another of Sabina's neighbours had turned up as well, but few other people besides. It seemed to Ellie a sad testament to an unhappy and lonely life.

The Vicar from a local Church led the service. Renata sat in the front row of the small Chapel with Ellie and Justin like sentinels on either side. Ellie slumped in her chair but listened intently, the words stilling her crowded head. Renata sat rigidly, her eyes brimming with tears, apparently giving the Vicar her full attention though in her numb state she barely heard a word. Justin stared into the distance, not even feigning awareness, lost in a bedlam of emotions.

In lieu of a eulogy John Claire's poem, 'I Am,' had been chosen as a poignant tribute to Sabina. Joanna, whom Ellie had decided would add a light touch to the occasion, went forward to the front of the Chapel and gravely read out the words:

I Am

I am: yet what I am none cares or knows,
My friends forsake me like a memory lost;
I am the self-consumer of my woes,
They rise and vanish in oblivious host,
Like shades in love and death's oblivion lost;
And yet I am, and live with shadows tost

Into the nothingness of scorn and noise,
Into the living sea of waking dreams,
Where there is neither sense of life nor joys,
But the vast shipwreck of my life's esteems;
And e'en the dearest – that I loved the best –
Are strange – nay, rather stranger than the rest.

I long for scenes where man has never trod,
A place where woman never smiled or wept;

There to abide with my Creator, God,
And sleep as I in childhood sweetly slept:
Untroubling and untroubled where I lie,
The grass below – above the vaulted sky.

By the poem's end Renata's tears had spilled over, Ellie's had welled up and Justin's face had finally buckled with pain. Renata reached out to grasp both her grandchildren's hands, which she continued to clasp tightly through the Vicar's address, the Commendation and until the final 'Amen' as he read out the solemn Committal and the curtains finally closed across the coffin.

From the crematorium they went to a small Italian restaurant near Ealing Common that Ellie knew her mother had occasionally frequented. Ellie had booked a large round table for eight that they almost managed to fill with immediate family and Mr Colman, who came along as well. Ellie sat beside Renata who looked suddenly frail.

'How are you?' Ellie asked her.

'It is a terrible thing, whatever the circumstances, for any mother to say, "Now I have no more children," so of course I am not feeling so good,' she replied wearily. 'But it is also a terrible struggle to watch one's child slowly destroying themselves. I have lived in fear of this moment for a very long time. At least I can now stop bracing myself for the worst, because the worst is now over.'

'I mourned her long ago,' added Justin thoughtfully. He had scarcely spoken all day, having barely emerged from his internal landscape since his mother's death. Ellie had wondered if he would even turn up to the funeral. 'But I still feel sad somehow. Her life's been such a waste,' he added in a regretful tone.

'No life's a waste,' Milo answered, trying to lift the sombre mood. 'Not even your mother's. Remember *It's a Wonderful Life* with James Stewart and the scene where he's shown how everything would have been so different if his character hadn't existed?

Well, equate that to your mother, and then look around this table. Only Renata and Mr Colman would be here. But none of the rest of us. Without your mother, neither of you would have been born, and nor would Joanna and Millie. And think what an impact Ellie's art has had, and how you made that happen. She created and shaped you both – she might have put you through the furnace to mould you, but she fashioned you nonetheless. Ellie would have been a very different artist had she had a different mother.'

A waiter poured mineral water and placed some *antipasti* on the table to eat while they decided what to order.

'I don't agree that the end always justifies the means,' declared Justin, 'She was brutal with us. Absolutely vicious with me. I never understood why she took so much out on me.'

'There is a simple and sad reason for that Justin, I'm afraid,' Renata said wistfully. 'You reminded her so much of her brother, Joachim. You were so like him in every way. His very image from the day you were born. I think at some level that's why she called you Justin – it's almost like an English version of his name. I think that at first she liked the fact that you looked like Joachim, but then when you got to four, which was when he was killed, you became a constant reminder of his awful death, and then the boy and man he would have become.'

'I never realised,' murmured Justin, clearly moved. 'I never saw pictures of him because of course none survived. I should have guessed – that's obviously why you called me Joachim so often,' he stated, looking at Grandma.

'It probably is,' she answered. 'I never did it intentionally. It was always a Freudian slip, I think. But there were times when it truly felt as if I had my son back again. It made you very special to me. That's why I couldn't bear to see your mother mistreat you.'

'That all makes sense, but it doesn't answer why she beat me because I looked like Joachim – I mean, it had the opposite effect with you.'

'I'm not a psychiatrist, but perhaps she was angry at Joachim for dying – and since she couldn't take her anger out on him, she took it out on you instead.'

'Angry with him for dying? It was hardly his fault!'

'No, it wasn't his fault, but she'd felt guilty for such a long time over his death that perhaps she was angry she'd had to shoulder all that guilt. I never really blamed her for his death – how could I? She was a small child caught up in a firestorm during a bombing raid. A few times afterwards I said things like, "You should have just yanked him up", or "Why on earth did you let go of him?" but that was out of frustration and not really blame. I was as much to blame, if blame's the right word under the circumstances, because if I'd made him wear his boots instead of allowing him to put on his shoes, he would probably have survived.'

'And she never stopped punishing herself,' Ellie added with a sigh. 'Created a prison called alcoholism from which she never escaped.'

'Well, she's free from that now,' said Milo pensively. 'Let's hope that she's found peace at last.'

'I think we should toast her memory,' said Ellie, attempting to lighten their spirits. 'Not all the unhappy ones, but her legacy that now happily lives on in us all.'

'I think that's a good idea, Ellie,' agreed Renata. 'I would like to propose a toast to Sabina, who is no longer with us but whose legacy is far richer than she ever realised, and whose life was very much fulfilled in you all.'

And with that they all raised their glasses.

MRS DIAMOND
13/6/12
MRS GREEN
18.2.15
Ms Wells
17/8/16